DRAGON SLEEPING

Ace Books by Craig Shaw Gardner

The Ebenezum Trilogy

A MALADY OF MAGICKS
A MULTITUDE OF MONSTERS
A NIGHT IN THE NETHERHELLS

The Ballad of Wuntvor

A DIFFICULTY WITH DWARVES
AN EXCESS OF ENCHANTMENTS
A DISAGREEMENT WITH DEATH

The Cineverse Cycle

SLAVES OF THE VOLCANO GOD
BRIDE OF THE SLIME MONSTER
REVENGE OF THE FLUFFY BUNNIES

The Sinbad Series

THE OTHER SINBAD
A BAD DAY FOR ALI BABA
THE LAST ARABIAN NIGHT

The Dragon Circle

DRAGON SLEEPING

THE DRAGON CIRCLE

DRAGON SLEEPING

CRAIG SHAW GARDNER

ACE BOOKS, NEW YORK

DRAGON SLEEPING

An Ace Book
Published by The Berkley Publishing Group
200 Madison Avenue, New York, NY 10016

Book design by Caron Harris

First Edition: May 1994

Library of Congress Cataloging-in-Publication Data

6/94

Gardner, Craig Shaw.
   Dragon sleeping / Craig Shaw Gardner.—1st ed.
      p.   cm.—(Dragon circle)
      ISBN 0-441-00049-5 (hard)
      I. Title. II. Series: Gardner, Craig Shaw. Dragon circle.
PS3557.A7116D7 1994   93-8723
813'.54—dc20   CIP

Printed in the United States of America

10   9   8   7   6   5   4   3   2   1

This one's for Kelly

○ Prologue

Deep beneath it all, the dragon slept.

Its jet scales had not seen the sun in so many years that people discounted stories of the creature. Old wives' tales, they'd say. Ancient myths. But others could feel the dragon's breath rumbling in their hearts. When they felt the earth move beneath their feet, they knew it was the dragon shifting in its slumber, and when the ground spouted fire, they knew the dragon was near to taking flight.

Still the dragon slept, within its home underground. The only light within that great cavern came when its eyes would flicker open, now and then, twin coals in the darkness that seemed to ask, "Is it time?"

The eyes opened more often now. The time would be soon. The dragon would arise again, as it had six times past, to destroy all before it.

And, as with every instance that the dragon slept, it grew, so it was always greater than the time before. Someday, on awaking, it would encompass all that is, and all that was, and all that might have been.

Its wings would darken the sky. Its talons would brush aside their weapons and crush their buildings. Most certainly, it would drink their blood. But the dragon would not be truly nourished until it fed on their souls.

The dragon slept, and the dragon dreamed. And in the dragon's dream, where there once were earth and trees and homes and lives, there was nothing but fire.

The dragon slept.

But it would not sleep forever.

PART ONE

O

A Short Visit to the Islands

◯ One

1967

The lights had gone out. The needle on the record had stopped dead, before the Turtles could even claim they were "Happy Together." Even the TV in the family room, his mother's constant companion, was silent. It was the first waking moment since Nick could remember that wasn't accompanied by the soft drone of news or comedies or quiz shows.

But it was more than just the power. When Nick Blake looked out the window, he saw that the storm had changed everything.

Not that it had been an ordinary storm. "A sudden summer hurricane," the TV weatherman had called it, before the whole street had lost electricity. Eight hours of torrential rain and fantastic wind, and then it was over as quickly as it had begun, the last of the wind blowing the storm clouds out of the sky by the fading light of evening. He could see the first glimmering of stars overhead between leftover bits of puffy grey, and a band of brilliant crimson on the western horizon: a band so bright that it looked to Nick like the edge of the world was on fire.

As to the street itself, the storm had left things rearranged. The rain had washed everything clean, leaving the houses almost glowing in the last light of dusk. Most of the damage seemed to have come from the wind. A couple of the trees had lost big branches, one right across Chestnut Circle up where it joined Oak Street, as if the storm had declared their particular cul-de-sac off limits. An old oak was leaning at a crazy angle against the top of the Smith house, its roots and a substantial piece of attached ground exposed at the edge of the street, obliterating that part of the sidewalk and gutter where the gale had tossed them aside.

Tossed aside—like a giant pulling up a toothpick, Nick thought. A giant who came in the night, crying a hurricane's worth of tears and rearranging the neighborhood with a single scuff of one huge shoe.

It was fantasies like that that made his father yell.

"What are you going to do with your life?"

Nick never had an answer; at least no answer that didn't come from his dreams. And his father didn't like to hear that kind of answer.

"Nick! For Christ's sake! You've got no plans for the real world."

He never replied. He couldn't even find his own voice when his father lectured him like that; his father looming larger and larger before him and Nick shrinking until he was hardly there at all.

"Your mother and I won't be here forever. Why do I even bother talking to you? Are you ever going to amount to *anything*?"

It was at times like that that Nick wished his father would just leave.

And three years ago, his father did exactly that.

He had divorced Nick's mother a year later, and gone off to face the real world all by himself, leaving Nick and his mother and the house on Chestnut Circle behind.

Sometimes Nick wondered if he'd driven his father away. His mother insisted it was something between her and his dad, that Nick had nothing to do with it. Nick supposed that made sense; he'd seen the same thing happen to the parents of other kids at school. But no matter how much sense it made, it didn't make the voice in the back of his head shut up; the voice that said Nick hadn't been good enough; hadn't lived up to expectations.

"You've let the team down."

That was the sort of thing his father would say.

But his father, Nick thought, belonged to the time before the storm.

The time before the storm. It might have been another of Nick's flights of fancy, but somehow the words felt right. Looking over the five houses that made up Chestnut Circle, he could almost imagine them as part of some little village, miles away from the rest of the world.

Nick stared past the dark houses to the even darker fields beyond: the surrounding farmland that hadn't yet become part of the subdivision. The trees out there appeared awfully close in the evening light, their silhouettes even darker than those of the houses before them.

The electricity seemed to be gone for miles. Nick couldn't see another man-made light anywhere. But the brightness of the sky made up for any lack below. Instead of the usual dozen or so stars that might make their way past the streetlight glare, tonight Nick could see thousands of them, so that the darkness was almost overcome by these countless points of light, the stars clustered together like a great mass of wildflowers on the field of night.

Nick had spent his last seven years on this street, ever since his parents had moved the family here, right after his tenth birthday. Never before had he heard this total quiet, seen this complete stillness. It was different after the storm. The rain-washed streets, the still houses, the incredible night sky, all made him feel that the world outside was something brand-new. And more than new. It seemed almost as if the whole street was waiting for something.

The phone rang.

Nick almost jumped out of his sneakers. Somehow their phone lines had survived the high winds.

The phone rang again. Where was his mother?

He ran from his bedroom and bounded down the stairs in the semidark, guided by the sound of the still-ringing phone. He reached the front hallway and grabbed the receiver midway through the sixth ring.

"Hello?"

There didn't seem to be anyone on the other end of the line. No one human, anyway. All Nick could hear was a distant whistling, and a rustling like leaves disturbed by a breeze. Nick said hello a second time, but there was no change on the line. He reached across to the base of the phone and pressed down the cut-off switch, then lifted his finger again. The rustling was gone. He had cut the connection. But there was no dial tone in its place. The phone was dead.

Nick replaced the receiver. Strange that the phone should ring like that. Maybe it had something to do with the lines going down. He wished he knew more about the way phones worked. Nick thought again of the street, and how it seemed to be waiting. He felt as if he had just gotten a phone call from the wind.

He heard another, distant sound in the evening quiet. It was bells again, but a different sort of bells than the phone this time, higher and fainter yet somehow more distinct, each bell tone separate from the next. It took him a moment to realize the bells were coming from outside the house, out on Chestnut Circle.

A dog barked. It sounded like Charlie.

"Nick?" It was his mother's voice. "Where are you, honey?" He heard the kitchen door slam.

"Here I am, Mom. I came down to answer the phone."

"The phone?" his mother called back in disbelief. He sensed more than saw her walking through the darkened kitchen toward the front hall.

He quickly explained how there hadn't been anyone on the line. He repeated his theory about there being some type of electrical disturbance.

"Can that sort of thing happen?" his mother asked uncertainly. Even in the now-almost-dark, her short, stocky form was reassuring.

She explained that she had gone over to commiserate with Mrs. Smith on the new placement of their oak tree. Mrs. Smith had been over there all by herself when the oak had smashed into their attic. Mr. Smith had been trapped in the city by the suddenness of the storm. Nick's mother imagined that a lot of people had been trapped by the storm in one way or another.

She went on to explain in some detail what the tree had done to the Smiths' back bedroom. His mother always liked details.

The ringing outside had grown so soft for a moment that Nick had almost forgotten about it. Now it was back, suddenly sounding much closer, a delicately high-pitched jingling noise, too strident to be wind chimes, like a happy but very definite call to attention.

"What on earth?" his mother murmured as she stepped past him to look out the front door. "Oh, my God. I haven't seen one of those in years."

Nick turned around as his mother opened the front door. She pushed open the screen door and walked out onto the front steps.

"Mom?" Nick called out to her.

She didn't seem to hear him. She kept on walking, down the steps and across the front walk. He pushed the screen door aside and followed her outside.

The last tinge of pink had left the sky. There was still no moon, but those stars were everywhere. The houses around them were nothing more than dark silhouettes against the brilliant sparkling white of the night sky. Nick looked down to his mother and saw a bright light beyond her on the street. It took him a second to make sense of that brilliant white box moving out there, like the time it takes your eyes to adjust from the shade to bright sunlight.

It was some kind of ice cream truck. No, not a truck; more like a wagon on the back of a three-wheeled bicycle. No, that would be tricycle, wouldn't it? It was pedaled by a stocky, bald man with a mustache so shaggy that it looked like he was trying to make up for the lack of hair on the top of his head. He was dressed all in white, not just shirt and pants, but coat and tie as well. His mother had said she hadn't seen one of these things in years. Nick hadn't seen one of these things *ever*.

As he walked down the steps after his mother, Nick was aware of other voices around him. He looked to see half a dozen adults and four other kids. The bells on this whatever-it-was had brought out the entire street.

The bald fellow in white used the handlebar brakes to come to a halt directly in front of Nick's house. The white box on the back of the bike sported large red and blue letters that announced:

MR. SERENDIPITY:
PURVEYOR OF TASTY TREATS
AND SMOOTH SURPRISES

The bald man swung his leg over the seat and smiled at the gathered neighborhood. "And what exactly can I get for you?"

Everyone started to talk at once.

"Where'd you come from?" Mr. Mills asked. You could tell he was the high school vice-principal. He always wanted to know everybody's business.

"Well," Mr. Serendipity replied. "I was hoping we'd all get introduced a bit more gradually."

"You got any ice cream sandwiches?" Mary Lou Dafoe asked. God, but she looked gorgeous in the starlight. Her long, dark hair framed her oval face, casting shadows that made her look older than her sixteen years; older and more mysterious, too. Nick sometimes wished the two of them didn't know each other so well. It was tough to ask out a girl who thought of you like a brother.

Todd Jackson sidled up to her. The starlight didn't make him look any different at all. He was still an overgrown, overmuscled lout.

"Hey, Mary Lou," he said in a voice just too loud for a whisper, "why don't you come over to my place? I've got tasty treats to spare." He leered in his usual offensive way, in case somebody thought he might actually be talking about ice cream.

God, Nick thought, how could Todd believe anybody would fall for that? But then, Todd was Mr. Attitude. Around school, he'd break your arm if you smiled at him the wrong way. He was big

enough to be a football player, too, although for some reason he
never tried out for the team. Back on Chestnut Circle, without his
goons at his side, he stopped being a bully and started being just
a jerk. Did he expect the adults to stand around quietly while he
made a crude pass at Mary Lou?

But the adults seemed too preoccupied by the ice cream truck
to pay any attention to Todd.

"Do you have Nutty Buddies?" old Mr. Furlong asked, his bald
head gleaming underneath the stars. His wife hung behind him,
probably waiting for her husband to say the wrong thing. There
was one thing the Furlongs knew how to do, and that was fight.
Some nights their arguments were so loud that the entire street
could hear them.

"How about Super Sundaes?" Mrs. Smith asked. She huddled
under a white cardigan that she had thrown over her shoulders,
despite the warmth of the evening. She was the oldest woman
on Chestnut Circle—somewhere in her sixties. Nick's mother
always referred to Mrs. Smith as "painfully thin." Somehow her
tall, skinny form made Mrs. Smith look even older.

Mrs. Smith glanced back at the other neighbors with a smile.
"I haven't had one of those in years."

"You wouldn't happen to have any Butter Crunch Bars?" Nick's
mother chimed in. "They don't seem to carry those down at the
market anymore."

Nick thought this was getting stranger by the minute. Now
would the bald man open up his freezer box and pull out anything anybody wanted? Ice cream treats that hadn't been made
for twenty years? Nick had seen this story before on *The Twilight Zone.*

The man in white pulled open the freezer compartment and
looked inside. Bright light poured from within. Steam formed
where the cold hit the humid summer air.

"Sorry," he said as he turned back to the neighbors. "All I've
got is vanilla ice cream covered with chocolate. Well, I might have
a couple of orange Popsicles in here somewhere." He shrugged
apologetically. "There wasn't much time, I'm afraid."

"What kind of ice cream truck is this?" Mr. Furlong complained.

"Well, actually, this isn't a truck—" the man in white began.

"Hey!" Furlong's son, Bobby, yelled as his friend Jason Dafoe
pushed him. "Get back in line, you scuz!" Bobby punched Jason's
arm. Jason giggled as Bobby grabbed for his glasses. Bobby took
a step forward, Jason a step back, as if they might chase each

other around the circle. The two of them were only three or four years younger than Nick, but they both acted like little kids.

"Look," Mr. Furlong insisted, "we'll take whatever you've got."

"That's just like you, Leo," Mrs. Furlong called out from where she stood behind him, ready at last to begin the battle. "You never think for a minute about what I really want."

Nick's mother had told him the Furlongs had been married for twenty-seven years. Nick sometimes wondered how they could have stayed married for twenty-seven minutes.

The ice cream man quickly distributed the bars to anyone who held out his hand. Even Mary Lou's parents came forward from where they had hung back silently.

"How much are these?" Mr. Mills asked.

"Oh," the bald man said with a start, "you mean money. Oh, dear, no, I couldn't. This isn't about money. I'm more of a—" He paused and frowned. "Oh, yes," he added as he smiled again. "That's what I am. A welcome wagon."

"What?" Nick's mother asked as she took a bite into her bar. "What do you mean? This is our street, we live here already. You must have that wrong." She paused to look at the ice cream. "You know, this tastes a little bit like that Butter Crunch Bar."

"Sort of like a Nutty Buddy, too," Furlong agreed as he chewed.

"Well, it is your street," the ice cream man said. He took a deep breath before he continued. "But something—well—I'm afraid that's what I've come to tell you about. When it gets light out here again, you'll see that things have changed."

"What do you mean?" Mr. Mills asked. "Because of the storm?"

"The storm? Oh, goodness, no. That was only a distraction, you see." The ice cream man grimaced. "I'm afraid I'm not explaining this very well."

Lightning streaked across the sky. Oddly enough, no thunder followed.

"Oh, no." The ice cream man studied the sky. "I had expected more time—you'll have to forgive me, but I can be found much too easily. That wouldn't be good, just yet. You'll be safer if I leave now, at least for tonight. I'll talk to you as soon as I can. Until then, well—remember, I was here first. And try to stay together. Whatever happens, please be ready."

He held up his hand, perhaps to wave to all the residents of Chestnut Circle, or maybe to stop all the questions that were pouring out of the adults. What Nick saw certainly stopped him,

for, in the shadowed part of the ice cream man's hand, he could
see the stars.

"Believe it or not," he called as if he was already very far away,
"we're all in this together!"

The man in white was gone. No, he hadn't pedaled away, or
even turned. He had simply vanished.

Mr. Furlong dropped his half-eaten ice cream bar on the street.
"I'm going home!" he announced.

Somehow, Nick thought, home wasn't the safe place it had been
a few hours before.

○Around the Circle #1:
A Visit with Nunn

Nunn didn't trust a soul. Those without souls, however, were a different matter.

The flash of crimson light seemed to agree.

It was there, waiting for him, when he opened the door to this, the most inner room of the place that he had built with his magic, half castle and half maze. But then the light faded, and all went back to darkness, as it was meant to be, safe from sunlight, and from spells other than his own.

The magician moved quickly into the lightless room. Nunn did not need to see his surroundings, at least in any ordinary way. Everything was stored quite carefully here, and anything that moved knew enough to stay out of his path. He paused at the room's center and clapped once, then twice more. A single point of light spread before him, and an image coalesced within: an elderly man in white giving handouts to the newcomers.

Nunn made a noise deep in his throat. "So quick," he whispered as he turned away from the image of his brother wizard. "How do you suppose he might have gotten warning?"

The air flashed red for an instant by his right shoulder.

Nunn rubbed at the single, deep furrow that ran across his forehead. "What do you mean? How could he have found out about the calling before I did?"

Another, longer flash of red lit the crowded workroom, a flash long enough to see the shape of the thing that made it, a shape that was almost human.

"Enough!" Nunn announced, his words increasingly angry. "This is no time for amusement."

The red light shifted to blue and then to green, as if it might entertain itself despite the wizard. Nunn reached out quickly with the flat of his hand, slashing across the illumination.

The green light screamed.

The magician withdrew his hand. His fingers tingled where he had made contact.

"Much better," the wizard added. "It pleases me so much when you choose to verbalize."

The green light shifted again and gained substance, defining itself into a small creature covered by fine hair. The light faded further as the hair turned brown, so that the creature might be mistaken for a large monkey or a small chimpanzee, unless one looked at the eyes. They still glowed with the same unnatural light.

The creature managed a ragged breath. "When you call me so abruptly," it spoke in a thin, high, and quite unpleasant voice, "it tears me up inside."

"So I'll put you back together," Nunn remarked dismissively. "It's not as if you could exist without me."

"One can dream," the monkey-thing replied with what looked like the beginning of a smile.

Nunn raised his hand to strike.

"Only using my wit!" the creature cried defensively. "You remember that! You're the one who gave it to me."

Nunn curled his fingers into a fist. The monkey was right. It was nothing more than what Nunn had created.

The monkey cowered, its eyes on the wizard's hand. Nunn half considered tearing the construct apart. It would be a satisfying bit of destruction. It would also be far too wasteful. Building it had been hard, intricate work. There were bound to be flaws. And every time he chose to tinker with this creation, he risked losing more of the energy he had bound inside the thing, until someday all that power would leak away and return to where it had come from. Nunn couldn't allow that, especially now. The monkey might not be an ideal vessel, but it would do. The Circle had begun, and even this creature was a part of it.

The monkey peered over Nunn's shoulder. "So Obar got to them before you?" The creature made a clicking noise with its tongue. "Such a generous soul."

Nunn spun about to look back at the glowing image. "Not for long," he replied after a moment's pause. "It's time for you to get to work."

The creature ambled over to the edge of the image and smiled.

"No killing," Nunn added quickly.

The monkey's smile vanished. Its eyes seemed to glow with disappointment.

"You'll have plenty of opportunity for that later," Nunn continued. "I'm sure that most of them are quite expendable. But we have to test them first."

The monkey's smile returned.

"Nunn," the creature said. "You're so good to me."

The thing vanished to do its work.

○ Two

"My lawn! What have they done to my lawn?"

The voice woke Nick up, but he didn't open his eyes until the pounding began.

"Joan!" another man's voice called. "I think you and Nick should come on out here!"

At first, Nick thought the second voice belonged to his father.

The thought brought him fully awake.

He forced himself to sit up. Why would it be his father? What did his father care about them anymore?

"Joan! Nick! Are you in there?"

No, certainly not his father. By the end of the second sentence, he knew that the voice belonged to Mr. Mills. He heard other voices, shouting somewhere down the street. It was quite a commotion for first thing in the morning.

If it was first thing in the morning. Nick noticed his clock radio still wasn't working; the dial seemed permanently stuck at 6:07. That meant the city hadn't gotten around to fixing the electricity. He glanced over at the bookshelf by the bed to that spot where he usually left his watch. There it was, and it was still ticking. Good old, cheap, wind-up watches; except that the face of this watch read 3:14. Either the sun was up awfully early or he had slept awfully late. Nick shook his head. Maybe his good old, cheap, wind-up watch had stopped for a while during the storm.

He heard the door open downstairs, and his mother's voice, speaking words he couldn't quite catch. He climbed out of bed and pulled on a T-shirt, a pair of jeans, and sneakers. He checked himself out in the full-length mirror on the back of his closet door. Not bad for a scrawny seventeen-year-old, he supposed; no new zits, and he hadn't sprouted fangs in his sleep.

He frowned. His hair looked different; even redder than usual this morning, almost like it was on fire. It must have something to do with the light. The sun lit the still-closed shade in such a

16

way that the pale paper seemed to glow with a pinkish tinge. He glanced back at his reflection. The only time he'd ever seen his hair look like this was in those old snapshots his father used to take. It was like the mirror was showing his hair in Kodachrome.

"Nick!" That was his mother's voice. "Come on down here, honey!"

Nick sighed. He'd regard his flaming locks some other time. He wanted to know what was going on. He swung his door open, crossed the upstairs hall, and took the stairs two at a time.

His mother waited at the bottom. She had her arms folded in front of her, a position that made her look short and imposing at the same time. He could tell from her expression that whatever was happening, it wasn't going to be fun.

"Hi, Nick," Mr. Mills said quietly when Nick reached his mother. Mills stood on the front walkway, just beyond the open door. He wasn't smiling the way he usually did when he visited. And his straight, almost gym-teacher-like posture looked definitely rigid.

Nick forgot to say hello back when he saw what was outside, past the vice-principal.

First off, the sky was green; well, more of an aqua. But definitely not blue. And all the colors beneath the sky were wrong, too. Nick thought again about his hair in those snapshots. The entire world looked like that now; like one of those pictures that hadn't been developed quite right. He went to the door, then stood and stared for a minute. Mr. Mills cleared his throat. Nick's mother didn't say a word.

"What's going on?" Nick asked when he found his voice.

"We don't know," Mills replied. He tried to smile reassuringly. Teachers could always smile reassuringly. Somehow, today, Mr. Mills' smile didn't work.

"Something's changed," Mills added after a moment. "Chestnut Circle is still here, but—well, it doesn't seem to lead into Oak Street."

Nick laughed at that, a quick, braying sound, louder than he'd meant it to be. What was Mr. Mills talking about? Nick tried to think of another question, something that would sound intelligent. Nothing came to mind. He decided he had to see for himself. He stepped outside.

"Something's changed"? That was all Mr. Mills could say? Nick felt the way he had when his first dog died and all the adults kept talking about his pet "passing away." It was more like *everything* had changed; like their corner of the world had gone crazy.

The sky had a green tint to it, and the sun was the kind of red you got at the end of a day in fall, except now that red sun was almost directly overhead. The houses around Chestnut Circle looked different, too, partially from the weird shift of colors. But some of the houses also had great strands of dark ivy crawling up their sides where there had been nothing but boards or brick the night before.

And there was more. At the far end of the circle, out where Oak Street used to be, but also in those spaces where he could see between houses, out beyond every yard, there was a forest made up of hundreds of thick, tall, dark trees; trees that plunged everything beneath them into shadow, so that the little clearing of Chestnut Circle was the only real point of light.

"My lawn!" that same voice yelled from down the street. "I'll call the city about this!"

Nick saw Mr. Sayre wildly waving his hands over his head. Sayre hadn't been out last night with the ice cream truck. It had probably taken his lawn to bring him out in the daylight. The only time Nick ever saw Mr. Sayre was when he was out working on his yard. Now, though, his manicured grass had turned a sickly blue, and a full quarter of his front lawn had been taken over by that same dark, thick ivy that attacked his house.

Sayre turned and glared straight at Nick, happy at last, Nick guessed, that there was somebody outside that he could yell at. "I'll call the city, I tell you!"

Nick had a feeling, even if the phones worked, that there would no longer be a city to call.

"What should we do?" Nick's mother asked from the doorway to the house.

"I think it's best if we get everybody together," Mr. Mills replied. "We all know each other here in the neighborhood, at least a little bit. We certainly know each other better than we know what's happened around here."

"That sounds good," his mother replied with a curt nod as she unfolded her arms. "Besides, I'm really worried about Constance Smith."

Mills nodded back. "Joan, if you can get Constance, and Nick goes next door and tells the Dafoes? The Jacksons, too." He turned to look out across the yard. "Why don't we meet in front of your house? I'll go up to the top of the circle and get the Furlongs. Maybe I'll even be able to talk some sense into old Sayre."

Both Mills and his mother started walking before Nick could say a thing. Not that he minded talking to the Dafoes. Heck, there might even be a chance that Mary Lou would answer the door. But the Jacksons? If Todd Jackson made Nick's skin crawl, talking to Todd's father made Nick's skin want to jump off his body. Todd would threaten you if you smiled at him the wrong way. Smile at Todd's father, and Mr. Jackson would start swinging.

Still, Nick supposed it was better than having to talk to crazy old Sayre, who was still out there screaming about his lawn. He had a job to do. He should get it over with.

He trotted over to the Dafoes' house. The door opened before he could knock. Mary Lou's little brother, Jason, stared up at him through his thick glasses.

"Jeez, Nick," Jason said, his voice cracking with excitement. "What's going on out there? Look at the colors, would you? Is it something about the hurricane?"

That was the longest speech Nick had ever heard from the fourteen-year-old. When Jason hung around with Bobby Furlong, Bobby did enough talking for both of them.

"Well, is it?" Jason insisted. He looked strange in this new light, too. His blond hair was almost white, his fair skin flushed a too-bright shade of pink.

"No," Nick remembered to answer. "I think it's something worse."

"Jason dear?" Mrs. Dafoe's voice came from somewhere deep inside the house. "Is that somebody at the door?" There was something about the way Mrs. Dafoe phrased things that sounded almost too polite.

"It's Nick from next door!" Jason called.

"Why, how nice to see you, Nick," Mrs. Dafoe said as she emerged from the kitchen. She looked like she would on any other day, her clothes perfectly ironed, her hair perfectly in place. "What can we do for you today?"

What can you do? It's the end of the world, is what he thought. What he said was, "Mr. Mills thinks there's something wrong. He wants everyone in the neighborhood to get together and talk about it."

"Oh, dear," Mrs. Dafoe replied, allowing herself the slightest of frowns. "I guess we could do that. Thank you, Nick. I'll get the rest of the family."

Nick thanked her back and ran to the next house.

"I see you!" Mr. Sayre yelled at his back. "Turn around when I'm talking to you! I want some *answers!*"

Nick banged on the Jacksons' door instead.

The door opened with such force that it slammed against the inside wall.

"What do you want?" Todd's old man demanded. He lurched forward into the doorway, squinting at the sunlight. Even though it was still the first thing in the morning (probably), he had a beer in his hand. "This better be fuckin' good."

Nick stumbled back down the steps, careful to keep out of arm's reach. The man stared over Nick's head, although it didn't look like his eyes were particularly focused. He also looked like he hadn't shaved in a few days. His rumpled clothing appeared to have been on his body just as long.

Nick looked to either side, ready to escape if Jackson made another move. "M-Mr. Mills," he stuttered. "He thinks something's going—"

Abruptly, Nick forgot what he was going to say next. He saw something in the woods and heard the same shouts he had heard before, sharp, short sounds; but now they were coming from around the corner of Jackson's house. Down the street, in the space between his house and the Smiths' next door, he could see men, dressed in brown, step from the shadows of the forest.

"Oh, shit," Jackson agreed. The door to the house slammed shut.

The newcomers seemed to be wearing uniforms of some sort. The brown showed on their sleeves and leggings and boots. They also wore breastplates and close-fitting helmets, but if these were made out of any metal, that metal was tarnished and dark. Once the men moved from their forest cover, they hardly made a sound. They reminded Nick of the scenes from Vietnam he saw on the news every night. Except the armor made the soldiers look a little like Spanish conquistadors.

Nick ran out into the street, toward the gathering neighbors.

"Mr. Mills!" he called.

"I see them," the schoolteacher said as he stepped beside Nick. He nodded to his right. "I thought I saw more moving farther up the street."

"*Now* you're out here!" Sayre was calling as the neighbors gathered on the street. "You took your own sweet time. Look at this. It's an outrage, I tell you! Someone is going to pay!"

No one looked at Sayre. By now, he seemed to be the only person unaware of the approaching army.

That's what Nick realized it was: a whole army of strange men dressed in brown, more than a hundred of them, he'd guess. He could see them now at the end of the street and in the yards between each of the houses, closing all the neighbors of Chestnut Circle inside their ranks.

"Someone is going—" Old Man Sayre shut up at last. He, too, had seen the visitors.

"If you would move forward?" a new voice spoke behind Nick and Mr. Mills. Nick started to turn his head. "Don't turn around," the voice continued. "Walk."

Nick walked. Out of the corner of his eye, he could see Mr. Mills walk as well. In front of him, he could see the other neighbors being herded toward the central asphalt circle.

"My lawn!" Sayre called out. "Watch where you're walking there! I've spent good money on this lawn!"

Todd and his parents walked from their house toward the others. Nick saw Todd wave at the lawn man to keep quiet. About ten of the men in brown moved forward and surrounded Sayre.

But the soldiers seemed to make him even more frantic. "You can't keep me quiet. I'll say my piece! This was a free country, last time I looked!"

Todd took a step toward the street, as if he might physically restrain Sayre. His father stepped in his way. Todd and his father stared at each other for a minute, but neither one said a word. Todd's hands tightened into fists, but he stayed on his own lawn.

For once, Nick thought, Todd had had a good idea. Sayre was going to get himself into real trouble. The soldiers were tightening their net. Nick didn't see any guns, but some of them had bows, with arrows notched and ready for flight. And all but a few of them had swords hanging at their sides, in elaborate scabbards of the same dark metal as the helmets.

Sayre's head began to twist from far left to far right and back again, as if he was trying to watch every soldier who approached him. "Who gave you permission? This is my house, and my yard. I warn you, I've got a gun. Another step, I'm going into my house, and when I come out—"

The soldier behind Nick shouted something to the men around Sayre. Two of the men in brown stepped forward and grabbed the lawn man's arms. A third pulled his sword. The handle was dark, but the blade shone bright silver in the strange sunlight.

"What?" Sayre called in disbelief. "You can't do this sort of thing on a man's—"

But the soldier in command had barked another order. The men to either side of Sayre pulled his arms away from his body so that he couldn't move. And the man with the sword drove the blade deep into Sayre's stomach, moving the double-edged weapon first right, then left, before pulling it free.

The other two men let go of Sayre's arms. Somehow Sayre was still standing. He moved his hands to his stomach, in a futile attempt to keep his insides from falling out onto the lawn.

"Yard," Sayre managed as blood bubbled between his lips. "Shouldn't. Oh, my. Sorry."

He fell first to his knees, and then to his face. His body spasmed twice, and then he was still.

Everyone in the neighborhood was quiet for a moment. It was the first time Nick had ever seen someone die.

He turned around to look at the man who had given the order. The man was dressed in the same dark uniform as the others, but wore no helmet. His pale face bore an even paler scar on each cheek, positioned as if they had been put there on purpose. The scars turned upward as the man smiled.

"We generally kill one," the leader said. "It makes the others follow orders that much more quickly." He shouted another guttural command to the swordsman, who leaned down and wiped the blood from his sword with Sayre's tattered polo shirt. "If you would all gather together in the circle?"

Nick turned back to see the neighbors moving toward the central asphalt. What else, he wondered, could they do?

"In this case," the leader of the soldiers continued conversationally, "I think that you would thank me. We shall never have to hear about his property again. Not that it's that much trouble to kill another one of you. It might be prudent to do as we say."

Nick looked from face to face of all the people from his street. Mrs. Smith was crying very quietly. The Furlongs were actually holding onto each other. He saw Mary Lou flinch as the leader shouted something else in the guttural tongue. Her brother, Jason, stared in confusion through his thick glasses, first at the soldiers, then at his sister and mother. Mary Lou grabbed his hand and led him toward the others. Todd Jackson walked backward toward the circle, his eyes half on the soldiers and half on his father, who pushed Todd's mother on in front of him. Mr. Mills and Nick's mother seemed to be staying close together as well.

Nick heard someone yell across the street. One of the soldiers had emerged from Sayre's house. He was carrying a revolver as if he didn't trust it, held away from his body, the handle pressed between thumb and forefinger, letting the gun dangle barrel-down.

He handed the gun to his leader, who placed the revolver in the palm of his hand as if he was much more familiar with this sort of weapon. The leader pulled something back on the rear of the gun, then pointed the revolver between the shoulder blades of Sayre's body.

He pulled the trigger. The gunshot sounded very loud in the silence. Sayre's body jerked, but Nick guessed that was only from the force of the bullet entering the dead flesh.

One of the neighbors, Mrs. Furlong maybe, shouted. Nick couldn't turn around to look. He was still staring at the gun.

"It is much quicker than the sword," the leader said as he looked directly at Nick. "While it won't work forever, it will work for now. I trust you won't require me to use it on you." He raised the nose of the revolver to point at Nick's chest.

Nick realized he still stood in the middle of the street. He hurried to join the others as the leader said something to his fellow soldiers in that second language. They laughed.

"And now it is time we moved along. It is not too good, these days, to stay in one place too long, or to have too much fun. We have no desire, just yet, to wake the dragon."

He turned to glance at the forest. "North, I think, will be the safest route. You can never be too sure, especially with the way things have been lately." He looked back at the neighbors. "But I'm quite sure you realize that things have changed around here."

This time it was the leader who laughed.

○ Around the Circle #2:
Todd at Fourteen

It was all crap, but some crap was worse than others.

"Who moved my tools?"

Todd knew that tone of voice. From anyone but his father, it might almost sound reasonable. He swore under his breath as he heard his father's heavy footsteps on the stairs.

He stared across the kitchen table to where his mother stood by the stove. Her gaze left the pot she was tending. She looked first at the floor, then at the ceiling. Hunting for somewhere to escape, Todd thought. Except that there was no escape around here.

She didn't look at Todd. Nobody in the family looked at each other when there was this kind of trouble. Todd and his mother both waited silently and did their best not to watch as his father opened the basement door and entered the kitchen.

Maybe, Todd thought, this would be the time he fought back. Something had kept him from doing it in the past. Maybe the fact the guy was his father, no matter what kind of a jerk he was. Or— and this was a better reason—the fact that if he made it bad for his father, his father would make it worse for his mother. And, no matter what happened, Mom wouldn't leave.

"Somebody's been using my fuckin' hammer." His father held the wooden handle in his hand like a club. "You know how I feel about somebody using my fuckin' things without per- mission."

Todd knew what he wanted to say: You get almost as angry as when Mom used to mention there was something broken around the house. His mother never mentioned when things were broken anymore. She didn't mention much of anything around her husband.

His father paused for a minute, waiting for a confession. There was total silence, punctuated only by the man's breathing—in and out, in and out.

Maybe this wouldn't be one of the bad ones.

24

His mother didn't look at him, and he didn't look at his mother. They both looked toward his father, without meeting his eyes.

The front step had been broken. His mother had been very upset about that loose board. She had been desperate to have it fixed. To his mother, it didn't matter what went on inside this house, but the outside of the house had to look fine. What would the neighbors think?

Todd had fixed the step when his father was out with the boys. His father was out with the boys a lot these days. Somehow Todd had put the hammer back wrong. He hadn't been careful enough; had hung it back wrong on its hook or disturbed the dust that covered half the workbench. Dad never really used his tools anymore. He would just go down to the basement from time to time to make sure nobody else had touched them.

"Answer me!" his father demanded as he slapped Todd's mother full across the face. At least he hit her with the hand that didn't hold the hammer.

His mother started to cry.

As usual, that only made things worse.

"I'll give you something to cry about."

His mother took a step away. His father closed back within striking range.

That was it. Todd couldn't sit here at the breakfast table and see his mother get another black eye. He'd had enough of his father's crap. He stood up and faced the old man.

"Dad, listen—"

His father spun to confront him. Both hands held the hammer now, as if he was holding the tool back from lashing out. He smiled, an expression of fury rather than joy.

"What do you want, Toddy boy?" The words came out slowly, his voice weighed down with sarcasm. "Why are you always getting in my way? You were worthless from the day you were born." He made a sound somewhere between a grunt and a laugh. "If your mother had had enough sense not to get knocked up, I wouldn't be in this mess today."

"Dad," Todd tried to explain, "the front step was broken. I had to—"

Dad's strange smile twisted deeper into his face. "So it was you, you little shit? You want to use my hammer so much? I'll give you my hammer!"

He swung the hammer wildly at Todd's head. This time Todd was faster. He ducked the blow as his father twisted around, carried by the hammer's momentum.

His mother screamed and tried to grab his father's arm. Dad pushed her to the floor and forgot about her. He turned back to Todd. He held a hammer, and his son was going to pay.

Todd took a step away, and found his back pressed against the shelves of the corner hutch where his mother kept her extra plates and cookbooks. There was nowhere else to run.

His father rushed forward, trying to tackle Todd first before delivering the killing blow. Todd's arms flew out from his body as he tried to escape. All three shelves came crashing down behind him. There were broken plates and cookbooks everywhere.

The dramatic noise stopped his father for an instant. Todd felt a tingling from where one of the heavy volumes had caught him behind the ear.

"Shit!" Todd screamed. He slammed his open palm against the now empty wall. The pain had brought his anger out at last.

His father blinked. "You're gonna break every fuckin' thing in the house." He tightened his grip on his hammer.

Todd had had enough. "You're the one who's broken, Dad." His father swung at him, but the broken plates around him gave Todd some space to move. He ducked the swing easily. He found his own hand forming a fist. One more swing and he'd knock his father across the room.

But his father's foot slipped on the broken china. He lost his balance and staggered three steps to the left.

Todd found himself laughing. "You're so lame! You could never catch me!"

"Lame?" his father screamed, fully lost in his rage. "I'll show you who's lame! I'm twice the man you'll ever be. My son the fuckup. You're all fuckups, every one of you!"

The hammer smashed a teapot on the kitchen counter. Todd saw that his mother had never gotten off the floor. She had curled into a fetal position in the corner. Father and son circled each other warily.

The doorbell rang.

Todd froze. All the rage and fear at his father drained from him, replaced by a different sort of panic. Somebody had heard. It was a hot day. Most of the windows were open.

"The neighbors can go to hell!" his father screamed.

There was a pounding on the door. The doorbell rang for a second time.

His mother got up, doing her best to straighten her clothes as she walked to the door. His father paused, letting the arm that held the hammer fall to his side.

Todd heard his mother open the door, followed by her reassuring response to a male voice whose words were not quite audible.

"No, Officer," she said brightly. "There must be some mistake. There's no problem here."

The door closed.

"Goddamned police," Todd's father muttered. "Who do they think they are, interfering in people's lives!" He pointed the hammer at Todd, but made no further move to strike out. "I don't want you talking to anyone about this, hear? Everything stays in the family!" He threw the hammer on the table and turned toward the family room. "I need to get a drink."

He staggered from the room, his anger forgotten.

His mother appeared at the other door, the one that led to the front hall. "I don't know what I'm going to do," she whispered. "I just don't."

There was no way to save his mother. Todd was as full of crap as the rest of them.

And there was no way for that crap to go away, unless he could get out of here.

○ Three

The dozen neighbors on Chestnut Circle were surrounded and prodded toward the forest behind Nick's house. The soldiers seemed to be very enthusiastic with their spears. The neighbors were much quieter than the night before; the Furlongs didn't argue, Bobby and Jason kept their hands to themselves, the Dafoes huddled around their daughter, muttering how "everything'll work out fine." No one else wanted to end up like Old Man Sayre.

There were some words between Todd Jackson and his father. Nick couldn't quite make out what they said. The leader of the men in brown sauntered over to the two of them and cheerfully waved his gun in their faces. Todd stared back at the soldier for a minute before looking away. His father hurried ahead. Neither said another word.

Nick's mother waved for him to hurry along. He felt something sharp at his back and decided he'd better follow her lead. He left the sunshine and stepped into the deep shadow of the woods.

Their forced march was brought up short by the line of trees and dense undergrowth before them. The dark ivy that had crawled into their neighborhood also curled here from tree to tree, creating such a wall of vegetation that Nick could barely see ten feet into the woods. If the soldiers had cut a path through the growth before, there was no sign of it now.

The leader shouted another of his guttural orders, and a pair of men freed axes from their belts and hacked away at the creepers. A high, shrilling sound filled the air, a noise with all the timbre and grating intensity of those early-warning sirens they had at school. Nick thought about covering his ears but didn't. He didn't want to draw any more attention to himself than he had to.

The largest of the vines separated with a final shriek, and then the forest was quiet again. The noise, Nick realized, had come from the vines themselves, as if they were calling out in pain.

The men with the axes pushed their way into the undergrowth.

"I suggest that you move quickly now," the leader addressed the neighbors. "These vines do like to rejoin."

As he spoke, Nick looked down at the pieces of vine, which had been severed in half a dozen places. Every piece of soot-colored vegetation was moving, twisting about on the ground like half a dozen blind snakes, their severed ends oozing a liquid darker than blood. A couple of the larger pieces sent out deep green shoots as well, leafy creepers that sought to twirl around other fragments of the vine.

"Shall we move?" the leader reminded them in a voice that sounded like anything but a request.

Mr. Mills led the way through the opening, and the others followed. The remaining soldiers took up the rear.

"Once in the forest," the leader continued conversationally, "the going gets easier. These vines climb higher and spread through the branches of the trees. They quite effectively keep anything else from growing down below."

It was quite dark under the trees. So little light filtered through the vines overhead that Nick got the feeling he was walking through some never-ending dusk. The crunch of leaves under their feet made their march anything but quiet.

Mrs. Smith stumbled on a root. Mr. Mills stepped back and helped her walk. She whimpered every time she put her weight on her left foot. The soldiers showed no indication of slowing down.

Their dark surroundings seemed to make the leader of their captors even more cheerful. He jogged ahead for all the neighbors to see. "Take heart!" he called as he opened his arms wide to include all his captives. "We are going to a place of some comfort. At least it can be quite comfortable if you wish it to be."

He laughed again as he hugged his arms to his chest. "You do not appear to be enjoying yourselves. Perhaps you would like to be entertained. I will answer questions. You may call me the Captain. It's not an exact translation, but it will do."

At first, the Captain was answered by silence. Nick heard other noises in the woods besides their walking. There was a kind of perpetual rustling going on overhead, as if something was moving through the branches of the trees. Nick wondered if there were animals up there, or something else like the wailing vines. He heard another noise in the distance, too, like a dog barking. Nick had forgotten about his dog. What had happened to Charlie?

There were still no questions. Nick wondered if anyone would dare to break the shuffling silence. To his surprise, it was his mother who spoke up first.

"Why are you taking us away from our homes?" she called ahead to the leader.

"Good, good," the Captain encouraged. "It is important that you speak up. It helps us to determine your true nature." He spent a moment frowning at the ground as he walked. "But your question is more difficult than it first appears. You see, your homes, as you call them, are your homes no longer, for they have been moved from familiar surroundings into an environment that might be— well—considered actively hostile."

He pulled Old Man Sayre's revolver from his belt and waved it grandly. "We did you a favor by liberating you from those places. In a few days, you won't be able to recognize those homes of yours." He looked up the nose of the gun into the trees. "That's what happens with these vines, you know." The Captain thrust the revolver back into his belt.

Nobody spoke for another period of time. Nick could no longer hear the dog. Maybe the vines were keeping Charlie trapped back on what remained of Chestnut Circle. Nick felt a moment of panic. How would Charlie survive in a weird place like this?

"Captain." This time it was Todd who spoke. "Why should you care what happens to us?"

"Even more impressive," the Captain remarked before he answered. "We care because what happens to you happens to us as well. There was a reason our worlds were joined. Not of course that common men like you or me are privy to those sorts of reasons. But I understand that one of you, maybe more, was needed."

"Needed?" Todd shot back. "Needed for what?"

Their captor shook his head ruefully. "I'm afraid not. Not yet." The Captain let his hand rest on the butt of his revolver. "Perhaps that answer should wait until we reach our destination." He turned forward to look at the men who led their band.

Todd balled his hands into fists, but his arms stayed at his side. He glanced over at Nick, but not with the sneer he usually wore. Todd's look was more one of appraisal, like he was getting ready to do something and wanted to know if Nick would go along.

"But come," the Captain called over his shoulder, "certainly there are more questions."

Nick decided it was time he asked a question. The more information they had, the more chance they had to survive. "Where are we?"

"The most forsaken spot on all the seven islands," the Captain said with a laugh. He added something in the guttural tongue, and his men laughed dutifully as well. "Dark and dirty and full of the most annoying—" He paused as he again pulled the gun from his belt. "It's time for a demonstration."

Nick half expected the gun to be leveled at him. Instead, the Captain pointed the muzzle up toward the rustling vines overhead.

"We have company," the Captain announced. "Maybe we can bring one of them down for your closer inspection." He pulled the trigger.

The roar of the gun was followed by a cry of pain far more human than the screams of the vines. Something fell with a thud on the packed earth ahead.

The Captain grinned at the neighbors. "Come on. Let's take a look at what I brought you."

He looked directly at Nick, then beckoned the teenager forward. The soldiers broke rank so that Nick could follow their leader.

Nick walked where he was supposed to. As he approached, the Captain pointed the gun at the ground.

"Here's the little piece of dung," the Captain announced jovially.

Nick looked where he pointed, at a pale creature on the leaf-strewn ground. The thing was still alive. It had curled into a ball, probably to protect itself from further pain. It made no noise, but Nick could see it breathing. Its skin was wrinkled, and closer in color to an albino white than the flesh of Nick's hand. It was small, too. Maybe, if the thing was stretched out head to toe, it would be three feet high. It looked exactly like a little old man.

The creature struggled weakly as the Captain grabbed it at its waist and lifted it off the ground. It bent and twisted its head about, its teeth snapping at the Captain's hand. The leader simply shifted his grip so that the teeth couldn't reach to do their damage.

"Filthy things," the Captain remarked with distaste. "You can't stop to rest anywhere around here. Men fall asleep, they don't wake again. And you should see what they do with the pieces of the body." He dropped the wounded thing onto the ground. "Their idea of a joke."

The Captain pulled back his foot to kick the body away.

And something happened. Nick saw the whole world blur around him. He felt dizzy, disoriented, like once when he had been struck on the side of the head by a baseball.

It was over as quickly as it had come. The other men in brown talked quickly, agitatedly. Nick heard one word over and over again in their conversation. It sounded like *ken-nak-ka.* "Kennake," maybe.

The Captain yelled at his men. He used the word, too. The men stopped talking.

The Captain frowned back at the neighbors. "Stupid. I am too full of myself." He looked down at the gun in his hand with disgust, then threw it away with a side-armed motion, the way Nick would throw a Frisbee. Nick heard the metal crack against the trunk of a distant tree.

The Captain barked an order. The brown-uniformed soldiers began to walk. That meant that the neighbors had better move as well. One of the soldiers yelled something at Nick. Even though he couldn't understand the words, Nick knew the soldier meant for him to rejoin the rest of the prisoners. One of the other soldiers walked past him toward the wounded creature, the soldier's spear angled toward the ground.

Nick hesitated a fraction of a second before he took a step. Maybe, he thought, he could escape. They no longer had the gun. Maybe there was some way he could get away, maybe even help the others.

But he was in the middle of a strange world, with creatures and a language that he couldn't understand. Where could he go? What might he do?

He could run. His skinny body could move pretty fast. He had even competed some on the junior varsity track team a couple years ago, before his father left. Some of the other kids had called him Fire Engine because of his red hair.

Would the soldiers kill him if he tried? He half imagined, if he got away, that this Captain would kill another of the neighbors for spite. He wouldn't want anyone else to get hurt because of him.

He saw the Captain out of the corner of his eye. And the Captain had pulled a knife.

Nick decided that it was better not to risk things now. He walked back toward the others. Somehow, though, he still felt like a coward. And he didn't want to look at Todd.

Nick's father had always called him a dreamer. He had a chance to act—and he hadn't. His father was long gone. But Nick realized he still wanted to prove him wrong.

Nick heard a shriek behind him. He didn't have to look around to know that the spearman had finished his leader's work.

The Captain increased his stride, then fell in at Nick's side. The soldier attempted to smile, but whatever had happened a moment before seemed to have undermined his smugness.

"It is too bad about the weapon," he said after a moment, his eyes scanning the forest to either side. "We will have to kill you now by more conventional means. It will be slower that way, and probably more painful."

The Captain looked back at the rest of the neighbors. He already appeared to be more cheerful, as if all he needed was the talk of death to put him in good spirits. "Not that we will have to kill any of you, so long as you see the justice of our cause."

They resumed their walk. But the new silence was almost immediately interrupted by the flapping of wings. Something swooped close over Nick's head. A soldier called out behind him. Then the wings were gone in the distance.

The men started to talk again. This time, the word they repeated sounded like *raven*.

The leader spoke harshly to his men, then added in English, "I am sorry. You must go more quickly now, or we will kill you."

The soldiers doubled their pace, pushing the neighbors before them. Nick didn't think Mrs. Smith could keep up. He didn't want her to be the second one to die. But what could he do?

"Watch out!" Todd called from behind him.

Nick looked up. A great tree trunk was crashing down toward them. He jumped back and saw another tree crashing to their left. The ground shook as the two great trunks hit the ground almost at the same time. Nick shielded his eyes from the flying bark and leaves. He started to take his hand from his eyes and saw another tree fall to earth in the space between his fingers. A second later, a fourth smashed down where they had walked only a minute before.

Nick felt a hand on his shoulder. He looked around. It was Todd.

"We can get away!" Todd whispered. He nodded toward their left.

Nick followed Todd's gaze and saw what he meant. The neighbors were still all pressed together in this new clearing made by the fallen trees. But the soldiers had scattered back in confusion, so that two of the great trunks separated them from their captives, and their left flank was completely open to the forest.

"Are you crazy?" Todd's father called after him. "They'll kill us if they see us run!"

"I don't think I can run," Mrs. Smith managed.

"Someone will have to stay with her," Nick's mother cautioned.

Todd took a step toward freedom. Another tree crashed to the right of the soldiers. The Captain yelled at his men. They didn't seem to hear him anymore, staring instead into the darkness of the surrounding forest.

"Get back here, you crazy fool!" Todd's father demanded. "You don't do anything I don't tell you to!"

"You're the one who's crazy, you piece of shit," Todd replied. He called out to the others. "Bobby! Mary Lou!"

"Mr. Mills!" Nick called. "Mom!" Todd was right. Now was the time to get out of here. He glanced back at the soldiers to his right and almost stopped dead. The Captain's orders were finally taking effect, and the soldiers, though rattled, were staring to fall back into line.

"All of you!" Todd yelled. "Let's try and get the fuck away from here. All they're going to do is kill us. It's either now or later."

Nick saw a couple of the soldiers notch arrows in their bows. He didn't want to die. But he also didn't want to meekly go along with this Captain fellow to whatever unpleasant future the soldiers had planned for them.

Nick had to do something.

The Captain screamed at his men as another tree smashed to earth behind them. Was there really any way Nick and the others could get away? Maybe, if they could only run fast enough.

"We have to go!" Todd urged. He took a couple more steps away, as if his lead would convince everybody else to run as well. "Hey, come on! What kind of losers are you? We get out of here now, we help the others later!"

"Get back here, you little shit!" his father called. "You'll get us all killed!"

Nick wanted to run, but he could almost feel the arrow in his back. He couldn't just stand here. He couldn't let someone like Todd Jackson get the better of him.

Nick heard the flutter of wings. He looked up and saw a bird, darker than the leaves overhead, fly low above them toward the bowmen.

The soldiers screamed. Somehow, Nick knew, the bird was there as a distraction, just as the trees were there to help them escape. If they were going to get away, this was maybe their last chance.

"Now!" Nick screamed, and started to run. He saw Todd right beside him, heard other footsteps to his rear.

The soldiers' angry voices receded behind them. Nick heard something whistle to his left. He wondered if it was an arrow. Nobody near him made a sound beyond their running feet. He heard a woman scream behind them, but he didn't dare look around.

"Not in a straight line!" Todd called out. He sprinted through an opening to their left between the trees. Other footsteps followed, but Nick guessed that there were only two or three neighbors behind him. The others must have been caught. Or maybe they hadn't had enough nerve to run.

Todd turned one way and then another. Nick followed close at his heels as they zigzagged between the trees, until Nick could no longer remember which direction they had come from.

They ran until they couldn't run anymore. Nick's ribs ached so hard he half imagined the onrushing air would crush them against his lungs and heart. Todd stumbled in front of him but kept on running. Somehow Nick caught up to him.

"Todd," he managed. "Enough."

"Yeah," Todd agreed. He broke his stride and almost fell. "I guess you're right. I guess we lost them by now." He made a noise that probably would have been a laugh if he had any breath left in him. He staggered to a halt, leaning at last against a tree. Nick fell down, exhausted, on the leaf-strewn ground.

"You know, Nick?" Todd said from where he was still barely standing. "I guess you're not as much of a chickenshit as I thought."

Nick forgot about anything he might say back to Todd when he heard new footsteps crashing through the leaves. He looked up and saw the two younger boys, Bobby Furlong and Jason Dafoe, Mary Lou's little brother.

Bobby waved at the older two, then turned around and looked at the forest, as if expecting others. Even though he was short and stocky, he acted like he did this kind of running every day of the week. Skinny Jason sank to his knees and pushed his glasses back up his nose. He seemed even more winded than Nick.

The forest behind them was silent and still.

"C'mon, guys!" Bobby called out to the trees. "Where are you?"

The kids were the only ones who had followed. What had happened to Nick's mother? Or Mr. Mills? Where was Mary Lou? There was no sign of any of them.

But there was no sign of the soldiers, either.

"What do we do now?" Jason spoke for all of them.

"We could go back to our houses," Bobby suggested with a big smile, like he was getting away with something. "That is," he added, his smile falling a little, "if we could find them."

Todd shook his head. "Bad idea. That would be the first place the soldiers would look. Besides, from the way that the Captain spoke, I don't think our houses are going to be there very long."

Something growled out in the woods.

"Oh, God," Jason whined. "What's that?"

Nick knew they didn't have any answer to that, either. He stood and felt in his pockets. "Do we have anything that we can use as a weapon?"

"I've got my dad's old Boy Scout knife," Bobby volunteered. "I was trying to learn how to whittle."

"Whittle?" Todd asked with his usual sneer.

"Yeah," Bobby said defensively. "My grandfather used to do it. I've got a couple of cool pieces of wood he fooled around with."

"Let me see it," Todd demanded. Bobby handed it over. Todd flipped out the biggest of the blades. "Not much." He crouched and held the open knife in front of him. "Maybe we'll get lucky."

Nick looked back at the spot where he thought he'd heard the growling. Was there a dark shape out there, running between the trees?

All four of them yelled when they heard a barking growl only a few feet behind them. Nick whirled around, ready to either strike out or run.

A dark brown shape barked back at him.

"Hey!" Nick called. "It's Charlie!"

He would recognize *his* dog anywhere, even looking as bad as that dog did now. Charlie's fur was ruffled and dirty, as if he had had to make it through briars or some other rough going. It looked like he might have a new scratch on his nose, too, like he'd been in a fight. Nick hoped it wasn't anything serious.

The dog bounded forward and leapt up to lick Nick's face. It was Charlie, all right. No other dog's breath could smell that bad.

"All right!" Jason clapped his hands and whistled. "Now we've got some protection!"

As if on cue, the dog gave up greeting his master to pace about in front of the four. He started to growl again.

"Charlie?" Nick called. "What is it?"

The dog turned to bark up at a nearby tree.

"Is that any way to greet your savior?" a voice called from a low branch overhead. Nick peered up, and made out a great black bird in the gloom.

It was Bobby who spoke this time. "Who are you?"

The bird—the talking bird—fluffed his feathers with pride. "I am Raven. I am the creator of all things."

A great, booming laugh erupted from the trees behind the four of them.

"No doubt you were about to mention my part in this?" a very deep voice added. All four sons of the neighborhood turned around. There in front of them was a well-muscled fellow who also happened to be eight feet tall. His skin was some tone halfway between tan and green, and his head was covered by something that looked more like tiny leaves than hair. His smile, however, was very friendly. Nick found his fear retreating again, to be replaced by a familiar confusion. How could someone that large not make some sort of noise as he approached?

The large man smiled. "Greetings, and many welcomes."

"Who are *you*?" Bobby asked once again.

The large man laughed as if the question was highly amusing. "There are those who call me the Oomgosh."

"There are those who call him other things, too," Raven snapped.

"Oomgosh is my preferred name," the large fellow explained patiently. "You may address me as such."

"And you can call me Raven," the bird interjected as if he wanted to regain the center of attention.

"You say you made all this?" Nick asked the bird with a certain skepticism. Todd snorted derisively.

"Raven does not make," the bird replied imperially. "Raven is, and all else follows."

Nick shook his head and turned to the Oomgosh. Somehow it was easier to talk to someone who looked at least vaguely human. "Why should we believe a bird?"

"Raven is very believable," the Oomgosh replied.

"The Oomgosh agrees with everything I say," Raven added drily.

"Of course," the Oomgosh agreed. "Raven is also a great liar."

The bird squawked. Nick wondered if that sound was Raven's laugh.

"Well, Raven did save you!" the bird insisted. "That is, Raven and the Oomgosh."

At that, the large green man lost his smile. "You were saved, but at a cost."

"Cost?" Raven protested. "What cost? Almost all the trees were dead."

"Not all, no," the Oomgosh replied sadly. "Not all. Still, it had to be done. The newcomers are most important."

Todd got an odd smile on his face. "More important than the raven here?"

This time the bird's squawk sounded angry. "Please. Address me as 'Raven,' not 'the raven.' The use of that extra word implies the existence of others." The bird ruffled his feathers and tossed his head. "Raven is unique."

Nick looked from one strange creature to the other. "You felled the trees, then. Did the two of you also do that"—he couldn't find the words—"that other thing, too?"

"Raven can do anything," the bird replied.

"What other thing?" was the Oomgosh's more pertinent response.

"I don't know." Nick tried hard to describe the feeling he had. "There was this moment, when everything seemed to fall away—"

"Yeah!" Bobby added with a yelp. "The whole place whirled around, and the air got funny—"

The Oomgosh laughed. "You give Raven far too much credit. That was the voice of the dragon."

"The dragon?" Jason piped up. "You mean there's a dragon around here?"

"Oh, most assuredly, no," the Oomgosh answered. "If the dragon were close, truly close, we would all be dead. But the dragon heard the soldiers. And the dragon called."

"Even Raven admits," the bird added, "as good as my ears are, the dragon's are better."

Nick still didn't understand. "What did the dragon hear?"

"Loud noises, perhaps," the Oomgosh ventured. "They make him stir in his sleep."

"Or the force of a great anger," Raven added. "Remember the stories."

"The dragon has slept for so long, no one quite remembers," the Oomgosh explained.

The bird fluttered its dark wings in agitation. "Even Raven's memory slips now and then. But we must be going."

"You are right," the Oomgosh agreed. "We are on a mission." He stretched out his arms to include the four boys. "We are all on a mission now." With that, he turned and marched off into the woods.

"Better keep up," Raven cautioned. "The Oomgosh can move quickly on those legs of his."

Charlie looked back up at the bird, a growl deep in his throat.

"And keep that creature away from me!" Raven cautioned. "You wouldn't want Raven to hit it with a bolt of lightning!"

"Lightning?" The Oomgosh's laugh boomed from up ahead. "Oh, Raven, you are most assuredly unique among birds."

"Most assuredly, my Oomgosh," Raven replied as he flapped his wings and flew from his perch to shadow the giant. "Most assuredly."

"What do we do now?" Jason whispered.

The four young men from Chestnut Circle all looked at each other for an instant. And then they followed.

○ Four

She should have gone with them.

Mary Lou looked at the spot where the four boys had disappeared into the woods. She had wanted to run, to get free of this nightmare, to go with her brother and the others, to somehow be away from everything.

But before she ran, she had turned and looked at her parents.

They clutched each other tight. Mother buried her face against Father's chest. And the way her father looked at Mary Lou; her parents were so upset, so afraid. What would they do if she left them?

Don't go. Mary Lou had seen it in her father's eyes. *Don't go.*

What a good daughter you are. Her father said it all the time. She did her best to make her parents happy. And a good daughter could never run away. Especially not now.

A man with a spear stepped between her and freedom. She took a step back toward her father and quickly looked around her.

For what? Whatever chance she had for escape was gone by now. The trees had stopped falling, and the leader of the soldiers had gotten his men to surround the remaining captives. Four of the soldiers cautiously climbed across the new barriers and followed Nick and the others into the forest.

"No more talking!" barked the man who called himself Captain. Mary Lou hadn't noticed anybody talking. They were all too scared. She twirled a strand of long brown hair around her finger. It was a nervous habit. Her mother yelled about it all the time.

The leader scowled at all of them. "I want nothing more from any of you," he added hurriedly. "Nothing." He turned away from them and marched ahead.

She heard something new in the Captain's last remark. She had expected him to be angry. She hadn't expected him to be as full of fear as the rest of them.

The soldiers prodded the neighbors on with their spears. Mrs. Smith had more trouble than ever keeping up. She tried to smile when Mr. Mills and Mrs. Blake helped her, but the pain showed through, making her look older than ever. Mr. Jackson looked angry. His wife and the Furlongs looked afraid. Only Mary Lou's parents managed to look cheerful. Her parents smiled in public, no matter what.

The Captain shouted something from where he marched at the front, almost out of sight of the rest of the party. A pair of soldiers hastily fashioned a litter from some dead branches and strapped the old woman inside. Mary Lou guessed that their leader didn't want to risk losing another one of them.

The neighbors started to walk, Mary Lou following close behind her parents, all of them surrounded by the soldiers. They marched quickly, and, to Mary Lou's surprise, not for all that long, halting a few moments later in the first clearing she had seen since they had left what remained of their homes. The open space was almost square, around the size of the baseball field behind the high school.

The clearing was also the first place Mary Lou had seen that was completely free of the dark ivy. In fact, nothing grew in the packed reddish-brown dirt, which looked as if it had been beaten down by thousands of boots. At the center of the clearing was a large building made of logs, topped by a tower; Mary Lou guessed it was a lookout post. No one emerged from the building as they approached. The place seemed deserted.

The soldiers stopped and pointed at the neighbors with their spears. The neighbors stopped as well.

"This is all of them?" someone spoke from their midst. "Was I misinformed?" The question was followed by a laugh. "I am never misinformed."

There was another man standing in their midst, although Mary Lou had no idea how he had gotten there. She blinked as the scene in front of her shifted, as if she was looking through a shimmer of heat or a sudden sheet of rain.

A moment ago, she could have sworn he was wearing some sort of dark-colored robes. Now he was dressed in a dark blue business suit with wide lapels, a white shirt, and a grey tie with silver stripes.

Did he think this would make them more comfortable? The new costume made Mary Lou trust him even less than before. He reminded Mary Lou of that salesman who'd sold them their new car. He smiled at the assembled crowd.

Mr. Mills stepped forward. He stood as tall as the soldiers as he stared at the other man. "What do you want with us?"

The man in blue nodded agreeably. "Only to help you, really," he said easily. "You've had the misfortune to be dragged from your homes, into a hostile environment. And that, I assure you, was none of our doing." He waved at the soldiers, who had now all put down their weapons. "Excuse us if our methods seemed harsh. Better, though, that you are physically moved from a dangerous place than to face some of the other things that live on this island."

"Then we're on an island?" Nick's mother asked.

"Yes," the man replied in a tone that reminded Mary Lou of her teachers, "one of seven islands, clustered together in this little corner of the world. Our world, that is."

"What?" Mr. Furlong demanded. He was so upset that his whole face turned red, all the way up to his thinning hair. "Where have you taken us? Is this some of that crazy flying-saucer stuff?"

"We haven't taken you anywhere. You have been brought by something else—" He paused and frowned for the first time. "Something difficult to explain. It is something very powerful, that tries to control everything that lives here, and everything that comes here. We call this thing the dragon, although it is more than a simple creature."

"Who's trying to control us?" Mr. Jackson demanded. "I don't take orders from anybody!" Mary Lou thought Jackson looked a lot like his son when he was angry, only thirty years older and thirty pounds heavier. With the way he held his fists, he also looked like he wanted to hit somebody.

"Carl, please," his wife said in a small voice. She backed away as she spoke.

Jackson whirled around to face her, as if he had found something to hit at last.

"Come on, now," Mary Lou's father interrupted, his face full of his peacekeeping grin. "I'm sure this must all be some sort of misunderstanding. There's got to be some way we can work this out."

Mary Lou's mother smiled, brushing a hand through her recently dyed hair. No matter what, her mother always managed to look her best.

"We most certainly can work this out," the man in blue replied smoothly. "But I'm being impolite. You have walked some distance." He clapped his hands. "We'll prepare a meal, find someplace for you to sit." As the man in blue spoke, three of the soldiers passed quickly into the structure behind him. "We'll have all the time you want to talk. After we've eaten, I'll make a proposition. I can help you. But you can help me, too."

He paused, letting the neighbors talk among themselves. Some of them, her parents included, wanted to hear this fellow out. Mary Lou was amazed. What were they thinking? He—or his men—had killed Mr. Sayre! How could they even talk to someone like that?

Two of the soldiers reemerged from the building, each carrying a pair of long, rough-hewn benches. Placing these before the neighbors, they went back into the structure and returned with a table of similar design; sort of a picnic table, Mary Lou thought, although the wood looked more green than brown.

"I appreciate the difficulties you've had coming here," the man in blue remarked as his soldiers continued their preparations. "I'm very glad you've decided to hear me out." Had they? Mary Lou couldn't remember the adults coming to any decision. Still, no one contradicted the man. "I understand that some of your fellows were not so polite. But, by running away from my men, they could inadvertently hurt themselves."

"What do you mean?" Nick's mother asked with a frown.

"This is a different place," he replied simply, as if this was all the explanation that was needed.

Nick's mother looked very upset. "But—" she began. "What—" she added, but couldn't find words to continue her sentence.

"We'll find them," the man in blue said reassuringly. "This is our home, not yours."

He strolled before the line of neighbors, regarding each one in turn. For some reason, Mary Lou thought he was going to ask for a volunteer. He paused by Mr. Mills, then walked over to Mary Lou.

She found herself staring into the eyes of the man in blue. For an instant, his eyes looked perfectly normal. And then they seemed to cloud over, and darken, so that her gaze was pulled deeper and deeper within, as if she was forever falling.

"Mary Lou," he said.

She started.

"So nice of you to share your name."

She had? She didn't remember speaking.

"You may call me Nunn," the man in blue continued. "See? We only want to work together."

Mary Lou shivered. Who did he mean by "we"?

"So, if we've all agreed to work together," Nunn continued, as if the neighbors had made another silent consensus, "I think we should eat."

Some of the neighbors murmured in agreement. Mary Lou's mother laughed, as if she wanted everybody here to be fast friends.

All three soldiers emerged from the building, each carrying a great, steaming bowl of something that looked like stew.

"We fight when we must," Nunn remarked conversationally, "but isn't it much better when we can work together?"

"I wouldn't worry about the boys," Todd's father added with a rough laugh. "They're all cowards. If they're like my son, they'll show back up here with their tails between their legs."

"Tails?" Nunn asked with his perpetual half-smile. "Ah, like animals, I see. Well, I certainly hope so, for their sakes."

Other soldiers had brought out smaller bowls and spoons for distributing the stew. Mary Lou couldn't help but wonder what the steaming bowls really contained. What did they use for meat around here? She remembered the small creature that the Captain had shot from the trees. It had almost looked human. Would they eat something like that?

She realized then that she hadn't seen the Captain since Nunn had begun to talk. Underneath his bravado, she couldn't help but think that the Captain had been very afraid. She wondered what had happened to him. She looked back at the bowls.

The stew could contain anything.

She shouldn't let her imagination run away like this. Still, she didn't think she could bring herself to eat anything. She wished again that she had run away.

Her parents and the others sat down on the long benches. Some, like Mr. Mills and Nick's mother, seemed guarded in their movements, while her parents seemed to want to treat the soldiers like they were old friends.

Her father thanked the soldier for the steaming bowl placed in front of him. The soldier grunted back.

Mr. Jackson laughed. "Just like the army."

"I understand you have already met my brother," Nunn addressed the others. He frowned when he saw the confusion on their faces. "Ice cream?" he added. The neighbors smiled as if they understood. They passed the bowls of stew down the table.

"Time may be very short," Nunn continued. "There are certain things that need to be done before the arrival of—well, something that's very important. We shouldn't let that confuse you."

"Then you sent for us?" Mr. Mills asked pointedly.

"Oh, no. We're not strong enough to do that. You were brought here—" He paused, as if thinking better of what he might say next. "—well, by others. I'll explain it to you soon enough."

He looked pointedly at the teenager.

"Mary Lou? Why don't you join us?"

She saw a bit of that same emptiness in his gaze. She quickly looked away. It was strange how quiet all the neighbors had been since they had come to this clearing; no stranger, she supposed, than anything else that had happened to them in the last few hours. She wondered if there was something about this Nunn that was affecting them all. Couldn't her parents, Mr. Mills, and the others see what was happening?

Perhaps they needed somebody to show them.

She remembered how the boys had run. Maybe, she thought, she hadn't lost her chance. Maybe the real battle would be here, facing this stranger.

Maybe, she thought, and the idea both scared and excited her, there were a lot of different ways to fight.

○ Five

"We're never going to get home, are we?"

Mrs. Smith was the first to say it. Although she was the oldest among them and sometimes had trouble walking, she had a lot sharper mind than half the other adults.

Mary Lou always hoped she'd have some of Mrs. Smith's spunk when she got that old. She looked at the faces of the others around the table. All had stopped spooning the stew into their mouths. Some looked at the old woman, while others were very busy looking somewhere else. For a moment, nothing moved but the wind.

"Nonsense," Mr. Furlong said. He made a noise that started as a laugh but ended as a dry croak. "We don't know that." Mary Lou's parents nodded from where they sat farther down the table, glad to agree with anything that was being said.

"What *do* we know, Leo?" his wife asked pointedly.

"I think this Nunn guy is here to protect us," Mr. Jackson said loudly. Mary Lou had noticed that Jackson almost always made firm statements like that, rather than asking others for advice.

"Did you see the way that guy talked?" Jackson insisted with his all-too-eager grin. "If we stick with him, we should all get back easy."

"But what about Bobby?" Mrs. Furlong said. "He's run away," she added quietly. She glanced out at the forest for only a second, as if the trees might object if she stared at them too long. "All our sons—what will happen to them?"

"And there's Jason, too," Mary Lou's father piped up. "But I'm sure the boys will be fine."

"Maybe they'll get some sense scared into them," Jackson replied. "The four boys went off together, but I'm sure Todd put it into their heads. Just wait until I get my hands on him—"

"We have to find them before we can do anything!" Mrs. Blake snapped with a surprising amount of anger.

"Nunn can find anything," the Captain interrupted from where he stood at the end of the table. Somehow, when he had disappeared a few minutes ago, Mary Lou hadn't expected to see him again. His expression was sour, almost angry, as he looked out over the neighbors. He seemed almost an entirely different person from the brash and boastful man who had brought them here.

"How?" Mr. Mills objected. "You haven't—"

"Nunn will tell you everything."

The Captain's sharp voice silenced everybody. Or maybe it was his mention of his master.

Nunn had disappeared after the food arrived, stalking inside the hut. Mary Lou now realized that, when he left, everyone— neighbors and guards both—seemed to relax. Nunn had certainly frightened her. After his strange actions, and his eyes that seemed to show the stars, the Captain and his soldiers appeared almost normal. And apparently, from the uniformed men's actions, getting to know Nunn better did not help ease that tension.

Some of the people around the table tried to get the conversation going again. Mr. Furlong made a remark about the kind of rations he used to eat in the war. People stared down at their stew. Mary Lou's mother looked up at her daughter and said she should eat something. Mary Lou sat down at the end of one of the benches and took one of the offered bowls. The food had done nothing to the other neighbors, except maybe quiet them down.

"This isn't bad," Mr. Furlong murmured.

His wife giggled nervously. "He never eats this well at home."

No, Mary Lou thought, the neighbors hadn't changed at all. She grabbed one of the wooden spoons the guards had provided and scooped up some of the dark brown stew from her bowl. She sipped at the gravy. It was both a little sweet and a little salty. Her mouth watered. She hadn't realized how hungry she was.

"Are you finished?" the Captain asked Mr. Jackson, who had placed his spoon inside his empty bowl. "When you are done, my men and I will eat."

Jackson patted his stomach and stared up at his captor. "I wouldn't mind stretching my legs. Maybe take a walk around the neighborhood."

Some of the other neighbors laughed at that.

The Captain didn't even smile. "You don't want to leave. It is far too dangerous out there. Here you have protection. And Nunn wouldn't like to lose any more of you."

"You killed one of them?"

The Captain stopped moving at the sound of his master's voice. He stood absolutely still, his gaze fixed somewhere beyond the clearing.

Nunn stood directly behind him. Once again, Mary Lou had been unaware of his approach. Instead, he had simply arrived.

"When you explained the escape," Nunn said softly, "there was no mention of a death. You will answer me now, Captain." The words seemed more ominous because of Nunn's very pleasant smile.

"I thought it best to ensure the others' obedience," the Captain replied. "The one we dispatched was obviously of no consequence—"

"Obviously?" Nunn interrupted, his smile showing even more teeth. "You, then, are gifted with that judgment?"

"Oh, no," the Captain said quickly. "I am not gifted at all. I am nothing but your soldier, doing my best to fulfill—"

"Your best?" Nunn nodded serenely. "Yes, you are only human, are you? All people make mistakes?" He sighed. "We need them all. Until we see them together, we have no idea who is chosen and who is not. You indicated that you understood that." He held his hands out before him. Mary Lou could swear that his fingertips glowed softly. Nunn chuckled, as if delighted with the sight. "But you will be happy to know, my Captain, that even this error is not irreversible."

"Sir?" the Captain asked after Nunn had paused.

"You can take a life, I can give one back," Nunn replied in a singsong tone. "There is one small problem. The restoration of life is a costly matter. However, I would think that, as the man who made the mistake in the first place, you would be more than happy to pay some restitution."

The Captain blinked. His mouth opened, then closed. A single bead of sweat danced the length of the scar on his left cheek.

"Sir," he replied at last.

"I am glad you agree." Nunn's smile was so broad by now that the lower half of his face looked like nothing but teeth. "But come. As I'm sure you realize, this conversation will best be concluded in private."

Both Nunn and the Captain turned toward the hut behind them, their movements so close that they looked like two puppets controlled by the same string.

Nunn strode quickly to the hut. The Captain followed, his walk almost too stiff, and no less direct. In a moment, both had disappeared into darkness.

"May eat?" one of the soldiers asked to break the all-too-familiar silence.

"Pardon?" Mrs. Blake looked up. The soldier pointed at the bowl before her. "Oh, certainly," she answered as she rose from the table. "I wouldn't want any more. Not now." Other neighbors followed her, one by one retreating from the table.

Mary Lou had lost her appetite as well. It sounded as if something horrible would happen to the Captain. She pushed the toe of her penny loafer into the packed earth of the clearing. She had seen the Captain order someone killed in cold blood. Why should she feel sorry for him?

Mary Lou knew the answer as soon as she thought of the man in the dark blue suit—the Captain's master. The Captain, at least, appeared to be human—human like Mary Lou and the rest of the neighbors. Who knew what Nunn was?

Half the soldiers sat at the benches that the others had just vacated. The other half of the men hung back, weapons in hands.

"Must stay," the new spokesman announced as he sat down among the other men. His accent seemed Slavic. He grabbed a spoon and waved it at those soldiers still standing. "Understand?" He pointed the spoon at the neighbors. "You go, our death." He screwed up his nose as if he smelled something bad. "Not pleasant. No." He turned back to the table, rapidly ladling stew into a clean bowl. "So quiet, please. We all live one more day."

With that, the soldier began to slurp his stew.

Mary Lou looked at her mother and father. She realized that, besides her mother asking her to eat, the two of them hadn't said a word throughout the entire meal. Her father shook his head when she looked at him. Why? The guard's broken speech had confused her. She wanted to ask the soldier if he was afraid of Nunn as well. But her parents looked as if they'd die if she opened her mouth.

Mary Lou glanced at those guards who still held their weapons. They had spaced themselves out at the edges of the clearing. A couple of them engaged in conversation, while another seemed busy refitting the shafts and heads of his arrows. A fourth stared out at the woods, his back to the gathering. Mary Lou had no doubt that, should she approach the line of trees beyond the clearing, she would get all of the guards' attention. But for now, they seemed involved elsewhere, as if they were saying, "You don't bother us, we won't bother you."

Short of some new distraction like those falling trees, she couldn't think of any way to escape. But there was no reason she couldn't simply stroll across the clearing and explore.

She walked away from the table, looking at the ground before her, the tops of the trees beyond the guards, the walls of the hut in front of her.

One of the guards looked her way. She took a few steps back toward the center of the clearing, and the guard looked away.

She turned back to her goal.

The hut seemed to be made of dried mud and straw. The wooden door, constructed from half a dozen logs tied side by side, had been left open. No light reached within. She could see nothing inside, even when her casual steps turned again and brought her closer.

She had a sudden urge to step through the doorway.

Why would anyone want to follow Nunn? Perhaps, she thought, because that was the one thing no one would ever expect. Maybe she could find out something about their captors, or find something inside that could help them with their escape.

She took a step forward. 'Quiet as a mouse, she thought. It was something her grandmother used to say when Mary Lou had become too excited as a child. Quiet as a mouse.

When she was younger, she used to creep from her bedroom and hide at the top of the stairs and listen to her parents. It was exciting, dangerous, forbidden, to be someplace she shouldn't.

The door was only two steps away.

No one called out to her, neither soldier nor neighbor. No one knew she was there. Everyone had stopped talking.

There was no noise anywhere.

Quiet as a mouse.

She risked a final glance behind her, waiting for someone to shout. Too close! Move away!

The guards were busy eating, or talking, or watching the other neighbors. Even Mary Lou's mother was busy, deep in discussion with the other women. Now that she looked back at them, she could hear voices, but only a distant murmur too faint to make out the words. Maybe the breeze made it hard to hear. It was almost as if they had all forgotten about her.

She stepped inside. She felt stone beneath her feet. She closed her eyes for an instant, willing her gaze to adjust to the dimness within. It was cooler in here; the air felt totally different from the forest outside. She opened her eyes with a start when she realized she could smell the sea.

She stood in a hall, made of dark and solid stone. She was at one end of a long corridor, lit with torches, that stretched as far as she could see.

The corridor must have been a dozen times as long as the hut. That was impossible. Well, she added, impossible in the world she had come from.

From somewhere far down the corridor came a terrible scream of pain.

Perhaps, she thought, this was more information than she wanted. Maybe she should step back and rejoin the relative security of parents and neighbors and soldiers who carried nothing more than bows and knives.

She glanced behind her. The door was no longer there. Instead, she saw another wall of dark grey stone.

It must all be part of the illusion. She pushed her hand against the wall, fully expecting her palm to pass on through to the invisible doorway that led back to the forest camp.

The wall was solid. Her fingers pushed against rough, cold granite.

A second scream came down the hall, even louder than the first.

◯ Six

"Nunn will not let us go that easily," the large green man said softly.

Raven's laughter stopped abruptly as the sun disappeared behind the clouds. They were dark clouds, their undersides a threatening blend of black and brown, hanging low as if they couldn't wait to release a torrent of rain. Somehow, Nick thought, these thunderheads, set against the greenish sky, looked even more ominous than they did at home.

"Nunn has avoided this before," the large black bird remarked, pointing his beak toward the approaching storm. "Something has changed. He's decided to test Raven."

The bird nodded at Nick and the other young men. "One of you must be very important."

The four newcomers all looked at each other. Jason appeared a little bewildered behind his thick glasses. Surrounded by these big trees, he looked even scrawnier than usual. Bobby shifted his pudgy body from one foot to the other, smiling like he wanted everything to be all right. Todd glared briefly at each of them, idly flexing his biceps before he turned away. Now that they'd gotten away from the soldiers, he seemed all too ready to go back to his usual anger. Nick didn't feel any different, either. Of course, with red hair and a gangly body that refused to stop growing, he supposed he could stand out in this place, too. Still, none of the four of them looked particularly "important." Maybe, Nick thought, they were all staring at each other to see if one of them had sprouted horns or something.

Raven shook his head and fluffed out his feathers. "Nunn will be very sorry."

Todd stepped forward from the ranks of the newcomers. "I've had enough of this. Who, or what, is a Nunn?"

"The boy is most perceptive," the Oomgosh observed with the most generous of smiles. "Nunn is both a who and a what."

"And the Oomgosh will talk and talk and never get to the point," Raven replied. "Sometimes I am amazed we are still in this battle."

The large green man smiled still. "Raven does make up for our weaknesses." But his smile vanished as he looked above.

"Nunn is looking for us now," the Oomgosh explained with a nod toward the clouds. "Nunn was once a man, much like one of you. But he has used his magic too long." He turned his head toward the sky as rain began to fall. "And the magic has used him in return."

Raven looked speculatively at the large raindrops, as if there might be a secret in the pattern of their fall. "If I were by myself, I would fly up there to take the lightning in my claws and thrust it back in the eyes of Nunn." He cawed softly. "Things become more difficult when I have four visitors to protect."

"Too true," the green man agreed. "Perhaps we should seek some assistance."

"Even Raven shares the sky," the bird said. "Follow me now, before this storm gets any worse."

With that, the great black bird took flight, his wings even darker than the clouds above.

"Come, friends," the Oomgosh urged from where he stood behind them. "It is for all our benefit."

Todd glared at the sky as he broke into a trot. Bobby and Jason scrambled to catch up, as if they both had elected Todd their leader. They all followed the path indicated by the low-flying Raven, which led from the clearing back into the forest. Nick started to run, too, afraid he'd get left behind. The rain was getting heavier. Nick blinked the water from his eyes.

Lightning flashed before them. Charlie barked at his heels. Nick's dog had never much liked lightning.

Nick waited for the great boom that always followed. There was nothing; no thunder at all.

"Come now!" the bird cried over his shoulder. "Keep up with Raven and we'll all be safe and dry." He cawed loudly as he flew, warning away the storm.

A second shaft of lightning crashed down in front of them. It was much closer than the first. The air smelled like something was burning. There was no thunder this time, either.

"Perhaps, O Raven," the Oomgosh called from where he took up the rear, "it would be better to take a less direct route."

Raven spread his wings and banked around before them.

"For once in his overgrown life," the bird called down as he flew overhead, "the Oomgosh might be right." He turned again, and flew a bit to the left of their earlier course, toward another opening in the surrounding woods. "Come on, my people! What say we outwit this storm?"

All four of them followed the Raven's lead, with the Oomgosh following them in turn. But Nick was finding it harder and harder to run. He had trouble breathing in the humid air, and the rain had soaked through his clothes. His jeans seemed heavier every time he lifted his legs. And the water kept falling straight down, a solid downpour, without any wind at all, as if the clouds overhead might stay there to unleash their torrent forever.

Lightning smashed into the trees directly in front of them, maybe a hundred feet away. One of the tree stumps that remained caught on fire, the flames sizzling beneath the rain.

"The storm does not wish us to go this way, either," the Oomgosh declared, his voice rising above the noise the rain made against the leaves.

Nick thought about Raven's saying he would outwit the storm. Maybe a storm that held no wind or thunder really could think, too. Maybe that kind of storm used the lightning for its fingers, for Nick felt as if those crooked lines of electricity were reaching out for all of them.

"So what will Raven do?" the bird shouted as he hovered overhead. "Perhaps it is time to challenge the clouds!" Still, as boldly as he talked, he made no move to fly up toward the thunderheads.

"The Oomgosh has had a thought!" the green man called from the rear.

"Another wonder in a world of marvels!" Raven chided. "Does the Oomgosh wish to share it with us?"

"We have said that one of the young men here with us is important to Nunn," the Oomgosh said with a grin so broad it threatened to split his face in two. "And Nunn has the storm throw lightning to send us back the way we have come. No doubt he wishes us to march back into the willing arms of his soldiers. But if these fellows are so important, the lightning cannot touch them. He can throw down all the slashing fire in the world, but it will be no more than a threat!"

"You mean this Nunn doesn't want to kill us?" Todd asked incredulously.

"Nunn doesn't dare kill you!" Raven cackled. "The lightning is nothing more than a sham, to lure you into his trap!"

Raven cawed loudly. "He is certainly the most excellent

Oomgosh!" He swooped above the green man, then fluttered his wings to gain altitude. "Of course," the bird added in a quieter voice, "Raven would have thought of that as well, had he not been so busy leading us all from danger."

"Most assuredly, my Raven," the Oomgosh agreed. "Now what say we go to meet the lightning?"

"Wait a moment," Bobby piped up, for once not smiling at all. "You want us to walk into that stuff?"

It was only when he heard Bobby's question that Nick realized how quiet the two younger boys had been since they had met the Oomgosh and Raven. But this last suggestion of the green man's was apparently too much even for Bobby, who looked as if he was about to lose it and run.

Jason stood by Bobby's side, content to keep silent and look miserable. His rain-soaked clothes made him seem even scrawnier than usual. His glasses were completely fogged over by the rain; Nick wondered if Jason could even see. Out of all of them, only Todd seemed eager to follow the large bird's lead.

Nick had to admit that even he had the kind of doubts that half made him want to run away. Not, of course, that he had anywhere to go.

"When Raven tells you a thing," the bird informed Bobby, "there is no need to worry. And when the Oomgosh tells you something"—Raven paused before continuing—"well, he certainly means well." He cawed to his assembled audience. "Step forward, and we'll test this wizard."

"*Test* this wizard?" Bobby asked even more loudly than before, his voice squeaking with disbelief. "Can I go home now?"

"None of us can go home," the Oomgosh advised, "until we deal with Nunn."

"I know," Bobby answered glumly. "I just had to say something."

Todd had turned around to look at the others. For the first time, Nick could see uncertainty in Todd's face, too. Bobby's outburst had brought out every fear all four of them had been so carefully hiding.

"Why do we wait?" the Oomgosh asked, as if he was oblivious to the feelings of the four visitors. Raven flapped his wings and flew up toward the glowering mass of cloud above.

Jason was the first to step forward. He didn't look at any of the others, but kept his face pointed toward their goal. "Let's go," was all he said.

"I see why Nunn prizes you so highly," Raven called from above. "Any of you could be what he is looking for."

"Come." The Oomgosh urged the other three forward. "We have no time to dawdle."

"Raven leads the way!" the bird called down from up above. "But Raven stays close!"

The others moved, urged along by the great, hard hands of the green man. Nick realized that he and the other humans were clearly outmatched. Disagreeing with the Oomgosh was like arguing with a force of nature.

"We go forward," the Oomgosh remarked. "Into the forest."

Shafts of searing white slashed into trees on either side of them, as if the lightning had been waiting for them to move. Limbs exploded from the trees to fall into the forest beyond.

"Whoa!" Bobby called. "Should we really be listening to a bird?"

The black bird dropped even lower in the sky.

"I believe it is time for Raven to come closer still," the bird announced. "Perhaps one of you fine young men would be honored to have Raven perch upon his shoulder?"

Nick found the large black bird flying straight toward him.

"This is not a privilege that I bestow lightly," Raven remarked as he settled down on Nick's rain-soaked T-shirt. "Your shoulder should consider this a rare distinction."

Nick didn't feel as if he or his shoulder had a choice in this. Raven's claws clamped down on his shoulder blade. Raven was not light. Still, the bird seemed careful not to dig his claws into Nick's flesh.

Another bolt of lightning flashed before them, so close and so bright that Nick couldn't see for an instant.

"Step away!" the Oomgosh cried. "Quickly!"

Raven squawked. Nick felt the green man's hard fingers grab his free shoulder and pull him back. He blinked as he saw something falling toward them from overhead. A great tree branch, as thick around as the Oomgosh's chest, fell less than a foot in front of them.

The green man stared down at the severed limb of the tree. "This is another injury that Nunn will pay for." When the Oomgosh didn't smile, his face looked frightening, like an angry mask carved from wood.

The others didn't speak for a minute.

"Maybe," Todd said for all of them, "Nunn wants to kill us, after all."

"At the moment," Raven answered drily, "I believe the magician has had a change of mind."

The rain stopped as the bird spoke, and the clouds broke apart to show the sun. The storm had ceased as quickly as it had come. It seemed that the last falling limb was too close even for the mysterious Nunn.

"This," Bobby remarked, "is just too weird."

"It is time to see Obar," was the green man's reply.

"Before Nunn gets other ideas," Raven agreed.

So they marched again, returning to the forest. Nick wondered who Obar was; but they were all so shaken that none of them, not even Todd, chose to ask their guides.

In the space of a dozen steps, the clearing sky was lost beneath the thick greenery. Once truly into these woods, Nick thought, they wouldn't know whether the sun was shining or Nunn was hatching the storm of all storms. Here, on the forest floor, it always seemed to be twilight.

Nick sloshed after the others. The perpetual gloom they walked through did nothing to help dry his clothes. Raven fluttered his wings but remained on Nick's shoulder. Now that he had found a form of free transportation, the large bird seemed to expect to ride forever more.

The Oomgosh held up his hand for the party to stop. In the sudden silence, Nick heard a rustling in the trees above. At first, he thought it might be the wind, back now that the unnatural storm had passed.

But when he looked up, he noticed that not all the branches above were moving. Only certain leaves shook on certain trees, shifting in lines over their heads. Something was moving with them up there, tracking their movements as it crept from branch to branch, always just out of sight. Nick suddenly thought of a great, undulating serpent crawling from tree to tree.

Nick looked at the others. Raven and the Oomgosh didn't seem at all concerned. Surely, they'd be aware of movement in the trees. Todd was too far ahead to talk to without shouting. Bobby looked as if he liked every minute here less than the one before, shifting from foot to foot as their marching had stopped. Jason simply shook his head and kept on moving, his eyes always on the Oomgosh, watching his every step, walking when he walked, pausing when he stopped. Maybe, Nick thought, that sort of resignation was the best way to go.

The rustling stopped overhead as well, and there was a moment of total silence, as if the trees that surrounded them masked sound as well as light. What was up there? It might be some of those small almost-humans; like the one that the Captain had shot down. The soldier had said the things were everywhere. Why couldn't Nick stop thinking about snakes?

"This is the way to Obar," the green man suddenly announced. He turned right and began to march. Raven squawked and rose from Nick's shoulder with a great flapping of wings.

Something happened with the next step Nick took. He felt what he thought was a breeze, maybe from Raven's beating wings. But it came and went suddenly, then flashed by again, the forest growing bright, then dark again. Nick got the feeling that they were passing through something, like walls of air and light. Even though he felt no real resistance to his movements, and still saw the forest all around him, he got the oddest feeling. It was like stepping from one room to another, one very definite place to somewhere else altogether.

The Oomgosh made a short sharp cry, as if he was in pain. But then he smiled and pointed ahead.

Nick blinked. The world around them had suddenly brightened and changed. Charlie barked sharply. Everyone but the Oomgosh had stopped to stare.

"Holy shit," Todd said.

Nick felt that Todd was talking for all of them.

◯ Around the Circle #3:
Mary Lou at Twelve

She should have known.

Mary Lou sat on her bed and stared at the small pink flowers that papered her wall. It was no use going downstairs. Her mother didn't want to talk to her anymore. Her mother didn't want to have anything to do with her.

A car passed on the street below, breaking the silence. Her mother wasn't even listening to the radio. Mary Lou couldn't remember the last time her mother hadn't turned on that little brown box in the kitchen, sounds of Frank Sinatra and Jack Jones wafting their way through the house. *Wives must always be lovers too.* Her mother would always sing along.

No one was singing now. Even the birds outside seemed to be sharing the silence.

Mary Lou had only wanted to know what happened to Susan. Was that so wrong?

Maybe it was. Over the past couple of weeks, every time Mary Lou had even looked at Susan, her older sister had burst into tears. Every one of Susan's tears seemed to make her mother angrier still. *People don't act like that in this household!* Susan didn't seem to care. Susan didn't even bother to retreat to her room. She cried in front of everybody.

What was wrong? Mary Lou was sure it had something to do with Brian. Their mother kept saying that Brian was no good for Susan. Mary Lou had thought that Brian was sort of cute, at least at first.

She remembered one night, when her parents were out and Susan was supposed to be baby-sitting. Mary Lou had been sent to bed, but she had snuck out to the top of the stairs. She stared at the two teenagers as they rolled around on the couch. Susan giggled and Brian moaned. Something was moving inside Susan's sweater, jerking around like some small frightened animal. It took Mary Lou a few seconds to realize it was one of Brian's hands. Mary

Lou's mother had told her to never let a man touch you like that.

Susan threw her head back over the arm of the couch. Whatever Brian was doing was hidden by the back of the sofa, but he couldn't have been doing anything bad. Mary Lou had never seen Susan with such a wonderful smile.

But that had happened long ago, back in the middle of last winter when all their father ever asked them about was school and their mother's radio played for the whole house.

This morning, when Mary Lou came out of her room, she found her father moving quickly down the hall, a suitcase hefted in either hand.

"Daddy?" she called after him. "Are you going away?"

Her father looked down the stairs as he answered her. "I'm not going anywhere, honey. These are—for Susan. She has to go—" His voice stopped abruptly, as if he wasn't sure what word should come next.

"Harold," her mother spoke from the bottom of the stairs. She looked up at Mary Lou as if her daughter had done something wrong. "I'll tell her later."

Her father walked quickly to the stairs. He grunted as one of the full suitcases hit against his knee.

Susan was leaving? Why hadn't she told Mary Lou? Susan was the one person Mary Lou could really talk to in this family. She rushed into Susan's room, but her sister wasn't there. It didn't even look like Susan lived here anymore. All her stuffed animals were gone, all her papers and schoolbooks cleaned off her desk, the poster of the Monkees taken down from her wall. Mary Lou had never seen the room so neat, or so empty.

Mary Lou hurried back out to the top of the stairs. Her father had reached the foyer below. Mary Lou rushed down the stairs and past her parents, glancing in the living room and kitchen, but saw no sign of her sister.

"Mary Lou!" her mother called sharply. For once, she didn't care. Where would Susan be going without her, without even *telling* her?

She saw Susan when her father opened the front door. Her sister was standing out on the front steps, her back to the house, like she couldn't wait to leave.

Mary Lou ran to her sister's side, her questions coming out all in a rush. "Susan, you're leaving? Where are you going? Why didn't you tell me?"

"Mom didn't want me talking to you," Susan replied, still looking out to the road.

"What's the matter? Have you done something wrong?"

"Wow." For some reason, a smile flickered across Susan's face. "I'm going to a place—for girls like me. Mom and Dad think it's for the best." She looked at her sister then. "Mary Lou, I wish you were older." She looked back to the road. A single tear worked its way down her cheek as her mouth formed a thin, hard line. "I'm never coming back here again."

Her mother had come out of the house then and ordered Mary Lou to her room.

But Mary Lou was too upset to go quietly. "Why?" she had demanded. "Why does Susan have to leave?"

Her mother hadn't spoken, but had only given her *that* look, the one she gave when you had really done something wrong, and then turned away, as if that was all the explanation necessary.

She had been sent to her room. She had done something really bad. She should have known better than to talk back to her mother, especially when her mother was in one of her moods. What was happening to all of them? Her sister would be gone, her mother would never talk to her again. Everything was wrong. Mary Lou felt like the whole house was spinning around her, spinning and spinning until it finally tipped over and everyone and everything fell out and was lost. Lost forever.

Everything was so bad. Her mother was so angry. There must have been something she could have done. Mary Lou hated feeling like this. She would have to be extra good from now on, so nothing could ever go wrong again.

○ Seven

Mary Lou found herself walking toward the screams.

There was nowhere else to go. The doorway she had walked through no longer existed. There was only this stone corridor, lit with torches to either side to guide her along.

She had stepped into it now. It would only get worse, so she might as well face up to it and get it over with.

The screams stopped abruptly. Somehow the silence was worse. The heel of her penny loafer clacked against the stone floor. She stopped, afraid to make another move. She saw a doorway ahead in the left-hand wall. That must have been where the screams had come from.

Now she heard a moan, followed by a gruff voice she knew belonged to Nunn.

"Thank you for your honesty," Nunn said in a tone that sounded both angry and tired. "Contrary to your assumptions, I did not make you Captain of my guard so you could exercise your stupidity!"

"Apparently," a high, childlike voice added, "he decided to do that on his own initiative." The second voice giggled.

"I was only," a third, very hoarse voice began, "trying to act in your own—"

"Talking back again?" the high voice asked brightly. "Don't you know that chattering only causes trouble?"

"Then I suggest that you stop chattering, too!" Nunn said more forcefully than before. "There are other ways he can be useful." He continued in a more reasonable tone. "I told you to bring all of them. Until I see all of them, I can't know which will be useful, and which can be discarded. Since you lost one of them, it falls on me to regain him." He paused before adding, "Of course, that sort of reclamation takes blood."

"Can you guess whose blood?" the high voice asked joyfully.

The Captain shouted something that Mary Lou didn't understand.

"He's clever enough for that," the high voice agreed.

The screams resumed. This time there was more than sound. The screams were like a physical force, shaking the floor at Mary Lou's feet. Waves of darkness washed through the air, dimming the torchlight. The darkness did more than simply cover her; it seemed to pass into her as well, each wave setting off a smooth electrical charge in her muscles and bones, freezing her where she stood. As long as there were screams, she couldn't move.

The screaming stopped. Mary Lou felt dizzy. She put her arm out against the wall to keep from falling. The stone wall was warm to the touch, as though it were a living thing.

Nunn's voice broke the silence. "Come in, my dear. After all, you're a part of this."

There was no doubt that he was talking to her. Mary Lou walked to the doorway.

There were only two men inside, Nunn and the Captain. The Captain sat in a chair, his hands tied behind his back. Someone had removed his shirt. For all the screaming she had heard, Mary Lou could see no blood or bruises. There was a dark circle drawn on the Captain's chest. The soldier's skin glistened with sweat. Mary Lou could see no sign of the child.

The Captain turned his face toward her and opened his mouth as if he might say something. Instead, he flung his head back and screamed, a scream that rose in both intensity and pitch and again froze Mary Lou. The circle on the Captain's chest began to glow, first dully, then with increasing intensity, the intense red of burning coals. The light spread outward from his chest and writhed about to form a figure, maybe half the height of a man, as if this thing had crawled out of the Captain's insides.

"Nothing to worry about," Nunn said in the most reassuring of tones. "It was a simple but necessary operation. We used a different knowledge than what you are used to, but that is all. The Captain is almost as good as new already." He reached forward and touched the Captain's shoulder. "Aren't you?"

The Captain's head nodded, although his eyes were still closed, awaiting the return of the pain. What would have happened to the Captain, Mary Lou wondered, if he didn't agree?

She found her gaze drawn back to that strange red light. It moved about like a living thing, prancing around the legs of the Captain's chair.

"But it is so good to have you here," Nunn continued smoothly, with such good cheer that it seemed that his fondest wish was to have people stumble upon him while he was in the midst of causing other men to scream. "I haven't really gotten to know any of the newcomers yet. I do appreciate when someone shows a little initiative."

The bright red light seemed to lose its shape as it rose quickly to hover above the Captain's shoulder.

"Ah," Nunn remarked. "It seems my pet would like some attention as well."

"You have not introduced us," that high, childlike voice whined petulantly.

"He is not the most polite of animals," Nunn remarked. "And his full name is quite unpronounceable."

The Captain whimpered, as if he was dreaming. If he wasn't conscious, Mary Lou thought, how could he have nodded his head?

"I am, however," the child voice protested, "very useful."

"Therefore," Nunn continued, "let's call this fellow Zachs, shall we?"

The red light writhed back to its animal form, and bowed. "At your service, Mary Lou."

She imagined that she was supposed to be charmed. Instead, Mary Lou wanted to get away from that thing and its master, and whatever they had done to the Captain. Still, where could she go? She tried to smile, and wondered if everyone and everything in this place was going to know her name.

"Very good," Nunn agreed, as if he sensed that she had made a decision. "We have a great deal to do in a very short time, and all your neighbors are part of it." He stretched out his hand toward her. "You will help us, won't you?"

As difficult as she found it to agree, she felt that she had to. It was more than just keeping herself safe. If she did something wrong, Nunn could do terrible things to her parents and all the neighbors. She stared at Nunn's outstretched hand, but she could not bring herself to touch it. She nodded her head instead.

"Good." Nunn withdrew his hand with a flourish, as if she was never meant to take it in the first place. He glanced briefly at the Captain. "It would be better if everyone in this place were so cooperative. Zachs and I will call on you when we need, then." He clapped his hands, and the light-being flew from the Captain's shoulders to Nunn. But the red glow did not seem to perch on Nunn's shoulder. Instead, it settled down over the other man's head, so that for a moment Nunn seemed to have a halo. Then the halo vanished, flowing inward, sucked within Nunn's skull. The wizard closed his eyes and shuddered. His eyes reopened and he smiled.

"Ah, Mary Lou," he said softly. "You'll be able to help us more than you'd ever imagine."

○ Around the Circle #4:
How Raven Stole the Sun

Once there was no light upon the world, and all was cloaked in darkness. But Raven heard that, at the source of the river that gave life to all things, there was one who had light but kept it all to himself.

Raven flew to this place and found there a rich man who lived with his daughter in a large house. As Raven flew by the open doorway of this house, he saw three large bundles, each a different shape and size, that hung upon the opposite wall within. Surely, Raven thought, these bundles contained what he sought.

"Caw!" he called down to the man below.

"And what would Raven want to do with me?" the man asked.

"Come, old man," the bird replied, "and give me a peek at your riches!"

But the old man was too clever for the bird, for he knew how Raven liked to grasp shiny objects within his claws and make them his. So he refused him, saying, "I have no riches that you can touch. My only wealth is what I see. There is nothing for you here, Raven."

So it was that the man turned away from Raven. But the man's refusal made Raven want these things even more. But how could he, a bird, convince the rich man to give him those things he desired?

It was then that Raven hit upon his clever plan.

"I will make myself very small," he said to himself, "and drop into the water in the form of a small piece of dirt."

And this he did as the rich man's daughter was about to take a drink, so that the dirt that was Raven found its way into the daughter's cup. The girl swallowed the dirt and soon discovered that she would have a child.

So it was, when the child was ready to leave his mother and join the world, her people made a hole for her, as was customary

66

in that time, in which she would bring forth the child. And her people further lined the hole with rich furs of all sorts.

But the baby did not wish to be born in such a hairy place. So the child's grandfather pondered this problem, and thought, "Perhaps it is best to line the hole with something else." So it was that he instructed his servants to remove the furs and line the hole with fresh green moss. Once this new covering was upon the hole, the baby promptly appeared. And the child's eyes were very bright, and it moved its head rapidly from side to side.

Thereafter the child grew, and learned to crawl, and, as he moved on his hands and knees around the great fire at the center of the house, he would cry. When the child cried, his grandfather would ask him what was wrong, but the child would only point at the first of the three bundles that hung upon the wall.

"Very well," the child's grandfather said, after listening day after day to the child's screams. "Give the boy what he is crying for, and we can have some peace."

So the first of the three bundles was given to the child.

"Gah!" the child cried in delight, and he clutched it and rolled upon the floor as the other people of the household went about their separate tasks. And the child looked inside the bundle and saw that it was filled with stars. Therefore the child let it go and gave the bundle a little push, and the whole package full of stars rose through the smoke hole at the center of the house and broke open above the roof, so that stars were scattered throughout the sky.

"Gah!" the child cried again, and he was happy that night.

But the following morning, the child began to cry again, with such force that it made his earlier noise seem like the meekest of whimpers. And, in those rare moments when the child paused to draw a breath, he would point to the second of the three bundles.

"Very well," his grandfather said at last, "untie that next one and give it to him."

So the child was given the second bundle, which contained something far more solid than the first. The child played with the bundle around and behind his mother as she saw to her chores. But when his mother looked away, he opened the edges of the bundle with his tiny fingers and saw something that glowed with cool light. So it was that he opened this second bundle to free what was inside and gave that orb a push as well, so that it rose up through the smoke hole and became the moon.

"Gah!" the child cried as he saw the cool light fill the sky, and he slept well again that night.

But on the following morning the child began to cry with such a ferocity that the people thought that he might die. And further did his eyes roll about in his head and change from one color to another color, so that those around him began to wonder if he was even human. But his grandfather said, "Very well. Untie the last of the bundles and give it to him." For what grandfather can deny anything to his grandchild?

So they brought down the last of the bundles, which contained a great box that held the daylight.

"Gah!" the child announced when he was given this last bundle. And then his cry of delight turned to the call of the raven.

"Caw!" he called as he grabbed the bundle and flew through the smoke hole. "Caw!"

"The bird has stolen my dearest treasures!" the old man cried as he realized what had passed. "When will I see my wealth again? May curses fall upon the thieving bird!"

But Raven took the bundle in his claws, flew up through the smoke hole, and was gone, leaving the old man's curses behind.

He flew with his prize back down the length of the River Nass, which was that place where all of the people of the world lived and fished.

Before this day, they had worked in darkness, but now they toiled by the dim illumination of the moon and stars. And while many of the people welcomed this light, to others it was far too strange and new, and made them uncertain of their place in the world.

Raven saw the people fishing in eight great canoes. Therefore he landed, and walked along the riverbank, and called out to the canoes:

"Give me some fish, and I will show you daylight."

But this only made the people laugh. "You try to trick us!" they called to the bird on the shore. "Daylight is owned by the richest man in the world. You are only Raven!"

"*Only* Raven?" the bird called out, for the people had made him angry. With that, Raven flew up into the air with a great cry. He let loose of the box when he was high in the air. The box fell through the air to break open upon the river rocks below. Once the box was open, the fiery ball burst forth and rose into the sky to become the blazing sun.

But the people had never before seen the sun, and many of them became afraid and dived within the water. An equal number ran into the woods that surrounded the river. And a strange thing happened to those people as they ran. Those people who wore hair-seal coats became hair seals, and those who wore fur-seal coats became fur seals. Before this time, you see, those were only the names of their garments. But now the people who had become hair seals and fur seals leapt into the water. And those who wore the skins of martens, and black bears, and grizzly bears, and all the many other skins of animals, became those animals as they ran into the forest.

So it was that the sun, moon, and stars came into the sky, and animals came into the world, and even the richest man in the world could once again see his wealth.

And Raven? He laughed, and admired his deep black feathers in the golden light of the sun.

◯ Eight

The sky was alive.

"Way to go," Jason murmured. The show up there was enough to get even the neighborhood shy kid talking.

Colors boiled forth from the clouds, blue to green to yellow to orange to red. Circles of crimson light spread from a central point like ripples in a pond.

"Psych-ay-delic," Bobby agreed, his smile firmly back in place.

Nick had to admit that it all looked like it belonged on an album cover by the Jefferson Airplane or Moody Blues.

"What's this all supposed to mean?" Todd asked, sounding much less impressed than the others.

"Obar is greeting us," the Oomgosh explained.

Raven cawed derisively. "Obar is showing off."

Whatever Obar was doing, Nick had to admit that the results were pretty impressive. The clouds above were shifting into recognizable shapes, first a crowd of yellow deer rushing across the sky, then a great green knight swinging a sword.

"This happens often with Raven," the bird remarked with disdain. "A mere wizard, confronted by my magnificence, feels challenged to perform some task worthy of my power." Raven ruffled his feathers. "Of course, such an undertaking is impossible."

"As is everything you do, my Raven," the Oomgosh agreed heartily. "But come. Our business is too serious for us to be distracted long." The large green creature led the way across a lawn that Old Man Sayre would have envied, marching to a great stone structure that seemed half house, half castle. The sky above erupted into a riot of wildflowers, then shifted to a scene of green dolphins jumping from a bloodred sea.

Jason and Bobby poked each other and laughed at the show overhead. Todd didn't seem to be paying any attention to it at all. Instead, he watched every move of the Oomgosh and Raven, as if the next thing they did might suddenly make sense. And

Nick? When he glanced up at the fabulous sky, all he could think of was that earlier strangeness overhead, the sudden storm with silent lightning.

Seven wide steps led up to a large wooden double door in the front of the castle. The two doors swung wide as the six approached. There didn't seem to be anyone on the other side of the now open doors. It was as if the two great slabs of wood had moved of their own accord.

Nick supposed he should expect no less from a wizard's home.

"You are invited inside," the Oomgosh remarked in admiration, "without reservation. You must indeed be important."

"Truly, then," the bird squawked, "you are fitting companions for Raven."

Todd looked doubtfully at the Oomgosh. He pointed at the darkened entryway. "We're supposed to go in there?"

"The door does not open for just anyone," the Oomgosh advised.

A loud cough came from the direction of the castle.

"Sorry," a disembodied voice remarked. "There have been unforeseen problems. I had no idea what time it had gotten to be. You see—well, never mind—" The voice cleared its disembodied throat. "Bobby and Jason, Nick and Todd, please, you are all most welcome to enter."

"Hey!" It was Bobby's turn to object. "How do you know our names?"

"Your names?" the voice continued in the same distracted fashion. "Oh, nothing to it. I've met you all before, haven't I?"

"Met us?" Bobby asked. "Where?"

"I may be one of the foremost wizards ever to grace this world of seven islands," Obar's voice replied. "I also deliver ice cream."

"Ice cream? You're the ice cream man?" Bobby started to laugh. Apparently, he thought the idea of an ice-cream-dispensing wizard was great.

Nick wasn't quite that easy to please. That explanation was still no explanation at all. On that strange night—had it really only been the evening before?—this Obar hadn't introduced himself. And no one had introduced themselves to Obar, either.

"But come inside!" the voice insisted. "The sooner we get started, you know—" Obar left the rest of the sentence unsaid, as if whatever he implied might be easily understood.

"All right," Todd announced as he hurried up the steps. "Let's get on with it." Bobby and Jason followed his lead again.

Jason frowned and looked back at the Oomgosh. "What about you guys?"

"Alas, I must stay here." The tree man pointed down to his toes, which indeed looked like roots. "My feet do not wish to leave the earth."

Nick felt Raven's wing brush his ear. Would the bird remain on his shoulder forever?

"Raven may go wherever he pleases," the bird intoned.

"Whether it pleases others or not," the Oomgosh added. "I will rest my toes in the soil. I await your return."

Nick decided it was time to get a little clarification here. "So you'll stay on my shoulder?"

"You will need a guide," Raven replied. "Obar's castle is much like Obar."

Yes, Nick thought, Raven would indeed remain on his shoulder forever.

Todd stood at the top of the steps, flexing his shoulders and cracking his knuckles, waiting for the rest of them to catch up. As Bobby and Jason joined him, he waved down at Nick.

"What's the matter, Nicky-poo? Scared of the dark?"

Nick stared, as startled as if someone had sucker-punched him. That was the old Todd for you, quick with a jab, Mr. High School Wise Guy. Bobby snickered at Todd's crack. Jason looked surprised and uncomfortable.

Nick suddenly wanted to jump up there and wipe the smirk off Todd's face. He never let Todd bully him into anything back on Chestnut Circle; he wasn't going to let Todd get away with anything now, either. He'd tell that guy just where he could shove it. If Todd could move fast, Nick could move faster.

Nick took two steps toward the doorway, then stopped. The darkness behind Todd looked total, as if it sucked the light from the surrounding air.

Todd glanced back at the doorway himself. "Hey," he added when he turned back toward Nick, "I don't think any of us are going to live forever." His expression had changed, too; his smile looked the slightest bit tentative. Like, maybe he didn't have all the answers, after all.

"It's time to go," the bird said close by Nick's ear, its voice surprisingly soft. A moment later, the creature added, "Only Raven lives forever."

Todd turned and strode into the darkness. Bobby was right on his heels, Jason a few paces after the others. Each, in turn, was swallowed by the doorway's lack of light.

Nick swore and hurried to follow.

Charlie barked and took up the rear. Raven squawked in alarm.

"No dog should—" the bird began.

Nick found the anger building in him again. "Charlie's the only thing I have left from home," he snapped. "I'm not leaving him behind."

"If you insist." The bird turned his head away. "Raven is more than a match for any dog."

"Sometimes," called the Oomgosh from where he stood in the sun, "Raven may even be more than a match for Raven."

Nick climbed the steps and walked into the pool of darkness.

"May good—" the Oomgosh began. His voice cut off abruptly. Nick realized that all the other forest sounds had ceased as well.

Charlie growled. Raven muttered something about wizard tricks.

Somehow Nick kept on moving. He stepped through into light that seemed as bright as that he had just left outside. He was in a large room with the others, a room bordered by grey stone walls, with no doors that Nick could see, only a pair of small windows on opposite sides, neither of them large enough to provide this kind of light.

Above him, quite close to the stone ceiling, was what looked like a miniature sun.

"Ah," Obar's voice said abruptly. "I see we're all together at last."

Obar had managed to walk in their midst during that second Nick had stared at the ceiling. He was the same old man who had passed out the ice cream, although now, rather than a suit of white, he wore a rumpled outfit of brown, clothes that seemed more fitting to a housepainter or plumber than to a wizard.

"I apologize for any disorientation," Obar offered as he smiled and pointed up at the tiny sun. "You've just passed through a protection and transportation spell. In these times, certain precautions are necessary." He glanced down at the neighbors. "But everything seems to be working now, doesn't it?"

A transportation spell? Nick took three quick steps to one of the small windows. They were easily a hundred feet above the manicured lawn; but it was still the same lawn. Nick could see the Oomgosh, standing still as a tree far below. He turned back to the neighbors as Obar continued to talk.

"I'm afraid that I have not prepared you as well as I might." Obar still smiled, but Nick noticed the strain in the wrinkles around his eyes. "I'm afraid I'm a bit distracted. It is an unavoid-able side product of those spells I must deal with." He made a noise that started as a laugh but ended as a cough. The wizard covered his mouth for a moment until the spasm had passed. "Excuse me. It does not do anyone much good to look at these things too directly."

Obar sighed as he sat on a stool that Nick hadn't seen before. "Let me attempt to explain your situation—well, our situation. You see, we have been waiting for you for quite some time. We have a most delicate situation here, and you are necessary to—well, whatever is about to happen." The wizard stopped and frowned, as if uncertain of what he might say next.

Todd was the first among them to speak. "So you sent for us, then?"

Obar waved his hands as if to rapidly dispel any such notion. "Oh, dear, no. I don't have that sort of power. Even Nunn doesn't claim that kind of control. No. I'm afraid you were chosen by the dragon."

Even Nick felt compelled to speak at that. "The dragon?"

"A real dragon?" Bobby said immediately after Nick.

"What's the dragon?" was Todd's question.

Obar sighed. "What is not the dragon?" He smiled at the expressions of the neighbors. "I do not try to be confusing. Well, perhaps sometimes I do, but that is another matter." Obar opened his arms wide. "The dragon hides, somewhere inside this world, or maybe somewhere above it. Even the greatest sorcery cannot find him. And even though the creature sleeps, we are—still—all controlled by the dragon. The dragon, you see, has brought us here for its own reasons."

He paused again, his eyes focused someplace far away from the tower room. "But we can fight it! The dragon is power. If we are to save ourselves, we will have to attempt to harness the power." He shook his head. "Eventually, we will no doubt all be destroyed by it."

He looked up at the neighbors. "We are not the first at this. Others have tried. Until now, every one has been destroyed."

"Wait a minute," Todd protested. "You're telling us we're going to have to do something that's going to get us killed?"

Obar chewed at a ragged fingernail. "Well, hopefully not. There is always hope, isn't there?"

Charlie growled again.

"Hey," Bobby broke in with a forced laugh. "Even the dog doesn't like it."

But Nick saw his dog staring out in the middle of the room.

"It's the magic, no doubt," Obar remarked. "The dog must sense it. It erupts with greater frequency, you know, as the dragon prepares to awake."

Nick followed the dog's gaze. There was a spot in the middle of the far wall that seemed hazy, where the sharp lines between stones blurred one atop another.

"You can use the magic sometimes," Obar continued as he stroked his shaggy mustache. His tone seemed more distracted with every word. "Or it can use you."

Magic. Nick saw a point of light growing on the wall, or maybe just in front of it, a point so bright it looked like the real sun had bored its way through from the outside world.

He turned back to Obar. Was this light the old man's doing? But the magician had closed his eyes, as if remembering.

"What if we don't want to use your magic?" Todd demanded. "What if we don't want to have anything to do with this?"

"Oh, you will," Obar replied with a quiet confidence, his voice now barely more than a whisper. "The magic is intoxicating." He chuckled softly. "And, of course, quite habit-forming."

Charlie started to bark.

The light burst forth like some tiny firework, except this was a firework with form, for the spreading light grew arms and legs and a head. The thing had lost its intense brightness now, but twinkled with countless points of light, like a creature made of stars. But it wasn't human; not quite. To Nick it looked more like an ape.

"What?" Obar called in confusion as his eyes snapped open. "This isn't—"

"Here?" Raven screamed on Nick's shoulder. "He dares?"

Charlie rushed the creature.

One of the creature's arms flashed forward, the still-moving light catching the dog as he leapt. Charlie was thrown back across the room, yelping in surprise.

The creature of light moved quickly toward the neighbors.

"Hey!" Todd struck out at the thing as the creature enveloped him. Bobby screamed and lost his footing, falling backward toward the floor. The light swallowed him while he was still in midair.

"Raven will not let this be!" the bird called angrily.

Nick felt an instant of intense pain as the bird's claws dug into his shoulder. The air nearby was filled with a great flapping of wings, mixed with the shouted words of Obar.

Raven cawed and flew straight for the thing.

Obar rushed after the bird. He stared at the light, both hands making rapid gestures as a hundred indecipherable words flew from his lips. There was an intensity about the wizard now that had been lacking before as he focused only on magic.

The light-creature stopped. Its hands flew up in front of what should have been its face.

Raven dived toward it as Obar made a noise so high and strange that it barely seemed human.

The creature screamed.

Raven struck the creature beak-first as the light broke apart like a glass shattering into tiny shards. One by one, the fragments of light flared and vanished.

The creature of light was gone as suddenly as it had arrived. But it seemed to have taken Todd and Bobby with it.

"Once again, Raven has saved the day," the bird announced as it attempted to resettle on Nick's shoulder.

"Raven had very little to do with it," Obar replied, trying to shake his brown costume more suitably back onto his shoulders. His efforts did little more than rearrange the wrinkles. "Nunn was simply not ready for my counterattack."

"But where's Todd?" Nick insisted, shaking off the bird. Raven squawked, either at Nick's unwillingness to be a resting place or at Obar's insistence that a wizard's magic had saved the day.

"And Bobby?" Nick continued. "And what's happened to Charlie?"

The dog lay against the far wall of the room. Charlie still breathed in heavy, rapid gasps. He whimpered softly, his eyes closed.

"Your dog I can cure," Obar remarked as he strode over to the fallen animal. "After ridding ourselves of Nunn's magic, patching up this canine will be the easiest and most delightful of tasks."

"But what about Bobby and Todd?" Jason insisted.

Obar blinked as if he had forgotten all about the two others. "Oh, yes. I imagine they've been shifted somewhere by Nunn. Perhaps not where Nunn wanted them. We did get to that creature well before he was done. It's always very satisfying when you can foil something nasty like that, don't you think?"

He knelt down by Charlie. Nick realized there was blood on the floor below the dog's forepaws. Please. He wanted Charlie to be all right. He hoped that this time the magician knew what he was talking about.

"Then you're just going to leave Bobby and Todd out there?" Jason demanded.

Obar placed a finger to the spot where his nose met his brow, and paused a moment in thought. "We will find them as soon as the effects of the spell dissipate."

Obar glanced up from the dog to give his remaining guests his very best smile. "Until then, we can but pray that they protect themselves."

Nick did not find the wizard's smile at all reassuring.

O Nine

Mary Lou was talking about the neighbors.

Afterward, she couldn't remember how she had gotten started. Well, she began by describing her parents and her brother, but that wasn't exactly what she meant. (And how about her sister? Somehow, because Susan wasn't there, she no longer seemed worth talking about.) She talked about how her parents were happier when she didn't bother them, and how they always paid so much attention to her brother, Jason, and his science projects. And that led to descriptions of Jason's friend Bobby, with his weird, braying laugh, and the two other teenage boys in the neighborhood, the cute (but shy) Nick and the handsome (but conceited!) Todd. She began to talk about Nick's mother, and the assistant principal, Mr. Mills, and how they seemed to be spending more and more time together, when another voice interrupted.

Mary Lou opened her eyes. When had she closed them? For an instant, she felt as if she had lost not only her voice but her breath as well, as if a tiny piece of ice had lodged in her lungs.

"That's quite enough, my dear," a third voice added.

She blinked and saw a smiling Nunn in front of her. Mary Lou found herself getting really upset. Why should she have wanted to say anything to him?

"Do you have any sense of them?" Nunn asked. His smile was gone; his brow wrinkled with a hundred creases.

Mary Lou didn't understand him. Was he still speaking to her?

A halo formed around the magician's head. Nunn's face relaxed as the light rose to form first a separate skull and then a body beneath.

"Oh, I will find them quite easily," the child voice replied as it hovered above the wizard. "Mary Lou is so helpful. We must find a way to thank her."

"Oh," Nunn agreed, "I think she will have a most important

role in what's to come. Especially if she continues to cooperate. But why don't you bring her friends to her now?"

"Then they will all be together?" The creature slowly became more solid as it hovered above the magician's head, so that its face now featured vague shadows for a mouth, a nose, and the sockets of the eyes. It glanced down at the still-unconscious Captain. "Well, almost all."

"I think the Captain will call back the other one without any further aid," Nunn answered with a chuckle.

The Captain nodded again, and smiled, as if he was glad to be part of the fun. He still didn't open his eyes.

"I'll bring them all together," the creature said in a voice that was almost singing. "Then, once we've made our choices, I can have some real enjoyment."

Two points of light flared on the creature's face, two red orbs where eyes should be. They stared at Mary Lou. "It's amazing how hungry you get when you're not allowed to feed."

"No complaints," Nunn reprimanded the thing, as if he was, indeed, talking to a five-year-old. "You always get what you want."

"I do, don't I?" The creature almost purred as its form, never that substantial, seemed to fade from where it hovered. After a moment, only the two glowing eyes remained. Then those blinked out as well.

"Now we wait," Nunn said. "It won't be very long. Zachs can be quite efficient when he is properly motivated."

Nunn turned away to examine a collection of vials crowded on one of many shelves.

Mary Lou felt like she had been dismissed. She was used to that; her parents were very good at dismissing her, getting her out of sight and mind. Except she was afraid that this time Nunn didn't want her to leave.

But this time she wanted, more than anything, to be out of here.

Nunn laughed softly as he picked up a jar filled with dark liquid. The Captain started to kick his feet out as if he was marching through the air. He still hadn't opened his eyes.

"I would like to see my parents," Mary Lou said.

Nunn turned to look at her. "You would?" Her remark seemed to have greatly amused the magician.

"I heard you say all the neighbors were important, at least for now," she continued quickly, knowing that if she stopped talking now, she might not have the nerve to start again. "Wouldn't it be better if my parents weren't worried about me?"

"A very persuasive argument," Nunn continued in that maddeningly agreeable tone. "I imagine you are very important." His smile turned down slightly at the edges. "I will speak frankly with you, Mary Lou. As you can see from our friend the Captain, I generally am able to get what I need from anyone, at any time." He nodded thoughtfully, and the Captain, still marching, nodded along. "However, I will admit that things go more smoothly when people are willing. Tell me, if you were to see your parents, would you be able to keep our little secret?"

"Secret?" Mary Lou asked.

Nunn swept his right hand in a great arc before him. "All of this. People are so much easier to deal with when they're not aware of complications."

She did not know if she could agree. She never wanted to say yes to anything this man might suggest.

"You are probably wise to be careful," Nunn said. "Not, of course, that it matters. Once you, or anyone, enters my castle, there is no leaving. Well, perhaps for someone very special. But you would have to prove yourself extremely worthy."

Special? She thought of the creature that had seeped out of the Captain's insides. Maybe there was something worse than being trapped here, after all.

"What?" Nunn asked sharply.

Mary Lou hadn't said anything.

Light filled the room, followed by a high scream that slammed into her with a solid force, lifting her from her feet and tossing her backward.

She landed flat on her back, stunned, the air knocked from her lungs.

"Hurt!" the child voice screamed.

She pushed herself up on her elbows. The magician's creature had returned. It sat huddled on the floor, its skin glowing a dull orange. The area around it was a mess of fallen shelves. The Captain's chair had tipped over on its side, so that his continuous stiff-legged marching pulled him around in a circle every time his left leg dragged along the floor. Nunn picked himself up and stared down at the thing.

"Where are the boys?" he demanded.

The thing looked up at the magician. "Hurt!" it screamed again, a great tongue of orange flame thrown from its mouth.

Nunn staggered away from the fire. He lifted both his hands. Mary Lou thought he would cover his face. Instead, he clapped them together, and a spout of green flame lanced forward to strike the creature's skull.

The thing's screams redoubled as it shrank close to the floor.

"There is more than one kind of hurt, my dear Zachs," Nunn said softly.

"Hurt!" the thing screamed sullenly.

"You haven't answered my question," Nunn continued in the same quiet tone.

"Slipped away," the creature replied quickly. "Zachs had them, the first two. But the magician. Hurt! Hurt!"

"You let them get away?" Emotion was returning to the magician's voice.

"No one hurts Zachs like that!" the creature continued its tirade. "I'll hurt them! Eat them slowly. Keep them awake so they know, so they see. Eat the head last!"

"Zachs!" Nunn's voice rose to meet the other. "You will answer my question!"

"Hurt!" The thing shot out another spit of flame. This one hit the pile of fallen shelves, setting them ablaze.

Mary Lou was afraid these two would destroy the whole place. She looked around for somewhere to hide, and saw that she had been thrown only a few feet short of the doorway. Carefully, she rose to her hands and knees.

Nunn clapped his hands again. This time his green fire was met by the creature's orange.

The second explosion caught Mary Lou as she rose to her feet, propelling her from the room, until she was stopped abruptly by the stone wall opposite the doorway. She managed to take a breath, swallowed, willed herself not to fall.

She stumbled to the side, trying desperately to get away from anything else that might erupt from the battle. She looked back the way she had come, but she knew that corridor ended in a solid wall. The hallway stretched off the other way as well. Mary Lou walked as best she could, fright making her forget her hurts. She would find some way out of here.

The way was quiet. As the cacophony behind her faded with distance, she could once again hear the slap of her heels against stone. She found it reassuring. Since that sound came from her, she felt once again in some control of what would happen to her.

The floor beneath her shook, as if Nunn's battle might destroy the castle.

She saw something flickering ahead, a light of some sort with a greenish tinge. She thought of the wizard's fire and almost stopped, propelled forward only when she heard another muffled explosion at her back. Maybe, she thought, there was window up ahead, obscured by a drape of some sort, blowing in the wind.

The light made her want to ignore her bruises even more, and she managed to break into a slow run toward the illumination. The fight behind her would not go on forever. If she was to get out of this place, it would have to be now.

The light flickered before her again, and she saw that it wasn't a window, after all. It was a door, and beyond that door were the trees and shrubs of the open woodland. But the door wasn't always there. When the light vanished, she saw a stone wall ahead of her instead.

She realized that these must be the only ways in and out of Nunn's castle: doorways controlled by the magician's sorcery. Nunn must have wanted her to join him inside his retreat; otherwise, she doubted if she could have gotten into the hut. For all she knew, he could also twist the corridors of this place around so that he could lead you to any place he wanted.

But, for a moment at least, Nunn had lost control. His spells flickered as he used his energy in a personal battle.

Mary Lou had no doubt it was a battle that Nunn would win.

The door flashed into existence before her again, looking bright and real and inviting. She broke into a full run toward it as the seconds fled by.

It vanished before she could reach it. Before her was the never-ending wall, stretching out into a new corridor both left and right.

From somewhere behind her, she heard a great, booming laugh, the sound, perhaps, of the magician's victory.

Then the doorway was back. Nunn hadn't had time to regain control of all his spells. If she was going to run, it had to be now. She had no desire to pass through that space as the magic stone wall solidified around her.

Mary Lou jumped forward, diving into a somersault as she had been taught in gymnastics. She hit the ground and rolled onto her back.

She looked back to where she had come from and saw nothing but a sheer cliff face. But she heard no sounds of battle, nor magician's laughter.

She did hear a great rustling in the trees overhead. She looked up and saw the branches bouncing about in an agitated fashion, far more than could be explained by a passing wind.

She screamed as something jumped from the tree, falling straight toward her.

O Ten

Now Todd was pissed.

Hey, he thought, maybe this whole thing was a way out, the kind of thing he'd always wanted to do, a way to get away from his bastard old man and his crying mother and all the things he couldn't stand in that house on Chestnut Circle.

But man, not like this. Now Todd didn't even want to open his eyes.

What had hit him? He had taken a swing at that light-thing. But his fist had been sucked right into it. The thing had fucking swallowed him up. God, did it hurt. His fist, then his arm, then everything. He never wanted to feel that kind of pain again, like he was burning from the inside out.

Then there was nothing.

Todd heard a groan.

He swore, and opened his eyes. It surprised him when he saw sunlight overhead. After that pain, he guessed he was surprised he could do anything.

He turned his head and saw he was lying in a field full of long yellow grass. Bobby was lying beside him, breathing like he was asleep. There was no sign of the light-monster, or of any of the others from the tower room.

Bobby groaned again. He shifted on the ground, but he still didn't open his eyes.

There were trees in the distance. For some reason, Todd was sure this had to be the same forest they had just come out of— maybe because that forest was all he'd seen since coming to this place.

It was much quieter than any place Todd could remember. Oh, there was some noise: the wind in the trees, the call of birds back and forth, the odd chirruping sound of some sort of insect. If this place was not the world they'd come from— and one look at the sky was enough to convince Todd that it

83

wasn't—there were still a lot of things about it that were awfully familiar.

But not familiar enough. This quiet didn't mean peace any more than one of his father's smiles meant you were safe from his fists. Todd was waiting for something to jump on him.

Unless he could find a way to jump first.

He tried to remember what had happened after he'd taken a swing at that thing. There was nothing there. He must have passed out. What, then? Why was he here, in some fucking field in the middle of nowhere, with Bobby? And where was that thing that had grabbed him?

Todd sat up, the anger making him move. Who cared what had happened? He just wouldn't let it happen again! Whatever that creep made of light had wanted, it wouldn't get it without one hell of a fight.

He looked around, suddenly aware of how exposed they were here, out in the open. He had to wake Bobby up. They had to get out of here. One thing you learned when you had an old man like Todd's—whenever things got weird, you made yourself scarce.

But how could you make yourself scarce when you didn't even know where you were in the first place?

Todd stood and flexed his muscles, surprised again that he wasn't sore from his recent battle. It felt as if, once he had left the light-creature, he had left all the pain as well. If anything, he felt rested, and ready for a fight.

He looked around carefully, ready to throw himself back into the tall grass if he saw anyone else. But they really did seem to be alone.

He stood up in the clearing. There was no way to tell if this was the same place they'd been attacked by the lightning storm, or if they were someplace else, miles away. There were probably a hundred fields like this in the forest, all surrounded by great trees.

Standing made Todd feel even more exposed. He wanted to get into those trees as quickly as he could, so they could hide from whatever was coming next. Maybe they could even climb the trees, get some idea of where they were. Maybe they could even see that big stone house the light-creature had snatched them from.

Or maybe they'd have to admit that they were lost. But Todd didn't want to just sit here. He had to move.

He knelt down next to the other boy. "Bobby! Wake up!"

"What?" Bobby's fist came up swinging. "Get away. I saw what—"

Todd blocked his friend's half-asleep swing with a well-placed arm.

"Cool it, Bobby," he said softly. "It's me. Todd."

Bobby finally opened his eyes. "Todd? Oh, wow." Bobby started to smile but stopped himself. "That thing—what happened to—" He paused again, afraid to describe the creature that had captured them.

"It's gone. At least I don't see it anywhere around here. And I think we should get out of here before it has a chance to come back."

Bobby shook his head, maybe to disagree, maybe to try to clear his own thoughts. "You want to run away? Aw, Todd, c'mon! It couldn't surprise us this time." He reached into the pocket of his jeans. "I've still got the knife."

Todd thought about the light, and the pain. "I think your knife would do as much good as my fists did. Better we make ourselves scarce." Todd didn't mention that, the way the creature had shown up in the wizard's room, they might not be safe anywhere.

Bobby started to say something else but ended up grunting instead. Maybe, Todd thought, he remembered that pain, too. Bobby pushed himself to his knees. Todd grabbed one of Bobby's hands and helped him to his feet.

"This way," Todd said as he turned to his left for no particular reason and started to march toward the forest. Maybe the trees looked a bit lower to the ground over here, a bit more climbable. More likely, though, it was just a hunch. He had to stop himself from looking around again. In a place like this, a hunch could mean a lot.

"So what do we do, Todd?" Bobby asked. "Go back with that bird and the Obar character?"

Todd didn't answer, concentrating instead on placing his feet on the uneven ground hidden by the grass. Bobby kept on talking, anyway.

"You don't think the knife's enough protection, huh? Maybe we could sharpen some sticks into spears or something." Bobby whistled softly. "I don't think spears would have stopped that glowing thing either, though."

Again Todd didn't bother replying. The way Bobby was going, he seemed to be able to hold up both sides of the conversation all by himself.

"What about our families?" Bobby asked. "I mean, what if something's happened to my parents? Maybe we should try to find them or something, too."

Todd grimaced at the very mention of parents. Now that he was out here, and free, there was no way he was ever going back to his father.

"We have to find out where we are before we can figure out where to go," he answered Bobby, his voice much more reasonable. "Now, quiet down. The less noise we make, the less likely something bad is going to find us."

Bobby seemed to consider the wisdom of that for a moment before replying.

"Anything you say, Todd," he said, his voice quieter already.

Todd frowned at the forest before them. They had almost reached the trees.

"So which one should we climb, huh, Todd?" asked Bobby, still not willing to shut up.

Todd didn't have an answer. The trunks were so thick and the limbs so high that there would be no way of climbing any of the trees on this edge of the forest. Todd looked speculatively at the great clinging vines that ran down the great boles. Would one of them support his weight?

Todd grabbed onto one of the vines, yanking it from where it hugged the tree.

"Remember those ropes in gym class?" he asked.

"I don't know if I can do this," Bobby said in a voice that was half astonishment, half misery. "How the hell are we going to get out of here?"

Something hummed close by Todd's ear as he hoisted himself off the ground. He froze.

An arrow thunked into the tree in front of him.

"Cripes!" Bobby yelled. "We're *not* going to get out of here!" He took a couple of running steps.

"Stay there," a voice called from somewhere farther along the curve of the forest, "or the next arrow won't be so polite."

Bobby froze, and looked back at Todd. The arrow had shut Bobby up at last, but his eyes wanted Todd to do something, anything, and do it fast.

Todd lowered himself carefully back to the ground, trying to figure out where that arrow had come from. He stood very still. What sort of a match were his fists, or even Bobby's knife, against arrows that came out of nowhere?

"Clever fellows," the voice called again from the wood, the words slow and deliberate, almost a drawl. "We're not gonna hurt you. At least, we won't if you can answer a question or two the way we like."

Without another word, four people stepped from the darkness beneath the trees, so silently it almost seemed as if they simply appeared. They were all dressed in ragged gear stitched together from dark brown pelts. It looked like they had covered their faces with mud.

"Whose side are you on?" one of the four asked sharply. His was the same voice that had spoken before. He was taller and thinner than the others, with a long, sour face. He looked like he never smiled.

"Side?" Todd asked. "We don't know anything about sides."

"They don't want to answer," another said. Todd realized from the timbre of the new voice that the speaker was female. With the shapeless clothing that they all wore, it was difficult to tell. She was shorter than the others, her hair cut close to her scalp.

She notched an arrow in her bow. "I think we can hasten their reply."

"Your side!" Bobby called. He raised his hands over his head. "We'll be glad to be on your side!"

"Sorry, fellas," the man answered lightly. "But that answer's too easy." He nodded to the woman. "Mary Margaret, you called it, you start it."

Todd wasn't about to let this happen. "Wait a moment!" he shouted. "We were dragged out of our home by soldiers, who were taking us to some guy named Nunn. But we got away, and ended up with some crazy old guy named Obar. Except something that looked like it was made of light grabbed us." Todd realized he was waving his arms. He let them fall to his side as he finished, "We ended up here!"

"Fair enough," the man replied, as if Todd's explanation was the sort of thing he heard every day. "But we still haven't heard your answer. Which do you follow, Nunn or Obar?"

"What?" Todd asked, incredulous. These guys were making him even angrier than he was before. "I don't want to have anything to do with either one!"

The long-faced man made a sound like a laugh, even though he still didn't smile. "Put down your bow, Maggie. That's the best answer of all."

The woman lowered her bow and resheathed her arrow, then turned back to Todd and Bobby.

"Name's Thomas," the first man to speak introduced himself. "You already met Maggie. Next to her are Wilbert and Stanley." The two other men nodded in turn. Wilbert had a heavy beard, the hair caked underneath the mud. He smiled as his name was mentioned, a flash of white against the mottled muddy brown. Stanley, on the other hand, had hardly any hair anywhere on his head. He squinted at the newcomers without expression.

"Together," Thomas continued, "we're all that's left of the Newton Free Volunteers. And just who are we speakin' to?"

Todd stared at the four for a moment before replying. He supposed he had to trust somebody here. What harm, after all, could come from giving these people their names? Todd introduced both of them.

"You don't come from here?" Bobby asked.

"Thankfully, no," Thomas replied. His expression softened a bit with that, as if he really did want to smile but had forgotten how.

"I don't think any humans do," Maggie added. "Of course, I could be wrong."

"You could be wrong about anything going on around this place," Wilbert said laconically. "We could all be wrong about everything. Probably are, too."

"We hail from the United States of America," Thomas said. "Newton, New Jersey; members of the Free State Militia. We were out on maneuvers one weekend—"

"War games," Wilbert added with a laugh. "Thought Teddy might need us! Never did get a chance to help."

"Never made it home." Stanley spat on the ground. "Ended up here, hey? With a bunch of self-styled wizards!"

"They told us the dragon brought us," Wilbert offered with a wry grin.

"The dragon?" Stanley grunted. "A bunch of mumbo jumbo, if you ask me."

Thomas opened his arms to take in his surroundings. "Mumbo jumbo or not, we ended up here. You boys don't look local, either. Where do you hail from?"

Bobby blurted out a short and confusing summation of the arrival of Chestnut Circle in the middle of the woods.

"So we're countrymen?" Thomas asked. "And you say there's more of you?"

"Yeah, a lot!" Bobby agreed. "There's probably still two guys with Obar, and then there's my parents and Mary Lou and all the other adults stuck with those soldiers."

"Nunn's men," Thomas remarked. The four Volunteers all looked from one to another, as if that meant something none too pleasant. "We know their camp a little too well. It ain't too healthy for your parents to stay there."

"Do we get them out?" Stanley barked. He rested his hand on the sword at his belt, as if he already knew the answer.

Wilbert smiled and pulled on the shoulder strap of the quiver on his back. "I haven't shot anyone in weeks."

"I think we gotta try," Thomas agreed.

"And then?" Stanley demanded.

"Things have changed," Thomas said as he nodded toward Todd and Bobby. "There're new people here. Fresh blood. Maybe we can all get home together."

"We can do some fighting for Teddy, after all!" Wilbert agreed.

"By now, that trouble in China's gotta be done, hey?" Stanley observed in a much less cheerful tone.

But Wilbert wasn't going to lose his good mood that easily. "There's bound to be a fight someplace! Bully and all that!"

Todd frowned, not really listening to their talk of battles and some guy named Teddy. The last thing he wanted to do was to go back and get his father.

He tried to calm himself down. Whatever these so-called Volunteers planned, he guessed that they wouldn't appreciate him wanting to split.

Maybe the others deserved to be rescued. He especially wouldn't mind rescuing Mary Lou. He thought about the way her breasts jutted from her chest, her dark hair fell across her shoulders, the warm, milky smell of her skin. Sometimes she acted like she didn't like him very much. But he saw the way she looked at him, out at the bus stop in the morning, when she thought he didn't notice.

But not his father. His father was crazy.

Maybe there was some way around this.

"So we go back and rescue those guys with Nunn," he said. "What about Nick and Jason? They're with the other wizard."

"Not the same problem at all," Stanley announced.

"Obar's a little easier to deal with," Wilbert explained when Stanley did not. "He tries to keep it under some control."

"Actually, I'm rather fond of Obar," Maggie said with a strange little smile. She ran a hand over her short and mud-caked hair.

"That's our Maggie," Wilbert said, the smile once again breaking out on his face. "Always the worst judge of character."

"Hey, it comes with my profession." She smiled graciously in return, then glanced at the boys.

"Former profession," Stanley snapped.

"Hey, now," Wilbert said more softly. "It's an ancient and honorable profession. Well, ancient, at least."

"Former profession," Maggie agreed. "I've retired to become a soldier."

"Still, you can live with some wizards," Wilbert said. "As long as you don't have to trust them."

Thomas glanced at the sun poised just above the trees. "We'd better get going if we want to raid them after dark. Tell me more about this light-creature that grabbed you."

Wilbert and Stanley shifted their bows onto their backs. Stanley took a moment to arrange the bow and a bulky pack he carried on the other shoulder. The two started to move without any further orders. Bobby shrugged at Todd and fell in behind the other two. Maggie smiled at Todd and tugged gently at his elbow. He started to walk beside her as Thomas took up the rear.

"Have you eaten lately?" Maggie asked.

Todd realized he hadn't had any food since the ice cream bar from the night before. "No, ma'am," he said. Even though Maggie was only a few years older than he was, "ma'am" seemed the proper way to address her. There was something different about her, about all of them, really, the way they held themselves, the way they talked. It reminded Todd of his grandfather, the major, when he was still alive.

It made sense, Todd guessed—the military connection, that is. Maggie said she'd retired to become a soldier. Todd wondered what she'd done before that.

"I've got some jerky here in my pouch," she offered as she opened a small bag at her side. "It's made from sand lizard, I'm afraid."

"Tastes sort of like dried squirrel," Wilbert added from up ahead.

"Well, I don't know," Maggie spoke up. "That might be an insult to the squirrels."

She passed him a piece of dried greenish-brown meat. As odd as it looked, Todd found his mouth watering. There was no reason they would poison him, was there? If they wanted him dead, it would be much simpler to use one of their arrows, or the knives that hung at their belts.

Bobby had started to tell the four what had happened with the light-creature. It wasn't quite how Todd remembered it. The way Bobby told it, there was more of a fight.

Todd took a small bite of the jerky, tearing the piece free with his teeth. It was a little salty, but not that bad. He swallowed, and tasted something sour.

"It's the aftertaste that'll get you," Maggie agreed, apparently reading the displeasure in his face. "Wilbert says you have to watch out, or the lizards will sneak up on you from behind."

"It gets better!" Wilbert called back. "After a while, your taste buds die!"

Well, Todd thought, it really wasn't all that bad. Sort of like strange Chinese food. He took another bite. He felt like his mouth was drying out.

"I could use a drink of water," he suggested.

"Ah," Wilbert called. "The food is free, but water will cost you!"

Everybody seemed to laugh at that but Todd. Todd's tongue felt like it would stick to the roof of his mouth. This stuff was salty.

He managed a grin when he realized that the pouch Maggie held out to him was a waterskin. The meat might have been sour, but he never tasted better water anywhere.

"Never go out on the sand without water nearby," Wilbert said soberly. "Stick with us, young fellow, and you'll learn a thing or two."

Like the fact that wizards couldn't be trusted? Todd thought.

Unless, of course, he couldn't trust the Newton Free Volunteers. Especially if they were taking him to see his father. Todd decided, for now, that he'd better keep his options open.

◯ Eleven

Evan Mills looked with up with a start.

Rose Dafoe stood so suddenly that even the soldiers who were still eating reached for their weapons.

"Where's Mary Lou?" she demanded.

"Rose, calm down," her husband, Harold, hurriedly reassured her. "I'm sure she's got to be around here somewhere."

Mills wondered how Dafoe could be so certain of his daughter's whereabouts when he refused to look up from the table.

"I will not calm down!" Rose Dafoe retorted. Her well-manicured hands pounded the table before her. "I want an answer!" Mills realized this was the first time he had ever seen the woman without a smile.

The soldiers looked at each other uneasily.

"Are all the children gone?" Joan Blake asked in a voice barely above a whisper.

"What's happening here?" Carl Jackson demanded. "We don't have to take this!" He rose to his feet as well, his hands balling into fists. It reminded Mills why nobody in the neighborhood ever talked to Jackson. He could be counted on to explode anywhere, at any time.

Two of the soldiers silently notched arrows in their bows and turned away from Mrs. Dafoe, pointing their shafts toward Jackson. Both soldiers looked much less uncertain than they had before.

"Carl," Constance Smith said softly. "This might not be the best time to object."

Jackson's jaw tightened. He looked at the elderly Mrs. Smith as if he was about to attack her instead. His eyes flicked quickly to the soldiers and just as quickly away. He nodded curtly and returned to the table.

In her way, Mills thought, Old Lady Smith was probably the bravest among them. Heaven knew, Carl's wife hadn't said a thing. She stared at the table in front of her, or looked deep into the forest, as if she wanted to get as far away from here as possible. Mills hated to think how Jackson must treat his wife at home. For all their talk of being neighbors, what did any of them really know about the others' personal lives?

Mrs. Smith turned to the soldiers. "But the children are gone, aren't they? There are things that you aren't telling us about."

The soldiers still did not reply.

Joan turned to Mills, a real panic in her pale blue eyes. He took her hand. It felt warmer than usual, and her palm was damp with perspiration. Evan had been pleased when Joan had stopped by more often over the course of this summer: a cup of coffee here, an afternoon picnic there. They had found they enjoyed each other's company. He had wanted them to get closer—but not because of something like this.

"Listen." Mr. Dafoe finally looked up at the soldiers. "I can understand. You've got a job to do. I was in the big one, myself. World War Two. Not like that mess we've got in Southeast Asia, no. That was—" He paused and stared at the confused faces of the soldiers. "You don't know about any of this, do you?" He looked around as if he expected an answer not only from the soldiers but from the huts and the trees. "Where the hell are we?"

"We fight for Nunn," said the same soldier who had spoken before. Apparently, now that the Captain had disappeared, this new fellow was to be the spokesman. "That is all we know. We fight, or we die."

It sounded, Mills thought, as if the soldiers weren't all that much better off than the rest of them.

"So they're doing their job!" Jackson turned to Dafoe, his eyes narrow, his voice low. "Why are you always criticizing our boys over in Nam, anyways?"

Dafoe smiled apologetically. "I'm not criticizing anyone, Carl," he said quickly. "I'm just trying to start some sort of dialogue."

"Dialogue?" Jackson retorted with a snort. "Better be careful you don't get us all killed." He nodded to all the other neighbors, as if they were all lucky to be alive after Dafoe's blunder. Dafoe looked as if he wanted to say something else, but turned his gaze back to the table instead. Jackson had an unerring sense of the best person to bully.

The soldiers lowered their bows, but all remained standing.

After a moment, another three sat down to eat.

Furlong shifted uneasily from foot to foot and tried to smile. "Hey, why don't we talk about something else?"

"And what would you like to talk about, Leo?" his wife asked in a way that implied anybody who would talk with her husband was an idiot.

"I don't know," Furlong said with a shrug. He looked over at Jackson. "Carl, you think the Packers have a chance this season?"

"Leo," Mrs. Smith said softly, "I don't think we're ever going to see the Packers again."

"What are you talking about?" Furlong asked, as if only now being confronted by the horror of the situation. "No football? Where the hell are we?"

"Well," Mrs. Furlong retorted, "I suppose there's some things to be thankful for."

A couple of the neighbors attempted to laugh at Mrs. Furlong's joke. It didn't sound very sincere. Somehow Mills expected someone to suggest charades.

The soldiers stopped eating again. Mills looked around quickly. Had one of the neighbors done something to upset them again?

But it wasn't any of them. Nunn had returned.

"Where's Mary Lou?" Rose Dafoe demanded as soon as she saw him. "Have you seen her?"

Nunn offered them the most reassuring of smiles. "Mary Lou is fine. She just took it upon herself to tour my home." He shook his head at Rose's expression of dismay. "Oh, don't worry, we had a little talk about places she shouldn't go. There are parts of my dwelling that are quite dangerous, I'm afraid." He chuckled. "But she's quite busy exploring."

"Exploring what?" Jackson demanded.

Nunn waved merrily at the hut behind him. "You see, my home is much larger than it looks on the outside."

"Nothing's happened to her?" Rose demanded, still not convinced.

"No, I wanted to assure you that she was safe. And to invite you to join her."

He stepped aside and waved for the neighbors to precede him into the hut.

Those neighbors who were still sitting stood to join the others. Dafoe and his wife led the way, followed by the Furlongs and the Jacksons. Joan walked over to Mrs. Smith and asked if she might like a hand.

The soldiers stood their ground behind them. Why weren't they following Nunn inside?

"Come now," Nunn called to the few who hadn't fallen into line. "You wouldn't want to miss the tour."

Mills followed Joan and Mrs. Smith as they joined the others. There was strength in numbers, he supposed, at least for now.

Besides, as far as he could see, Nunn was not giving them much choice.

The pain had stopped at last.

The Captain opened his eyes. He felt as if his insides had been pulled out and hastily stuffed back inside. Nauseous and weak. But still alive. And still able to think. Thank whatever gods there might be that Nunn had not chosen the Captain for some of the experiments he had seen.

He supposed he had always known that this would happen. As long as he had used Nunn's power, and it had been a very long time, someday that power would turn against him. Nunn had been generous before today. The Captain had authority, the use of certain devices, and the first choice of all newcomers. That had been the bargain. The Captain had been looking forward to spending time with that young girl, Mary Lou, before Nunn began his experiments on her.

Instead, Nunn expected the Captain to give of himself.

He screamed again, pulling uselessly at his bonds. The fire had moved from his body to his head. He felt as though his skull might explode, spewing bits of brain like so many pieces of ripe melon.

The pain receded, and the Captain realized he wasn't alone.

No. No one else was in the darkened room.

There was someone sharing his mind. Someone whose thoughts had slowed, and stilled. Someone who was waking from the deepest of sleeps. Or returning from somewhere far away.

The Captain thought about what the wizard had told him as the creature of light had done its work. The Captain had taken a life without the wizard's permission. Now he would have to bleed his own life away to give an existence back.

The Captain sensed another body, so stiff it almost felt brittle.

Somehow, though, his new form lifted his new head, then sat upright, swaying a bit as he recalled how to use his balance. His bony arms pushed him up from the forest floor. Awkwardly at first, as if he only remembered as he moved, he began to walk toward Nunn's castle, and the Captain.

His new voice—or was it two voices together?—formed words that surprised the Captain at the same time that he spoke them.

"My lawn," his new voice muttered in a tone filled with equal parts of pain and anger. "What have they done to my lawn?"

○ Twelve

Mary Lou was too scared to call out again. Things were falling all around her: living things that hit the ground running and called out in high voices: voices that sometimes sounded like laughter, and sometimes like screams.

She whirled around, looking for some way to get past these pale creatures. Each one was only as tall as a two-year-old. But there were so many of them. They were everywhere.

These were the same sort of creature that the Captain had shot. Did they remember that? Did they blame her for the death of their brother?

As if to answer her, they began to leap about her in a circle, repeating one word over and over again.

It sounded like "Nunn? Nunn? Nunn?"

Mary Lou suddenly found her voice, the words rushing out of her. "No, I don't want Nunn! I don't want any of you! Now get away from me!"

She took a step forward, determined to break free of the circle. But how? Where once there were a dozen of the tiny, cavorting things, there now were over a hundred, and more were dropping around her from the trees: a downpour of creatures. The circle was tightening as their numbers grew, and she saw the wizened things look up at her and leer as they rushed past, their hairless heads with tight pale skin looking more like skulls than faces, the same singsong word chanted by all their almost human lips.

"Nunn? Nunn? Nunn?"

Mary Lou shifted her left foot forward. She would break through these things if she had to, push them aside. She had to get out of here.

"Nunn? Nunn? Nunn?"

One of the things ran across her toes.

Mary Lou jerked her foot back so quickly that she couldn't

quite keep her balance. She yelled as she twisted, falling toward the ground and the tiny dancing things.

They were quick. They jumped out of her way as she fell in the dirt. She waited for the circle to close, for them to run over her, tiny feet trampling her hands and feet and wrists and ankles, climbing across her arms and legs and back and head until the hundreds of bodies overwhelmed her, suffocating her beneath their weight.

But she didn't feel anything. She didn't hear anything, either. Her fall seemed to have ended the dance, and the chanting as well.

"Dobbit?" one of the high voices inquired.

Mary Lou was afraid to look, afraid that if she raised her head, she would see one of those things staring back and leering, eye-to-eye.

The things didn't talk again. Silence surrounded her, replaced by the growing sounds of the forest. Maybe, Mary Lou thought, the things could have gone away as quickly as they had come.

She lifted her face from the dirt.

The things were still there, but they had moved a few feet away and were staring at her with closed mouths, their fierce smiles gone. The circle shuffled quietly as she watched, and the creatures opened a space in their ranks before her. Were they giving her permission to leave?

Mary Lou put her arms under her and pushed away from the ground.

She saw something else in the space the creatures had left, something soft blue that seemed to glow in the center and shine on its darkened edges, like a neon sign reflected in the rain.

The blue glow widened and deepened, and from its center stepped a young man, close to Mary Lou's age. He was dressed in robes of a darker blue, almost black, and his long hair was gathered behind his head with a ribbon of the same color. He seemed at that instant to be the most handsome man Mary Lou had ever seen.

"They don't want to hurt you," the young man said in a voice that was both calm and deep, perfectly suited to his looks. "That's what they want me to tell you."

Mary Lou found herself standing. She tried to brush some of the dirt from her blouse. It was quite hopeless; her clothes were ruined. She looked back up at the handsome face, not sure if this man was real.

"They?"

"The People," the apparition replied with a smile. "That is what they like to call themselves." He paused, his forehead creasing for an instant before he continued. "They are aware that you have escaped from Nunn. That, they imagine, would hurt the wizard." He smiled again. "They are greatly in favor of anything that would hurt Nunn."

It was Mary Lou's turn to frown. "These—uh—people have told you this?"

"They're telling me that now," said the man, still smiling. Mary Lou very much liked the way he looked at her. "These People do not talk entirely with words. But I've been here long enough to understand them, if I concentrate a little." He paused again. "They are sorry if they frightened you. Sometimes they are overcome with joy."

Mary Lou wasn't even thinking of the three-foot-high creatures anymore. "But who are you?"

This time the apparition's frown looked truly perplexed. Somehow it made him look far older. "I'm afraid—I don't know. I only know what the People tell me."

"You're dressed very nicely," Mary Lou mentioned, almost half to herself. "You could almost be a prince—or something."

As soon as she had said the words, Mary Lou felt she wanted to snatch them back. A prince? How could she say something so embarrassing? It was like something out of a fairy tale!

But, then again, this whole place held as strong a resemblance to a fairy tale as it did to anything else. Especially, she thought, the bad things that would happen early on in those tales, like the wolf eating Red Riding Hood's grandmother, or Hansel and Gretel getting threatened with the witch's oven. This prince (for she realized she already thought of him that way) had called Nunn a wizard. Where would you find a wizard except in a fairy tale?

"A prince?" The apparition continued to frown as he looked down at his fancy clothes. "Well, I suppose that explanation is as good as any other. If you would like me to be a prince, a prince I shall be."

He looked back at Mary Lou and gave her a smile that made her embarrassment disappear, as if it had been blown away by the wind.

"But the People have apologized," the prince said after a moment's silence. "Do you accept this?"

"Well, yes," Mary Lou said quickly, her thoughts suddenly pulled away from the prince. "I mean, there are so many strange things happening, it all can be a little frightening. I'll try to understand them better. I think I can if you are around."

"I shall be around whenever you need me," the prince replied with the same wonderful smile. "At least so long as we are here. I'm not certain how far I can travel." He shrugged and looked up at the sky, as if the clouds might hold the answer.

In a way, he was the one who seemed helpless. And Mary Lou very much wanted to help him. What could she say to him that didn't sound too forward, or too foolish?

The prince waved to the hundreds of creatures quietly waiting. "But our hosts have some questions."

"Questions?" Mary Lou remembered the prince had said these creatures spoke with more than words. She hadn't heard any voice beside the prince's. "Well, they can certainly ask them."

The prince nodded. "You were a prisoner of Nunn?" he asked, his voice deeper, empty of emotion.

She nodded back.

"Did they capture you alone?"

"Oh, no," she replied, "there were others, a lot of them. Almost my whole street." She wondered if she should explain that. Would these creatures know about streets?

Apparently they did, or the exact words weren't important, for the prince's next question was, "Then the others are still prisoners?"

She nodded again. "As far as I know."

She realized she was surprised that these "People" had to ask her these things. She guessed she had imagined that they had been following all of them through the trees, spying so that they would know everything. It made her feel better that they weren't quite as all-seeing as she had thought.

"The People are not happy with this." With that, the prince fell silent.

She looked at the handsome young man. He seemed to be looking somewhere beyond her, his face without expression. What were these so-called People getting at? And what did they do to the prince to make him act this way?

"You really don't know who you are?" she found herself asking.

"I don't even know what I am," the prince said, his face once again lighting with that same self-deprecating smile. "I remember waking up one day and having the People all around me. Somehow they had brought me out of—wherever I was. They gave me a brand-new life."

She should thank the People for that, she guessed. Mary Lou always judged too much by first impressions. Her parents were always telling her that. The prince—no matter what he looked like—might not be any more human than any of the People.

But Mary Lou really wanted to trust him and spend time to get to know him better. So she decided she would.

"We may be able to rescue some of them," the prince said suddenly. "We may not."

"You mean the neighbors?" Mary Lou suddenly felt guilty for not thinking about them before. "My parents are there. Is there something I should do?"

"Can you use a bow and arrow?" the prince asked.

"Actually, I can," she said, delighted that she could be of help. "Three years on the high school archery team."

"That certainly sounds impressive," the prince agreed.

She shook her head. "You really don't know what I'm talking about, do you?"

"There are more things I don't know than I do," he said with a smile and a shrug. "It is nothing new."

There he was, acting helpless again—her lost prince of the forest. She stepped forward and reached out to take his hand. Her fingers passed through his ruffled sleeve. He really was an apparition.

He was frowning again, but not at her attempt to touch him. His attention was focused somewhere else when he said, "You are one of the three. And one of the seven."

"Now I'm the one who doesn't understand," she answered.

"Neither do I," the prince said as he smiled at her again. "But the People do. Or they will. And they'll explain it to both of us in time. But there are things we must do. You've been in Nunn's castle. You'll realize that you don't want your parents to go there, too."

Mary Lou almost shivered when she thought again about the Captain's screams, and the ape-creature who seemed to be made out of light. Yes, as little as she really knew about it, Nunn's castle was a place that she understood far too well.

○ Thirteen

Charlie whimpered where he lay on the ground, still in a deep sleep.

"Your dog will heal," Obar pronounced as he rose from his work with the patient. "How do I put this?" The magician looked up to the ceiling. "The recovery will take a different course than what you are used to. There are certain things about this place that are unlike—well, I suppose you realize that, don't you? However, I should be handy to make any—shall we call them adjustments?—that you may deem necessary."

Adjustments? What was Obar talking about? Nick wasn't even sure what the wizard had done already, save for some business where he moved his hands up and down along the length of the dog's body while he chanted something in a voice so deep that it was almost a growl.

"Excuse me," Obar remarked as he lifted his palms toward the ceiling. "This can be a bit distracting."

Two flames of light shot from the wizard's palms, flaring up to brush the ceiling. He closed his hands into fists and the light was gone.

"I have to get rid of it somewhere," he explained.

There was a dark smudge on the stones of the ceiling where the light had hit. There were dozens of other similar smudges on the stone above. Apparently, the wizard dealt with this sort of thing all the time.

Obar made a soft clicking sound in the back of his throat. "Would that I could have dealt with that creature of Nunn's as quickly."

Nick found himself suddenly angry with the wizard; like he had been holding back his feelings until he was sure that his dog was all right. But now that the worst of his worry about Charlie was out of the way, he thought about everything else that had happened—especially the way that creature had snatched Todd and Bobby.

"What kind of wizard are you, anyway?" he demanded.

"Apparently, not a very good one," Obar confessed. He looked around at the overturned furniture and papers scattered across the floor. "At least we rid ourselves of that thing before it did some real damage."

"And you have Raven to thank for that," the bird insisted again from where he now perched on a high shelf.

"Why are we thanking you?" Nick asked, more skeptical with every passing minute. Todd and Bobby were gone, Obar couldn't find them, and Raven didn't even seem to want to try. He stared back at the wizard. "What have you gotten us into?"

"No need to raise your voice," Obar replied a bit testily. "We— that is, this bird here and myself—haven't gotten you into anything. We're trying to—well—let all of us survive it."

Nick simply didn't want to accept this. "Well, you've got a funny way of trying. I mean, where are Todd and Bobby? Are they even still alive?"

"Oh, I'm sure they are still alive. Otherwise I could tell, you see. Well, perhaps you can't. However, it is not in Nunn's best interest—that was who captured them, you know—but Nunn would not kill anyone—quite yet. They were destined for Nunn's stronghold, I imagine." He paused for another of his frowns. "But I'm certain they were tossed someplace else, thanks to the combined efforts of this bird and myself, since we managed to foil Nunn's creature, didn't we? Of course—I'm not certain where that someplace else is—well, at least for the moment." Nunn resumed the clicking noise at the back of his throat.

"Combined?" It was Raven's turn to make a derisive noise.

The wizard clapped his hands together. "Well, I certainly hope that helps to ease your fears. I should be able to find them soon enough." Obar frowned at Jason's and Nick's less-than-comprehending expressions. "Not clear enough, is it? I suppose it must be time for some—uh, deeper explanation, heh? That always does come up eventually."

"Raven needs no explanation," the bird said to no one in particular. "Raven simply is."

"Then I would thank Raven to be still for those of us who do require clarification," Obar said in a bit of a huff. "I will speak to Nick and Jason." For an instant, Nick was surprised that the wizard even remembered their names. It made him wonder how much of the magician's constant confusion was playacting.

"We have certain advantages in this situation," Obar continued. "First, we have experience."

"The dragon has done this before?" Jason asked.

"Far too many times," the wizard agreed. "You see, he stirs in his sleep from time to time. And, when he stirs, people arrive. And this sort of thing has been going on for"—Obar paused to chew on his mustache—"well, quite some time. Generations, at least. Some surmise that everyone here has, in one way or another, been brought to this place by the dragon."

"Raven is not dependent on any dragon," the bird cawed. "Raven was here first. The dragon has only followed."

The black fowl stared moodily at Nick's shoulder. Did Raven want an invitation to return? Nick could still feel the places where the bird's claws had dug into his flesh.

Obar turned and frowned out the window. "I do wish that tree man didn't always want to stand around outside. He seems to be the only fellow who can control this squawking creature." He cleared his throat. "Anyway, as I was saying, we have advantages. We come equipped with a little knowledge, a certain amount of experience, and—oh, yes—we also have one of these."

He opened his fist to reveal a small green stone resting on his palm.

Nick saw the stone, and then he didn't. He felt that the tiny stone suddenly grew large so that it surrounded him—and not just him, but the whole room, and maybe the space beyond the room as well. Everything was diffused in a haze of green, a haze that did more than cover things in color. It seemed to change the nature of everything Nick looked at, as if rather than acting as camouflage, the green light revealed, showing the true objects that hid inside their everyday coverings. Jason had an aura that glowed faintly green. The light that hovered about the still-sleeping Charlie was red. Obar's aura was not so clear. At first, it appeared to be almost blinding white. But, beneath the glow, Nick thought he saw another layer, so dark that it showed no light at all.

Nick blinked. The green tinge was gone, the world looked as it had a moment ago, and the stone was just a stone.

But he had seen the others through the green light. Now, if he could only make sense out of what he saw. Something about Obar reminded him of sharp edges, like a piece of slate so pointed that it could cut, and Raven looked like nothing so much as a clear black flame.

"The dragon!" the bird squawked. "Raven has no use for the dragon!"

Nick blinked again and shook his head. Now that the light

was gone, he felt dizzy, disoriented, as if he had been suddenly snatched back from looking down a bottomless well.

"I don't believe any of us would like to meet the dragon," Obar said drily. "At least in person." He examined the green jewel in his palm. Nick braced himself for another burst of light. "This, however," the wizard continued, "is another matter entirely." He closed his fingers over the stone and raised his fist into the air. "In this hand, I hold an eye of the dragon."

Jason snickered behind him. All this dragon talk must be too much for him. Nick was surprised how ready he himself was to accept it.

"This is nothing to laugh at," Obar remarked, more to himself than Jason, as he stared at his closed fist. Nick wondered if it felt strange to hold onto a stone like that.

Obar looked up and smiled, as if a bit embarrassed by all this. "This is the root of all my power. It comes from the dragon. At least that's the story, as I heard it. I doubt this is literally one of the eyes. Yet, I don't question that the dragon can somehow sense through these things, that in a way they are an extension, shall we say, of that entity." He tightened his fist around the stone, and his smile grew, more in ferocity than joy. "And through this, the dragon gives the bearer a portion of its fire."

He blinked and lowered his arm to his side, his expression again losing its intensity. "There are supposed to be seven of these things. At least that's what I suspect. When you are dealing with the dragon"—he laughed abruptly—"well, no one ever wants to get close enough to make sure."

"All right!" Jason said with a sudden enthusiasm. "This finally makes some kind of sense. So we just have to go and get these things, huh?"

Obar shook his head. "I don't think you could, well, 'get them' so easily. Unless, of course, you are the correct person. Then, these 'things,' as you call them, will find you."

"So these things will look for us," Jason insisted, "and once we get them, they will give us power?"

"Indeed they will," the magician agreed, "if you can learn how to handle them. They can just as easily kill you."

The bird became increasingly agitated. "Raven will steal these shiny baubles!"

"There are certain things that even Raven doesn't control," Obar snapped, his own irritation now evident.

"If we can't go after these things," Jason pointed out, "why are we here?"

"I didn't say you couldn't try," was Obar's somewhat gentler reply. "We have to try, no matter what the risks. Otherwise, the dragon might kill us all."

He laid the stone carefully on the table beside him. Jason took a step toward it.

"Don't touch it!" Obar said sharply. Green fire danced at the ends of his fingers.

Jason quickly stepped away.

"Sorry." For once, Obar's smile faltered. "It must be tended to most carefully. Wouldn't want to see it fall into the wrong hands." He ran his index finger gently across the face of the jewel, almost as if he stroked the skin of a loved one.

The magician looked directly at Nick, perhaps the first time the magician had made eye contact. "If you encounter any of these things, you would be well advised to return them to me."

He stroked at his ragged mustache for a moment before he continued. "Nunn has two of these. I only hold this one. There are four more, somewhere on the seven islands. By themselves, they bequeath a certain amount of the dragon's power on anyone who possesses them. But, on some level, I feel that the dragon might be the one really in control, and that it might possess us instead." Obar seemed to shiver slightly. "Ah, but what if you were to possess all seven? Then, if my readings are correct, the situation changes. The seven eyes are the dragon's true power. Whoever holds all of them should control the dragon—absolutely!"

Obar looked quizzically at the two newcomers, as if he expected questions.

"So that is the whole story?" Nick asked.

"Well it is." The magician paused to rub at his bald head. "That is, the story is as whole as I think you will understand at present. There are some things, quite frankly, that I do not understand myself. But that—what I told you—is what you'll need to know."

Nick didn't feel right about all this. "So we have to trust you?"

"I would hope you'd do so, yes." Obar frowned suddenly. "Oh, dear. You know, it is unwise to trust any wizard—fully."

Nick felt the ground shift beneath him. The disorientation he'd felt when he first looked at the jewel returned, like someone had flip-flopped the floor and the sky, and then put them back in place again. This was far worse than he had felt when looking in the jewel. But it reminded him of another shift of time and space, when he'd first come to this place.

Raven squawked and took to the air, landing quickly on Nick's shoulder. He didn't object. It seemed proper, now, that the bird should be there.

"At last," Obar said, and now his smile was back completely.

"At last?" Jason demanded. "At last what?"

"I think we have what we've been looking for at last," Obar answered. "You see, the dragon is calling you."

○ Around the Circle #5:
The Day the Oomgosh Met His Match

Once upon a time there was a man who was more than a man. And it wasn't just that he was taller than other men, with skin the color of leaves and bark. One day he had simply stepped from the wood, from the darkest part of the forest where the shadows always seem to hold onto a little piece of the night. He had walked straight from that maze of greenery, as if the forest itself was his mother and his father, and all the trees his brothers and sisters.

The people from the village rushed to meet him.

"Greetings, stranger," their leader called, holding forth his proud oak staff, which was his badge of office. "How may we welcome you?"

The tall man looked down at them and smiled, and when he opened his mouth to speak, his voice boomed from one side of the valley to the other.

"What is this place," he called as people gathered around, "which is made out of wood which no longer grows?"

And the people told him that this was the village where all of them lived and farmed, and that they used the wood to protect them from the rain and wind and cold.

The large man thought about this for a moment and at last replied: "If the wood must be taken, then this is a good purpose."

So he stayed in the village for a time, to learn the way of his human brethren as well as he knew the way of the woods. And as he stayed the days and weeks and months, the children of the village would follow him about, like a dozen acorns rolling about a great oak. And the children called him Oomgosh, because he was a man and a half. After all, what else would you call someone so big and surprising?

So it was that the Oomgosh learned about the human ways of sowing seed and growing grain, and taking the wood and stone and mud of the earth and building things with their hands.

"You give to the earth as well," the tall man remarked when he saw the villagers sow their seeds, and again when he watched them bury their dead. "This, too, is good."

And the people found a certain peace with the Oomgosh, for he moved slowly and gently for all his size, like a great maple swaying in the wind.

So it was that all was peaceful in the village until another came: a man who was constant movement, as if he wanted everything that his eyes fell upon, and whose face was so bright that you would have to turn away or be blinded by its brilliance.

The villagers gathered again to meet this stranger and to marvel that their home could attract two such wondrous visitors.

"Greetings, stranger," the village leader called, once again holding forth his proud oak staff, which was his badge of office. "How may we welcome you?"

"What I want," the newcomer said, "I take."

He touched the leader's staff, and with a single flash of light, that staff was reduced to a pile of ash.

All in the village shrank back from this new arrival, save for their tall visitor, for the Oomgosh did not seem acquainted with fear.

The tall man of green and brown stared down at the ashes with a frown. "This, then, is not good at all." He looked at the one who was new to the village and asked, "Are you a man, or are you something else?"

The newcomer's smile was horribly bright as he replied, "I am nothing so pitiful as a human. I am Fire."

At this, the Oomgosh nodded, for he had met this creature's smaller cousins, who helped the people with their cooking and gave them warmth in the cold of night.

"Welcome, Fire," he said in his gentle voice. "There is a place for you in the village, too."

But Fire replied, "I need no welcome. I go where I will and take what I want!" And, having said this, he strode to the nearest of the village's dozen huts and stroked the wall of the hut only once. In an instant, the whole wall was consumed by flame.

The villagers cried in alarm, but the Oomgosh took another step forward. "You have done what you must," the tall green man called. "Now move on, so that the villagers may live as well."

But the bright one only shook his head and grinned even more fiercely than before. "Fire only grows. I eat a staff and I want a wall. I take a wall and I want the house. I consume the house and I desire the village. The more I eat, the more I hunger."

"There are no new beginnings here, only endings." The Oomgosh stepped between this Fire and the rest of the village. "I must say no."

The tall man clapped his hands, and branches of nearby trees reached out to grab the bright one. But where their wood touched his arms, they burst into flame, and the limbs quickly turned to blackened stumps.

"Whether my food is living or dead," Fire replied, "makes little difference to me." With that, great flames shot from his fingers to engulf the Oomgosh, so that there was again nothing left but a pile of ash.

Night fell, and those villagers not burned in the conflagration fled, as Fire took one house after another, until he had consumed half of the village.

But when the morning came, there was movement in the ashes, and a tall man of green and brown stood once again.

"I am still here," the Oomgosh said in his great slow voice, "as all things grow, and all things must die."

Fire only laughed. "How can you challenge me? Not even your great strength can stand against someone like me!"

"You take," the Oomgosh replied, "but you cannot learn. Now I have seen you destroy both the village and its people, I have found pain and suffering."

"What good will that do you?" Fire chortled, ready to burn the tall man all over again.

But the Oomgosh thought of the pain, and felt the suffering, and he began to cry.

And Fire screamed, for the Oomgosh's tears fell from the sky, and the rain came down in torrents to kill the bright one's flame.

And where the fire had been, there was nothing, but where the trees and houses had stood, new green shoots rose from the ashes.

"This, too, is good," the tall man said.

And then he returned to the wood.

◯ Fourteen

Todd was ready to kill something.

He felt like he was trapped again. These new soldiers held them prisoner as surely as those earlier troops who had been leading them to Nunn. Sure, they acted friendly enough, but Todd was sure if he tried to leave he'd end up with an arrow in his back.

There was no way to get away. And the soldiers were taking him back to his father.

Even on this broad dirt road that they traveled, he felt like the woods were closing in around them. Every step seemed darker than the one they had taken before, the wind above their heads no longer giving a glimpse of the sun, but only shifting layer on layer of dark branches and leaves.

"About this dragon," Wilbert said abruptly. "We talked about the mumbo jumbo, wizards telling us the dragon was to blame. Didn't tell you the important part, though."

Todd looked ahead and realized that Wilbert and the others, Bobby included, were already twenty steps in front of him.

No one was paying much attention to him. He glanced over at the moss-covered bank by the side of the road and what looked like another path to a brand-new clearing. Maybe, if he was quiet enough, he could get away, after all.

"Todd!" Thomas called sharply. "Don't leave the trail!"

Todd froze, waiting for the arrow. None came. He still almost stepped off the road, just to piss them off.

A rough hand pulled him back to the center of the dirt pathway. "Lord, Todd!" Stanley shouted in his ear. "Can't you see the Man Trap?"

"If he could see the Man Trap, he wouldn't be wandering off by himself, would he?" Wilbert ventured.

Wandering off? Todd was sick and tired of these guys patronizing him. "Man Trap?" he demanded. "What the hell are you talking about?"

Stanley looked around quickly, then picked up a good-sized branch that had fallen from above.

"Watch," he instructed as he tossed the branch four feet in front of Todd. The moss-covered ground collapsed. There was a pit down below, maybe six feet deep, filled with sharpened spikes.

"Man Trap," Stanley remarked.

"Hey," Wilbert added. "Wolves have got to eat, too."

"Wolves?" Bobby called out in a voice every bit as upset as Todd felt.

"Clever things," Wilbert continued by way of explanation. "Vicious, too, when you get them in a fight. Not that they like to fight."

"Wolves are all cowards, hey?" Stanley said. He turned away in disgust and paced back up the road.

"They'd rather kill their prey through tricks like this." Wilbert paused to scratch at his beard. "At least they do around here."

"So stay close!" Thomas called from up ahead. "We want to keep everyone alive as long as possible." He turned away and marched on, as if used to having the final word on a subject.

"But about these wolves," Bobby insisted. "You mean they build these traps themselves?"

The wind stirred the branches above them, not so much a breeze as a whisper. Todd thought about clever wolves. He had already accepted them, and he knew why.

"Bobby," he called. "Think about Raven."

Maggie, Stanley, and Wilbert all groaned at the mention of the bird's name.

"Not that bird!" Wilbert exclaimed.

Maggie laughed. "Oh, he'll be in the middle of it. He always is—"

"Is either of you any good with a bow?" Thomas interrupted as he scanned the forest before them. Todd wondered what Thomas could see that he couldn't. "Or a sword?" He glanced back at Todd. "We may need to use them shortly."

Todd shook his head. There was an archery team, and a fencing team, at high school, but he had never found much use for them. He guessed he never expected to find himself—well—here.

"I've tried them some," Bobby admitted. "Bow and arrow, that is. Jason's sister, Mary Lou, showed us how. She's really good. She came in second in an all-state championship."

Thomas waved for the others to follow as the road they traveled narrowed to a path. They would have to walk single file.

One Man Trap was enough for Todd. He decided he would keep up with the rest and deal with his father when they came face-to-face.

Wilbert followed Thomas. Todd and Bobby took up the next two places in line, then Maggie, with Stanley watching their rear.

"There's other ways to defend yourselves, too," Wilbert offered. He tugged distractedly at his matted beard. "I was going to tell them about the dragon's eyes."

"Damn the dragon eyes!" Stanley objected with a surprising vehemence. "You remember what they did to Douglas?"

"He was one of us," Maggie explained to the newcomers. Todd glanced back at her and saw her looking from Wilbert to Stanley and back again, as if willing the both of them to calm down. "A dragon's eye killed him."

"He was our leader, hey?" Stanley snapped. The anger seemed to rise in his voice with every word. "Eye didn't kill him. Used him up!"

"But he went out blazing," Wilbert replied with a firmness of tone Todd hadn't heard before. "Not left behind like us, to eke out whatever miserable existence we can manage."

Thomas stopped abruptly at the head of the line. "We will get back to our homes," he stated firmly. "Never forget that." His voice held the kind of finality Todd's father used when he didn't want an argument. Thomas pulled a flat-bladed sword from his belt and turned away from the others. He gripped it with both hands, hacking at a mass of vines that blocked their way. His next words were shouted over his own effort and the screams of the vines: "We will get back to our world!"

"And pigs can fly!" Wilbert retorted. He paused and looked at the top of the trees with a grin. "Well, actually, around here, maybe pigs do fly. Haven't seen it yet, but you can't take anything for granted."

"Exactly," Thomas agreed as his arm swung down toward the greenery. The vines separated with the same pained cries Todd had heard before. "You can't assume anything. Not even about the dragon's eyes." His arm rose again, the sword rising in a great arc above his head. "We'll be more careful than Douglas, but we'll use them if we must." The sword fell again. "We'll use anything to get back to where we belong."

Thomas stopped abruptly, his sword suspended in the air. "Hold it!" he whispered.

Todd looked around the trail, waiting for wolves or dragons or

God knew what. In the distance, he heard a high, bloodcurdling wailing. It lasted for about a minute, then faded away.

"Sounds like the Anno," Wilbert said after another minute had passed.

Stanley shook his head. "That's not the Anno. Least not the way I've ever heard them."

"Maybe," Maggie added, "this place has some other new visitors."

The noise had gone as quickly as it had come. Whatever it was, Todd wasn't looking forward to meeting it. The forest was quieter than before, as if even the small animals and insects were waiting for what might come next.

"Prepare for the worst," Thomas ordered. He pointed to Todd and Bobby. "Give them a couple of knives. Make young Bob a bow when we get the chance."

Stanley lifted the dark animal-skin pack from his shoulder and pulled loose the rope that held it together. The pack unrolled on the ground before him. There, in a couple dozen pockets, were knives, short swords, hatchets, a whole arsenal. For some reason, Todd found himself thinking that the pack had to weigh a ton. Maybe skinny Stanley was stronger than he looked.

He pulled out two more or less identical knives and handed one each to Todd and Bobby. Bobby curled his hand around the leather-clad handle. The knife felt remarkably light for something with that large a blade. It looked something like a Bowie knife. That was one thing that Todd knew something about; he had seen *The Alamo* three times.

"Use them to defend yourselves," Thomas said to the boys, "only if you have to." He paused and listened for another moment to the woods around him. Satisfied, he unsheathed his sword and attacked a new mass of vines.

"Often—the best thing—to do," Thomas continued as he cut, his words matching his rhythm, "is to run—so that you—can fight again."

He waved for the others to follow. "Let's get through here before the vines close up!"

The others moved swiftly and silently to follow, only Todd and Bobby making noise walking over the fallen leaves and branches. Todd was glad for the quiet. It gave him a moment to think about what had happened to his anger.

One thing this place had showed him: He was becoming very aware of the possibility of death. His death. Anybody's death. Death constantly surrounded them, waiting.

Todd felt the weight of the knife in his hand. Maybe he could give as well as receive. Maybe there was some way he could learn to survive, to go beyond orders given by parents or soldiers or volunteers. The leather hilt felt warm in his hand. Maybe, Todd thought, he could kill something, after all.

For the first time in a while, it was easy to smile.

◯ Fifteen

Mary Lou opened her eyes. Someone had shaken her shoulder. She realized she was still in the clearing where she had met the People, except that now the small folk were gathered on the far side of the open space, beneath the trees. With their pale, bald heads, they reminded her of nothing so much as a field of mushrooms. They were marching to the edge of the clearing, toward a mass of vines between two of the larger trees. Dozens of them turned, one after another, and waved for her to follow. For some reason, Mary Lou thought of *The Wizard of Oz*.

The little people must have shaken her awake. She shivered, and felt embarrassed because she had. There was something about their small, wrinkled bodies that still made her want to keep away.

In her dream, she had thought she had been woken by the prince. She wished it could have been his hand on her shoulder—if only her insubstantial prince could actually touch things. She looked around as she stood, hoping to catch a glimpse of him, but he seemed to have disappeared.

Where could he be? Mary Lou was surprised how much she missed him. He was the only one she could talk to in this place.

Maybe, she thought, someday, somehow, they could do more than talk.

"Mary Lou!"

Startled, she turned and looked at the People. One of their high, thin voices had called her by name.

The prince must have told them. Just as he spoke *for* the People, he had to speak *to* the People as well. He must have introduced her to this tiny tribe. She found herself smiling. In a way, he was still helping her, even though he wasn't here.

"Mary Lou!" The way they said it, quickly, breathlessly, her name sounded like a single word. "Mary Lou!" *Merrilu.*

The People called her name over and over, much as they had called Nunn's name, but there was a difference, too. Their cries of

"Nunn! Nunn!" had been frantic and angry. The way they shouted her name was gentler, almost playful. She smiled all over again.

The first of the small folk had reached the vines, climbing them with surprising speed. Those still on the ground continued to wave for her to follow. As she walked toward them, a pair of them pulled a vine free from the rest. They brought it toward her, calling her name even more excitedly than before.

"Mary Lou! Mary Lou!" (*Merrilumerrilu!*)

They wanted her to climb up with them, like scaling a rope in gym class.

But the thought of leaving the ground made her hesitate, as if, in taking this step, she'd be at the mercy of these small creatures.

What should she do? She wished the prince was here to help her make a decision.

Maybe, if she stayed with these creatures, she could keep from being recaptured by Nunn. No matter what they looked like, the People seemed to have her best interests at heart.

Best interests? She was starting to sound like one of her mother's lectures.

She reached out for the vine they offered her, grabbing it firmly with both of her hands. Before she could even begin to pull herself up, she found her feet off the ground as the vine was yanked from somewhere up above. She almost let go in her surprise but found herself gripping the vine even more firmly as the ground grew farther and farther from her feet. She was hoisted quickly aloft, maybe a hundred feet in the air in a matter of seconds. She looked away from the ground, suddenly so far below, afraid she might fall if she panicked, and saw herself lift past the lowest level of leaves.

There was a mass of branches directly above her. On one of the broadest of the limbs was a line of the People, all pulling on her vine, which they had looped over another, slightly higher branch to give them leverage.

Small hands grabbed at her legs and arms, pulling her back onto another massive branch, as wide across as one of the paths in the forest below.

"Mary Lou!" Those same small hands plucked at her sleeve. "Mary Lou!"

She turned and saw a dozen or more of the three-foot-high People scrambling from branch to branch in front of her. They waved again for her to follow. The branches grew so close together here that it was easy to move from tree to tree, like climbing a slightly uneven set of steps. She strode carefully up to the next tree, using another, higher branch to grab for support, as the People raced forward like mountain goats along a cliff.

They climbed that way for a while, Mary Lou slowly gaining confidence as she stepped from branch to bole to branch. In places where there was a gap between the trees, the People had used the vines to tie together bundles of branches into rough bridges.

She stepped carefully on the first of these. She stopped as it swayed with her weight.

"Merrilu!"

Three of the People stood at the far side of the bridge and beckoned her on. Their dark eyes seemed very concerned as they stared out from their wrinkled faces. Maybe, she thought, she might trust them, after all.

She placed her other foot on the bridge. Her penny loafer slid a bit as the bridge swayed, but the ropes that held the logs to the tree trunks showed no sign of breaking. The People held their hands above their heads and screamed in delight.

And so she rose from bridge to bridge, branch to branch, tree to tree, with the excited calls and laughter of the whole tribe around her, until she noticed that the world was brighter than before. Soon, as she climbed, she caught a glimpse here and there of the sky, and once a corner of the bright red sun above. She and her escort were nearing the top of the trees.

She followed the branch path around another large trunk and stopped abruptly. There, before her, was a whole expanse of the tied logs, entire platforms, some with other structures built atop them: tiny huts, she guessed. She saw a central area where stones had been piled upon the deck of logs, with smoke curling up from the middle of the pile. It must be an oven. She was surprised that the People had control of fire.

But what did she know about the People, except what she had heard from Nunn's Captain and the prince? Here was a whole village, hundreds of feet above the forest floor.

"Merrilu!" the People called. She stepped onto the edge of the first platform. She had expected it to sway like the branch bridges, but it felt very firm beneath her feet, wedged and tied between the trees. The People continued to wave her toward the center of their village. She stepped forward and realized that she was walking fully in sunlight. The branches ended here, and she could see the almost blue sky stretch before her. She looked out beyond the far edge of the platform and saw the whole of the forest spread below.

The trees seemed different from up above. In places they appeared like leaf-strewn hills; in others, where the branches grew sparse, they looked like intersecting clouds of green. It seemed to Mary Lou that this place was almost a whole magic kingdom above the earth.

The People called and waved for her to join them at the edge of the platform. There was a row of log stools with a triangle of branches at their back. All seven stools faced toward the village, six of them proportioned for the three-foot height of the People. The seventh and central chair was much larger, so big that Mary Lou might almost have fit into it herself.

As she approached, seven of the People climbed onto the stools. The one in the center gained a boost from a couple of his fellows. He wore a necklace of leaves and stones around his neck. Besides the small breechcloths that they all wore, this was the only article of adornment Mary Lou had seen on any of these creatures. She must be getting an audience with their chieftain.

"Merrilu," the Chieftain said.

"Merrilu!" all the rest of the People echoed. "Merrilu!"

The Chieftain made a high, keening sound, and all the People joined in as well. It was so shrill it hurt Mary Lou's ears. She tried to smile, and not let them know that she would much rather run away.

The Chieftain and the rest of the People stopped their shrill cry, all at the same instant. Mary Lou took a deep breath, worried about what might happen next. There was no way out of here if something went wrong.

The three to the left of the Chieftain—maybe they were village elders—passed an object from hand to hand to their leader. The Chieftain looked up at Mary Lou and, showing all his teeth, offered it to her.

Mary Lou looked at the gift. It was a bow; a bit smaller than she was used to, but probably gigantic for creatures of this size. The largest of these creatures was maybe a foot and a half shorter than she, but their arms were much longer in proportion to their bodies. She could easily use this bow.

She lowered her head slightly, hoping that this was the right sort of thing to do in front of a chief, and took the curved wood in her hands. The string was surprisingly taut. She'd be able to get some distance with this thing.

There was another flurry of movement to the right of the Chieftain as a second gift was passed along the row of elders. Their leader held this out to Mary Lou in turn. It was a quiver, made from tree bark, that held seven arrows. Mary Lou wondered what mystical symbolism that number had for the tribe.

"Merrilu!" the Chieftain said again.

She expected the rest of the tribe to repeat her name the way they had before. Instead, the People were eerily quiet, so that all Mary Lou heard was the noise of the leaves, a heavy rustling now, the branches whipping about as if they were about to have a storm.

The silence was broken by a scream: the sound of all the People together, more like a single voice than the hundreds gathered around.

The Chieftain spun around in his chair to peer over the edge of the platform. They all seemed far more agitated than they had a moment before. Mary Lou wasn't at all sure that this was a part of the ritual.

"Nunn!" the Chieftain shouted.

"Nunn!" his tribe replied. "Nunn! Nunn! Nunn!"

What were they saying? Had the wizard found her? Mary Lou took a step away from the edge of the platform. But there was no sign of Nunn. Instead, three new creatures, much the same size as the People but covered with a fine, red fur, vaulted onto the platform from somewhere below.

The People were in an uproar, no longer screaming anything in unison, but screaming nonetheless. There was something familiar about these newcomers: their large shoulders and chests and the way they shuffled more than walked, more like apes than men. Mary Lou realized she had seen one of these creatures before, changed somehow by Nunn's magic: the creature of light.

Another dozen or so of the creatures had scrambled onto the platform during the confusion. And all of them carried either knives or spears.

"Death to Anno!" one of them cried in a voice that was shrill, but far deeper than that of the People. The other red-furred creatures took up this cry in turn. "Death to Anno!"

The People fell back before them as the red-furred ones jabbed at them with their spears. A couple of the newcomers threw their spears in their excitement. One of the weapons clattered on the platform between two of the People as one of the village elders swatted the second away with a defiant hand.

The elder stiffened suddenly, grabbing at the hand that touched the spear. Mary Lou couldn't see any blood. At most, the elder had gotten a scratch. He fell to the platform, shrieking in a way that made all the other cries of the People seem like nothing more than conversation. The People fled as he rolled back and forth.

Mary Lou realized, as the People retreated from the attack, that the red-furred creatures were turning toward her.

The elder stopped screaming and rolling, and lay very still. He looked quite dead. The red-furred creatures raised their spears above their shoulders as they rushed toward her.

Mary Lou slipped on the logs as she tried to back away. She almost fell. She realized she still held the bow and quiver in her hands. Did she have any time to defend herself?

"Mary Lou!" the first of the creatures cried quite distinctly. "No one leaves Nunn without permission!" The creature's tone was in an odd singsong, like this was a message from the wizard himself, something that this creature was only obediently parroting.

Mary Lou felt she should be petrified. But Nunn's message only made her angry.

The wizard would not control her. She grabbed an arrow from her quiver.

"You are Nunn's," the first of the creatures shrieked. "Capture first!" It barreled toward her, leaping across the logs with short, muscular strides, the arm with the spear raised to throw.

"Nunn will do what he wants!" the creature continued in the same fierce monotone. "She is nothing without Nunn!"

As quickly as she could, Mary Lou fitted an arrow to the bow, aimed, and released the string. Maybe too quickly. The arrow veered left, striking the creature in the shoulder.

"Capture?" the creature cried, pain giving his voice emotion at last. It stopped to break off the shaft of the arrow as it stared at Mary Lou. "No capture! Die! Die! Die!"

Half a dozen more of the creatures joined their wounded leader in a rush toward Mary Lou.

⊙ Sixteen

Charlie stirred as Nick gently patted his head.

He looked down at the mutt. His mutt. Plug-ugly, that's what some of the other kids in school called him. And while he might not have the greatest face—the pushed-in nose, the floppy ears— he did have great soft fur and deep brown eyes that somehow helped Nick through his worst days at home.

In some ways, he was closer to this dog than he was to any person. Whenever Nick was really upset, he and the dog would take off together.

There was a part of the woods behind his house where he only went when he was angry, a part where a fire had roared on through, leaving great hollow pieces of wood in its wake. Whole trees still stood, except their wood had turned to charcoal. A branch as tall as he was would weigh a dozen pounds; a tree trunk could be tossed around like he was Hercules. Nick would go there when things were really bad: when his parents would have those screaming fights that seemed to go on for days.

His parents were staying together for him. That's what they always said.

That's why he had to leave. If he wasn't around, they wouldn't be fighting, would they? His mother said that didn't make sense, but it made more sense to Nick than half the things his parents said to each other.

Out in the woods, behind his house, was the only time he ever felt free. He could run and yell and smash things, and Charlie would run and bark and jump alongside. Nick would fall down laughing, and the dog would collapse down next to him and lick his face. In his simple, trusting way, Charlie knew Nick better than anybody. Certainly better than anybody in Nick's family.

Nick felt something wet. Charlie was licking his hand.

"Ah, our patient is recovering nicely," the magician said bright-ly. "Obar's cures always work!"

"Except when they don't," Raven replied drily.

"Well, most of the time, certainly," the magician replied as he busied himself brushing nonexistent dust from his sleeve. "After all, what in this world, or any world, is truly certain?"

"The dragon," Raven answered.

"Well, possibly the dragon," Obar allowed. "But, even if that's the case, what can we do about it? Except what we are doing?" The magician answered his own questions as soon as they were out of his mouth. "Well, knowledge is the only thing that will beat the dragon. It does like to keep us ignorant. Still, we can use a bit of my skill to discover what else goes on."

He spread his hands before him and waved his fingers at the floor. Whirls of dust danced toward his palms.

"If you watch carefully," Obar explained, "you may see some pictures in the dust." His lips curled into the slightest of smiles as he glanced at his audience. "What is dust, after all, but tiny little particles from this whole world round? The dust keeps a bit of every place it's been. With the proper care, it can even help show us these things." He clapped his hands as the dust swirled before him. "This is also one reason it never pays to keep this place too clean."

Dust leapt upward, forming a flowing curtain that rose to Obar's waist.

"Oh, wow," Jason murmured. A second later, he inhaled sharply, as if he'd been startled.

Nick frowned. As good as the magician's trick had been, Jason still seemed far too appreciative. Did Jason see something beyond the swirling dirt? Nick moved over next to the younger boy to get a better look.

"Nunn is speeding his attack," Obar said with a frown. He nodded brusquely. "He has a number of allies, pressed into service through promises—or fear. Mostly fear, I would imagine. However, his first effort might not be entirely successful."

"Is that Mary Lou?" Jason asked.

"Well, yes," Obar said with a touch of surprise. "That's very good, you know. The untrained eye. My, my. We'll have to keep you as far away from Nunn as possible."

Where was Mary Lou? Nick squinted, but still could see nothing more than shifting dust.

"And those red creatures?" Jason added.

Red? The only color Nick saw was a swirling yellowish grey.

"Nunn's minions," Obar explained. "They come from his home island. He must have brought them over for this first assault."

He peered over at Nick. "You seem less than pleased. You see nothing? I assure you, that is far more ordinary."

That, Nick thought, was exactly how he felt. Ordinary. Being upstaged by Jason Dafoe was too much.

A great roar came from outside the window: the sound of some creature in pain.

"Oomgosh!" Raven called. He flew from Nick's shoulder to the stone windowsill. Nick followed him to see what had happened.

"There is a disturbance!" the Oomgosh called back in a voice that seemed to quaver more than before.

Raven glanced back at Nick. "The trees tell him when they are hurt. Sometimes he is even hurt himself."

"I am quite all right, my Raven!" the Oomgosh's booming voice replied. "More startled than damaged. The voice of the trees is very strong."

"The Oomgosh informs us that the battle is quite nearby," Obar explained.

"What isn't nearby?" Raven snapped.

"It's one of the advantages of living on an island," Obar admitted. "It cuts down substantially on travel time."

"But Mary Lou—" Jason objected.

Obar frowned. The dancing dust was gone. "Yes, she is involved. And she is holding her own." He looked up, straight at Nick. The intensity of his gaze was startling. Nick realized this was one of the few times the wizard had made direct eye contact.

He smiled again and the severity was gone. "But if Nunn is beginning the attack in earnest," he asked wistfully, "what can we do but defend ourselves?"

The wizard clapped his hands again. This time the far wall vanished, the stone dissolving to show a great area beyond, although most of it was lost in shadow. Nick had the feeling, though, that this new space went on forever.

Obar peered critically at Nick and Jason. "Can't use a bow?"

Nick began to feel inadequate all over again.

"Never mind," Obar continued before either of them could reply. "You'll be fine."

He turned away from the two to regard the great shadowed hole where the wall had stood. A single point of light appeared through the shadows, small at first, but growing rapidly larger.

"Eager, are we?" Obar called.

Nick didn't feel the wizard was talking to them. He realized that the light wasn't simply growing larger, it was coming toward them, a long, narrow shape rushing toward the room.

There was a ripping sound as the light flew into the daylight and Obar's hand, like the air was solid between this room and the space beyond.

The light vanished as the object settled against the magician's palm, gone as quickly as the flick of a switch. Nick realized the flying thing was a sword with a long, flat blade, slightly curved. Obar looked soberly at the weapon as he began to speak again.

"You remember our bargain," he said quietly. "Even though you will have a new master, that bargain remains, and you will share it with him as well."

Nick's first reaction had been right: Obar was talking to the sword, and despite the darkened room and the way the weapon had flown into the wizard's grasp, it was this conversation that made Nick really nervous.

The wizard held the sword out to Nick.

"Everything is understood," the wizard said gently. "This is for you."

What? Maybe the sword understood what was happening, but Nick was totally in the dark. Nick wasn't sure he could trust either wizard or weapon, and the fact that Obar was smiling made this whole exchange even worse.

"But I can't—" Nick began. Even as he protested, his fingers gripped the hilt. It felt surprisingly warm in his hand.

"Nonsense," Obar interrupted. Nick was less than pleased to see that the wizard was pointing a warning finger at the sword. "Don't even think it."

"What is this—sword?" Nick asked, feeling that the word didn't begin to describe the thing in his hand.

"Simply one of those special objects I keep in storage," Obar answered. "A good weapon for someone who lacks experience. It has a bit of a mind of its own. Not that it's alive—really. Think of it more as a simple machine. I just had to give it a bit of instruction. But it knows its job. And it wants to be used."

The sword suddenly felt heavier in Nick's hands. He looked down to see that the weapon was now settled in an elaborate sheath made from the skin of some golden animal, sewn in a zigzag pattern with inlaid studs of silver. And the sheath was tied to a belt, no doubt just the right size for Nick's waist.

"It's best to keep your sword covered when not in use," Obar continued. "Otherwise, there might be some—complications."

Nick had had quite enough of these half-explanations. "Wait a moment. You say I can use this sword. But you make it sound dangerous."

"Do I?" Obar replied, as if startled that anyone could think such a thing. "Well, then—no, of course the sword won't hurt you." He paused again before adding, "Unless of course you want it to."

Obar frowned and looked perplexed, almost as if he was trying to explain things to himself at the same time as Nick. The magician turned away from the shadow space to frown at Jason. The stone wall re-formed, stone by solid stone, to hide the shadows again.

"Your friend, I'm afraid, is destined for greater things than enchanted swords." Obar looked over at a cluttered table in the corner and picked up a short dagger he found in the middle of the pile. "Here," he said as he offered the blade to Jason, "take a knife to defend yourself. For emergencies, you know."

"Raven!" Oomgosh called from below.

"My tree friend grows restless," Raven called. "The battle must be growing fierce." He cawed loudly and rose from Nick's shoulder with a great flapping of wings. "Join us when you can!" he called over his shoulder as he flew from the window.

"Join them?" Jason called. "Shouldn't we go?"

"You'll catch up with them in a minute," Obar replied. "This is only the beginning of the battles." He turned his palms upward and stared at them, as if the answer might be there. "Nunn is very active. This might very well be the time. The dragon is close. He wants to be ready. As do we. But even Nunn doesn't have unlimited strength." He looked back at the boys, his forehead creased. "Please excuse some of my answers. In magic, it often pays to be indirect."

He clapped his hands and the castle disappeared. Nick and Jason found themselves on the edge of the forest.

"Get away from him, you apes!" the black bird called behind them. "Or you'll know why so many fear Raven!"

Both boys turned to see Raven perched on the Oomgosh's shoulder. Three short, red-furred things, looking like a cross between ape and human, advanced slowly toward the tree man. Each of the red-furred creatures held a spear in both of its hands, ready to jab at the Oomgosh.

"They need us!" Jason called as he rushed forward.

"Wait a minute!" Nick called as he hurried after his neighbor. These ape-things had spears. Jason only held a knife. Maybe, Nick thought, he could scare the things away with his sword.

He grabbed the sword hilt. The weapon made a noise as it pulled free of its sheath, half the clang of metal on metal, half a whistling moan.

The apes stopped and stared at Nick. The sword felt remarkably light in Nick's hand. A well-balanced blade. That's the sort of thing it would say in those swashbuckler books Nick used to read. He swung the sword in a great arc above his head.

The apes shrieked and threw their spears. The sword jerked in Nick's grasp, the weapon guiding his hand, as the flat of the blade quickly deflected each of the projectiles. The sword pulled violently, as if it wanted to fly from Nick's grip to embed itself in one of the red-furred enemy.

The apes screamed again, this time more in fear than rage. They ran. The sword jerked again, as if eager to follow. Nick held it firmly as he watched the creatures flee.

The sword wrenched to the side, leading Nick's arm in another great arc.

"Ow!" Jason called.

The sword suddenly felt limp in Nick's hand. He looked over and saw that the swing of the sword had sliced through Jason's shirtsleeve.

"What have I done?" Nick asked. "Jason?"

The younger boy pulled apart the fabric to look at his arm. "It's only a scratch," he said with a stoicism that wasn't matched by the fright on his face.

"You haven't done anything," the Oomgosh said more softly than usual. "It's the wizard's sword."

"The sword?" Nick looked down at the weapon in his hand. It still moved easily, but it no longer tugged at his grip.

"No doubt it needed blood," Raven explained.

"Blood?" Nick felt that his brain was much too slow to accept what had happened here.

"Maybe because it hasn't been used in a long time," the Oomgosh added.

"Perhaps it needs blood every time it is drawn," Raven suggested.

Nick almost dropped the sword. Instead, he pushed the blade back into its sheath with exaggerated caution.

"No doubt that sword will give you great skill," the Oomgosh said. "But all skill has its price."

What had the wizard given him? Nick looked over at his friend. "Jason, do you want to sit down? Maybe we should look at that."

The younger boy shook his head stubbornly. "It really is only a scratch. It only bled a little." He looked away from Nick, toward Raven and the Oomgosh. "Mary Lou needs us."

The great black bird cawed. "Raven will show you the way!"

Nick saw the others turn to hurry after the bird. They had to save Mary Lou. But how? Nick looked ahead to where Jason held his wounded arm. If the sword would do something like that, how could he risk using it again?

◯ Seventeen

One of the attackers at the edge of the front line screamed as an arrow hit him in the back. Other arrows fell into the red-furred crowd behind him. Some of the People had gotten to their weapons as well.

Mary Lou fitted a second arrow to her bow. She wished she had had a chance to test her gift before she had to use it. More of the invaders clustered behind their wounded leader as he renewed his charge for Mary Lou.

"Die!" he cried again.

Five of the red-furred things pulled back their spears in unison as they rushed toward her.

Blue light flashed to her right.

"Don't you think you're being a little hasty?" the prince asked by her side.

The enemy leader and his spear carriers shrieked even more fiercely as they shifted their charge to the newcomer. Five spears launched toward the prince. Mary Lou glanced to her side to see the weapons pass through the apparition and clatter harmlessly on the bundled logs of the platform.

The leader of the reds backed away from the spirit in front of them. His troops massed behind him, but their forward momentum had been startled out of them.

"Poison sticks," the prince said calmly. "That is what the People call them."

"The spears?" Mary Lou asked.

The prince nodded. "Their tips are dipped in a poison that is instantly fatal to the People."

"And to someone like me?" She kept her bow drawn, ready for the next attack, but she couldn't resist at least glancing at the prince.

"Who knows?" He shrugged his broad shoulders. "I don't imagine it would be pleasant." He smiled at her and pointed back at the enemy. "Maybe it's time you shot that arrow."

128

The red-furred things had begun to move forward again, more slowly than before, and more as a solid group, as if their numbers might overcome their fear of the apparition.

Their leader had another spear in his hand. He held it before him now with both hands, pointed straight toward Mary Lou's midsection.

Mary Lou pulled back the bowstring as the leader charged. She loosed the arrow.

This one went straight for the creature's head, embedding itself deeply in the thing's eye.

The creature wailed and dropped its spear, clawing at the shaft that stuck out from its head. Blood poured down the creature's face: brown against the red of its fur. It staggered toward Mary Lou, its mouth open wide, baring its fangs. No words came from the creature now, only guttural noises from somewhere deep in its lungs, a cry that turned into a bubbling moan. Mary Lou froze, her hand on a third arrow in the quiver.

"Die," the thing managed at last, its voice barely a whisper. It fell forward onto the logs, as still as the village elder.

The next moment seemed to stretch on for a very long time. Mary Lou had never killed anyone, or anything, before. All her arrows had been shot at straw targets, not at things that struggled and screamed.

The moment ended. The creatures, disoriented by the death of their leader, rushed forward again in a ragged line to engulf everything on the platform.

But now the People were ready. They rushed at the invaders from either side, forcing them to press even more tightly together. And where the People pressed, their arrows traveled before them, a black rain that fell into the enemy. The red-furred things hurled their spears in turn, but there were too few too late to stop the onslaught of the People protecting their home.

The People held knives and hatchets as they jumped into battle. They hacked at their enemy with a singleness of purpose, slicing throats, cutting deep into arms and thighs and bellies, pressing the red-furred things back so that they had no way to free themselves or even reach for weapons of their own.

It was no longer a battle. To Mary Lou, it looked more like a slaughter. And the People were the executioners, slashing the life out of each and every red-furred thing; the last survivors of the attacking party slipping on their fellows' blood as it ran along the furrows of the logs and fell to the forest below with the patter of a summer shower.

Mary Lou was startled by the People's brutality. She had thought of these little men (and women, maybe; she had no way to tell if there were two sexes) as "cute" simply because they were small. But she watched now as the People methodically chopped through the necks of their fallen foes. Once each head was free of its body, it was passed to the crowd, and tossed from hand to hand like a beach ball as the People whooped with delight.

She remembered now how much the Captain had disliked these creatures; enough to use that gun to shoot one and bring on the wrath of the dragon.

She turned to the prince, who seemed not to dislike this at all. Instead, he was watching the slaughter with a great deal of amusement.

"Do the People use the same sort of things on their enemies?" she asked, trying not to sound too upset. "You know, like poison sticks?"

The prince shook his head with the same good humor. "They would never use poison. It would be a waste of perfectly good meat."

She realized they were carrying the headless corpses over to the fire stones. No doubt that was where they also kept the cook pots.

Mary Lou leaned back against one of the great tree boles that supported the platform. She felt quite suddenly and completely exhausted.

She had to calm down. Why was all this so terrible? She had seen films in science class where different species of predators attacked each other: a shark eating a barracuda, lions ripping the meat from a wild dog.

She looked at the bow still in her hand. All the killing had begun after she had shot the leader, as though that arrow in the eye was a signal to wash the village in blood.

"Why are you distraught?" the prince asked her. She looked over to him and saw that he was no longer smiling. "Those red-furred things would cheerfully have devoured you given the chance."

Mary Lou shook her head. For all of the prince's concern, she couldn't find her voice. She didn't think she could ever eat anything that talked, no matter what it said.

"It was strange that those things should be here," the prince continued conversationally. "At least in such force. Their stronghold is on another of the islands." He paused for a moment, watching the People sing as they began to skin the carcasses. "The People are concerned. It's not a good sign."

Mary Lou remembered the leader's parroting voice. "These others—work for Nunn?"

"Almost everything does," the prince affirmed. "We would expect him to have a plan. It startles me that we defeated this plan so easily."

Thick smoke rose from the stone ovens of the People's cookfires. Mary Lou thought she could smell cooking meat. The People jumped up and down, waving their enemy's heads above their own.

"Merrilu!" they called. "Merrilu! Merrilu!"

The prince waved cheerfully back at them. "You're the reason for their victory. They honor you. They never want to let you go."

Mary Lou couldn't smile back. She was still thinking about what the prince had said.

"So we caught Nunn by surprise?" she asked.

"Perhaps," the prince replied. "It takes a great deal to surprise a wizard, and he is the most powerful wizard alive."

Mary Lou found herself even more upset than before. How could she have escaped someone like Nunn if he was all-powerful?

Maybe she hadn't escaped at all. Could the wizard have let her go for some other reason? Perhaps this was some sort of test. Nunn talked about those who were chosen. How did he know who was chosen and who wasn't?

On impulse, she asked the prince, "Do you know anything else about Nunn?"

He hesitated before he spoke. "I feel—we've met." His handsome frown deepened. "I don't really have any memories. Although there is something up here." He touched his broad, uncreased forehead with a long-fingered hand. "It's hard to explain. It feels more like the echo of memories." He sighed, and waved again at the revelers around the cooking fires. "All my real information comes from the People. Somehow I imagine that I'm happier that way than I was before."

Nunn had a plan, Mary Lou thought. Maybe they had foiled it, or maybe they had helped it along.

Maybe, through her escape, Mary Lou was condemning not only herself but the prince and the People as well.

◯ Eighteen

"Let me out!"

The King of the Wolves was happy. It was the most pleasant of days, not too cold, not too warm, the afternoon sun shaded by the greenery above. And one of their traps was full, angry shouts bursting up from the pit. Human shouts. They would have fresh man for dinner tonight.

"I'll get you for this!"

The man was very angry. This man was also very lucky. He had survived the stakes: long, sharpened pieces of wood that the wolves had planted at the bottom of the pit. Some humans did survive, every once in a while, the younger ones mostly—they were more agile, and tender to the taste. It amused the King to hear their cries, always angry at first, but more and more pleading as the time passed, as the only answer those cries received was the howls of the wolves.

"I can hear you out there!"

Still so angry. This new man was stronger than most. They would leave him in the pit for a while, until he lost a bit of his spirit. Fresh man. It was their screams for mercy that gave the meat its flavor. The King of the Wolves drooled in anticipation.

"You haven't heard the end of this!"

He did go on and on. The man in the pit was beginning to grow a bit tiresome. The King of the Wolves would enjoy ripping this one apart.

"Who's there?" another human voice called from somewhere upwind.

The seven other wolves in the pack looked to their leader. He willed them to silence with his gaze. Perhaps they could eat two fresh men rather than one.

"Let me out of here!" the one in the pit called even more loudly than before. "You have no right to keep me!"

132

"Where are you?" The second voice was getting closer. "Maybe we can get you out."

The King heard movement, rough man feet crunching dead leaves. There were at least two. The King of the Wolves smiled. The pack could easily handle two.

"Wait a moment, Thomas," a new voice said softly.

"Wilbert?" the first voice asked.

"Wolves," the second voice replied.

The pack grew nervous around the King. They had lost surprise. These new humans knew how to find a scent, or how to see where someone had passed before them. Things were becoming far too equal.

The King pricked his ears forward. There were more than two coming, but the others knew how to walk to keep from making noise. That, too, was rare in humans. There might be half a dozen of them approaching, almost as many men as wolves. The pack would not like those odds.

"I know my rights!" the man in the pit screamed. His angry cries would last forever. He would lead the others straight to his prison.

The King of the Wolves would not have it. The fresh meat was theirs by right of capture. They would not give it up no matter how many humans confronted them. The King growled deep in his throat. Three members of the pack replied in kind.

"Wolves," the second voice said again as he stepped into view. He carried a bow with an arrow notched and ready to fly. Others crowded behind him: two more full-grown males, a female, and two males that were younger. The two that had not reached maturity looked uncertain, afraid. The King wished he could get them away from their grizzled elders, catch their tender flesh in one of his traps. He ran his great red tongue along his fangs.

"You'll regret this!"

The voice from the pit drew the other humans closer. All four of the elders now held bows in their hands.

The youngsters would have to wait. The wolf pack already had fresh meat. The King of the Wolves wouldn't let the one in the pit get away.

The King moved between the newcomers and the traps. The pack followed. They were brave now. They growled and barked defiance at the gang of men. Would they stay that brave when the arrows began to fly?

The King lifted himself onto his hind legs, to walk in that way that men walked. It hurt his throat to talk like men, but he could do it if he had to.

"Staaay awaaay," he announced, his voice closer to growl than bark.

"Cripes!" one of the youngsters yelled. The King's voice seemed to have startled the two of them. The others didn't look impressed at all.

"Not if you've got somebody in there," replied a gaunt man with dark hair. He was so thin, the King mused, he'd barely be worth killing. He'd have hardly any meat. What there was was bound to be stringy.

"I know it!" the voice cried triumphantly from the pit. "I know you want to ruin my lawn!"

The bearded man with the bow screwed up the top half of his face into a mass of wrinkles.

"Fella doesn't make any sense."

"Yes, he does," the short, pudgy youngster said excitedly. "It sounds like Old Man Sayre."

"Screw it!" the other youngster—taller, with more muscle than fat—said with a shake of his head. "It can't be! He's dead!"

"Dead?" the gaunt man asked sharply. "You're sure of that?"

"Who can be sure about anything?" the muscular youth exploded.

"We saw him die!" the pudgy one insisted. "The Captain stuck him with a sword. And then he shot him!"

"Sounds pretty dead to me, hey?" said a bald man standing behind the others.

"Wolves can make traps, and dead people can walk around," the bearded man explained. "Just some of the extra benefits of a place like this."

"What's his name?" the gaunt man demanded. "Sayre?"

"Don't try to be nice to me!" the pit man's voice demanded. "I know you were on my lawn!"

"How could he still be yelling about his lawn?" the taller youth said, his voice cracking midquestion.

"Not doing it of his own accord," the gaunt man answered. "Nunn's helping."

The King of the Wolves stared up at the gathering of men. Dead? They said the wolves' catch was dead? Was this some sort of man trick?

"I know who you are!" the man in the pit raved. "I'll kill every one of you!"

The King of the Wolves backed up to the pit as the other

members of the pack gathered before him, teeth bared against the intruders. The King pushed the curtain of branches out of the way with his snout to stare down at his captive.

"What?" the thing in the pit screamed up at him. "How dare you?"

The King of the Wolves stared down into the pit, openmouthed. The thing in the pit had once been a man, but it was man no longer. Its skin was a pasty white, as if no blood ran through the body to give it color or warmth. Its head sat upon its shoulders at an odd angle, like its neck was broken. It had a hole in its belly, too, where a bit of something from inside hung out, torn at the end as if it had been gnawed at by some animal.

And it hadn't avoided the stakes. One of the long, jagged poles had impaled the creature through the back and stuck out of the thing's chest. There was no sign of blood here, either. The impaling seemed only to have made the thing angrier. The King almost choked on the smell: rancid, like three-day-old meat.

"How dare you!" The thing's mouth worked furiously. "Everyone knows I don't allow dogs on my lawn!"

The King glimpsed movement within the creature's mouth, too. Either there was something wrong with the thing's tongue or the worms were already at work.

"Let's back out of here," the gaunt man said.

The one with a beard waved his bow at the wolves. "This Sayre is all yours. May he rot in good health."

The real men disappeared behind the trees as quickly as they had come.

The King of the Wolves howled. There was no fresh meat here. This thing was an abomination. He would have to destroy the trap; none of the pack would eat from someplace where a dead thing— or maybe not-dead thing—had waited.

"I've had enough of this!" the thing in the pit called.

The King looked down to see that somehow the thing the others called Sayre was pulling himself up off the stake.

"I'll show you what happens when you cross me!" The Sayre-thing's bony fingers reached for the top of the pit.

The King called to the others as he backed away. It was time for the pack to leave this part of the forest altogether.

Nunn fled from the mind of the leader of his furry army. The creature was in too much pain. They had failed in their assault. It was worth nothing to Nunn to save them now.

Other parts of Nunn's consciousness still coaxed those creatures that would have a part in this later. Some were easy to motivate, like the dead man who was driven by his own fury, or those things beneath the sea that waited so impatiently for action and their promised rewards. Others needed a closer watch, especially those of the various races that he had recruited, through greed or fear, to act as spies. And then there was Zachs, his brightly illuminated assistant, who showed all the restraint of a blazing fire.

There were too many images in his mind, and all of them led to exhaustion. Nunn felt a great weariness, as if all the vigor in his form had been blown away by the island wind. Perhaps he had attempted too much too early in the campaign.

But he had so much to gain. If he could only determine why these newcomers were here, before the great dark one was ready to use them.

The room was filled with glaring white. Nunn turned his head, willing his tired eyes to remain open and alert.

"She's getting away!" cried Zachs' singsong. The creature flashed like lightning before him, as if Zachs could no longer contain the energy pent up inside him.

"Only for a moment," the wizard managed, stretching out the weary muscles in his arms. "She has wonderful potential. I will let her think she is free for a little while longer."

Zachs' light dimmed enough for the wizard to see the petulant expression upon the creature's face. "You're not going to give me the girl, are you?"

Nunn tried to keep the annoyance from his voice. Zachs was far too useful; he had to be treated gently. "I never said that I would."

The light-creature wailed. "You won't give me Mary Lou? I'm so hungry! You haven't fed me in so long!" Light pulsed along the creature's trunk as its voice rose and fell. "I must have another."

The wizard stared at his minion for a long moment. "We both will need to replenish our energy."

Nunn felt a tingling where the light-creature rubbed his head against the wizard's sleeve.

"Nunn is so good to me," the creature purred. "Zachs is so happy."

Nunn stood, feeling the slightest bit light-headed. Still, the weakness was passing, for now.

"I have spent too much and gotten too little," he said, more to himself than to his minion. He felt a lancing pain in one of his calves. He was seated for so long that the muscles must have fallen asleep. It surely wasn't any more than that. "Perhaps I was too sure of myself."

"Nunn will win!" Zachs cried loudly, as if any other outcome would be unthinkable. "Nunn always wins!"

"It will all come to me, sooner or later," the wizard agreed. "I have made too many plans, forged too many alliances, corrupted too many officials. All that is left is for me to sort through our new uncertainties—our guests, if you will."

He shivered, and quickly placed a hand upon his chair to steady himself. "We both need new energy—new strength. I have been far too gentle with those around me of late."

"Food at last!" the light-creature cheered. "Where do we begin? We have so much of it at hand." He jumped to the rafters, swinging back and forth like a pigeon trapped in a bell tower. "I am famished! I can help! Who is dispensable?" Zachs beat a wild rhythm on the broad oak ceiling beam. "The Captain would be quite tasty. And he'd offer hardly any resistance at all."

Nunn sighed. This great display of Zachs' only seemed to make him feel still more exhausted. "No. It would be a waste of resources to kill the Captain—just yet. He has worked for me too long. He has a certain knowledge that I might need."

He smiled, looking out beyond the small windowless room that served as his work space. "I think it is time to test the visitors. I am sure we will find a few of them who are expendable."

Zachs giggled from the rafters.

Nunn sat back down upon his stool. "I will need to rest for a moment. Then we will determine which of our guests will survive."

Zachs returned to the floor to dance and laugh in delight. Nunn closed his eyes at last. For a moment. Only for a moment.

Then he would let the dragon's eyes fill him again.

◯ Nineteen

Had it all been a dream? The forest, the soldiers, the cabin in the woods, their slick but sinister leader—and how about Sayre? Evan Mills remembered how the old man died, the way he tried to keep his intestines from spilling on the ground, the way the body jerked when the Captain had shot Sayre in the head. That was much more graphic than Mills' usual dream.

But if it wasn't a dream, what was he doing back at school? He was at the blackboard, writing out the beginning of the lesson on sines and cosines. He could smell the mix of chalk dust and floor wax, hear the shuffle of bodies in the classroom behind him, Homeroom 409. His room for twelve years, scribbling lessons on the board.

There was always something very reassuring about trigonometry. But he had no idea why he was here.

He hadn't spent any time in the classroom in the last three years, since his promotion to vice-principal. Well, he had made a couple of emergency substitutions. Could that be what this was? He couldn't remember being given this assignment. He couldn't even remember getting up this morning.

He finished his notes on the board and turned to face the class.

Carl Jackson was passing a note to Joan Blake. That Jackson always was a troublemaker. But Joan was a sweet girl. If he could call her a girl. Joan was almost his age. In fact, the whole class was much older than usual.

Somebody snickered in the back of the room. Leo Furlong, that was who it was, always waiting for the teacher to screw up. This new classroom had shaken Mills more than he liked to admit. He had to start his lesson, get control of the class.

"Class," he began, his voice sounding oddly hollow in the classroom, "today we will continue to study the determination of angles in trigonometry. Sounds pretty long-winded, but we've got a couple of tools to help us." He pointed with his chalk to the spot where he'd written the words on the blackboard. "Sines and Cosines."

"Long-winded?" Jackson piped up from his seat. "That's our teacher, Mr. Mills the blowhard!"

Most of the class laughed. Harold and Leo and Rose and Margaret all thought it was hilarious. Even Rebecca grinned. Only Joan didn't smile. Mills was losing control. Leo threw a spitball at Margaret Furlong.

Margaret and Leo were husband and wife.

"Blowhard! Blowhard!" Jackson called in a singsong. "Blow it out your rear, Millsy!"

Evan had dealt with worse discipline problems than this. He was over at the side of the student's desk in an instant.

"Do we have a problem, Mr. Jackson?" he asked in a very even tone.

"Hey," Jackson sneered up at him, "I don't have any problem that couldn't be solved by me walking right out of here."

Maybe this was going to be even more of a problem than Mills had thought. "Would you like to say that to the vice-principal?"

Evan Mills was one of the vice-principals.

"Hey, I'll say it to anybody!" Jackson pushed his chair back from his desk. "I never had any use for school. There's no way for you to keep me here." He stood, balling his hands into fists. "I'm too old to be kept caged in like this." He took a step toward Mills, but the teacher stood his ground. He wasn't going to let any punk get the better of him. He stared straight at Jackson, teacher and student locked eye-to-eye.

"We're all too old!" a woman's voice cut in.

Mills blinked, startled from his stubbornness. Jackson took a step away as Mills turned to look at Constance Smith. He hadn't seen her before. The sun that poured through the classroom window showed how little grey hair she had left on her head.

"Can't you see what's happening here?" she demanded. "Don't you remember where we are? This has to be some sort of trick!"

"A trick?" Mills murmured.

"Incoming!" Jackson screamed.

A hand grabbed Mills' fatigues and pulled him roughly to the jungle floor. Something whistled overhead. The ground lurched below him as the forest exploded with a deafening roar. His helmet was pelted with rocks and mud and pieces of wood.

"Jeez, Millsy," Jackson shouted over his ringing ears. "What are you thinking about? You've been in Nam long enough to know when to get out of the way of their little presents."

Mills frowned. He had never been in Vietnam. It had been Korea, when he was in the army. But he was in the hospital corps, stationed in Germany. There had been rumors of a transfer, once or twice, but the orders to ship out never came.

"No casualties, Sergeant!" Harold Dafoe stood close behind them. His uniform seemed three sizes too big for him. He stood at attention, but his eyes darted back and forth as if he wanted to watch every inch of the jungle.

"We've got our orders!" Jackson shouted. The ringing in Mills' ears had subsided enough for him to hear distant machine-gun fire. He slapped Mills on the shoulder. "You're going to take the point!"

"Nobody's going to take anything," a woman's voice interrupted. Constance Smith stood beside them. She looked strange dressed in army fatigues. "Can't you remember?"

She paused, as if she couldn't remember herself.

"Remember that we should all be on our best behavior," she continued. Somehow she had managed to change from her uniform into a pink dress with a lacy front and sleeves. And who had given Mills a cup of tea?

"After all," Constance continued politely, "I think it was very generous of my mother to allow us to have this party, one with both boys and girls. Thank you so much, Mother!"

"Oh, good," another of the girls whispered a moment later. It was Joan Blake. Evan thought Joan was pretty. He smiled at her when he could in school, but he could never think of much to say. "She's gone. Now we can have some fun!"

"Fun?" Constance frowned. "What kind of fun?" She shook her head sharply, as if trying to get rid of some bad thoughts. "I don't think my mother would allow dancing."

"I'm not talking about dancing." Joan giggled.

"Dancing?" Margaret made the word into a groan. "I'm not dancing with Leo!"

Joan's voice lowered to a conspiratorial whisper. "I'm talking about kissing games!"

"Wait a moment," Constance said sharply. "It seemed so much like my childhood." She shook her head again. "Don't you see—" Her voice was cut off by a great wind.

Mills felt himself pushed away from the others by the gale.

"Fight it!" Constance called. "This is no more real than the school, or the jungle, or my tea party!"

Things were flying through the storm: great black birds, whose slowly flapping wings seemed to cut through the gale. Their calls were very much like human screams. Their beaks, when they opened them, were lined with razor teeth. They were flying straight toward Mills.

Maybe the wind could carry him faster than those birds could fly.

A hand grabbed his. It startled him even more than the sight of the birds. He had thought he was all alone.

"Listen to me." He looked over at the face of Constance Smith. "This is the work of Nunn. I think he wants us to fight, to panic, maybe somehow betray ourselves. Somehow I can see this is all wrong. We are still in the clearing, behind the table. Let us all join hands. Maybe there is some way I can get us to safety."

Mills blinked. He could see the others now, quite close, as if Mrs. Smith's words had broken the spell. He reached for Carl Jackson.

"I'm not taking your hand!" Jackson screamed, as if still shouting over the storm. He grabbed his wife, Rebecca, by the shoulder. "I have all the help I need right here!"

"I'll take your hand," Rose Dafoe announced firmly. She smiled. Her hair, no longer windblown by the storm, was once again perfectly in place. Mills felt her strong grip on his fingers.

"Harold?" Rose added, more an order than a question. Her husband took her hand in turn.

"Why are they doing this to us?" he cried in a voice near hysteria. "What have we done to them?"

"Calm down, Harold," Margaret Furlong said as she took his hand. "The wind is going away. Leo? Take my hand, too."

"Snakes!" Jackson screamed, pointing at the ground before him. "Dozens of snakes!"

Mills couldn't see any snakes, or any great black birds anymore. The windswept, featureless plain that they stood on did not seem so vast as before. He could see dark, still shapes in the distance, but, unlike the howling wind and the fanged birds, these shapes held no menace. Mills guessed they were the trees at the edge of the clearing.

"Why is this happening?" Jackson howled. "We don't want to hurt you! Maybe we can make a deal!"

"I don't see any snakes," Harold Dafoe said in a much more reasonable voice. He smiled a bit sheepishly. "Thank you, Constance, whatever you did."

"Rebecca!" Joan Blake called from where she held onto Mrs. Smith's other hand. "Come join the circle now! It's the only way to fight it!"

"I'm not—" Carl Jackson began. "I'm nobody's—"

Rebecca broke free of his grip and ran to Joan's side. She smiled ever so slightly as she joined the circle.

"No!" Jackson screamed. "You can't have her! You won't get me!"

"Carl Jackson!" Rebecca called. "If you ever loved me, take my hand!"

Jackson shook his head, then looked to his wife as if he only now saw her. "You're still—I thought—" He walked to her, his steps labored as if he was still fighting the wind.

"Where?" he asked, as if suddenly woken from a deep sleep. "What happened to—"

The last vestiges of the wind were gone. They were back in the clearing in the woods.

"Interesting," a deep voice remarked. Mills had no idea where it came from.

Someone screamed. Maybe it was Constance Smith.

The forest was gone again. Everything was dark and cold. And the others' hands were gone.

Mills was alone.

○ Twenty

Knife or no knife, Todd's hands were sweating.

He remembered this feeling. He used to get this way before he got into fights in junior high. He was the new kid then. His parents had moved into town right at the beginning of seventh grade. He was the outsider at school, and he had to get in. He was short, too, when he was thirteen. But he was fast.

Most of the time, he won.

All that stuff he couldn't let out at his father came right out when he was fighting in the playground. He wasn't much on technique. He just started swinging until the other kid was on the ground. One or two of the other kids called him nuts. That helped him, too.

Most of the time, he won.

That is, until he met Bruce the Mouse. Bruce was huge, especially by seventh-grade standards. The Mouse nickname was somebody's idea of a joke, a joke that stuck.

It had started with a pushing match in gym class, in one of those games of dodgeball they used to have on rainy days. Todd had tripped over the Mouse's big feet. A few words had been exchanged, and a few more words after that. Todd called the big kid a stupid ox.

Mouse had replied, "Get out of my face, you little faggot." Fighting words. The gym teacher, Mr. Pinelli, broke it up for a minute. But only for a minute. Nobody called Todd a little faggot and got away with it.

And then Mouse laughed at him. That was it. Todd could take anything but somebody laughing at him. A meeting was arranged in the locker room: the far side of the baseball diamond, out of sight of the school building, ten minutes after the end of classes.

The Mouse was waiting for him, and a couple of the Mouse's friends, two guys named George and Tony.

143

Todd thought he'd better get this over with fast. He closed in on the other guy as soon as he got there.

Hitting the Mouse was like banging your fists into a brick wall. The larger kid didn't even seem to move. Bruce the Mouse swatted him casually. Todd found himself on the ground.

Todd got back up. He wasn't moving fast enough, wasn't hitting hard enough. He kept punching, punching, punching. Bruce the Mouse took a half-step backward. A left hand swung in on Todd from nowhere.

Todd was down again. The ground seemed a lot closer this time than it had before.

He wanted to groan when he pushed himself up this time, but he kept silent. Better not to let them know what he was feeling, or if he felt anything at all. Mouse wasn't laughing anymore. But his friends were.

The Mouse's fist knocked squarely into Todd's jaw. Hey, Todd wasn't even ready yet. His legs twisted under him as he went down this time. He saw tiny points of light when he opened his eyes.

Somehow he was back on his feet. His pants were torn, his nose was bleeding, he swayed when he stood. He made a noise every time he swung his fist. He couldn't help it from coming out anymore. He'd land one good punch on this guy yet.

"Hey!" the Mouse yelled, opening his fists to flat palms. "You win, okay?"

The Mouse laughed then, and Todd found himself laughing with him. God, but he hurt! He didn't have an ounce of strength left in him.

That was the start of his gang. George and Tony and Bruce the Mouse. They all hung out together and shared Todd's brains. He was the idea man, they were the muscle. Not that anyone would ever think of getting in their way once they were upper grads in high school. They didn't just win most of the time.

They won all the time.

Todd had grown after that, close to six feet by his senior year. Todd's gym teacher had suggested he try out for the football team. But Todd had better things to do.

He learned how to use the system. Todd the winner. High school was no different from any other place. Todd the boss. If you knew how to play it, you could have your very own kingdom. Todd, the guy who could figure out any angle, anywhere. He learned how to use his mouth rather than his hands. A simple threat was enough to get just what he wanted. He had it worked so he would never have to fight again. Or so he thought.

But now he—or he and the Newton Volunteers—had to rescue Mary Lou.

He looked up at the trees that seemed to close over him. There were new rules here, complete with talking ravens and wolves, and magicians who only told you half the truth—if there was any truth at all.

Todd wished he had George and Tony and Bruce the Mouse with him now. He'd gotten too used to depending on others to slide through his difficulties.

But he didn't have anybody else anymore. He had to be ready for his own fights. He wiped his hands on his jeans.

"Your Mary Lou would be this way," said Wilbert as he pointed at a spot in the woods where there didn't seem to be a path.

"The wolves have gone this way, too," Stanley added. "See their tracks down there?"

Todd looked down at the place Stanley pointed to in the dirt. The smudge there could have been a pawprint, if it wasn't a footprint or a mark made by a branch.

"What tracks?" Bobby asked over Todd's shoulder. Todd was glad he wasn't the only one having trouble here.

"You'll figure that out sooner or later," Stanley replied. "That is, if you manage to live long enough. Hey?"

"Stanley's such a cheerful sort," Maggie said with a snort. "But he's right. Most of the Volunteers died before they could learn a thing."

"Nunn killed them," Thomas announced abruptly. "Or they died trying to escape. Nunn was responsible, one way or t'other."

The others increased their pace without a word. So they weren't simply helping Todd and Bobby out of the goodness of their hearts. They had a score to settle with this wizard.

"Douglas Nutman," Maggie said, talking more to herself than anyone around her. "Lieutenant Nutman. He was our commanding officer. Nunn tortured him to death."

"In front of the rest of us, hey?" Stanley added. He spat. "Wizard wanted us to know how serious he was."

"Now we have to show him how serious we can be our own selves," Thomas summed it up for them all.

"Truth be known," Wilbert said easily, "we've avoided him till now. Didn't think we stood a chance against him."

"Dragon eyes and all, y'know." Stanley grunted as if he still didn't believe in all that mumbo jumbo. "But things have changed."

"They have?" Bobby asked.

"Yep," the bearded man replied. He scratched at his neck for a moment before he continued. "We got a chance of winning this time around." Wilbert offered Bobby and Todd his biggest smile. "After all, you're here."

This was the second time Todd had heard this sort of thing. He was already getting tired of it. It sounded like he and the other neighbors from Chestnut Circle were expected to save everybody. Why should he be responsible for a bunch of losers and freaks in someplace nobody had ever heard of?

He'd already managed to leave his father behind. If only he could figure out some way to get rid of the rest of these guys—

And do what? Todd reminded himself that meeting these guys was probably what was keeping him alive. And how could he possibly hope to rescue Mary Lou?

The Volunteers were moving more quickly now, gliding through the dense growth as if it were a city sidewalk. Only Todd and Bobby made noise as they crunched through leaves and stumbled over branches that the others missed without effort.

Somehow Thomas managed to find a path where Todd could have sworn a second before that none existed. And Thomas did it all without slowing down.

Perhaps there had been a road here before the trees and vines had taken over. Todd thought about how all the neighborhood houses had just been plunked down in the middle of this forest, and, how, within hours, they were half covered with those dark vines that draped from the trees. By now, the houses were probably completely lost beneath the undergrowth. Maybe other houses and bits of streets were lost here, too. This island might not just be full of people from other places, but little parts of all the places as well.

They broke into another clearing. Birds sang back and forth in the late afternoon sun.

"Even if we can't stand up to Nunn and his tricks," Wilbert began, as if the sunshine was a signal to restart the conversation, "one of you newcomers can."

"Wilbert is right," Thomas said. " 'Twould seem you are your own best defense. One of you, at least, controls a great deal of power. Otherwise, you wouldn't be here. Simple as that."

"In other words," Maggie explained gently, "you can be our shield. Nunn doesn't dare kill you."

Todd thought of the silent lightning storm but didn't say anything aloud.

"I know how difficult it can be, being someplace so far away from home."

Todd looked up, surprised that Maggie was still talking to him.

"It's happened to me a couple of times, you know," she continued. "I came from quite a good home, in Boston. A complete public schooling." She brushed at her pant leg. "You wouldn't think that, to see me now. My life changed twice. First when I left home—" She hesitated before adding, "And then this—"

She paused and smiled self-consciously, as if she realized she was talking more to herself than to Todd.

"We're glad to see somebody from the States, after all this time," Maggie resumed in a brighter voice. "We've been here for months."

"At least," Wilbert snorted.

"It's hard to keep track of the time," Maggie admitted.

"Weather never changes, hey?" Stanley grunted. "No seasons at all."

"It was as cold as hell when we left New Jersey," Wilbert added.

"Well," Maggie said, "it *was* almost Christmas."

Todd told the Volunteers it was August in the neighborhood.

"Eight, maybe nine months?" Stanley said. A moment later, he grunted again. "I suppose it could have been that long."

"Sometimes seems like it's been years," Wilbert agreed. "You know, there were more than twenty of us when we started."

"Twenty-one," Maggie added. "We told you what Nunn did with most of us."

"Six, maybe seven months?" Maggie said softly, almost to herself. "It still doesn't seem so long ago."

"It was December 19," Wilbert offered. "Middle of the afternoon."

"Isn't that Pearl Harbor Day?" Bobby asked.

Todd glanced at the other boy; he could never remember that sort of thing. Like his father said, he was a lousy student.

"Pearl Harbor?" Wilbert asked with a frown. "Who's she?"

Todd glanced even more sharply at the bearded Volunteer. That had to be another one of his wisecracks.

"Hold it!" Thomas called, one hand upraised.

The line stopped so abruptly that Todd almost plowed into Bobby. In the distance, he heard a high, bloodcurdling wailing. It lasted for about a minute, then faded away.

"Sounds like the Anno," Wilbert said after another minute had passed.

Stanley sniffed at the air. "I'd say we're getting close to the wolves. Human smell here, too."

"Mary Lou?" Bobby asked.

"Too soon to tell," Thomas replied. "If it is, we'd better get to her soon."

They were going after Mary Lou. The handle of Todd's knife was damp. His palms were sweating all over again.

"Keep your knife ready," Thomas addressed him directly. "We'll tell you when we need it."

Now they were ordering Todd around. Well, they could, he guessed, until they found a way to rescue Mary Lou. But these Volunteers were going to do some things for him, sooner or later. No matter how strange this place was, he'd figure his way around here. He'd been on top before, he'd be on top again. Todd the boss, the guy who could figure out any angle, anywhere.

After all, he usually won.

He dropped his knife hand to his side so nobody else could see the way his hand was shaking.

○ Twenty-one

She didn't know when she had felt so sick.

The People—or the Anno, as the red-furred creatures had called them—were chittering happily around the cooking pots. A number of them waved to Mary Lou. Some of them held hanks of raw meat in their hands.

"We have vanquished the enemy, behind your example." The prince smiled at the calm and good cheer. "Now it's time to eat."

Mary Lou couldn't. The things that had attacked them had been fierce, their weapons had been terrible, but they had talked! Even with their fine red fur, they had been almost human.

Mary Lou made no move to join the others around their cooking pots. At the moment, she didn't want to go anywhere.

"Mary Lou!" the People called, even more wildly than before. "Merrilu! Merrilu!"

"You should eat something," the prince said softly.

"I suppose—" Mary Lou said hesitantly. "It's only polite." She sounded like her mother.

"Politeness has nothing to do with it," the prince replied. "It's part of the initiation."

"Initiation?" She turned to look at him. The prince seemed fainter than before, more transparent. She could see the outlines of the leaves behind him through the folds of his cloak, as if he was slowly fading away. Maybe, Mary Lou thought, it was a trick of the late afternoon light slanting through the trees. After all, the prince was never solid at the best of times.

He still had the most reassuring of smiles. She wished she could really tell the color of his eyes.

"You fought by their side," he explained. "To the People, that makes you one of them. A few formalities, and you are a part of the tribe."

"Formalities?" she encouraged. She still had the feeling that the prince was avoiding speaking about something.

"Only when you eat the enemy have you truly vanquished him," he explained with that same smile. How could he smile when he talked about something like this? She wanted to shiver. It was almost as if the prince was trying to fool her somehow. But he had been trying to help her. She had to remind herself of that.

"You would only have to take a bite," he continued, his voice soft and reasonable. "It could help you in a place like this. The People are fiercely loyal."

"Are you going to stay for the meal?" she asked. She would feel so much better if he was here, but she had no right to insist.

The smile actually disappeared from his face. "I'm afraid—I'd rather not. If the People allow it, there are certain things I'd rather avoid."

Mary Lou felt a rush of relief. No matter what the People had asked him to say, she knew the prince would understand. "So you feel it, too? The way they're eating their enemy—it's almost like cannibalism."

"I'd never thought of that." The prince seemed to grow paler still. "Actually, I'd like to avoid eating altogether. I don't need to do that anymore, you know, eat or drink. And I don't like to be around others who do. Sometimes it's too painful to watch things that remind me that I was real."

Too painful? She looked away from him, out over the tops of the trees. The leaves had turned a russet brown against the brilliant red of the setting sun. Maybe she didn't understand the prince as well as she had thought. She would try to do better.

"You're real to me," she said quietly.

"The celebration is coming to you," the prince's voice called back to her over her shoulder, so soft it was almost a whisper.

She turned back to the encampment and saw the Chieftain striding toward her, a large bowl carried in each hand. Steam rose from the bowls into the cooling evening air. Mary Lou was all too sure what was in those bowls: the victor's stew, full of what was left of the vanquished.

"I can't," she whispered to the prince as she turned back to him. "How can I tell—"

She stopped. The prince was gone.

She didn't know what to do. She wished he wouldn't disappear like that. Still, from what he had told her, his comings and goings weren't entirely in his control. But who did control them? The People?

"Merrilu!" The Chieftain's smile was so broad that his face looked like nothing but teeth. Before now, Mary Lou had never realized how sharp the People's teeth were, sort of like a whole mouth full of fangs.

The leader of the People held the bowl under her nose. Mary Lou had expected the stew to smell terrible. Instead, the odor reminded her of meat loaf.

She wished the prince was still here. She wished anybody could be here to tell her what she should do. But the prince had already encouraged her to eat this stew. Just one bite, he had said. It was important to the People. And the People had protected her. She didn't know how she could survive in this strange place without them.

Only one bite. That would be all she would have to take for the People to be happy. How different was this from all those times her mother had ordered her to clean her plate? If she could get past lima beans, she could eat anything.

The Chieftain handed her the bowl and a squat wooden utensil shaped like a broad spoon.

"Merrilu!" he cried.

"Merrilu! Merrilu! Merrilu!" the People called from the surrounding trees.

If she could just close her eyes and think of anything but those red-furred creatures. She smiled and nodded at the Chieftain, which seemed to please him no end. All the People called her name, over and over again.

Merrilumerrilumerrilu.

Her stomach growled. She hadn't eaten in quite a while. The smell of the stew filled her nostrils. Her mouth was watering.

The Chieftain bowed before her, then retreated, walking backward toward the rest of his tribe.

She looked down at the stew, scooped out a single piece of meat with her spoon. The piece was coated with a thick brown gravy. She turned the spoon to her mouth.

Don't think about it, just eat it.

Merrilumerrilumerrilu.

She opened her mouth and placed the stew on her tongue. The gravy was surprisingly pungent, spiced with something Mary Lou had never tasted before. The People were going wild around her, screaming her name ever more loudly and quickly.

Merrilumerrilumerrilumerrilumerrilu.

She took a deep breath and sank her teeth into the meat. It was hardly cooked at all. Sour juices spilled out over her tongue.

She gagged. She couldn't have this thing in her mouth. She felt whatever was left in her stomach rise up in her throat.

She dropped the bowl, spitting out the barely chewed piece of meat. She was going to throw up. Whatever happened, she didn't want the People to see that. It would be like spitting in their faces.

She had failed the initiation. She had let them down.

She ran to the edge of the platform. The People were still chanting.

Merrilumerrilumerrilu.

Hadn't they seen what had happened? She wanted to hide, like she used to run to her room when her mother started to accuse her. But the camp was all one flat platform, completely open on this side. Maybe, she thought, if she found the place where she had climbed up, she could go down to someplace quieter among the trees.

She saw one of the swaying bridges off to her right. Why didn't the People stop chanting her name? Maybe, if she could just step out onto the branch here, she could cross over to the trail through the trees without having to go back and face the People on the platform. She'd explain this to the prince, somehow. She just didn't want to be here now.

She waved back to the People, hoping her gesture could somehow mean "I'm all right. But don't follow me." And she stepped from the platform out onto the thick tree limb.

Merrilumerrilumerrilu!

The People's chant was growing closer. She looked over her shoulder and saw they were moving as a group, one great wave of creatures that would surround her and pull her back into their middle.

Couldn't they understand that she wanted to be alone? She almost laughed at the thought. Without the help of the prince, she and the People didn't understand each other at all.

Maybe there was some way she could show them that she wanted to be by herself, someplace quiet. Sign language, maybe, could tell them how upset she was. Or maybe they'd simply recognize the misery on her face. She turned around on the branch so that she could see the approaching tribe.

Her loafer slipped on the bark. Her shoes were never meant for climbing. She grabbed a small branch to steady herself. The new branch bent strangely as she shifted her weight. Her foot shifted under her. She felt as if she might slip down both sides of the limb and land on her rear end. She pushed her right foot toward the top of the broad limb, pulling again on the supporting branch to regain her balance.

Leaves ripped free in her hand as the branch snapped away from her.

She couldn't keep her balance. Both her feet slid from the limb below her. She was falling.

Merrilumerrilu. The People's voices followed her down as she crashed into another mass of leaves immediately below. Another good-sized branch whipped into her stomach, knocking the breath from her. She grabbed at the branch as she fell again. She held on, gasping for air, as her body swung beneath her. But her fingers held no strength. They slid down the smooth bark, and she crashed, back-first this time, into another mass of leaves.

And she stopped.

She lay on a bed of branches, limbs from two or three trees intersecting so thickly that they easily supported her weight. She groaned. That meant she was getting her breath back. She shifted ever so slightly to get a better look at where she was. She could no longer hear the People call to her. She guessed she had fallen maybe thirty or forty feet, although the branches and leaves above her had broken her descent into a number of small falls rather than one big one. She was surprised that nothing felt broken or torn. She hated to think how many scratches and bruises she'd have.

Maybe, she thought, it would have been better to face the People, after all.

She laughed. It hurt a little. She still didn't have much air in her lungs, and she might have bruised her ribs in the fall. She groaned a second time.

Still, all the groaning in the world wasn't going to get her out of this. It was too quiet here, the only sounds her breathing and the wind. She wished now she could have heard the People's nonstop chatter in the distance. She shifted again, ready to grab onto one of the thicker limbs if this set of branches gave way like the ones above.

Her resting place held as she turned herself over. There, perhaps ten feet farther down and ten feet to her right, were the worn bark and tied vines of one of the People's tree trails.

She would have to crawl across her temporary resting place, then push herself through the jumble of branches to drop down to the trail. From there, she could climb back up to the platform, and safety.

Another noise, the howling of an animal, rose from below. She hoped it came from the ground and not the nearer trees. She wondered if the People would come looking for her, or if she had offended them so much that they wanted nothing more to do with the strange girl from Chestnut Circle.

She heard a second, fainter howl, as if in answer to the first. She remembered the setting sun above. The forest was growing darker around her. She should get over to the tree trail while she could still see her way.

She inched forward, trying to keep her weight above a large branch that pointed in the right direction. The mass of branches swayed but held. She grabbed a joint between the branches and pulled herself along, kicking with her legs like she was swimming. It was quiet again. Leaves rustled. Small branches snapped as she crawled toward her goal. But the howls were gone. Why did she feel like something was waiting for her down below?

There was a groaning sound, like a door with rusty hinges. One of the branches was giving way underneath her. The foliage that supported her was dropping away. Her feet still rested against a substantial branch. She pushed out with her legs, wrapping her arms around another sizable limb as a mass of branches and leaves fell from where she had been a second ago. She hung from the great tree branch, her feet dangling in the air.

She heard the limbs crash on the forest floor, some distance below, followed by a chorus of howls.

Something *was* waiting for her below.

But she had almost reached the trail. If she could simply swing herself forward, she could drop right on the vine-lined path and get out of this place.

She swung, feeling her sweat-damp fingers once again slipping over the too-smooth bark. She let go when her feet had swayed to their farthest forward point, and fell straight toward the trail, and the huge trunk the path wound around.

She yelled as she hit the trunk, her hands in front of her to break her fall.

Her cry was answered by a new series of howls. She looked down and was surprised that she could see the ground, maybe forty feet below. She hadn't realized she had fallen so far.

She pushed herself away from the tree and cried out again when she tried to put her weight on her right foot. She must have twisted her ankle. At least, she hoped that was all it was. The howling cut off abruptly as a dark figure stepped from the shadows below to look up at her.

The thing below stood like a man, but looked more like a great, shaggy dog. It held a bowl in one of its paws. Mary Lou realized it was the same bowl that had held her stew.

"You feeeast withhout usss," the creature said in a slow, grumbling voice. "Youu should inviite usss to the parrttyyy."

"Too mucchh foood forrr succhh aa sscrawwnny creeeaturrre," a second voice called from the darkness.

"Nooo neeeed tooo coook," a third voice added. "Ggllladd tooo eeeat rrrraww."

"Whyy donn't youu comme dowwn annd joinn usss?" the creature with the bowl called up. "Wee cann havvve ourrr parrrtyy herrre."

Mary Lou looked away from the creature below. Maybe, if she leaned against the tree trunks on her way, she could manage to climb back up to the People's camp.

"Vverrry wwelll," a new growl came from below. "Ifff youuu willl nnott commme tooo meee, I willl vvissssit youuu." Mary Lou glanced back down as she heard a rustling below. The creatures were moving across the ground, dim shapes in the gathering shadows. Their leader smiled up at her, its great teeth putting the tiny fangs of the People to shame. "Unnlliike ourrr ffourr-leggedd brrotherrrs, I cannn climmb a treee."

"Merrilu!" the People called from somewhere overhead.

"I'm here!" she called back. "Here!"

Two more of the doglike things had leapt into view. They seemed quite agitated.

"Theeyyy folllowww!" one of them barked. "Theeyyy folllowww!"

Mary Lou was startled by the fear she heard in that cry. Maybe these things would be scared away by the very thought of the Anno.

"She's up here, hey?" another clear male voice called from down below.

"Wolves!" a second voice, this one female, added. "If you offer us any resistance, we will shoot you. And we are very good with our bows!"

These creatures were wolves? The things howled below her, six or seven voices joining in the chorus, as the leader stalked away, still on two legs. The other wolves that Mary Lou could see followed on all fours.

"Mary Lou!" a call came from below. She recognized that voice. Two figures came out of the shadows. One of them was Todd Jackson!

"Merrilu! Merrilu! Merrilu!" the People screamed as they streamed down around her.

"Todd!" she tried to call out over the frenzied calls of the Anno. But their calls of "Merrilu!" seemed to drown out everything. She turned to her would-be saviors. A moment ago, she couldn't wait for them to arrive. Now she wished they would just shut up!

"Please!" she called to the People. "Could you stop your calling for a minute?"

But their cries of "Merrilu!" grew in intensity, as if it was some war chant. She saw that many of the Anno carried their bows, and a few even held spears taken from their enemies. Poison sticks.

"Merrilu!" the People all called in one great, united voice as they drew their bows and shot their first arrows toward the humans on the ground.

What were they doing? They could hurt Todd and his friend, maybe even kill them!

"Back off!" the other man below shouted. He dragged Todd toward the safety of the surrounding trees.

"No!" she shouted with every ounce of strength left in her. "No!" she screamed at the People as they swarmed around her. "Can't you understand?" She tried to move forward, to rip the bows from their hands, but pain shot up from her ankle. She leaned back against the tree, gasping. "No," she whispered, her voice much softer than before. "I don't want you to hurt them!"

"Merrilu!" the People called. "Merrilu!"

The People kept firing their arrows down to the earth, even though Todd and the others had long disappeared.

○ Twenty-two

Evan Mills was wrong. This was more than darkness.

The world was changing around him, and changing again. He saw flashes of light in the darkness, bright strobes in the black. And in that light were objects, places, people, things that he thought he might recognize, if only he could concentrate on them for longer than the instant they were illuminated.

One flash showed an expanse of green, maybe a grassy hill. Mills thought, for some reason, about being a boy, taking a walk through a meadow on a hot afternoon.

Another flash, full of grey. Mills thought of a city street, the first place he kissed the woman who would be his wife.

A flash, almost pure white, and he was in the doctor's office at the moment that he and his wife, Cathy, were told they would never have children.

One more, in red, as he yelled and cursed until he lost his voice as Cathy threw everything in their living room to the floor.

Another in brown, an autumn day washed in rain, the day Cathy left. He wanted to say something, simply call her name, but that great weight in his chest kept his mouth closed, his voice silent.

Flash piled upon flash, giving Mills ten, a hundred, a thousand pieces of his past. It was like that old cliché about your whole life passing before you, except in this case, Mills got the idea that his life was being replayed for someone else's benefit. He thought he heard a deep chuckle, but he couldn't tell if that was any more real than those strobed scenes he might be making up in his head.

"Don't believe any of it," Mrs. Smith cautioned.

At least, Mills thought she had cautioned him. Her voice sounded like she stood right next to him. How could he hear her like that if she was nowhere to be seen?

"Where are you?" he called.

"Oh, dear," she replied. "Wait a moment. I believe I can take care of this."

The light strobes ceased abruptly. The air was filled with a chorus of sopranos as Mrs. Smith descended from somewhere high above. Her housecoat had been replaced by immaculate white robes, even more brilliant in the bright light that seemed to hang around her like a halo.

She glanced self-consciously at her attire as she landed in front of Mills. "Oh, dear, that was rather melodramatic, wasn't it? I'm sure there must be some way to adjust that sort of thing." She smiled and shook her head. "I'll simply have to work on it."

Melodramatic wasn't the word for it. She had looked like some angel in one of those old biblical epics.

"I do have a fondness for Cecil B. De Mille," she admitted. "It's not something I'm particularly proud of."

Mills had had enough of this. Maybe he shouldn't have gotten angry at Mrs. Smith, but she was available at the moment.

"What do you mean?" he shouted at her. "I need to know what's going on here, and I need to know now!"

"You need an explanation?" Mrs. Smith's wistful smile faltered a bit. "I'm not quite sure I could. I simply seem to have a knack for this sort of thing." The wrinkles around her eyes deepened as she reached for words. "It's a certain way of thinking about things. That's all I can tell you now."

"Interesting," Nunn's disembodied voice commented once again.

"Be quiet, will you?" Mills yelled, throwing his anger in a more appropriate place. "We are not here for your amusement!"

"Well," Nunn's voice replied. "Perhaps some of you aren't."

"Now, he is so sure of himself," Mrs. Smith chided. "Let's see what we can do about that, shall we?"

"What? You can't—"

Nunn's shouting voice abruptly stopped.

"There." Mrs. Smith's head bobbed up and down in a no-nonsense nod. "That should give us a little privacy."

Mills had no idea what to say. Mrs. Smith picked up the conversation for him.

"Sometimes, as I've grown older, I notice that my mind has begun to wander. It's a frightening thing, to discover you don't remember how you got somewhere, even where you are." She paused for a second as she looked out to the woods beyond them. It was only with that gesture that Mills realized the forest was there again. No doubt Constance had brought that back as well.

"My mind seems to wander just as much here," she continued, "maybe more so. But back home on Chestnut Circle, I'd lose myself. Here, when I wander, I find things."

She paused again and frowned, waving her right hand in an impatient sort of way that seemed more directed at herself than at Mills.

"Here, I should explain this to everyone."

She closed her eyes. The forest was filled with the rest of the adult neighbors.

"What's going on here?" Jackson demanded. His wife flinched at his anger, but she didn't seem to shrink away the way she had before.

"Harold," Rose Dafoe called to her husband. "I was so worried!" They stepped together so that Harold could take her in his arms.

"And where were you, Leo?" Margaret Furlong demanded of her spouse.

"Trying to survive, like the rest of us," Furlong retorted sharply. "If you could look at what was happening to the others, instead of simply thinking about yourself—"

"Now, please!" Mrs. Smith announced in a voice remarkably strong for one so frail. "There's no reason to fight. This was all that—Nunn person's doing. Some sort of trickery. However, I seem to be able to counter it. I always was strong-willed. You should ask my husband—Arthur."

She paused for a moment, as if only with the mention of her husband's name did she remember the world they'd all left behind. Arthur had been trapped in the city, cut off by the storm from returning home. Maybe Constance realized she would never see Arthur again.

"But, Constance?" Joan Blake broke the silence. "You brought us here? How?"

"Oh, Joan," Mrs. Smith replied in her usual self-deprecating way. "I don't think I brought anyone anywhere. I believe we were all here all along. We simply couldn't see each other. Trickery, like I said."

"But what about Mary Lou and the boys?" Rose Dafoe asked hopefully. "Do you think you could find them, too?"

Mrs. Smith considered the question for a moment, her aura dimming with thought. "Well. I don't think I could conjure up the children, if that's what you mean. I can see through the things that are happening here, but I'm not able to create anything of my own. I don't understand enough of this yet. Perhaps I never will."

Half the neighbors seemed to want to talk at once. Margaret Furlong demanded an explanation of everything. Her husband told her to stop bothering people. Rose Dafoe talked about how they had to look on the bright side: They were all together, and they all seemed healthy. Mills thought he heard Jackson murmur something about the "crazy old lady."

Somebody had to get some sort of order. Mills thought he was as good a candidate as any. "People!" he called in his best teaching voice. "Now listen. We have a moment's peace here, but it may only last a moment. We need to make some sort of plan."

"How can we plan," Leo Furlong complained, "if we have no idea where we are or who's in charge?"

"We have to find our children!" Rose Dafoe demanded. Harold moved close to his wife, tried to take her hand, but she brushed him away.

"First," Mrs. Smith said evenly, "we have to find some way to protect ourselves from Nunn."

"Nunn?" Mills felt like laughing. "But he's gone! You simply sent him away!"

"Yes, but how? And why does it work?" Constance shook her head. "I have to figure out how I manage these things before they will do us much good."

"Why do we have to protect ourselves from Nunn?" Jackson demanded. "Seems to me he's willing to work with us."

"At least he's talked to us and fed us," Margaret Furlong agreed. "That's more than could be said for that other fellow!"

"And one of Nunn's men killed Sayre!" Leo pointed out venomously. "You'd forget about anything as long as you get three square meals!"

"I don't think it's time to trust anyone just yet." Everyone stopped speaking as Mrs. Smith's voice cut through their arguments. Mills couldn't remember when he had heard her voice sound so strong. "I like what Evan had to say. Yes, we certainly should try to find our children. But we must have a plan."

"Yeah, we have to keep ourselves safe here, too," Furlong interjected, his smile faltering as he looked to the others for support. "I mean, none of us want to die!"

Margaret Furlong gave her husband a look reserved for cockroaches after you had squashed them with your heel. "Leo, why do you even try? I have never seen anybody so ineffectual."

"I tend to agree." Nunn stepped forward so that he stood between the Furlongs. Mills hadn't even been aware that he had arrived.

Nunn turned to the male half of the couple. "Leo, you do seem ineffectual to me. You'll be the first. After you, the choices get harder."

"What?" Leo's voice squeaked as he tried to frame some sort of question. "Where did—how did you—"

"None of that matters anymore," Nunn replied smoothly, "at least not to you." He turned to Furlong and held out his hands. "Leo, you are mine."

"What?" Leo looked surprised. "I won't! Constance, can't you—" Leo Furlong began to waver, the way a television image did when the reception was bad.

"No!" Mrs. Smith shouted. "I won't let you!"

"Really," Nunn answered her in a tired voice. "Try me again when you've figured out what you're doing." He waved his right hand and Mrs. Smith vanished. He turned back to the wavering shape that had once been Furlong. "Now, Leo, it's time for you to do something of value."

"Nooooo!" What was left of Leo's voice turned to a moan as his image shrank and swirled, then bounced like a child's ball into Nunn's open palms.

"Oh, yes," Nunn said. He closed his eyes as his hands encircled the ball. His frame shook as he breathed sharply. His eyes opened, and then his hands. The ball was gone.

"Leo!" Margaret called.

"He's gone, I'm afraid," Nunn said with a grin, "but his passing has served a greater cause. I need energy to complete my work. Those of you who agree with me will see benefits as well, believe me."

"What have you done?" Mrs. Smith popped back into existence at Mills' side.

"A bit too late, my dear old dame," Nunn said smoothly. "I'm afraid you'll have to do better than that if you want to compete. I ate him, of course. Everyone needs to keep up their energy. Especially after having to fend off a raw power such as your own."

Mrs. Smith looked as angry as Mills had ever seen her. "Are you saying that my actions helped lead to Leo's death?"

"Does that disturb you?" Nunn said, his smile growing with every word. "I have ways of making it easier."

Mrs. Smith's aura flared behind her. "No. I can't blame myself for something I didn't understand. But I'm beginning to understand you all too well."

"You will be difficult, won't you?" Nunn looked to the rest of the neighbors. "I will be blunt with you. The old lady is a remarkable exception. Most of you show very little potential. However, even what little you have can be molded. I am going to leave you on your own for a bit. You will be given nothing. You must make choices to survive.

"You can join me, and you will have both comfort and my protection. I will take my victims from those who refuse me. I will warn you that, as the battle intensifies, so does my hunger."

He waved to all the men and women of Chestnut Circle as he began to fade. "Welcome to the seven islands. I hope you enjoy what little stay you have remaining. Now, if you will excuse me, I believe it's time for my nap."

He was gone. For a long time, the only sound in the clearing was the deep sobs of Margaret Furlong.

The sharp pains were gone. The Captain had thought they would never end.

He tried to open his eyes. Light flashed before him. The Captain grunted, the only sound left in him.

"Not fair!" a shrill voice screamed. "Not fair!"

Zachs was here with him. The Captain was glad the creature was angry about something else than him.

"He feeds, but there is nothing for me!" the glowing ape screamed. "I do all his work. What would he be without me! Where is my reward?"

The Captain opened his mouth. It was far too dry. He managed to gasp out two words.

"From Nunn?"

"What are you saying?" Zachs demanded. "Nunn doesn't give rewards? Maybe not to you, but to me, I've been loyal, I do everything for him. Surely, he knows what I'm worth!"

The Captain managed another grunt.

"I won't listen to you!" Zachs shrieked. "I'll wait for our master to return! He'll know what to do to you, what to take from you next. And I'll be so happy to help, oh, yes, I will!"

Zachs flared again. Then the light was gone.

The Captain enjoyed the darkness.

Take from him? he wondered between painful breaths. Perhaps they had at first. But then there had been additions. A new set of arms and legs, a new vision of the world outside this stinking room. That vision was the only thing that had allowed the Captain to survive the pain. Otherwise, he surely would have lost his mind.

But now he knew a new truth, a truth that would unite his two selves, a truth that placed him high above the petty pains and concerns of a Nunn or his creatures.

The Captain relaxed, more at ease with every moment he thought of his newfound vision. He opened his arid mouth again, his ruined voice speaking two more words, the mantra that would help him survive.

"My lawn," the Captain whispered.

○ Twenty-three

Charlie's barking snapped Nick from his reverie.

He hadn't realized the dog had followed him.

"My," Obar remarked as he somehow stepped into their midst. The magician and the dog must have come together. "That all happened rather quickly."

Nick wondered if it had happened quickly enough. Obar seemed to be able to accomplish almost anything with remarkable speed, yet he hadn't been there in time to join in the confrontation with the red-furred creatures. Had the wizard waited until the danger was over before he joined them?

"What have you given me?" Nick demanded when it seemed that the wizard was only going to stand around and smile. "This sword—" He pointed accusingly at the scabbard that slapped against his jeans. "It felt like it wanted to act on its own. Like it was going to kill those red-furred animals whether I wanted it to or not."

"And did it kill them?" the wizard asked with that same annoying smile. He snapped his fingers, and another miniature sun lit above them to take away the evening shadows. Somehow the new light made Obar's expression even more irritating.

Nick shook his head. "When I held it back, it jumped from my hand and cut Jason!"

"Oh, dear." The wizard frowned and immediately turned to the younger boy. "Jason?" The boy showed him the place the sword had nicked him.

"Well, it really is only a scratch," Obar said, the cheerfulness already back in his voice. "Sometimes the best of weapons can have a will of its own. Well, you do have to be firm—you saw how I handled it?" He chuckled. "Well, I can be firm, I'm a wizard, aren't I?"

He waved a finger at Nick. "Sometimes you might need to let the sword have its way. It generally only acts out when somebody or thing really needs to be cut." Obar scratched at the neck under his beard. "It doesn't do, Nick my lad, to be squeamish."

"Squeamish?" Nick blurted out. "I try to control the sword, and you call me squeamish? What do you want from me?"

"Only what you can give," Obar replied sharply. "Do you want to have control, or do you want to survive? Around here, I'm afraid, you usually can't have both."

"Raven only does as Raven wants!" the black bird interrupted.

The wizard glared at the bird. "I suppose there must be exceptions to every rule."

"Raven's whole life is one great exception," the Oomgosh's voice boomed.

"So few understand, my Oomgosh," Raven replied.

"And Raven is truly beyond understanding!" the tree man agreed.

"I don't think that even I have time or energy to understand." Obar nodded in grudging agreement. "Or to continue this argument. Besides, there is that other matter to attend to, this—Mary Lou?"

His forehead creased for an instant.

"We should get to her as soon as possible. She is in some danger from her surroundings. But she is in the most jeopardy from Nunn."

"Well, let's go," Jason piped up. Nick wondered if he was trying to be as cheerful as Obar.

Obar shook his head. "I can't take all of you."

"Raven flies alone," the black bird agreed.

The wizard paused to glance at his companions. "And my magic doesn't suit the Oomgosh. At least not in this particular case."

"It is not good if my feet leave the ground," the tree man agreed.

"Dirt is his life," Raven added.

"I think it best that we send a delegation," Obar continued. "Mary Lou seems to be in a delicate situation. She's been taken by one of the local tribes, the Anno." He raised both hands, waving away any questions that might come from Nick or Jason. "I don't think she's in immediate danger. The Anno will protect her, until they get tired of the novelty. Unfortunately, they also wouldn't appreciate it if we approached them too directly." His right hand stroked his shaggy mustache. "No, this is certainly a sensitive matter."

"So what should we do?" Nick asked.

"I'm glad you agree," Obar remarked.

Nick wasn't aware of agreeing to anything.

But the wizard's hands danced before him, the motions so quick that his fingers blurred. "I think it important to have one of the—what did you call them?—neighbors, yes, neighbors present for the negotiations."

The world shifted around Nick. He felt like he had left his stomach behind. The trees seemed to be in different places than they were before. Or maybe they were different trees.

The wizard coughed beside him. And it was only the wizard and his portable sun. Raven, Oomgosh, Jason, and Charlie were nowhere around. The wizard had brought Nick somewhere else.

"It is a bit disconcerting, isn't it? Well, you get used to it after a while." Obar cleared his throat. "At least, you pretend you get used to it. But we have company."

The tiny sun darted away from them to illuminate a crowd of people farther down the trail. Mary Lou wasn't with them, but Nick recognized two out of the six. Nick and Obar had gotten more than just the attention of the crowd, too. Four arrows were notched in four bows, all aimed straight for them. Four of the six seemed quite ready to kill them.

The other two were Todd and Bobby.

"Hey!" Todd called. "I know this guy! He's my friend."

"He was your friend," one of the bowmen replied, "till he got involved with a wizard."

"Wait a moment, now." Obar frowned for a moment. "Thomas? We need to talk."

"Hey?" another of the bowmen spoke up. "You know what we do with wizards. It doesn't have a thing to do with talkin'."

Obar walked forward, his hands folded before him. "I am no threat to you. We have had our differences in the past, a certain failure to communicate."

"You let half of us die!" A woman's voice spoke this time. If anything, she seemed angrier than the men.

"A sad thing, but unavoidable," Obar continued in the same neutral voice. "If I had stepped in, Nunn would have killed us all."

"And all for those damned dragon's eyes!" the fourth bowman chimed in. "And what good have we seen from those things? Tell me that!"

"What good?" Obar opened his arms, spreading his palms to the sky. "The fact that Nunn has not yet gained the power to kill us all. Believe me in this, if nothing else. My brother has two of the eyes already. If he was to acquire three, especially when I had none with which to fight back, he would do whatever he wished."

"Your brother?" Nick whispered at Obar's side. "The evil wizard is your brother?"

"Oh, did I neglect to mention that?" Obar replied in a voice almost as soft. "You can't trust someone just because they're in your family."

Nick thought for a second about the night his father had walked out on his mother and him. Somehow he imagined that wasn't quite what the wizard meant.

"So you tell us!" the first of the bowmen called back to Obar. "But Maggie's right. The only thing we've gotten from you and your brother is death! And for what?"

"For what?" Obar sputtered, "But I've shown you all that Nunn is destroying—"

"Pictures in the dust!" the bowman countered. "Conjurer's tricks."

"And you know exactly what is real?" A smile threatened to curl the corners of Obar's mouth. "That is the true trick around here."

None of the four with bows seemed to have an immediate answer for that.

"Hey." It was Todd's voice that broke the silence. "I know one thing, and that's that I'm glad to see Nick again. I want us all to get back together again." He paused, then added, "Well, most of us, at least."

"You should listen to this—Todd," Obar said. "The only way we will win is if we fight Nunn together."

"And what do we win, wizard?" asked the bowwoman the other had called Maggie. "The return of our dead comrades? Will you give us back all those months we've been here, just barely surviving? Or maybe a way to get home?"

Obar managed to look down on the bowmen, fifty feet farther along the trail, as he replied. "We win the power of the dragon. With that, you can gain anything."

So that's what they were really here to do. Why hadn't Obar told him all of this? Not, of course, that Nick would have understood much of it.

"I do not underestimate your strength," the wizard went on to the bowmen. "I know what you did to our third compatriot. That's why I've come to you, so that we can work together." Obar smoothed his mustache again. "There is great power here, in almost all of the newcomers. An amazing amount of power. In fact, I've come here not only because you are here but to help rescue a young woman who is a part of that power." He paused midscratch to stare at Todd and Jason. "A young woman named Mary Lou."

"Mary Lou?" Todd interjected in sudden excitement. "I did see her, then, up in the trees! It was hard to tell in the darkness, and there were all these little hairless things screaming and throwing things our way."

"The Anno," Obar agreed. "They think a lot of Mary Lou as well. But I think she'd be happier with us. Besides, we need her more than they do."

Todd turned to the bowman called Thomas. "You have to listen to him. We have to save Mary Lou!"

Thomas frowned. "Are you sure you saw this girl in the trees?"

"Thomas!" a bald man at his side demanded. "How can you listen to him, hey?"

"Now that I know she was there, yeah," Todd answered the question with a shake of his head. "I thought I was imagining things."

"Don't you see what the wizard's doing?" the bald man demanded, his voice getting higher and wilder with every question. "Don't you remember what happened when Douglas trusted them?"

Thomas looked to the bald man. "I'm sorry, Stanley. I don't think it's quite that cut-and-dried." He nodded at Obar. "Maybe we will have to call a truce, then."

"What?" Stanley shrieked in disbelief. "I'm not working with a wizard. I'm not going to let a wizard live!"

With those final words, he released his bow. Nick saw the arrow, headed straight for them.

Todd saw things shift in front of him.

"Come now," the magician said. Except the magician had somehow moved behind them, on a completely different part of the path.

"You should know that nothing as simple as an arrow can stop someone like me," Obar continued. "Stanley does not seem to care for me. I assure you, the dislike is mutual, but we do have to put these differences out of our minds."

Todd felt something was missing even before he looked back up the path. "Wait a moment," he called to the others. "Where's Nick?"

"Nick?" Obar frowned as he looked to either side. "He should be right by me. I caught him in my dislocation spell, too. Wouldn't do to have one of our new arrivals killed by accident, or even by a fit of pique. Nick?"

The wizard's brow furrowed as he hesitated.

"He's gone," Obar announced, his voice far less sure than before.

"Gone?" Bobby piped up behind Todd. "Where could he go? Why would he leave?"

"Not of his own free will, or mine," Obar continued. "This is Nunn's work." He waved a fist at the Volunteers. "Now do you see that we have to work together?"

The Volunteers stared back at the wizard without answering. As far as Todd could figure out, Stanley's arrow shot seemed to have startled everybody, Stanley included.

"Nunn knows we are here," Obar went on, his voice more clipped and direct than before. "Mary Lou will have to wait for a few minutes. I think we need to challenge Nunn more directly, don't you?"

The wizard paused again. "At least we will, if we want to save Nick." He stopped tugging at his mustache to point at the Volunteers.

"I'll say this once more: If we don't work together, Nunn will win."

○ Twenty-four

Jason wanted to cry.

Nick and the wizard were gone. One minute, old Obar was standing right next to them, pontificating. The next, poof. And they had taken the light with them, too. He didn't like that much at all.

Much worse, though, they had left Jason behind.

It wasn't totally dark here in the clearing. He blinked up at all the stars. There were thousands of them up there, bathing everything with a soft glow. Actually, he could still see pretty well.

"Just like a wizard!" Raven said with even more disdain than usual.

"Where did they go?" The words escaped from Jason's throat before he could stop them.

"I don't think wizards want us to know," the Oomgosh answered. "It adds to their mystery. And he has taken young Nick!"

"That is a greater disappointment," the Raven said. "Nick had the most excellent of perching shoulders."

Jason's heart beat loudly in his chest. Nick was his connection to what he knew, the world they had left behind on Chestnut Circle. Somehow, with Nick around, Jason could imagine he'd see his parents and sister again, and maybe, with a bit of a walk, sleep in his own bedroom again.

Without Nick here, Jason felt lost and alone. And scared— very, very scared. What had he done to deserve this?

He hadn't done anything. He never did anything. Maybe that was the point.

He was always the quiet one. If he kept out of the way, everything would be fine. At least that's the way Jason always felt around his family. His parents and sisters got along perfectly well without him. Problems started when he came in the room. Oh, sure, sometimes they'd be fighting before he got there, but that only made things worse. "Go away, Jason. This isn't for you." Or "You'd never understand." Nobody wanted him around for anything. Sometimes he felt that maybe it would be better if he just disappeared.

He looked up at the Raven perched on the large man's shoulder, a man who seemed to bear more resemblance to the dark forest around him than to the people Jason had left behind. This, Jason realized, was the sort of place you disappeared to.

"So we should start, Jason." The Oomgosh lifted his great feet, first one, then the other, slowly from the dirt. "Some can vanish and reappear, some can fly, but only the best creatures walk."

Charlie barked as the tree man shook himself.

"Raven walks whenever he wants," the bird cawed. "Which is not very often."

Actually, Jason thought, you couldn't really be alone when you were with characters like Raven and this tree guy.

"Now there are three of us," the Oomgosh continued. "We will find your neighbors in our own way."

The black bird bobbed its head. "Raven will fly on ahead. Raven's eye sees all."

"And I can direct him," the green man said as he smiled at Jason. "For the forest tells me everything that happens on this island."

"The forest?" Jason asked, amazed. "You can talk to every tree?"

"In their way, every tree speaks to me," the Oomgosh affirmed. "The messages will be passed from root to root, until they reach me. I know where Nunn has kept all your fellows." He pointed ahead of him into the forest. "We can be there in a day."

"Even with the slow gait of the Oomgosh!" Raven made a low call that sounded like a chuckle. "Another advantage of living on an island!"

The Oomgosh frowned. "Undue haste has been the downfall of many."

"Raven is the exception." The bird fluffed his feathers.

"Raven is always the exception," the Oomgosh agreed. He waved his gnarled fingers toward the trail. "Come, Jason. Together we will perform heroic and no doubt impossible tasks."

"I will return as soon as I have found them!" the bird called. "Raven will know everything!"

The dog barked as Raven took to the air.

"Come on, Charlie," Jason said as he leaned down to pat the dog's head. "I guess I'd better take care of you, too. We're all in this together."

"Indeed we are, Jason," the Oomgosh replied as he took his first step to follow the bird. "Indeed we are."

The wizard's light was gone.

"Obar?" Nick called. There was no answer. Apparently, the wizard was gone as well. "Todd?" he tried. There was no response to that, either.

Evening had been turning to night as the wizard had created his magic light. Now, with the magic gone, the darkness closed around him. The magician had left him alone, deep in the woods.

He heard the rustle of leaves. Was something out there? Nick felt at his belt and found the handle of the sword. There was another sound, a low rumbling, like the grumbling bark of an animal on the prowl.

Leaves crunched beneath his toes as Nick edged one foot forward. His eyes struggled to make sense of his surroundings. He looked up and saw a single point of light, one star that managed to show through the foliage above. There was so little light beneath the leafy overhang that all he could really see were dark shapes in front of lighter tones of grey, trees in front of trees.

Other leaves rustled, closer this time. The grumbling sound, when it came again, sounded even more like a growl. He couldn't move. It was so dark, he didn't know if he could walk safely across the uneven ground. Even if he could make it to a tree, their trunks were so thick that there would be no way to climb one.

Nick expected an attack, a heavy animal shape knocking him down, a set of sharp teeth ripping at his throat.

But Nick found he was more angry than frightened. He had had enough of being pushed around by this brand-new world.

"Are you coming?" he shouted out at the darkness. "I'm ready for you!"

If he was going to die, at least he could take his killer with him. He drew his sword.

The blade glowed dully with a light of its own, a pale grey light that made Nick think of ghosts.

Something howled out in the woods.

The sword flared for an instant as bright as day. Nick threw his free hand in front of his face to protect his eyes. A chorus of cries came from the forest as the light startled whatever stalked him.

"Onne of the neww onesss," the same animal voice somehow grumbled in words.

"He hass a ssworrdd," a second voice growled.

"Fressh meeat," the first voice reassured. "Fressh meeat."

"The girrl wass too farrr," other voices joined in the conversation.

"The menn werrre too mannyy."

"They taunnt ussss, ssso taassty, but alwayss beyond ourrr rrreach."

The voices circled Nick now, coming from half a dozen points in the darkness.

"Thisss onne isss alonnne."

"Ssso he hasss a sssword? We outnummber himm ssseven to one."

"Beforrre he can ssstrike uss dowwn, we will have himm on the ground."

Nick took his sword in both hands. The ghost glow brightened slightly. Nick thought he could see dark shapes pacing on all fours, shadows circling him through the trees.

"Hisss fresssh blood will slaake ourrr thirrrsst."

"Hisss meeat will sstill the grummble in ourrr belliesss."

Nick turned slowly. The moving shadows were all around him.

"Commme, booyy. Therrre isss noo hope forrr youuu."

"Wee will ennd it quickly!"

"Fressh meeat," the first voice chánted once more.

"Fressh meeat," all the voices growled together.

As if that were a signal, two shadows separated from the surrounding gloom to rush toward the sword light. Nick made out legs and heads and matted fur as the shadows turned to wolves.

"No!" he yelled, swinging the sword before him. The weapon tugged in his grip, making him stumble to his left. The closer of the wolves veered to meet him. The sword jerked Nick to the right as it rose and fell, slicing the onrushing wolf on its flank. The first wolf yelped with pain as it rolled away, but the sword was already guiding Nick's hands toward the second attacker.

The second wolf leapt from the ground with a sharp bark, ready to tear out Nick's throat. The sword jerked forward so suddenly that Nick fell to his knees. The sword point swept upward, catching the now falling wolf full in the belly. The wolf screamed as the blade slipped through to its spine. The wolf's momentum carried it over Nick's head, tearing the sword from his hands.

Nick stood and turned, running the quick three steps to the fallen wolf carcass. He was dead if he didn't rescue the sword. He placed his sneaker against the side of the dead animal as he grabbed the sword with both hands. The weapon came out slowly, almost reluctantly, the metal making an odd whistling sound, like the soft rush of air when you drink through a straw.

The sword glowed, no longer a pale grey but a vibrant, pulsating red. Oddly enough, the metal edge looked clean and dry, as if it had taken the blood that should be smeared there and drawn it into the blade.

None of the other wolves attacked. In fact, he could no longer see any movement in the shadows.

Instead, those creatures that remained all lifted their voices together in one great howl.

Nick held the sword before him at arm's length, confident that the blade would lead him in whatever battle was to come.

"Ssommeday youu will not havve the ssword," the first voice said. "Fressh meeat."

The wolves vanished as quietly as they had arrived. There was a long moment of silence.

Nick heard a rustling behind him. He whirled around to see the wounded wolf whimper as it tried to drag itself away.

The sword tore itself from Nick's grip and flew to the injured wolf, plunging itself into the animal's upper body. Straight for the heart, Nick thought. The wolf shuddered once and then was as silent as the rest of the woods.

The two wolf bodies lay side by side on the forest floor. The first carcass was oddly flat, as if all the blood had been drained from it.

The second body shrank as Nick watched. The sword hilt rocked gently back and forth until it was done.

When the sword had what it needed, he stepped forward and pulled the blade free. The sword was there to save his life. If it wanted blood, he had to give it, one way or another.

He wasn't home anymore.

Nick retreated to stand, back to a tree, the sword gripped in both his hands.

If he had to, he'd wait this way until morning.

○ Twenty-five

Somewhere deep inside, she was as upset as she had ever been. But Mary Lou didn't dare cry.

She had seen Todd down there. If there was only some way to get to him. She wanted to bolt from these creatures again, to run after Todd and his friends, calling for them to stop.

But she could barely move her foot. Her ankle hurt that much. And what if somehow she did manage to get down to the ground from here? Those wolves were down there, too. The minute she was alone, she was sure something terrible would happen to her.

Mary Lou winced as the People gathered around her, pushing her back up the path, waving with their torches for her to follow. She wanted to scream at them to leave her alone, to cry out with the pain, use all the grief and hurt and anger inside her to make everybody go away.

Crying and screaming were never the answer to anything. That's what her mother had always said. *You can't run away from your problems, Mary Lou.*

She didn't know what else to believe.

The People had come to rescue her, after all. She didn't want to hurt them. They just didn't understand that she had been threatened by the wolves, and not the people—the real people— with Todd.

She had to talk to the People, make them see what she needed. They could work something else out—after all, hadn't the prince said that they considered her some sort of hero? They thought she was the reason they won against the red-furred creatures. A heroine should be granted anything she wanted. Shouldn't she?

It was all a matter of making them understand. But, in order to do that, she had to wait for the prince. In an odd way, this was the most frustrating part of all the things that had happened to her. She wished there was some way she could call him herself, without waiting for the People to bring him to her. But then, she always wished for all sorts of things.

The People had stopped screaming when the humans disappeared. They tugged at Mary Lou's blouse now, urging her to follow them back up the path they had built through the trees.

She let the People lead the way. She winced as she put her weight on her ankle. She'd twisted it, just like she had when she played field hockey in junior high. She was lucky she hadn't done anything worse.

Lucky? Anything worse? That sounded like her mother talking, too.

"Merrilu!" the Chieftain called to her when he saw her limp.

"Merrilu!" the other People echoed as they flocked around. "Merrilu!"

Small hands pushed gently against her legs, stopping her from taking another step. Others pushed at the backs of her legs below her knees. She felt herself losing her balance. They were going to push her over! She tried to fight against the press and tug around her, but cried out the moment she put pressure on her ankle.

She didn't fall. Instead, she was lifted, a dozen or more of the People gathered beneath her to carry her back to the stronghold.

"Merrilu!" they called her name over and over, but much more slowly and rhythmically than they had before, like a call to march. "Merrilu!" They paused for a beat. "Merrilu!" Pause. "Merrilu!"

She knew she should try to relax. Perhaps, in the morning, the prince would return, and she could convince the People that they had to take her back to the others of her kind.

Her eyes closed despite herself. She started to drift. She was exhausted.

Pain lanced from her ankle. She jerked awake and discovered she was back on the great platform where the People had built their village.

"Merrilu," the Chieftain urged. He held a wooden cup filled with dark liquid in his hands. Other hands pushed at her shoulders, urging her up into a sitting position. The Chieftain thrust the cup forward so that it rested against her chin. Her mouth was so dry that the skin tore as she pulled her lips apart. The Chieftain tipped the cup to her mouth.

For an instant, as the liquid touched her lips, she was afraid it might be blood.

It was sweet to the taste. She guessed it was some sort of fruit juice. So much else had been going on, she hadn't thought how thirsty she might be. She drank everything that was in the cup, and nodded her thanks.

The helping hands lowered her back to the platform. She noticed that she had been placed on a pile of furs. She didn't want to think about where they had come from. At least the People didn't offer her anything else to eat.

"Merrilu," they called, although their voices were so quiet that the chant almost sounded like a lullaby.

She felt a gentle pressure on her shoulders as her ankle was suddenly jarred with pain. She could only raise her head slightly, barely enough to see that a crowd of the People were taking off her shoe and sock. Another crowd rested on her shoulders, keeping her from rising.

Mary Lou fought against panic. What were they going to do?

"Merrilu," the People whispered. "Merrilu."

She stopped struggling. The whole tribe had rushed down the trail to save her. Why would the People want to hurt her now?

Two more of the people approached her resting place. One carried a bowl, another, two great fistfuls of the huge dark leaves that grew on the ever-present vines. Working quickly, they applied a gooey mixture to the leaves and wrapped the great green foliage around her ankle, one leaf right after another.

"Merrilu," they whispered. The leaves wrapped around her ankle felt pleasantly warm. The healers finished their work, and the Chieftain waved them and all the others away.

"Merrilu," they whispered as they bowed their heads and backed away.

The Chieftain opened his arms to the sky. "Merrilu!" he called once in a high, piercing tone. Then he, too, bowed to her and backed away, the last of the People to disappear from her sight.

The furs beneath her were cured. They were soft and warm. She exhaled, doing her best to relax, and looked up beyond the village. From here, Mary Lou could see the whole sky filled with stars. She was on a whole different world now. Were all the stars different as well?

She wanted to know more about this place, figure out how she fit in with all that was happening around her. She seemed to have a reason to be here. At least Nunn and the People seemed to believe that. The wizard wanted her, the People wanted her, too. Only the prince seemed above using Mary Lou for his own selfish ends.

She wished again that the prince could be here with her, right now, in this quiet moment under the stars. If only one thing could come true in all her life, she thought. Oh, how she wished!

"Mary Lou?" a deep voice whispered by her ear.

She turned and stared at the apparition, even more like a spirit in the starlight.

"Prince?" she asked.

"That's what you still choose to call me," the prince replied, amusement in his voice. "One name is as good as another. Better, really, if the name comes from you."

Mary Lou blinked. That was the nicest thing the prince had ever said to her. It was so warm wrapped in these furs, so quiet without the constant chattering of the People, so calm compared to everything that had gone before. She wondered if all of this was really happening.

"No, I'm not a dream," he replied as if he could read her thoughts. "I'm as real, well, as I ever am."

She liked the way he gently kidded himself. And the way he smiled when he saw her.

"And yet you called me, didn't you?" He looked down at his ghostly hands. "Somehow I could come here without the People's aid. Strange, isn't it? As though the two of us are developing some sort of bond."

Mary Lou had felt that—or wished for that—from the very beginning. She was so glad to learn it was true.

"What will the People say?" she whispered back to him.

The prince turned to look across the platform. "I doubt they need to say anything just yet. I don't think they'll even notice us, at least for a little while. They've had a great victory and a great feast. I have been among them long enough to know their habits. In the morning, a few of them will salt the remaining meat. For the remainder of the tribe, it will be a day of rest."

But the prince is here! a small voice said inside Mary Lou. She should change things now, call the People to them, let them know that the humans were her friends and that she had to see them.

Somehow, though, finding Todd and the others didn't seem anywhere near as urgent as it had a few minutes before. Any conversation she and the prince might have with the People could certainly wait until morning.

The prince smiled at her, then turned to study his dark surroundings. "It's good to be here, with no work from the People. My life, or whatever you would call this, is filled with performing the wishes of others. But now"—he laughed—"at this minute, I've nothing to do but talk to you and stare up at the stars." He paused for a long moment as he did just that. "It seems to me

I used to know something about the stars. Maybe I'll remember what it was someday." He looked back at Mary Lou. "I have a feeling that things are changing. Many things will change, now that you are here." He paused again, then chuckled. "I wonder if I will remember where those feelings of mine come from as well."

Mary Lou yawned despite herself. "Excuse me," she said quickly. "I've had a—busy day."

"Much more than that, I would think," the prince replied. "You should sleep. The way things are changing, I think we might have a great deal of time—together."

Mary Lou smiled at that and lay back in the furs. She drifted, and in her sleep she felt her prince take her by the arm and lead her to a castle built high in the clouds, much closer to the stars.

Mary Lou opened her eyes to a clear sky and a hint of sun peeking through the forest leaves. She remembered how the prince had come to visit her during the night. It had been such a wonderful dream.

"Well, good morning." The prince's face materialized above her. He greeted her with a smile.

"You were here last night?" she asked as she rubbed her sleep-puffed eyes.

"And I still am," the prince answered with a nod. "When you want somebody around, you can be pretty persuasive."

Mary Lou blushed.

"The People have checked on you from time to time," the prince continued. He didn't seem to notice her embarrassment. "They haven't seen me. I have—well, ways to hide when I'd rather people didn't know I was around." He lowered his voice to a whisper. "I thought it best that nobody shared our little secret, at least not yet."

They were sharing this secret life together, then? Now she felt both embarrassed and thrilled. It would be wonderful to really share something with the prince.

"I should get up," she said quickly. Maybe, if she could walk around, the prince wouldn't notice how flustered she was. That is, if she could walk at all.

She sat up and felt the dried mixture that coated the leaves wrapped around her ankle. The stuff had dried there, like a plaster cast. She flexed her toes, then her whole foot, waiting for the ankle to complain. There was no pain at all.

"I'm going to stand up," she announced abruptly. She wished

there was some way that the prince could reach out a strong hand to help. Still, she managed on her own, getting her feet beneath her in a squat, then raising herself up slowly, careful of her balance. She felt the slightest twinge when she put weight on that foot, but the leaf cast seemed to keep all the muscles in place. Whatever was in that concoction with the leaves, it seemed to have taken away all but a slight tenderness from the sprain. In another day, she bet she wouldn't feel any pain at all.

"They used Garo leaves," the prince said suddenly, as if it was something he had just remembered. "They come from those great dark vines that hang from the trees. When used in the proper way—well, you see what they can do."

The prince smiled in delight. "This is very strange. Over the course of the past few moments, I feel as though memories are coming back, like I'm coming out of—" His hands waved around as if he might grab the missing words out of the air.

"Some sort of magic spell?" Mary Lou prompted.

"It could be." The prince laughed as he looked through his ghostly hand. "Appropriate to our surroundings, I'd guess. But I was going to say that I was coming out of a cave, or a tunnel. It's like I've been living in darkness for a long time, and for the first time I can see the slightest bit of light."

Mary Lou was happy for him. She wondered if she had anything to do with it.

"You talked about a spell," the prince said after a moment. "I knew both the wizards, once. I think their magic does have something to do with what has become of me." He laughed, waving his transparent fingers in front of his eyes. "Does any of this mean anything? I still don't even know if I'm truly alive. What if I am no more than some sorcery—some memory of what I was when I could claim flesh and blood?"

"Merrilu!"

Mary Lou turned her head to see a small cluster of the People waving at her. They had finally noticed that she was standing.

"Prince," she said as she turned back to him. But he was gone.

"Merrilu! Merrilu! Merrilu!"

The People gathered together in the middle of the platform, calling to her but waiting before they approached.

The crowd parted, and their Chieftain, complete with his many-colored beads of office, walked in front of them. He approached her, and the rest of the People followed. They called her name over and over again.

She tried to smile at the approaching entourage, but couldn't help feeling disappointed. She and the prince had barely begun to get to know each other.

"Hello again," the prince's voice said at her side.

She turned to him. She wouldn't have any trouble smiling now. He came back so quickly. Was it her thoughts that had brought him back?

"The People have called me this time," he explained quietly. "Now I have a job to do."

And, Mary Lou realized, she had something to explain to the People as well.

"First," the prince began, "I extend a morning greeting from the tribe. They are very happy that you could be with them."

"You should thank them for coming to my rescue last night," Mary Lou replied. "It was a very confusing situation. Dangerous, too. But—"

She hesitated, unsure how to put what she wanted into words.

"But?" the prince repeated gently.

"But not all of those on the forest floor were my enemies. Some of those I saw last night were my friends. Friends that I very much would like to see again."

The prince nodded, then paused for a second, as if listening. At last he added: "The People want to make sure you know how pleased they are that you have chosen to join their tribe."

Mary Lou nodded, smiling at the Chieftain and those around him. She still hadn't let them know what she really wanted.

"But you have to understand," she added quickly, "I need to find my friends again."

The prince frowned slightly, then remarked: "Nothing could have been better than your arrival at this most propitious of times."

"But I can't stay here," Mary Lou said a bit more forcefully. "I need to find the people whom I came here with."

"It is so important that you arrived now, before the Ceremony," was the prince's answer. "Nothing else would have done."

"Why aren't they answering me?" Mary Lou asked. "Don't they know that I want to leave?" She almost felt like screaming at the People again.

"Merrilu!" the People cheered.

The prince spread his hands in a gesture of total helplessness. "I am trying to tell them, the best that I know how. They seem incapable of understanding. Or maybe they simply don't want to."

She felt calmer the minute the prince talked to her in his own

words. "It has something to do with this Ceremony?" she asked.
"What kind of ceremony?"

"It is a great event," the prince explained with a frown. "I don't
think I've ever felt this excitement in the People over something
that was yet to come."

He looked over at the quiet yet expectant crowd. "They do get
excited when their hunters return with a kill, or when they have
a victory like the one of the day before. But the People never
seemed to plan for their future. Their lives always seemed as
timeless as my own existence, until you came along." He turned
back to Mary Lou. "But this Ceremony? I don't know a thing
about it. It has never happened in all the time I have been here.
Maybe they had to wait for someone like you before it could
occur."

And, she thought but didn't say aloud, now that they had found
her, they weren't going to let her go.

She didn't know what to do. She knew that Todd was somewhere in this part of the forest. Maybe other neighbors were out
there, too.

She remembered again what Nunn had told her. She seemed
to have a purpose in this place, far greater than anything she
had ever had at home. Or so everybody said. She wished she
could learn what it was for herself, beyond Nunn's plans and
the People's ceremonies. And, she realized, she didn't want to
wait around for the People's wishes any more than she wanted
to satisfy Nunn.

If the opportunity presented itself, she might have to try to
contact Todd and the others on her own. She might have to leave
this place without the People's permission. For some reason, that
made her feel guilty.

She looked back to the Chieftain again and did her best to
smile. But her mind was turning over everything that had happened. She wondered if Todd had seen her in the trees. She
wondered if the others were searching for her now.

She looked over at her companion, his bright robes turned to
pastel by the morning sun. She seemed to have broken through
whatever spell or curse the prince was under. He said his life
would come back to him slowly. And she wanted to be there to
share it with him.

She could feel her heart beating quickly in her chest. Maybe,
Mary Lou thought, when she left, she wouldn't have to face this
world alone.

Maybe the two of them could leave together.

⃝ Twenty-six

Todd didn't like the silence. Back home, this kind of quiet meant there was going to be a fight.

"So how do we rescue this—Nick?" Thomas asked abruptly, as if he had decided to cooperate for all of the Volunteers.

"I should be able to do it," Obar replied, "as soon as Nunn turns his attention elsewhere."

Wilbert laughed. "So what do you need us for?"

"I need you to find the Anno," Obar replied simply. "We have to rescue the girl, too. Mary Lou. The only way we're going to win is if we work together—the way we did before."

"Oh, there we have it at last," Wilbert said as he shook his head. "There's something else you can't do. I knew the little creatures were talented. So the Anno really are wizard-proof?"

"I can no longer see them," Obar admitted. "They seem to have found a way to deaden my spells."

"We can find them, easily enough," Stanley volunteered as he looked up at the trees. "Wouldn't be surprised if they were closer than you think, hey?"

Obar started. "Nunn is letting down his guard. There he is. Nick, I mean. He's been fighting the wolves. I'll only be a minute."

The wizard light blinked out as Obar disappeared.

"Gone again," Stanley said. He paused a moment to spit. "You sure this is such a good idea, hey?"

"Admit it, mate," Wilbert replied gruffly. "You were getting tired of day-to-day survival, anyway. Besides, how much sand lizard can a person eat?"

"Mary Lou," Thomas said as he moved silently off into the darkness.

"Let's go meet our fate," Wilbert agreed as he followed Thomas down the path. "Bobby and Todd, my boys, I trust you know your way around a knife."

What did he mean by that? Todd had played around with a switchblade for a little while, but never in a fight. Before this, he'd never used anything but his fists. Maggie followed Wilbert, and Stanley waved for the boys to follow.

"Maggie's good at this," Wilbert went on. "She'll show you how to get in close, slash 'em quick."

"What's that?" Maggie said, as if she wasn't really listening. "What are you talking about? I can't really train the boys in the dark, can I?"

"Then they'll have to learn on the job, like the rest of us." Wilbert laughed. "You see, fellows, the Anno don't trust the four of us much. Comes from certain disagreements in the past."

"And the fact that they're filthy, murdering swine!" Stanley added.

"Well, that, too," Wilbert allowed. "The Anno recognize the four of us. And they know how hard we are to take advantage of."

"That's where they come in?" Maggie asked.

"We need bait," Wilbert agreed jovially. "Newcomer bait."

This time Stanley laughed. "Against the Anno. Bobby and Todd, you got my respect, hey? You folks are about to become full-fledged Volunteers!"

"Geesh, Todd, what are they going to have us do?" Bobby asked softly, as if there was any way Todd could know what was going on.

"Enough talk," Thomas ordered from the front of the line. "Gettin' close."

Todd didn't like this silence any more than the earlier one.

Even the greatest wizard in all the seven islands would have to sleep.

Nunn laughed, half from the feeling of power within, half from the giddiness of exhaustion. Furlong's energy had revitalized him, given him the kind of warmth he could only get from those fully alive. But he had so many uses for that living energy, and that small portion of him that held onto its humanity needed regeneration as well.

There were so many things to control. Too many, perhaps. Even when the two dragon eyes—his two eyes, more a part of him now than those feeble orbs in his skull—even when the eyes would let him split his consciousness in two, it was not enough. So many pieces, and all had to be manipulated before the dragon arose to reclaim his seven jewels.

And that pitiful woman—that meddling woman—Smith. Oh, she had a certain raw power, that was undeniable. She might become a formidable foe if given time to learn the arts. But it was time that Nunn was not ready to give. Soon, after he had rested, he would gather his awareness into a single sphere and cause the old crone to wither in front of all the others. Nunn chuckled. Oh, yes, that would be most pleasant. Her death screams would be so satisfying. He would attend to it first thing, after he had rested.

A second giggle came from within him, from a throat that wasn't his.

Nunn felt the familiar shiver as the separation began. If Furlong's life had filled his veins with warmth, Zachs' passage through his form filled the wizard with ice and electricity. Nunn took a ragged breath, steadying himself against a chair, letting his whole self be taken, if only for a second, with the pleasure and the pain. Zachs had stayed within him, sharing in Leo Furlong's gift, but the wizard had things for his creature to do. A single scarlet flash, and Zachs would flow out from his brain to regain his almost solid flesh. The wizard always considered this moment a sort of rebirth. His light-child was leaving him, ready to do Nunn's bidding.

"They hurt me," the light-creature whined. "Zachs will kill them all!"

"No, you will not," Nunn replied with more patience than he felt. It would not do to let his exhaustion lead to anger. "You will find those among the newcomers who have escaped. And you will bring them to me, one at a time."

"You want the girl!" Zachs cried in sudden excitement. "You need Zachs to get the girl!"

Nunn took a deep breath. Everything his creature said made him want to fly into a rage. It was his exhaustion, surely, or maybe that the light-child told the truth. It was more difficult to reclaim Mary Lou than he had imagined. Even with two dragon eyes, he could only get the faintest hint of her whereabouts. Then, when he had sent some of his creatures to capture her, it had not gone well. He lost too many of his troops, too quickly.

Not that it really mattered. Nunn controlled so many, he could attack the Anno a hundred times, killing every one of them, and smashing whatever childish device they had contrived to cloud his vision. Except for the dragon. Nunn had to be ready for the dark one, whenever it chose to appear.

"Yes," he said at last. "I want you to bring me the girl."

"Yes! Yes! Nunn will let Zachs capture them all! Zachs gets to bleed them! Zachs gets to feed!" The light-creature screamed with pleasure, and disappeared.

Nunn sat heavily on the pallet he used for sleep. Things would be simpler after he had captured all the newcomers and had a chance to study them, and to dispense with those that had no special talents. Their little lives would give Nunn strength for what was to come. These little setbacks would seem very small once he had rested.

Nunn would have everything, after he had slept.

○ Twenty-seven

"I know one thing," Evan Mills said to the neighbors grouped around him. "I'm not going to take this anymore. I don't think any of us should."

"Just like that?" Carl Jackson laughed derisively as he paced around the others. "Mr. Vice-principal. You've been running your students' lives too long. Just what do you expect us to do?"

Margaret Furlong looked up from her misery. "What would Nunn do to us if we tried—" She couldn't find the words to finish the sentence.

"Nunn isn't here now, is he?" Mills retorted, more toward Jackson than Mrs. Furlong. Every time Jackson spoke, Mills wanted to have less to do with him than the time before.

"I'm not sure it's as simple as that," Constance Smith interrupted from where she still sat upon the bench. Everyone, Jackson included, stopped to listen to her. In a way, she had become their real leader.

"It's difficult to remember exactly what happened," she continued. "One minute, Nunn was leading us to his hut. Perhaps we even stepped inside. And then?"

No one tried to explain the rush of events that had followed.

"I can't argue that Nunn can do remarkable things," Mills answered after a moment of silence. "But he only seems to be able to do them for a very short period of time. Have you noticed that he limits his time among us, abruptly appearing and disappearing?"

Jackson rolled his eyes at that remark. "What are you talking about? So he can show up here whenever he wants to! And look what happened to Leo!" He smacked his fist against his open palm. "That guy Nunn can do anything!"

"That's certainly what he wants us to believe," Mills replied quickly. "But I think his entrances and exits are designed to startle us. He's obviously a man with great power in this place, but I don't know where his power ends and his sense of drama begins."

Mills looked at the unconvinced faces gathered around him. "Look. Mrs. Smith has been able to stand up to him, and she has barely begun to understand her own potential."

"We *are* out in the woods again," Joan agreed with the slightest of frowns. "Constance seems to have completely stopped whatever Nunn was doing to us."

Good old no-nonsense Joan. Of course she'd see what Mills was talking about. Now, if he could only convince the others, maybe they could do something constructive.

"And this time," Mills pointed out, "we're all alone."

Rose Dafoe turned to look outside their little group. "The soldiers are gone, aren't they?"

"Actually," Harold Dafoe admitted, "I'd feel better if the soldiers were here. They seemed to know when Nunn was going to do something. Why aren't they guarding us, anyway?"

"Perhaps it's because we actually beat Nunn," Mills insisted, "if only for a minute. I wonder if anybody's ever done that before. It might have been the one outcome he didn't expect."

"And how long will that last?" Jackson shot back. He started to pace again. "I imagine someone like Nunn doesn't make many mistakes."

"He seems able to show up whenever, and wherever, he wants to," added Harold Dafoe as his eyes followed the restless Jackson.

"I think Evan has a point," Constance Smith said softly. "Nunn is powerful—far too powerful for me. But he does seem to have his lapses. I think we'd be foolish if we didn't take advantage of them."

"Advantage?" Rose Dafoe asked. She patted nervously at her well-combed hair.

"Let's get out of here," Mills answered. "I say we leave here together. See if we can find the kids, and maybe even that fellow with a mustache who visited us last night."

"But look what Nunn did to Leo," Margaret Furlong insisted. "Won't Nunn get angry if we try to leave? What will he do then?"

"Poor Leo," Mills agreed. "I imagine Nunn will do that sort of thing to all of us if we stay here. And to our children as well, if he can catch them again."

Rose nodded her head at that; little, no-nonsense lines formed at the corners of her mouth. "I want my children back."

"We all do," Joan agreed. "Nunn hasn't been able to find them, either. Maybe, if we get out of his camp, he won't be able to find us."

Constance Smith considered this. "There may be some way to find the children, but only if we leave this place. There's something about this place where we stand that—isn't right."

"Nunn will kill us," Harold Dafoe whispered.

"There's no way to tell what will happen next in a place like this," Mrs. Smith continued. "The best we can do is guess. And not give up."

"Nunn rules through fear," Mills added. "If we let that fear overcome us, he's won."

"So what do we do," Jackson demanded, "just walk out of here?"

"I don't see anybody stopping us," Joan replied, looking sharply at Jackson. Mills was glad that others were getting annoyed with his attitude.

"I'm afraid somebody will have to help me," Mrs. Smith said, her tone suddenly apologetic. "I still can't walk very well."

Mills looked around, but saw no sign of the litter the soldiers had fashioned to bring Mrs. Smith here.

"We'll just have to take turns carrying you," Mills said with a smile. "Harold, why don't we put our arms together and give Constance a seat of honor?"

"Well," Harold murmured. He shuffled forward slowly, as if reluctant to do anything at all. "Where do you want my arms?"

Mills showed Dafoe how they could grasp each other's arms above the elbow to give Mrs. Smith a firm place to ride while distributing the weight between the two of them. It seemed to be the most dignified way to transport her. After a bit of fumbling, they got their arms organized and squatted before Mrs. Smith. Joan helped to guide the old woman the few steps from the bench to her new seat, and Mills and Dafoe rose to a standing position with her between them. They could probably travel some distance with her weight distributed like this. She was remarkably light. Mills guessed she couldn't weigh much above ninety pounds.

"Let's go, Harold," Mills said.

"I guess so," Dafoe agreed.

"Let's get out of here for good," his wife insisted. Harold tried to smile. Her resolve seemed to get him moving a little faster.

Jackson already started to pace ahead of them, while his silent wife held back with the rest of the group. Joan walked over to Margaret Furlong and helped her to stand and join them.

They started to walk toward the surrounding forest.

Harold grunted. "Trees are farther away than I thought."

"No, they're not," Mrs. Smith said from her perch between Dafoe and Mills. "The trees just aren't getting any closer."

"What are you talking about?" Jackson demanded from the front of the line.

"Carl?" she called to him. "Would you be willing to run on ahead to the edge of the woods? Maybe you can find an easy way in among the vines, or a trail we can take."

"Sure," Jackson replied with a bit of surprise. "I guess so." He trotted on ahead, twenty, fifty, a hundred feet.

The trees seemed farther away than they had before.

"What the hell?" Jackson yelled. He broke into a run, as if he might be able to catch the forest with speed.

"Carl!" Mrs. Smith called out. "Never mind! It's no use!"

Jackson broke off his charge and turned, taking great gasps to try to force air back into his lungs.

In half a dozen steps, he made it back to the group.

"What's going on here?" he said softly.

"It's another one of Nunn's illusions," Mrs. Smith replied. "I didn't realize it until now. I think we did enter his home, after all, and we're still there. He only fashioned the illusion of the camp to get us to relax."

"Have us let down our guard," Harold Dafoe added, looking quickly around as if he might catch a glimpse of what really surrounded them beneath the illusion. "Why did I listen to you? What's Nunn going to do to us now?"

"Nothing," Mills said. "He still isn't here, is he? He's left us here while he takes care of other things."

"Take care?" another voice called to them. "Oh, Nunn will take care of you, all right. Just—" The voice broke off in a fit of coughing.

A figure stepped out of the forest before them. It was the Captain. Mills hadn't recognized him at first. He looked like one of those emaciated famine victims you saw on the evening news. His shirt was gone, and so was his attitude. But the two scars still sat on his now sallow cheeks.

The Captain more staggered than walked as he approached. Mills half wanted to rush out and help the other man, but he imagined he'd get no closer to the Captain than he did to the trees.

The Captain looked up at the neighbors. His smile no longer held any hint of certainty. "Have to—sit," he managed. His legs shook, then collapsed beneath him, throwing him to the ground. He groaned.

"Oh, God," Dafoe whispered. "This is what's going to happen to all of us!"

Somehow the Captain pushed himself up to a sitting position. "An interesting coincidence—" he managed. "Finding you here. I imagine—you're looking for a way out—as well."

Mills stepped forward. As he suspected, the Captain grew no closer. Still, even if they couldn't meet, maybe their old adversary could give them some information.

"Captain?" Mills called. "Where are we?"

"Um? Now?" A spasm of pain crossed the Captain's face before he continued. "In a room. Just another one of Nunn's rooms. He has so many rooms."

"So we are in his fortress? Nunn's castle?" Mills didn't know what to call it.

"Just another room," the Captain answered. "Nunn's saving you."

"What?" Jackson demanded. "What do you mean—saving?"

"Maybe that isn't so bad," Dafoe added hastily.

The Captain tried to laugh but ended up coughing. "You are kept very safe. He has uses for all of you. Just like he used me."

His head fell back as his body was racked by another spasm.

"Using me. Made a little mistake. Never should shoot some-one—without permission."

Mills tried to make sense from the Captain's ramblings. "Nunn is punishing you for shooting Sayre?"

"Never should," the other man agreed. "Bad Captain." His lips trembled as he tried to smile. "So I'm bringing him back."

Constance Smith quickly asked the next question. "Bringing him back? What do you mean?"

The Captain spasmed again, but when he spoke this time, his voice was stronger.

"I know about all of you. You stood by while they did those things to me."

"What things?" Rose Dafoe asked. "I don't understand."

The Captain's voice rose to a shriek. "Not a single one of you cared about what happened to my lawn!"

"His lawn?" Jackson called back in disbelief.

"My lawn!" the Captain continued at the same fever pitch. "All these years of work! But did you care? I knew you were laughing behind my back." He pushed himself off the ground and rose unsteadily. "I'll show you what happens to people who laugh at me!" He shook his fists as he swayed before them. "A bunch of scum, bringing the neighborhood down!"

"That's Hyram." Constance Smith softly confirmed what they all were thinking. "Hyram Sayre."

Rose Dafoe looked at the older woman. "You mean he isn't dead?"

Her husband laughed nervously. "I think he's worse than dead."

"I'm coming to get all of you!" the Captain screamed.

Mills looked at the others. "Not if we can get out of here first."

"Nunn did this!" Dafoe shouted, working himself to a state close to the Captain's. "He's going to make us all like that!"

"As long as we're here," Mills replied, "all we'll see is Nunn's work."

"Then we have to leave," Mrs. Smith said firmly from where she still sat in the men's arms.

"How?" Dafoe demanded. "When Nunn can twist everything we see."

"We'll simply leave without using our eyes," Mrs. Smith replied. "Or our feet. I might be able to do something, now that I know about the nature of this place. But not by anything as simple as walking, my, no. Dear, you should put me down. I must be getting heavy."

Mills and Dafoe carried her back to the bench, a half dozen steps away.

"I'll have to think a minute," Mrs. Smith admitted once she was back on her bench. "This is all a bit too new to me."

"All right," Rose Dafoe agreed, looking almost as nervous as her husband. "But please hurry, would you, Constance?"

"My lawn!" the Captain howled. He reached his hands out toward the neighbors as he stumbled forward.

"Maybe there's some other way we can help Constance," Mills said as he studied the forest. "Nunn's done his best to scare us, then left us to look at this illusion." He turned back to look at the confused faces of the neighbors. "And then there's this— thing in front of us—this fellow who may or may not be the Captain. Do you believe he just stumbled in here? I don't think so. This is all supposed to scare us." He waved back at the surrounding woods. "I wonder if this stuff around us is kept up by our fear?"

"What kind of line are you trying to feed us now?" Jackson demanded.

"Maybe," Mills persisted, "if we were to stop being afraid, this fake forest would disappear. We could simply walk out of this place."

"An interesting theory," another man's voice said behind Mills. "Pity it is wrong."

Mills turned around. Nunn had returned.

The Captain started to laugh, a rasping sound that again degenerated into a coughing fit.

Harold Dafoe made a noise like something was caught in his throat. "We didn't mean anything!" he shouted. "We were just trying to—to—"

"Escape," Nunn replied calmly. "I don't particularly blame you. I haven't exactly been the perfect host. And, while you may not entirely agree with my methods, you don't have enough information to realize that what lies beyond these walls can be so much worse."

The forest faded away as he spoke, replaced by bare stone walls.

Margaret Furlong pushed herself forward. "Worse? What could be worse than what you did to Leo?"

That only made Nunn smile. The dark orbs where his eyes should be opened wide with innocence. "Really? What did I do to Leo?"

He shuddered slightly. When he spoke again, it was with a different voice.

"Margaret? Can you hear me?"

Margaret stared at the wizard's mouth. "No," she said.

"Margaret," the unmistakably nasal tones of Leo Furlong continued. "I'm sorry we fought so much. Having this happen to me has made me see things so much differently."

As Nunn talked, his face changed. It was rounder, the severe cheekbones replaced by pudgier circles of flesh, his nose no longer straight but slightly crooked, just like Leo's.

"Leo?" Margaret asked softly. "But I thought—"

"That I was dead?" Leo laughed, a dry sound. "So did I, for a while. But this isn't death. It's something much stranger. And it may be wonderful." His voice rose, both wistful and excited at the same time. "I wish I could explain it to you. Margaret, I wish I could explain so many things."

Didn't she realize that Nunn was trying to confuse them? To demoralize them?

"Margaret!" Mills called. "Don't be fooled. It couldn't be!"

"No, Evan," Constance Smith said solemnly. "Actually, somehow it could. Every new feeling in me tells me that voice does belong to Leo. Somehow he's now a part of Nunn."

The Leo-thing smiled. "Thank you, Constance. I knew you'd understand."

Margaret began to cry again.

"What are we going to do?" Joan asked.

"Yes, what are you to do?" the Captain called from the far corner of the room. "No matter what you try, you will pay!" He took three steps toward the others, steps that seemed to bring him nearer at last. Nunn, his face suddenly his own, glanced at the emaciated soldier. The Captain froze, midstep.

"Sorry for this inconvenience," the wizard remarked with a gracious smile. "Even for someone like me, there will be an occasional loose end. But I, too, believe it's time for a decision. Will you work with me"—he paused, his smile fading slightly—"or not?"

Jackson sneered at everyone, as if there was only one choice. "We've got to join him. Look at his power. He can get us anything we want."

"You heard him," Harold Dafoe agreed. "If we don't join him, he's going to kill us, do whatever he did to Leo."

"Leo," Margaret said in a voice that was little more than a monotone. "What am I going to do without Leo? People thought we fought all the time. Oh, nobody understood!"

"I would like to consider my options," Mrs. Smith remarked coolly.

Nunn's smile grew even broader. "And give you a chance to get away? I think the time for your little surprises is over."

"What can we do?" Dafoe asked those around him. "He's strong enough to kill us all."

Evan Mills stepped forward from the group. "I think, then, that we should get ready to die."

"No, Evan!" Mrs. Smith called. "I can do what we talked about."

"You're not doing anything," Nunn said. Small lights danced in his dark eye sockets. "I've had enough interference from a pitiful old crone."

"What?" Mrs. Smith called. "Keep away!" She swatted at the air around her, as if surrounded by insects. Her body shook. The wrinkles on her face and hands grew into spiderwebs of age. Her cheeks hollowed, her teeth retreated into her gums, until her skin was no more than a thin parchment coating over her skull. She was withering away to nothing.

"Why are you hurting her?" Dafoe demanded. "We'll stay! We'll do whatever you want!"

"Of course we will," Jackson agreed. "We'll work together, just like you said!"

Margaret looked guiltily at the others around her. "I'm staying with him, too. I have to stay—for Leo."

Mrs. Smith's eyes had sunken deep into their sockets. Worms crawled from the empty holes.

"No!" Mills screamed. "I won't let this happen!"

Constance Smith raised her hand to brush at her face. She stood, her legs unsteady at first. She took a deep breath and stood up straight as a soldier. "We will not let this happen, Evan."

"You will not let anything happen, crone," Nunn retorted, "once you're dead."

Mrs. Smith cried out.

Mills couldn't stand this anymore. He rushed toward the wizard.

"Evan!" Joan Blake called out as Mills ran headlong for Nunn. Everything was moving faster and faster.

The Captain groaned and shook himself. He was no longer frozen. He put his foot down, one step closer. The crazy glaze in his eyes had been replaced by anger.

"I will not be taken over by someone else!" He spoke between clenched teeth as he, too, headed for Nunn. "If I'm going to die, let it be as a soldier!"

Nunn's hands, both stretched out toward Constance Smith, began to shake.

"No!" Nunn shouted back at all around. "This won't happen. I am too good for this!"

"Enough of this nonsense," Constance said calmly. She looked over at the other neighbors, once again her sixty-year-old self. "Shall we try to leave?"

"I have only begun!" Nunn shouted back.

"Then begin with me!" Evan shouted as he jumped for the wizard. Evan's hands went around Nunn's throat. But they passed on through, as Evan's forward momentum carried him into the wizard, his arms and legs first, then his torso and head disappearing within Nunn's robes, as if Evan Mills was being sucked inside the other's form.

"Evan?" Joan called out again.

The wizard's eye sockets were filled with white light. Nunn screamed.

"Who is with me?" Constance Smith called. "Now!"

What was Constance saying? Joan was with her, no matter what.

Nunn, and the room around him, disappeared.

⊙ Twenty-eight

Mary Lou woke with a start. She hadn't remembered even feeling tired.

She couldn't have slept for long. The sun still hadn't reached too high in the sky. It was midmorning at the latest. The last she remembered, the prince had been there with her, talking about how the People were so excited about some upcoming Ceremony that involved her, too. She had hardly thought about that Ceremony at all, though, because of the prince; her prince, who now seemed able to come whenever she called, as if she had broken through whatever spell controlled him.

Why had she slept, then? She studied the branches overhead with half-closed eyes. Exhaustion, maybe. She had only dozed the night before, especially with all that had happened with the prince.

The People had given her something to drink. More of that fruit juice from the night before. Had that put her to sleep?

Did this have anything to do with the Ceremony?

She was suddenly very wide awake. The Ceremony, so distant in the early morning hours, seemed more real with every moment the sun climbed up in the sky.

She had no idea what the People wanted to do with these planned festivities. All sorts of things could happen with something like this. She saw how brutal the People could be with that other tribe, and how they had hurled spears and arrows at her fellow humans. Why were they being so kind to their Mary Lou?

A chorus of the People called out her name.

She pushed herself up on her elbows. The tribe stood in a circle around her sleeping place, all maybe ten feet from her. The words "a respectful distance" came into her head.

The two People who acted as healers each held one-half of the leaf cast in their hands. She looked down and saw they had

196

taken it from her ankle. The healing must be complete. The tribe shouted out her name three times in triumph.

Mary Lou smiled. What did she have to worry about from the People and their Ceremony? Why would they plan to harm her after going to such pains to help her heal?

The Chieftain took her hand. His skin was very warm and very dry. Where it rubbed against the skin of her own palm, it scraped ever so slightly, a bit like being licked by a cat's tongue. The Chieftain pulled at her, calling out her singsong name again. The People responded in kind.

Mary Lou realized they wanted her to stand up.

She let the Chieftain's strong grip pull her into a sitting position. He was very strong for one so small. Letting go of his hand (*Merrilu!*), she gathered her legs beneath her (*Merrilu!*) and carefully stood up on the platform (*Merrilu! Merrilu!*).

She wondered if this could be the beginning of the Ceremony the prince had told her about. The way the People celebrated her every movement, could she even tell if something special was about to happen?

When the cries died down, Mary Lou realized there was one voice crying out something completely different. Something high and quick, like words of warning.

"Lodda!" the Chieftain announced abruptly.

"Dobble!" the others called back. "Lodda!"

The People moved quickly, and silently, away from her.

Before she could really wonder why, she heard another voice, calling her name as it should be called.

"Mary Lou!" The voice cracked as it shouted. "Mary Lou!" It sounded like Bobby from the neighborhood.

"Bobby!" she called back, walking to the edge of the platform. She felt no pain at all in her ankle.

"Yeah!" Bobby called. "She's up there, all right!"

"Okay, shrimp!" a second voice said. It was Todd. He'd found her again. "Mary Lou! We want to talk to you. We understand you're not alone. Can you convince the others that we won't hurt you?"

Mary Lou squinted through the leaves. She couldn't see anything of the ground through the heavy foliage.

"Todd!" Bobby more shrieked than called.

"Mary Lou!" Todd added. "Could you call your little bloodhounds off? We just want to talk! Shit!"

She saw the People now, swarming through the branches beneath her, bows and quivers in their hands. Occasionally, one would stop to fit an arrow to its bow and shoot it toward the ground below.

"No!" she called to the People directly below her. "Don't do it! No!"

The People paid no attention to her. They were totally immersed in their attack.

"Christ!" Todd called with rising panic. "They're everywhere. We gotta go!"

"No!" Mary Lou shouted at the top of her voice. "Why don't you listen to me!"

Somewhere in the distance, she heard a group of the People chant her name like a battle cry.

"No!" Mary Lou replied. "Shut up! I don't want to have anything to do with you again!"

"Then why don't you leave?" a deep voice said at her side.

With the first word, she knew it was the prince. He smiled at her. He seemed to come more quickly every time she needed him. This time she didn't even remember calling his name.

"Could I?" she asked.

"You seem to be healed," he replied gently. "And I know where all the People are. It is one of the advantages of my earlier condition. I think we could avoid them, easily, if we move quickly. The People seem very intent on driving your friends away."

She hadn't realized, until that moment, how much she really wanted to get out of there. "Then I can get down to my friends?"

The prince considered this for an instant before answering. "Perhaps, eventually. For now, I think we need to take a way down that gives us some distance from the People's battle."

Her name echoed in the distance as hundreds of high voices sang it in triumph.

At that instant, Mary Lou thought she would be happy if she never heard her name again. "Let's go, then."

"We must leave from the far corner of the platform," the prince said with a mischievous grin. "Come, I will walk beside you."

"I've never seen you walk," Mary Lou mentioned as they crossed the logs.

"Well, I could float, I suppose, or pop in and out of existence every fifty feet or so," the prince agreed. "The act of walking, though, seems so human. It feels so free." He laughed out loud. "It also feels rather good to do something to the People rather than for them."

"Were they horrible to you? I mean the People?" Mary Lou would hate them twice as much if they had done bad things to the prince.

"Oh, no, they were neither particularly bad nor good. To have them treat me one way or another, they'd have to consider me a thinking, feeling being." He shook his head. Mary Lou thought she could see anger behind his smile. "I've been their slave, a tool, really, to use when they see fit and to ignore the rest of the time. I am finally—*finally!*—doing something from my own choice." He threw his arms open to the trees before him. "Let me tell you, the illusion of free will is a wonderful thing."

"Illusion?" Mary Lou asked with a frown.

"That sounds cynical, no doubt." The prince tossed his head up toward the sky, a chuckle in his throat. "Every hour since you called me, I remember more. Especially, I remembered the dragon. When you are dealing with a power as strong as that, all questions of free will are doubtful."

"The dragon?" Mary Lou looked into the prince's transparent eyes. "What does the dragon want?"

"There are still some things I can't remember. Or perhaps things I never knew." The prince turned away. "But here's our escape route." He waved at a rope bridge before them, another of the People's pathways to the world below.

"Where are the People?" Mary Lou asked. She could no longer hear her name.

"They seem to be pursuing the others," the prince replied. "It will give us a few extra minutes to get away."

Mary Lou hoped that Bobby and Todd would be all right. She'd never forgive herself if something happened to them while they were trying to rescue her.

But there was nothing else she could do but leave. The People certainly wouldn't listen to her. She had to be in charge of her own life now. And maybe she could learn something more about the prince.

The young man in blue led the way across the tree path that spiraled down toward the forest floor. His feet never quite touched the bark and branches that they passed over. She was glad he made the effort to act like the human he used to be. It was a nice way for them to feel closer.

As they descended, the prince pointed out things near the path: the leaves the People used for Mary Lou's cast, the call of a certain bird renowned for its plumage, the manner in which many of the limbs of the great trees grew out almost horizontally, so that they could walk with little difficulty along the People's road. It seemed to take no time at all to reach the forest floor. Mary Lou truly enjoyed listening to the sound of the prince's voice. And he often seemed as surprised as Mary Lou by the information he had at his command.

"Obviously," he said as they reached the lowest branches of the tree road, "I was once a person of some learning."

"I imagine your earlier life must have been fascinating!" Mary Lou enthused. "I hope you remember all of it soon."

The prince's smile seemed a little strained. "Let's hope I don't remember something that I don't want to know." He pointed to the thick vines that hung to the forest floor. "But now it's time to stop walking and start descending."

Mary Lou knelt on the great branch. Her fingers barely touched when she put her hands around the nearest vine. She supposed she could shinny down one of these things, just like a rope in gym class.

"I'll meet you below," the prince announced abruptly. Then he was gone.

Mary Lou swung down on the vine quickly, afraid that if she took too long she might lose him. These past few hours, when the prince and she had had a chance to be alone, she had been as happy as she'd ever been, either here or back in the neighborhood.

She half climbed, half slipped down the vine, reaching the ground in only a minute. It had been growing darker as they descended from the People's stronghold. Now, on the forest floor, it seemed like dusk, even though it was far closer to noon.

"Prince?" she called.

"Here I am," a voice called back, but it seemed to come from everywhere, the great tree boles, the hanging vines, the leaf-strewn ground. "I could be a part of everything—"

His voice faded as he spoke.

"—or I could be right by your side," his voice said, suddenly strong. She looked to her right and saw her prince with his ever-present smile.

Mary Lou shivered. In a place like this, she wouldn't mind if her prince was a little more solid. "I wish we could get out of these woods. This darkness is creepy."

"Maybe you'd like to go home?"

She glanced at her companion. Prince or no prince, part of her would.

"Maybe we can find a way," the prince added gently. "I wish I could remember more!"

He looked down at his transparent hands. He chuckled, deep in his throat.

"I don't have to stay here, either. You've let me break free of whatever held me there. I can go and find out where I come from, who I truly am. Oh, God, to be free of everyone!"

And with that, he was gone again.

"Prince?" Mary Lou called. "What are you doing? Is this your idea of a joke?"

There was no answer.

"Prince?" Mary Lou didn't like this. "I have to find Todd and Bobby! I need your help! I don't know where I am!"

She only heard the sound of the wind, blowing the leaves far overhead.

"It's dark here!" she called, hearing the panic rise with every word. "Don't leave me alone!"

There was a sudden flare of light before her. Mary Lou threw her hand in front of her eyes. When she looked again, the light had shrunk and taken on a two-legged form.

"Ah, dear Mary Lou," Zachs purred. "I'll be very happy to light your way."

○ Twenty-nine

Nunn screamed.

This one, this human, this Evan Mills, had invaded his body. The fire he gained when he took life was no longer sweet. It was devastating. Pain shot from the core of his bones, as if his skeleton would shatter into a thousand pieces, ripping his flesh apart in a great explosion of organs and blood.

"No!" the magician called. And he heard the voice of Evan Mills inside his own, the pain of Evan Mills a part of his pain. This human had somehow thrown himself within Nunn with no idea of what he had done. But Nunn had knowledge, and the knowledge would let him survive. He opened his palms, and the dragon eyes that hid within there rose to the surface of his flesh.

"I will not die!" he screamed, but it was still both voices, crying out not so much in unison as in confrontation. But no one could overcome the power of the dragon within him. The second fire flowed through his body to consume the first, the cleansing heat swallowing the pain and absorbing that entity within that had once been Evan Mills, breaking that one defiant voice into a dozen, a hundred, a thousand smaller voices, each one less able to cry out against the wizard, against the fire, against the hack and hew, as his soul was sundered into a thousand bits, and the voices could not be heard at all, and only the energy remained.

Yes, much better. Yes. Nunn looked up and banished the Captain with a wave of his hand. Pity he still had enough energy for insolence. It wouldn't last long.

Nunn saw three of the neighbors before him: Carl Jackson, trying to stand before the onslaught; Margaret Furlong and Harold Dafoe, cringing before what they saw. He had uses for someone like Jackson. With the Captain busy elsewhere, his troops could use a new leader. Jackson seemed vain and cruel enough to be ideal. And the others? Well, Nunn could use anyone, one way or another.

But the others. They had left. No one had ever escaped from him before. Not that he couldn't pursue them, capture them all over again. But he had never found anyone to be so problematic as this batch of newcomers.

This time the dragon had outdone itself.

Obar smelled blood.

A wave of his hand, and his portable sun returned.

There, in front of him, were two carcasses, two hollow shells that had once been wolves before they had all of their blood drained away. Their draining was so complete that Obar was a bit surprised there was an odor of blood left to smell.

Still, a wizard's senses were sharp, at least some of the time. Nick and the sword had certainly passed this way. So where was the boy now?

Obar was about to call Nick's name when he realized he wasn't alone. No, it wasn't the boy, unless he had learned to transport himself by magic. For Obar always knew when magic was around. Something in the air, he thought. And that something was directly behind him.

The magician snapped off the sun. Obar wouldn't be caught that easily. He squeezed the dragon's eye deep within his robes, letting the fire fill his veins.

Leap, he thought.

And he leapt some hundreds of yards into the woods.

He turned, hoping to seek out his adversary at a safe distance.

Except his adversary was no longer back where Obar had come from. The magician sensed that same tingling of sorcery, once again behind him.

The fire of the dragon was still within him. He waved his hands in a quick protection spell as he turned to look at what followed him.

An old woman, glowing faintly with a light of her own, stood before him in a pink housecoat. She smiled at him.

"Excuse me," she said with a slight nod of her head. "I didn't mean to startle you. You did leave a very pretty trail. I thought it would be a shame not to follow it."

"I see—pardon?" Obar replied. Quite frankly, he didn't see at all. "You followed my trail across the forest?"

"Well, eventually," she admitted with the slightest little grin.

As the woman talked, Obar realized he had seen her before. She was one of the neighbors he had visited the other night with the ice cream wagon. He had hoped that wagon was an appropriate choice—and they had seemed to trust him, at least a little. Damn that meddling Nunn and his two dragon's eyes! You had to be careful when your opponent had twice the firepower you did. But this woman—she looked quite different with this inward glow; far less frail than before, for one thing. Obviously, life in this place had begun to bring out her talents.

"You see," she continued, and then paused again.

Constance Smith, yes, that was her name. Obar made a point of remembering names. When you were in his line of work, so many things passed your way that you simply had to forget some of them.

"I found myself someplace else," she went on. "I'm afraid I'm not explaining this very well."

Obar smiled and nodded. Sometimes there was no explaining magic, even to yourself.

"We were getting away from this Nunn person," Mrs. Smith explained. "And I've discovered a way to—well, remove myself from a place and then deposit myself someplace else. This is the first time I've ever brought others along with me, though." One of her hands fluttered protectively before her throat. "Oh, dear, I'm afraid I'm a little giddy here. Should I be telling you all this?"

She got away from Nunn? Yes, this woman had considerable talents.

"Please," Obar encouraged. "We have met before, you know."

"We have?" Her frown was replaced by a sudden grin. "The ice cream man! I'm so sorry. Sometimes it's difficult to recognize someone when you're in a new situation. And I'm certainly in a new situation!"

"It is nice to see you again," Obar replied, trying to bring the conversation into some kind of focus. He had much the same problem with magic sometimes, as if he had far too much on his mind for one thought to follow another. "But you were telling me how you followed my trail?"

"Yes, once I had brought myself—and the others, of course—to this other place, wherever it is, I saw a brilliant trail streaking past me. It really was lovely, you know. I couldn't help but follow and see where it led."

"Well, thank you," Obar replied, a bit more flustered than he had expected. Until this moment, he had no idea any of his spells left a trail. "And that's how you found yourself here?"

"Precisely," she agreed.

There was still something bothering him. "And you said you brought others?" he asked.

"Well, I have, and I haven't." She smiled again, rather like a child telling a secret. "You'll have to forgive me, but I had to wait until I thought things were safe. But I can't leave them waiting, can I?" She waved up at the trees overhead. "Rebecca? Rose? Joan? Can you hear me?"

Three women floated down from the branches to land beside Constance Smith.

"Only four of you?" Nunn asked.

"Some of the others stayed behind," a short blonde woman announced. Joan Blake, Obar recalled. "I think they were too afraid of Nunn."

"My husband, Carl, is back there," a pale woman with dark hair added. The way she stared at the ground with her shoulders slumped forward, she looked like she didn't want to be here. Obar wondered if she wanted to be anywhere. Rebecca Jackson, that was her name. "He thinks Nunn has all the answers."

"My husband stayed behind, too," the third, well-groomed woman added very quickly, almost as if she wanted to dismiss what had happened. "I don't know why. Harold always wants to do the right thing."

"Margaret Furlong remained behind, too," Constance Smith added. "Poor thing. She was quite distraught. Nunn did something to her husband."

"He ate him!" Rebecca said with surprising vehemence.

"Did the same thing happen to Evan?" Joan asked.

"I don't know," Constance admitted. "Somehow I sensed that was a little different. I don't think we'll see Evan again."

"So Nunn has taken two of you?" His brother wizard absorbed the energy of others when his own needed replenishing. So much more efficient than eating or drinking. Or so he claimed. Obar repressed a shudder.

"I'm glad he hasn't taken more," Obar added after a moment's pause. "Maybe, now that you're here, we can all work together. Actually, I came here to find one of your sons."

The three younger women all looked at him.

"Nick Blake," Constance said suddenly. "Yes. I'll fetch him now."

She disappeared. How, Obar wondered, could she locate Nick when he was still having trouble unraveling Nunn's spells? Of course, he knew the answer. He just didn't want to admit it.

The dragon brought people here it could use, people with wild talents that the beast could mold to its own purpose. When Obar and Nunn had come here, so very long ago, both of them had had a certain innate sense of the second world that existed here, that invisible web of the dragon's power which covered all of the seven islands. This Constance Smith had the same sense, but much more finely tuned than any of those who had gone before her. Nunn and Obar had had to teach themselves the way of the dragon. This Constance seemed ready to walk the web as if she was born to it.

Obar and Nunn had had to grow into their power. What would Constance be able to do once she had discovered the nuances of the dragon?

Obar suddenly felt very cold. Perhaps this time the dragon would truly get its way.

"The children," one of the other women was saying. Obar snapped from his reverie. It was Rose Dafoe. "What about the other children?"

"Oh, yes," Obar replied, doing his best to collect himself. "They have all had adventures, but I believe them all to be reasonably safe. Todd and Bobby are with some friends who have gone to fetch Mary Lou. And Jason is with two of the best guardians one can find in this place. No, we'll all be together soon."

Constance Smith popped back into their midst, the displaced air making a soft *whump* with her arrival. Soon, Obar imagined, she'd learn to silence that as well. A visibly upset Nick stood by her side.

"I'm sorry it took me a minute to get him back," Constance said softly. "But he was afraid to come at first. Something about not trusting his sword."

"Nick!" his mother called.

"Mom!" he said, the sound more of a gasp of pain than a word. "I don't know!" he murmured. "Have to be—so careful!" He walked slowly toward his mother, his hand firmly pushing the hilt of his sword down into its scabbard.

"I told him not to worry," Constance continued. "Whatever problems we have, we'll find a way to correct them."

Obar was afraid that she was right. So right that it might destroy all his carefully laid plans. He rather liked this Constance Smith and her no-nonsense attitude toward this world she found herself in.

It would be a shame if he had to destroy her.

⭕ Thirty

The tree man stopped abruptly in front of Jason.

"Danger," the Oomgosh said.

Jason froze. He wished the Oomgosh would tell him what to do. He always felt better when someone else led the way.

Charlie growled at his side. His eyes seemed to glow in this strange half-light.

"Good boy, Charlie," Jason whispered. "We'll get whatever it is."

"It is three short, red-furred creatures," the Oomgosh explained. "They are not from here." He paused, listening. "They are tired and frightened. They have recently lost a battle. And they have weapons."

"What do you mean, they're not from here?" Jason asked. "Do they come from the same place I do?"

The Oomgosh shook his great, leafy head. "They come from another of the islands. There are seven of them, clustered together in this part of the world. They are home to a number of different peoples. And not all those people are friendly."

Jason started when he heard something crashing through the forest. "Should we hide?"

"We could try to avoid them if they were not so close. For someone my size, hiding is a difficulty."

The Oomgosh paused and frowned again. "Raven should know of this. I will inform the trees."

Charlie started to bark furiously.

Three red-furred creatures came running from between the trees. They hunched forward as they ran, their long arms almost touching the ground, so that they looked more like apes than men. The lead creature shrieked as it looked ahead, as if it never expected anything like the Oomgosh.

"Enemy!" the red fur exclaimed, waving at Jason and the others with a short spear.

"We do not have to be," the Oomgosh replied calmly.

"All here are enemies!" the red fur insisted. Its two fellows seemed to shriek in agreement. The three things looked ready to attack.

"Stand behind me," the Oomgosh told Jason. Jason did as he was told, wishing he could do more. Obar had given Nick a sword. Why hadn't he given something better to Jason?

Charlie strained forward, his bark turning to a growl deep in his throat. Jason knelt down, putting his arms around the dog's neck and chest. "Charlie," he whispered. "Stay. Please stay."

The dog looked up at him, even wagged his tale slightly. but he didn't stop growling.

"We do not wish to harm you," the tree man said to the others. "Why don't you go home?"

"Home?" The leader of the ape-things grabbed its spear with both hands. "We have no more home. We have been defeated. Nunn no longer needs us."

At the mention of the magician's name, the Oomgosh stiffened, looking even taller and firmer than before. "Ah, Nunn."

"We must kill or be killed!" the leader cried.

"Kill!" one of his companions shouted. All three repeated the word together. "Kill!"

"Let us be done with this, then," the Oomgosh remarked, stepping forward with one of his great, root-shaped feet. "And let the forest return to peace. Do what you must. Not, of course, that I can be killed."

The three red furs launched their spears. One fell far short; the second landed only inches from Jason and Charlie. The third flew straight for the Oomgosh. He lifted his arm before his face. The spear embedded itself there with a solid sound, like metal lodged in wood.

"You are dead!" the lead creature shouted in triumph. "Poison stick! Poison stick!"

"The Oomgosh does not die," was the tree man's reply. "The same cannot be said for those who no longer hold weapons."

As if all three followed some hidden command, the red-furred things reached for their waists. Jason realized each wore a belt, partially hidden by their coats.

"We have our knives," the leader remarked as all three waved short but jagged blades. "We have our teeth. We will tear you apart."

The Oomgosh laughed as he moved more quickly toward his

enemy. "Would you tear a tree apart with your teeth? Run away, little men, while you—"

The tree man stopped suddenly, bending forward like a sapling beaten by the wind. He groaned.

"The poison begins!" the red leader cheered. "We have killed you!"

The Oomgosh shuddered as he once again stood erect. "Then the least I can do is return the favor."

The tree man stepped forward again. His movement seemed to set Charlie off as well, as the dog leapt forward with a tremendous growl.

Jason was left alone behind them. He clutched the small knife Obar had given him. He would fight these creatures off with his bare hands if he had to.

The creatures ran forward. One leapt for the Oomgosh. The tree man swatted it away with the arm that still held the spear. The Oomgosh stepped forward quickly, placing his great foot on the fallen creature's chest. Bone snapped as the Oomgosh pushed down, collapsing the thing's rib cage beneath his great weight.

Jason looked down at the spear embedded in the ground before him. He didn't have to use his bare hands.

Charlie ran to meet the second of the rushing things. The dog leapt toward the creature's chest, his teeth reaching for the red thing's throat. The creature threw its arms out at the dog, trying to fend off the attack. Charlie's snapping jaws latched onto one of those arms. Both dog and ape-thing were surrounded by a flash of crimson light, a glow so intense that Jason almost thought the creature of light was visiting them again.

The third thing was rushing toward Jason. He dropped the knife and grabbed the spear, pulling it from the earth with both hands, and turning it quickly so that the poisoned point faced his attacker.

The thing made no attempt to veer away, instead throwing itself forward so that the spear took it straight in the stomach.

"This is far better," the creature remarked, its voice calmer than before. "We no longer have to live, defeated. Now we die." The thing went suddenly rigid, its arms reaching for the spear. Then that, too, passed, and the thing slumped. Jason let go of the spear. The lifeless creature fell to the ground.

Jason looked up from his fallen foe and saw that the crimson light had vanished from around Charlie. The dog now stood above a withered, blackened thing, like some corpse rescued from a fire. He barked joyfully, as if this was a great game.

The Oomgosh was not so happy. He swayed back and forth

above his dead foe, like a tree cut through at its base and ready to fall.

"Jason," his deep voice called, far less forceful than usual. "I need assistance."

Jason rushed over to the tree man's side.

The Oomgosh nodded to the ground. "Take the knife."

Jason looked down to see one of the red furs' short knives lying near its former owner. It was much longer and sharper than the one he discarded. He bent down and grabbed the hilt in his hand.

"Good," the Oomgosh continued as Jason straightened again. "Now cut off the limb."

The tree man held his arm forward. Except that it no longer looked like an arm. It had shriveled and blackened, like a branch riddled with disease.

"We must get rid of the poison before it spreads," the Oomgosh urged. "Cut it now!"

Jason swallowed. How could he use a knife on a friend?

The Oomgosh moaned. "In a few days, the limb will return," he managed.

"It'll grow back?" Jason asked.

"The Oomgosh's limb will—grow again." The words were coming more slowly from the tree man's lips. "Now cut!"

Jason grabbed onto that part of the arm which still resembled human muscle. The skin was rough and hard beneath his fingers. He took the saw-toothed edge of the knife and ran it across the tough skin. It split easily.

"Good," the Oomgosh managed. He made a constant noise, like a low, mournful hum. Jason wondered if that was something the tree man did to keep from screaming. The sawing motion of the knife went quickly. There seemed to be no bone in this arm at all.

Jason's mouth was completely dry. Sweat from his forehead ran into his eyes. But he had to keep on sawing—otherwise, even someone as big as the Oomgosh would die.

Suddenly, the knife broke through the hard skin below, and the withered arm fell away. The Oomgosh gasped. There was no blood. Instead, the stump oozed something thick and green.

"It will stop in a moment," the tree man said. "I thank you. The trees thank you." With that, the Oomgosh closed his eyes and was still as the forest around him.

Jason stood there for a long moment, trying to get his heart to stop beating so fast. He heard the rustle of leaves in the trees above him. Was this the way the forest spoke?

He wiped the green liquid from the knife with his shirttail. Now that he'd used the knife like this, he figured it was his to keep. He walked a few feet away from the red-furred corpse and the withered limb. But only a few feet. He had no energy left. He sat heavily against one of the great trees.

He felt something wet. Charlie was licking him, as if nothing at all was wrong.

Except, when Jason looked up to the dog's eyes, the deep brown pupils had been replaced by two orbs of glowing red.

◯ Thirty-one

"Pretty Mary Lou," the creature of light whispered. "Let me touch you."

"Keep away," she replied in a much louder voice. "If you don't, you'll be sorry." Mary Lou looked to either side, her eyes only leaving Zachs for a second. She didn't even know what she was looking for. If only the prince would come back. Or the People. Or anybody.

When she looked back, the creature was much closer.

"Your smooth skin would feel so good beneath my fingers," the creature murmured softly. "Your long hair would be so lustrous, reflected in my light. Let me caress you. My light will surround you."

She stared at him, afraid that if she looked away again he would overwhelm her. "I have friends here!" The softer Zachs' voice became, the louder hers was in reply. "They'll make you sorry you were ever born!"

"I wasn't born—exactly," Zachs continued, his glowing form gliding across the forest floor. "How could I ever be sorry around someone like you? You don't know how good you can feel, until we get really close."

The creature reached out an amber finger. Mary Lou jerked her arm away.

"No!" she shrieked. "Help me!"

"Some creatures can certainly be tiresome," the prince said by her ear.

Mary Lou was so grateful that she almost collapsed. Her rescuer had returned. This time it felt like he came straight out of a fairy tale!

"You!" Zachs screamed.

"Then we've met?" the prince inquired.

The creature made shooing motions with its bright orange hands. "You're supposed to be dead!"

"No doubt I am," the prince replied smoothly. "Pity for you that I'm still around." He chuckled. "I almost went exploring, until I sensed you in the neighborhood. One has so many choices when one is granted his freedom."

"How could you know?" the creature whined. "No one knows! Zachs is fast. Zachs is clever. Zachs is silent."

The prince shook his head. "We are more similar than you think. A creature like you lives partially in my world as well." He took a step toward Zachs. "That is, if you can call this living."

"Prince!" Mary Lou shouted, surprised at her own confidence. "Make him tell you who you are!"

"Prince?" Zachs asked. The creature tried to laugh, but its voice shook so much it came out as a strangled choke. "You are no prince!"

"No doubt I've had a promotion," the prince replied slowly. "Don't you think it's time you bowed down before royalty?"

"Zachs bows for no one!" The creature's light flared and dimmed as its voice grew more disturbed. "Zachs will leave you all behind!"

"Why don't you try to disappear?" The prince's smile grew. "I know exactly where you go. I'm much more comfortable in that realm than this."

"You will have to catch Zachs!" the creature demanded. It waved its arms about wildly, like a two-year-old trying to fight. "He who catches Zachs catches Nunn!"

"It's everything I hoped for," the prince replied.

Zachs shrieked and disappeared. The prince silently vanished as well.

Mary Lou thought, before he left, her rescuer had winked at her.

She supposed that he had to go, to chase Zachs down so she wouldn't be threatened again. But now she was all alone again, lost in this perpetual forest twilight.

"Bobby!" she called, hoping that somebody she knew might be in hearing range. "Todd! Anyone?"

For one long moment, she was met with silence.

Then, in the distance, she heard another, shrill cry, one that she didn't want to hear again.

"Merrilu!"

She felt suddenly cold. The People had rescued her before, but for what purpose? Now that she was away from them, on her own on the forest floor, she couldn't let them take her again. Without the prince there by her side, she'd feel like a prisoner.

She thought the call came from somewhere behind her. She didn't dare call out again herself, for fear that she would lead the People right to her. She had to run, to get as far away from the People's village as she could, and hope that she found the neighbors somehow. Maybe, if she could just avoid the People long enough, the prince would return and help her find the way.

"Merrilu!"

This time the call sounded as if it had come somewhere far to her right. She kept on in the same direction that she had begun her escape. She really had no idea where the People's village was hidden overhead. One direction was probably as good as any other. She just needed to cover some distance.

"Merrilu!"

The voice shouted to her left. She wanted to cry. She remembered how, on their first march through the woods, the Captain had said that the People were everywhere overhead. She hoped that wasn't true. She kept on moving, careful to avoid hidden roots beneath the piles of leaves.

"Merrilu!"

This time the call came from directly in front of her. But there was nothing to do but to keep on running. Maybe, if she moved fast enough, she could still leave the People's voices behind.

There was a rustle of leaves above her.

"Merrilu!"

Something dropped to the ground far to her right. She looked over, even though she already knew what it was. Two short, pale, near naked bodies rushed toward her, calling her name. Two of the People. But only two. Maybe she could still outrun them.

She heard another noise in front of her. The Anno were going to surround her!

But it wasn't the People. It was something else. A dark beast of some sort, whose dark eyes glowed in the half-light. It was headed straight for her. Maybe, she thought, the People would have to save her all over again.

She stopped running, stumbling to her left. She looked around and saw the two People fitting arrows in their bows. The beast rushed forward with a great, rumbling growl, flying past her, straight for the nearer of the two Anno.

It jumped on the pale thing. There was a great flash of light. Mary Lou screamed in surprise.

The light dimmed. The beast still stood there, but all that was left of the first Anno was a twisted pile of ash.

The second of the People shrieked and jumped up a nearby vine. The beast turned to look at Mary Lou, its eyes twin beacons of scarlet light.

Mary Lou screamed again.

"Good boy, Charlie!" another voice shouted. Mary Lou looked out beyond the beast and saw her brother, Jason, approaching through the trees.

"Jason?" she called. "Oh, God, Jason!" She never thought she'd be this happy to see her brother.

But that thing was Nick's dog, Charlie? Now that Jason had said something, Mary Lou could recognize the bits of white in Charlie's brown-black fur. But the head was wrong, and it was more than just the eyes. It was larger than Charlie's head, with too many ridges above his eyes, as if the dog's skull bone had decided to explode.

Charlie barked happily. Whatever was wrong with him, he didn't seem to feel it.

"Oh, Jason!" Mary Lou called again, running toward her brother. She could feel the tears streaming down her face.

"Yeah, it's good to see—" Jason stopped abruptly as something swooped down overhead. Mary Lou looked up, afraid the People were back for her again.

But it wasn't the pale People. It was a great black bird.

"Calm down! Calm down!" The bird actually spoke. "Raven is here to make things right."

Rather than surprise, Jason reacted with anger. "Well, it's about time you showed up! Oomgosh almost died! And we just barely saved my sister!"

"Awk!" the bird protested as he settled on an exposed root. "Raven can see everything, but Raven can't be everywhere! Raven is much in demand, for Raven is unique!" He turned his head for an instant, pecking at his shoulder with his beak. "But you say my Oomgosh is in trouble?"

Jason told a story about how he and this Oomgosh person were attacked by the same red-furred things that had assaulted the People. Apparently, Mary Lou thought, she had only begun to see the strange things around here.

"And you had to hack off his arm?" The bird made a clucking sound deep in his throat. "Poor Oomgosh! That will tell him not to go into battle without Raven at his side."

"You had to cut off his arm?" Mary Lou repeated in disbelief.

"Yeah," Jason said in the matter-of-fact tone of someone who cuts off arms every day of the week. "It was pretty easy, actually.

Like sawing through a log. And he says he can grow a new one in a few days."

"Of course he can," Raven agreed. "After all, is he not the Oomgosh?"

"I see we have company," the prince's voice said in her ear.

Jason yelped. "Where did he come from?"

"You're not the only one who's made friends around here," Mary Lou replied. "This is one of mine. Unfortunately, he doesn't remember his name."

"She calls me her prince," the spirit said with a smile.

Mary Lou blushed. "Well, he could be a prince, couldn't he? I mean, look at his clothes!"

"We apparitions are always careful about our grooming," the prince agreed.

"Hey, Raven," Jason said. "You know everything. Ever seen this guy?"

The black bird cawed softly. "Raven knows you from somewhere. Indeed Raven does. Just can't remember where." He ruffled his feathers. "If only Raven didn't have so much to think about."

Mary Lou was fascinated by this creature. "If I may ask, what is on your mind, Raven?"

"The Cosmos, Mary Lou," the black bird replied. "The Cosmos." He fluttered his wings. "But come, we need to see to our Oomgosh. I imagine you simply left him standing there?"

Jason nodded. "That's what he wanted to do. He said it gave him time to heal."

"The Oomgosh can be very boring in that way," Raven said.

"Then Charlie jumped up," Jason continued, "and ran over here."

"Filthy beast!" Raven replied. "Still, this Charlie seems to have done some good this once. But we should return to our Oomgosh. We don't want his life to become too tedious. And Raven tells you this: Those who hurt the Oomgosh will pay."

"I hope you don't mind if I tag along," the prince said. "My existence has often wanted for excitement."

"Your dull lives are over," Raven promised as he took to the air. "It will get very exciting, very soon."

◯ Thirty-two

Nunn awoke with a start, his robes drenched with sweat. Something was wrong. He hadn't felt this disoriented since he was human. He needed to sleep far too much. Somehow, when he had taken Evan Mills, it had led more to exhaustion than nourishment. He rose from his sleeping pallet and began to pace, not bothering to light the darkness. Why did a wizard need light?

Nunn didn't like this weakness, this almost being human. He wondered if this was the dragon's doing.

Nunn knew more about the dragon than anyone, and he knew very little. Those few who had survived its last attack had been driven half-mad. When Nunn and Obar had been pulled into this world, it had taken forever to pry free the knowledge from those who had gone before them, knowledge that only came when they had also freed the dragon's eyes and learned how to harness their power. Pity that when the three wizards had been deprived of their eyes, the three had also shriveled and died.

But, as little as he really knew about the dragon, he could sense the creature. The dragon was close, far closer than ever before. That was surely one of the reasons for the change Nunn felt. Could the dragon take back its power as it approached, drain it from the dragon's eyes? This was something Nunn had never considered. It was all the more reason to collect as many of the eyes as he could, to hoard that power, to try to control the dragon before the dragon controlled all of them.

Light spilled into the room. Light! Nunn spun to confront the intruder.

This was impossible. He controlled everything in this castle. Someone had opened the door. Light flooded in from the hall.

Margaret Furlong stood in the doorway.

"I need to talk to Leo," she said.

217

"I see," he replied, lifting an eyebrow to fill this room with light. He thought he had locked her safely away with the others while he took his rest. But, impossible or not, here she was.

"Please," she said. "This is very difficult for me." She did not look at all happy.

The only way she could have left that other room and found her way to this place was if he had shown her the way. Perhaps this was the reason he couldn't sleep.

"I'm lost without my Leo," she whispered.

She did look lost in that doorway, both vulnerable and alone. Nunn was surprised to find how attractive that made her. When he had gained power, he had dispensed with these simple physical pleasures. He had had power for a very long time.

But a part of him wanted her. A very human part. Apparently, Nunn thought, there were still some things that could surprise him.

"Yes," he said in Leo's voice. "Why don't you come over here?" He held out his hand. "We haven't been close in a long time."

"Oh, Leo," she said as she walked toward him. "I'm so sorry for everything."

For an instant, Nunn felt sad himself, as if it really was Leo's voice that spoke through his mouth. Perhaps he was splitting himself into too many pieces. If only he could take a few moments to rest. If only the dragon wasn't so close.

He watched Margaret cross the room toward him. She looked deep within his eyes. His eyes, in Leo's face. Perhaps he could rest for a minute. Perhaps he could find some human warmth.

"NOOOOOO!"

A scream smashed into the room. Nunn stumbled back, assaulted by the light.

"Zachs hurt! Zachs screams in pain!" The room pulsed with light: red, then blue, then yellow-green. "He tried to kill Zachs! But Zachs still too fast, still too clever! He protected Mary Lou! He called himself a prince, but Zachs knew better! Zachs knew what he really—"

Nunn threw a burst of energy back at the cascading creature of light, causing its shrieking to redouble.

"You do not—" Nunn began.

But the creature was beyond listening. "Zachs hurt!" A ball of fire grew in its hand. "Zachs hurts back." It hurled the fireball at the floor. Margaret cowered, covering her head. "Zachs kills everyone!"

"Enough." Nunn opened his palm to expose the jewel. Zachs' light shrank back into its monkey form as it spun to face the wizard. Nunn held up his palm to face the creature.

"No! Zachs will be good! Zachs sorry!" Zachs cried as if Nunn was crushing its soul. Not, of course, that the creature had a soul to crush. Its glowing form flowed toward the jewel. Its arms and legs thrashed wildly, as if it was swimming hopelessly against the tide. And then with a final shriek it was gone, sucked deep within the jewel.

"I apologize—" Nunn remembered who he was supposed to be. His voice changed again. "I'm sorry, Margaret."

"Leo?" Margaret replied.

"It's safe now, Margaret," Leo said in his most reassuring tone.

"Leo," she replied, and then again. "Leo, Leo, Leo." The tone of her voice slid up and down, as if she sang a nonsense song.

Nunn reached out a hand for her. "Margaret?"

"No!" she shrieked at the touch, cowering even more than before. "Leo," she sang. "Leo, Leo."

Nunn stared at the woman curled on his floor. Humans were so fragile. He would be better without them. This attraction was a momentary weakness, nothing more.

Margaret Furlong was still in the room, but she was no longer with him. Nunn thought for a second of taking her energy as well. But something still wasn't right, something to do with Mills. Nunn didn't want to stuff himself.

Besides, a part of him wanted her to recover. He could still think of other things to do with this one.

He sent her back to the others with a wave of his hand.

The room was quiet once more, and dark. But Nunn could no longer sleep. The jewel with his creature throbbed where he had lodged it in his palm, as if even the dragon's eye didn't want to hold the light-thing. Zachs was becoming too difficult to control. Nunn would need new allies. He had to change. He had spent so much time planning, he had forgotten how to act. He could not mistake weakness for strength. He was not doing too much. He wasn't doing enough.

He opened his right hand and accepted the strength of the eye. His mind reached out across the island.

None of the red furs were left. All were dead. Three quite recently.

The thing that had been the neighbor Sayre was using the Captain's energy quite well. He would be here shortly. He could be very useful. Nunn would have to introduce him to the other neighbors. Jackson had wanted to work for Nunn. He wondered how eager Jackson would be to work with Sayre.

Other things had changed while Nunn slept. He could see the Anno. Mary Lou wasn't with them. He let the dragon's eye roam. She was still on the island somewhere. His other abilities could sense her presence. But now she was the one that he couldn't see.

But the Anno were giving their special greeting to other members of the neighborhood. Two of the boys, two of the first to escape, Todd Jackson and Bobby Furlong. Arrows, stones, spears, twigs, anything the Anno could grab was being thrown at the two running youngsters.

Perhaps it was time to save them. Nunn would particularly like to get these two back and reward them for their initiative. Maybe the boys would like to join their parents. Or not. The young ones held a lot of potential. And a lot of energy.

But he could no longer use Zachs; at least not until he had a chance to make a few adjustments. And his other allies had disappointed him as well. They had died so easily. If the boys were to be fetched, Nunn would have to do it himself.

It couldn't be helped. He'd have to go and fetch them back.

Perhaps, as a reward, he'd eat one along the way.

◯ Thirty-three

"You are very talented, you know."

Nick looked up from where he sat huddled against a tree. Obar's voice had broken the silence. But the wizard wasn't talking to him.

Nick hugged his arms close to his body. He couldn't stop himself from shaking.

He never thought he'd be this glad to see his mother. She had hugged him; he found himself surrounded by warmth and familiar smells. For a second, he'd felt like he was a teenage boy on Chestnut Circle. For a moment, he'd forgotten all the blood.

He'd sat down against one side of a great tree, and his mother had sat down beside him, just past one of the great roots that jutted from the ground. She had fallen asleep, as had some of the others.

And Nick had begun to shake. There was no way he could sleep. Every time Nick closed his eyes, he saw his sword plunge into the belly of a wolf. The animal struggled, howling with a voice that knew it was already dead, its blood sucked from its veins.

"You don't wish to talk?" the wolf said with Obar's voice.

Nick's eyes opened with a start. Obar stood in the small clearing only a few paces from Mrs. Smith. The old woman stood with her back to the wizard.

"I don't want to be here," she said.

Obar laughed. "Do you think that any of us came here by choice? Once we learned there was no going back, we taught ourselves how to survive. You'll have to learn that, too, if you want to save your neighbors."

With that, Mrs. Smith turned and looked at him. She did not seem happy.

"Oh, yes," Obar continued. "You're the only one with enough power to save them, if you choose to use it. Nunn is much more

221

powerful than I am. I can hinder his actions, but I don't know if I can stop them. With the two of us working together, well—" He smiled and shrugged.

Mrs. Smith didn't reply.

"Nunn has two of the dragon eyes, you know," Obar went on quickly. "And he wants all the rest of them, and all of us too. I think he believes, if he controls all the parts of the dragon, he'll control the dragon as well."

"And what will that give him?" Mrs. Smith asked sharply.

"Everything, perhaps," Obar replied. "At the very least, a chance to survive." He sighed and stared for a moment at the trees beyond his miniature sun. "I've been here for a very long time—not that time means much to this place. I was one of the first to arrive, after the last visit of the dragon. I saw the devastation of the islands— cities leveled, forests uprooted, people torn to little pieces. A very few survived. One of them became my tutor."

The mage laughed again, a much more sour noise than before. "I did not trust my predecessor, even as he taught me so much about the powers that we all consider magic. Never trust a wizard, you know.

"But I believe one thing he told me: If you use the dragon, you will become a part of it. But if you do not, the dragon will destroy you." He waved at the trees around him. "It's a little game the dragon plays with humans. This whole world is his board, and the stones we call the eyes are the pieces. If you can find a stone, you can be a player. Maybe, if you find all of them, you can win."

"Stone?" Mrs. Smith asked. For the first time, she seemed interested rather than angry.

"Seven stones. So my tutor said. I have one. Nunn now possesses two. The other four are somewhere on the seven islands. Should we be able to find them, we should be able to defeat Nunn."

"And if we don't find them, we don't survive?"

Obar nodded. "If Nunn doesn't destroy us, the dragon will."

"You don't paint the most pleasant picture." Mrs. Smith thrust her hands into the pockets of her housecoat. "I suppose you would like us to work together."

"Well, I was getting to that," Obar replied hurriedly, as if the slightest bit annoyed. "I think that if we don't, we will all die. And, perhaps, if both of us can search, we can find the remaining stones and outwit Nunn at the same time. But we must begin at once. The dragon is close, and there are four of the eyes left."

Mrs. Smith pulled a hand from her pocket. "Three."

Nick forgot to shiver. Mrs. Smith held a stone in her hand that shone with brilliant light. Nick glanced away quickly before he could be drawn in again.

"Where did you get that?" Obar demanded.

"I don't know," Mrs. Smith admitted. "I reached in my pocket once, and it was there. You don't mind if I put it away, do you? It's all a bit melodramatic."

Nick looked up as the clearing once again dimmed to the light given off by Obar's tiny sun. The magician was staring openmouthed at the old woman.

"I believe," Mrs. Smith said after a moment's silence, "that the dragon gave me this."

"What are you talking about?" Obar blustered. "The dragon doesn't hand out gifts!"

"How do you know that?" Mrs. Smith asked.

"I just—that is—everything I've learned about the power—" Obar stopped abruptly. "I don't, obviously. Everything I know is really built on assumptions." He smiled at Mrs. Smith. "Apparently, our dragon has decided to play favorites."

Mrs. Smith nodded her head, as if bowing in acknowledgment. "Perhaps the dragon will also guide me to the others."

"Then you will work with me?" Obar hopped from one foot to another, barely containing his excitement.

She patted her pocket. "How could I ignore this sort of invitation?"

"Many of the others have talents as well, you know," Obar continued gleefully. "The dragon picked you all very carefully. If we work together"—this time his laugh was full of joy—"Nunn doesn't have a prayer!"

"Is there something else?"

"I was thinking about the eye." He looked straight at her with the warmest smile Nick had ever seen. "I don't suppose you'd give that to me?"

○Thirty-four

Todd wouldn't cry out, no matter how much he hurt.

Something had hit him in the back. Part of it was still sticking out of his shoulder. Todd didn't have time to look at it. He had to keep running.

"I don't want to be here!" Bobby was screaming enough for both of them. "Stop throwing things! Get me out of here!" The kid had managed to avoid everything those creeps were throwing at them from the trees. But with every one of Bobby's shouts, a hundred high-pitched voices taunted them from up above.

And still the missiles fell. Something glanced off the back of Todd's head.

"Over here!" a deeper voice called. Thomas stepped from behind a tree, an arrow flying from his bow. There was a scream above. Something fell to earth behind Todd. He still didn't want to look back.

The other Volunteers appeared from cover to fire their missiles in turn.

"God, are we glad to see you!" Bobby enthused. "These things wouldn't listen to us at all!"

"Not very social, are they?" Wilbert boomed. He, Maggie, and Stanley fired their arrows together. They were greeted by more screams overhead and the crash of small bodies falling through the leaves.

Bobby looked at the bowmen in wonder. "How do you see them up there?"

"Don't have to see them," Thomas replied. "Way the Anno crawl all over the branches up there, you almost can't help but hit 'em."

"Like fish in the barrel," Wilbert agreed. "Wish I still had my Winchester. Now, that would make them run!"

Todd realized that the arrows had stopped falling around them. The shrieks of rage from the Anno were becoming less frequent, and farther away.

"Plus, you hit a couple of them, hey?" Stanley surveyed the trees. "Next thing you know, they've skedaddled!"

The screams had stopped completely. Stanley looked like he almost might smile.

"What do we do about Mary Lou?" Maggie asked as she slung her bow over her arm.

"Have to find another way to get her," Thomas answered. "Something's going on with the Anno. Never knew them to get so skittish, so fast. Usually take their time sizing up newcomers."

"Don't want to turn down any potential meals," Wilbert agreed.

Todd heard a moan. It took a second to realize it came from his lips.

"The boy's been hit," Maggie called.

"I'm all right," Todd insisted. But he wasn't. His knees wobbled as he tried to walk the last few feet to the others. The back of his shirt was heavy and damp. Todd hoped it wasn't blood.

Todd fell to his knees. Except his knees didn't hit the ground.

"Is this any way to treat your guests?" said a voice behind him.

"Nunn!" Maggie shouted as she reached for her bow. The other three were already fitting arrows to theirs. Todd realized that he was drifting away from them, toward the voice to his rear. Bobby was moving, too, his arms and legs flailing wildly three feet above the ground, like some puppet doing a mad dance.

"Nooooo!" Bobby wailed.

"Most assuredly yes," Nunn's voice replied lightly. An arrow whizzed past Todd's ear. There was a soft whoosh behind him.

"You boys were very rude not to accept my earlier invitation," Nunn continued. Todd realized that he was spinning slowly as he floated toward the wizard. Soon he would be face-to-face with Nunn.

Two more arrows flew past. This time Todd was able to turn his head enough to see them burst into flames and disintegrate before they could reach their target.

"Help us!" Bobby shrieked. His fists had swung forward, like he wanted to pummel Nunn. Todd twisted his head a bit further to get his first glimpse of the wizard. Nunn was tall, with a long, thin face, his skin a bloodless white against his black robes. His eyes were jet-black as well, all darkness save for tiny flecks of white, as if his eyes held part of the night sky.

The wizard pointed a finger, and another arrow burst into flame. Nunn reached out for the two of them.

"I believe we will be going now."

"No!" Bobby lashed out, striking Nunn's shoulder.

Todd wished he had the strength to fight back. His shoulder throbbed with a heat that seemed to drain all the energy from his body.

Somehow, through his frantic movement, Bobby managed to twist away from the wizard. Nunn turned with the boy, grabbing him before he could float any farther.

An arrow struck the wizard's shoulder.

Nunn spun back around to stare at the archers, the darkness of his eyes turned to a molten red. "I will be back for you!" One of Nunn's hands grabbed Todd's shirtfront. The light flared out from the wizard's arms, enveloping his face, then rushing across his shoulders and arms until it encompassed Bobby and Todd as well.

Todd felt a great pain, starting in his back, then exploding out to include the world.

Nunn was annoyed. That was not done well at all. Rushing to grab the children, confronting the Volunteers! He had been too sure of himself, and impatient to be done with his work.

He reached back and touched the arrow that protruded from his shoulder. It crumbled to dust. Nothing more than a minor aggravation, really. Except that the pitiful Volunteers had managed to get one of their tiny weapons past his defenses. They knew that he could be reached. That was unfortunate. The more Nunn looked all-powerful to those around him, the easier it would be to become truly all-powerful. Now he would have to find some more-inventive ways to reignite the humans' fear.

First, though, it was time to bring some fear to those close to him. He snapped on a light above his head, a ghostly moon, as cold as a light could be. Despite his anger, he had to admit it was a nice effect.

It was time to discuss how his two newest guests might be useful.

"Where are we?" the younger one—Bobby—cried out against the sudden light. "You can't do anything to us!" The tone of Bobby's voice said that Nunn would be able to do whatever he wanted.

The wizard looked around his study, to see where the other one—the quieter one, Todd—had fallen. Nothing but silence.

Maybe Todd's wound was more severe than the wizard thought. Nunn should be careful not to let him die. It was such an arduous process to reanimate these people.

He waved a finger to increase the illumination of the moon, driving the shadows from his study.

"Where's Todd?" Bobby demanded. "What have you done with him?"

For an instant, Nunn couldn't believe it. Todd was nowhere in the room. The second child had not come with them.

It couldn't be. Something had taken Todd away, away from the power of Nunn! No one could do that. No one had ever dared.

Nunn was no longer simply annoyed.

Nunn was angry.

Everything was blinding white. Yet Todd felt there was no light anywhere.

Todd couldn't see a thing. But, in another way, he could see everything. He saw the woods where he had left the Volunteers behind, and the castle where his father slept. In the blink of an eye—but he wasn't seeing with his eyes—he was in the clearing with Nick. There was Todd's mother, waking up with the morning light. Somehow she'd gotten away from his father at last.

He saw Mary Lou, now with Jason and the black bird and the tree man. It surprised him how much better he felt to know she was safe. And he saw someone—or something—that reminded him of that crazy man Sayre, although this guy seemed even more intense than the lawn man, dragging himself across the island toward Nunn's castle, pushing himself through bushes and clumps of vines as if he no longer realized they were there.

Todd could see all of the island, and everything that happened there; not so big a place, really, with a deep green ocean all around. He could see everything, except a couple of the neighbors, Bobby's father and Evan Mills. Todd didn't want to think about what that meant.

Instead, he wondered what had happened to him after the wizard had shown up. He saw Bobby then, huddling in a place far away from Todd. The kid cowered in another corner of the great structure that also held Todd's father.

Nunn was in the same room with Bobby, and Nunn didn't look happy. He screamed, his arms high in the air. And the room seemed to respond. Small objects were flung around the raging Nunn to smash into the stone walls, even though no one touched them. Bobby looked like he wanted to cry.

Todd imagined he was the cause of all this. He had a talent for making people angry.

He blinked again, or his mind thought he blinked, as he tried to look closer. There was simply nothing there, nothing, at least, that his eyes or mind's eye could focus on. Todd could see everything, except for where he was.

But, wherever he was, he felt he wasn't alone.

There was a vibration that he felt in his fingers and toes and teeth, a deep rumble, as if he was close to some great machine. Except the rumbling rose and fell, not like machine noise, but some living, breathing thing.

He thought about the strange light he more felt than saw. It made him think of fire. Light and fire. Suddenly, as certain as if someone had told him out loud, he knew he was with the dragon.

While he looked at the world around him through the dragon's gaze, the dragon was looking at him.

The rumbling went deeper now, so that he could feel the vibration in his bones. And Todd knew that these tremors were only the slightest hint of the creature's power. He was being judged by the creature. One wrong move, and Todd could be obliterated by flame.

Somehow, though, he wasn't frightened. Instead, he found he was angry. Not at the dragon. It would be useless to get mad at something as powerful as that. No, his anger lashed out at Nunn, and the way he tried to use people; at Nick, for being the good boy on the street, the A student he could never match up to; at Mary Lou, for turning away from him when he made his clumsy attempts at getting to know her better; at his mother, for being so weak that Todd felt weak as well; at his father, whose own drunken anger bled over all those around him and poisoned everything he touched. And Todd found his anger turned inward, too, at the boy who could beat up those smaller than he was, but was always beaten—when he was young, with fists, and later, with looks and words—by that monster who was his father.

The rumbling deepened and grew closer, shaking Todd so hard that he felt his skin would separate from his bones. Todd opened his mouth in surprise, and hurt, and anger, and heard his own voice mix with the great voice of the dragon.

Todd, and the dragon, roared.

PART TWO

The Dragon's Request

○ Thirty-five

Jason was so glad when the Oomgosh opened his eyes.

The tree man smiled. "It's good to be with friends." His broad brow furrowed when he looked down at Jason. "Don't be so concerned. I'm bound to recover. One way or another, there always has to be an Oomgosh."

Raven cawed at that. "So true! The Oomgosh is the second most important creature in all the world!"

"After all," the tree man agreed, "if I were not here, who would keep Raven in his place?"

Jason quickly woke his sister. She was the only one who had really slept during these last couple of hours before morning.

She sat up with a start. "Oh, Jason. I'm glad to see you're really here." She smiled slightly. "Since I've come here, I think I have difficulty figuring out what's real and what isn't."

"I'm sure I don't have anything to do with that feeling." Jason turned around to see the ghost-man standing behind him. The transparent fellow had disappeared soon after they'd found Mary Lou. Now he was back. Charlie stopped sniffing the surrounding trees and started barking.

"I've done some exploring," the phantom said to Mary Lou, ignoring Jason completely, "but without much success."

He waved to the dog. Charlie's bark stopped abruptly, replaced by a curious whine. A moment later, though, the dog started wagging his tale. This ghost-fellow seemed to have a way with everybody but Jason.

"My real self-discovery seems to have begun with your arrival," the phantom said to Mary Lou. "If I'm going to continue to find out more about myself, I suspect it will be around you."

Jason couldn't believe the smile his sister gave to this guy. It was the sort of look she usually saved for those rock stars she always had to watch on TV, especially when Jason was watching a cowboy movie on another station. How could anybody get that

231

kind of sick-cow expression on their face, especially about some guy who wasn't even there?

He glared back at the guy, who still didn't seem to notice. Mary Lou referred to him as "the prince." Well, maybe that deep blue costume of his could look royal, if you studied it in the right light. Otherwise, the pants and jacket looked like a set of baggy, fussy Levi's.

"Jason," the Oomgosh called, "it is time to leave. There are people to meet."

"More people?" the black bird called in protest. "Raven knew this wasn't going to be the best of days."

"Do you have something against people?" Mary Lou called as she stood.

"People are difficult," Raven acknowledged. "People are ignorant."

"Mostly," the Oomgosh added, "people do not recognize Raven for what he is." He smiled as the bird flapped his wings. "Raven is the most singular of beings."

"It is a great burden to bear," Raven agreed. "And it takes these great black wings to bear it."

"Raven will bear it with us, as we walk this way," the Oomgosh said, taking his first step forward. If he was feeling any ill effects from the past night's injury, Jason couldn't tell. The tree man's strides were as bold and steady as they were the day before.

Jason turned back to his sister, who smiled at him and shrugged, and then started to walk after the Oomgosh, as if she was game for anything. The prince, however, was nowhere to be seen.

"What happened to your friend?" Jason asked.

"Oh, he's still around," Mary Lou replied as if she had known this ghost-man all her life. "The prince doesn't have to travel like regular people, one foot after another. He can leave one place and reach another like that!" She snapped her fingers. "He'll be there when we need him."

"And the rest of the time, he'll just be spying on us?" Jason asked. He didn't know what had gotten into his sister. To him, this ghost-guy was definitely creepy.

"Brothers!" Mary Lou raised her palms to the sky, as if she was imploring the heavens. "Why do I even try?" She laughed, unable to seem really upset. "You don't know, Jason, how happy I was to see you last night."

"Sure, Mary Lou," he replied. "As long as we stick together, everything's going to be fine."

Charlie barked then and looked up at Jason with his red, glowing eyes. Even if they survived, Jason had the feeling that they would change in ways they couldn't even imagine.

"We will find the others." The tree man's deep voice seemed very reassuring. "And, as we walk, I will tell you a story of long ago, and how the Oomgosh first discovered rain."

"How you discovered rain?" Jason asked.

"Well, yes," the tree man admitted quietly. "Either myself or someone very much like me."

Raven flapped his wings and took to the air. "I have heard this one before!"

"And I have heard all yours as well," the Oomgosh noted. "The difficulty with being friends."

"Old friends!" Raven called as he lifted himself to the trees.

"Almost older than either of us can recall," the Oomgosh explained to the others.

"Raven should recall the prince," the bird shouted down from up above. "Except he wasn't a prince. That much Raven remembers. It will come back to me. It always does, sooner or later, come back to Raven."

With that, the great black bird flew up until he was lost beyond the leaves.

One minute he was all the world.

The next he stood in the forest.

"Todd!" Maggie called. She strode quickly but cautiously toward him, as if she expected Nunn to pop from the bushes at any second.

Todd shook his head. He didn't seem able to speak. The immense feeling of well-being he had had only a moment before was gone. Instead, he felt as though he hadn't slept in a week.

But he was back with the Volunteers, delivered by the dragon. He had the feeling that everyone who visited the creature wasn't that lucky. It was as if he had passed some sort of test, like he was a piece of some great puzzle the dragon was putting together.

Todd fell to his knees. Wasn't this where he'd come in?

He heard other voices around him.

"Todd, boy." That was Wilbert. "Someone's taken the arrow from your back."

The arrow? Todd had trouble thinking about what had happened to it. He must have lost the arrow when he was with the dragon. It was all so clear just a minute before. As tired as he was, Todd realized there was no soreness in his shoulder.

"Shirt's pretty much a waste, though." Stanley this time. "I didn't know people could have this much blood, hey?"

Hey, he thought, you'd be tired, too, if you didn't have any blood. Todd managed a smile as his face pitched forward toward the forest floor. Strong hands caught him before he could reach the ground.

Todd could hear something being dragged. He managed to open one eye. The trees were moving above him. It took him a moment to realize that the trees were standing still, and he was moving. He was on some sort of litter, like the one the soldiers had built for Mrs. Smith. He tried to remember what had happened. The Volunteers had to get somewhere in a hurry. Time was important.

Other things were important, too. There was something at the edge of his consciousness, more feeling than thought, that seemed urgent. It had come to him on the edge of waking, almost a dream. He felt it there, in the back of his mind, like he could reach it if he only knew which way to turn.

Damn it! If only he had more strength.

When he thought of strength, he thought of fire; fire and the dragon.

Whatever was in his mind came from the dragon. The creature had given Todd something that needed to be passed on to all the other players in this drama. But the dragon didn't speak in words. It spoke in emotions, and actions, and finally in destruction.

The images of destruction were very strong in Todd's mind. But, even as they swept through his memory, Todd realized they were only a small part of what the dragon had to say. A new feeling welled up in Todd's chest: a sure thing, why this was so important.

Somehow the dragon had told him the only way he, or any of them, could survive.

○ Thirty-six

Bobby had to get out of here. It seemed as if this whole room would come crashing down around him.

Nunn took a deep breath. Books and vials and jars and feathers and stones and shells, the ones that hadn't yet smashed against the walls and floor, all froze for an instant in midair before settling down to those surfaces from which they had come. The wizard frowned as he looked around the room. A jar that had been smashed knit itself back together on the floor, the golden powder spread around it funneling back inside. Torn parchment knit itself back together and rerolled itself into a scroll. A great black bird reinserted its cotton stuffing and flew back to a perch high on the wall.

"Now that we have that out of the way, we can get back to business." Nunn sighed. "But what are we going to do with you? Oh, any number of things, most assuredly, but where shall we start?"

Bobby sat up straight in the corner where he had taken refuge from the flying missiles. This wizard wasn't going to scare him! Well, actually, Bobby was plenty scared. But he'd do his best not to let it show.

"What have you done with Todd?" he demanded.

Nunn laughed softly at that. The wizard's grin looked forced, but the lightly teasing tone was back in his voice.

"I suppose I could take credit for his disappearance, but I really wanted to bring both of you boys here together. This Todd business—" Nunn waved his hand as if shooing away a fly. "I'm sure this is all my brother's fault. Obar, I mean. You see, I snatched someone away from him not long ago—one of your friends. Nick. I'm sure he only wanted to return the favor. Something to do with his idea of fairness."

"Is Nick here?" Bobby looked around the room, as if he might find his friend hiding in another corner.

Something like annoyance crossed over the wizard's face; it reminded Bobby of his father.

"Oh, no," Nunn said, his voice far lighter than his expression. "He was only visiting. Unfortunately, I believe you might have to stay here more permanently."

More permanently? Bobby wanted out of here now. He bet there was some way he could do it, too. And Nunn would tell him what it was. Just like with his parents, Bobby had to listen not for what Nunn was saying, but what Nunn really meant. He wondered if Nick had escaped. That could be exactly what Nunn meant by "visiting." If Nick had done something like that, Bobby could, too.

"Bobby, wouldn't you like to see your parents?" Nunn asked suddenly.

Bobby felt like he'd been punched in the stomach. His parents were here? When he'd run away the day before, he hadn't even had a chance to say goodbye.

"They've missed you ever so much." Nunn smiled again. This time the grin seemed to fit much better on his face. "Oh, I know you've had some troubles with them in the past. You might say I'm intimately acquainted with them. But you see, they've changed."

"Changed?" Bobby repeated, his voice barely a whisper. What had Nunn done to them? "Where are they?"

"Oh, your mother's just in the other room. And your father's even closer than that."

Nunn waved a hand and one of the room's walls went away. In its place was another room with three people, all looking upset. Mr. Jackson paced back and forth across the stone floor. Mr. Dafoe wrung his hands, his gaze following Jackson as he paced. And Bobby's mother sat on the floor in the far corner of the room, her knees tucked up close to her body so that she could rest her chin on top of them. She didn't seem to be paying any attention to the two men. In fact, she didn't seem to be looking at anything at all.

"Don't you think we should get her to eat something?" Dafoe asked Jackson.

Jackson stopped his pacing long enough to stare at the other man. "How can we get her to eat when she won't even recognize that we're here?"

Dafoe nervously glanced back at Bobby's mother. "I don't want her to die."

"Whatever's happened, she brought it on herself," Jackson

insisted. "Nunn told us, if we worked with him, he'd see we were rewarded. She just didn't try hard enough."

"I don't know," Dafoe said. "I don't know about anything. I wish I'd never seen this place." He moved over to a table in a corner of the room opposite Bobby's mother. He looked at the dozen or so objects cluttering the tabletop: an assortment of bowls and cups and a large pitcher. "As long as we're stuck in this place, I'm going to try and get her to eat something."

"Suit yourself." Jackson glanced one more time at Bobby's mother, then began to pace again. "I'd like to do something, too. All this waiting reminds me of the army."

Dafoe grabbed one of the bowls and carried it over to the woman huddled in the corner. "Margaret? You really should eat."

Bobby's mother looked up at the sound of the man's voice, a little startled, as if she only now realized there was someone else in the room.

Bobby couldn't stand this anymore. He had never seen his mother look so miserable.

"Mom?" he called.

"She can't hear you," Nunn announced abruptly. "Why don't you just sit here and watch, like a good boy?"

"Come on," Dafoe urged as he approached her. "This is some more of that stew we had the other day. You remember how good that stew was?" He held out the bowl.

She ignored it, staring instead at Dafoe's face.

"Leo?" she asked.

"No, Margaret," Dafoe said patiently, "Leo isn't here. You need to eat something." He offered the stew to her again.

She pushed the bowl out of the way and struggled to get to her feet. "I need you to stay, Leo."

"Now, Margaret—" Nervous, Dafoe took a step away.

She stood more quickly, clutching at his sleeve. "Leo, please don't leave me again."

Dafoe pulled himself away from Margaret's grasping hands. She stumbled, staring dumbly at her fingers, as she once again collapsed to her sitting position on the floor.

"I don't believe this shit." Jackson had turned away from the two others in disgust. "You can't talk to her, Harold. Leave her alone."

Dafoe stared down at her. Her eyes were unfocused again, as if she didn't even want to think. "Why has this happened to her, Carl?"

"Why?" Jackson made a snorting sound. "That's one question

I can answer. She didn't listen. She stood up to Nunn."

Dafoe turned away from Bobby's mother. He put the bowl back on the table. "No, no," he said, more to himself than Jackson, "can't stand up to Nunn."

Bobby looked up at the wizard. "What did you do to her?"

Nunn chuckled, as if this was all some merry joke. "She'll be fine, once she meets your father." He waved his hand again.

"Dad?" Bobby asked as the other room disappeared.

"He's right here, you know," Nunn said softly.

Bobby turned away from the now empty wall.

His father stood behind him, but he was wearing the wizard's robes.

"Bobby?" his father's mouth said. It was his father's face, too, but it was on the wrong body. "We need to talk."

Bobby was no longer frightened.

"Things have changed around here," his father's voice said, "but they've changed for the better."

Bobby looked at the thing before him and knew, in that instant, what he had to do.

"We just have to talk about things," his father's voice droned on. "We never did talk much about things in the past, did we? That's another thing that'll change. Soon you'll understand."

Bobby understood already.

He had to kill Nunn.

○ Thirty-seven

Constance Smith did not care for Obar.

She had known men like him before. Women, too, for that matter. People who said one thing while they meant another, who kept up a line of happy chatter to cover up what they were really looking for. Actually, when she thought of it, there was one particular gossip in her church, a woman close to Mrs. Smith's age who always wanted to talk "in all confidence." Unfortunately, that confidence only lasted until the woman found someone else to gossip with.

There were simply certain people who you couldn't trust. And Mrs. Smith felt that Obar fell firmly within this group.

"We will talk no more about this stone," she announced, tired of the man's constant whining. When she wouldn't give him this dragon's eye outright, he had resorted to arguments, cajoling, even all-out pleading.

And the look on the man's face when he talked about anything having to do with the stone! It was more than a simple matter of want; more like an obsession. It seemed that everything Obar did or thought had something to do with his dragon's eye. She was quite sure he would steal the new eye from her if given the chance.

"The stone was given to me," she continued. "It is mine. We will have to work together, using our own dragon's eye, if we are to succeed."

"Oh." The wizard did his best to smile and nod. "Most certainly," Obar agreed all too heartily. "I would have it no other way. It doesn't do to argue with the dragon."

"And we have more pressing business," Mrs. Smith added. "We need to put these stones to use. I came with a number of people. Some of them Nunn has killed. Others have stayed with him out of fear. And anyone not with him now he tries to capture."

"Capture?" Obar frowned at that. "Bobby Furlong," he said after a moment.

So the dragon's eye told him that, too, if Obar reached for it. Constance had seen Bobby's kidnapping the moment it had happened. Perhaps it was because she was closer to the other neighbors, especially the children.

"Someone has to put a stop to Nunn," she said, not just to Obar, but to the other neighbors. "He cannot come in and take us like that, with such impunity."

"Certainly, that's a worthy feeling," Obar agreed. "But we must save the rest of us first. We must find the other dragon's eyes, to get ready for the battle to come."

"We are already in a battle," Mrs. Smith replied abruptly, "and I think we need to fight every battle we can if we are going to win the war. I will not sacrifice a single one of my friends to this Nunn; especially not the children." She took a deep breath. This was the sort of thing she never admitted out loud; the sort of thing she wouldn't ever have thought of admitting, before her life changed. "I never had any children of my own. In an odd sort of way, all the people on my little street were my children. They are my family. And I will fight very hard for my family."

Joan Blake looked up from where she had been talking to her still upset son. "Thank you, Constance. I think we're all going to have to pull together if we're going to get through this."

"B-but the stones," Obar blustered. "We'll need more of the stones than Nunn! We need more power!"

"Why?" Constance asked, becoming more exasperated with this man by the minute. "We have just as much power as Nunn now."

"But he could destroy either one of us!" Obar insisted.

"Then we'll just have to fight him together, won't we?"

"Approach Nunn directly?" Obar's voice cracked at the very thought. He patted his chest, as if to calm himself. "I suppose it could be done, if we did so carefully, and there was something to gain."

"We gain Bobby's freedom, at the very least. And maybe we can convince one or two of the others that have stayed with Nunn that we have a chance to win. Every one of us is important." She caught Obar's gaze with her own. "Remember, you said the dragon brought us—all of us—for a purpose."

"Well, I did, didn't I?" Obar hesitated at that. "No one really knows the exact elements necessary for the dragon's arrival. But people are very important. In fact, in some way, they seem to add power to the dragon's eyes. Or so I've heard." He shrugged, as if this was all really beyond him.

This time, Constance thought, Obar appeared genuinely flustered. "This is all new to you, isn't it?"

"It's that obvious?" Obar sighed. "This is new to all of us. The few who survived the last visit of the dragon are now dead. But they did survive, and they had ideas of not only how to survive but how to thrive through control of the dragon."

"Ideas?" Mrs. Smith asked. "Do you mean theories?"

"Well, yes, there was no way for them to prove them," Obar admitted. "That means they could be wrong, doesn't it?"

She pressed her point. "So people could be even more important than the stones?"

Obar looked frightened at the very thought. "Well, I suppose they could."

Mrs. Smith allowed herself to smile. For once in this godforsaken place, a conversation was going her way. "Good," she said, careful to look at all the neighbors as well as Obar. "Then this is what we'll do. I'll be glad to help you locate the other dragon's eyes. With the two of us working together, we should be able to perform a much more thorough search than Nunn. But first, we must rescue our fellows—brought here by the dragon— before Nunn can use them."

Obar looked at her in defeat. "We?" he said weakly.

"Together, we equal the power of Nunn. Together, we cannot be defeated."

Obar sighed. "Who am I to argue with logic like that?"

She nodded. "Tell me what you know about Nunn's fortress and how he protects himself. Then we will get to work."

"And attack Nunn," Obar said softly, as though those were the last three words he wanted to hear.

"It is the only way we'll win," Mrs. Smith insisted.

Obar shook his head, totally bewildered that it had come to this. "It was much simpler when I was on my own, with the single eye. That way, I was only trying not to lose."

But then he told them all that he knew.

Mrs. Smith smiled to herself. The first skirmish had been won. Now it was time for the real battle to begin.

At first, he was in darkness, surrounded by silence. Total darkness, total silence. Like he had died and been sent to limbo. Like all his senses had been cut away from his brain. Like there was no way out, and nothing left to do except fall into despair.

But Nunn had done this sort of thing to him before. Evan Mills wouldn't let appearances deceive him again. He knew all about the wizard's tricks. And he knew those tricks could be defeated.

He remembered how Constance Smith had handled Nunn's will with a discipline of her own. If he could gather that same mental strength, maybe he could conquer this illusion on his own.

Last time he thought he was all alone, the rest of the neighborhood had been all around him, suffering from the same illusion. He wouldn't be surprised if something similar was happening all over again. Perhaps, if he thought about the others, he could find them, too.

As soon as the notion entered his head, Mills realized he wasn't alone. He sensed another nearby, some vibration perhaps. But he felt a shape, like in this total darkness there was a space that was darker still.

Mills found he didn't want to speak. He felt his voice wouldn't work.

What could the doubt be but more of Nunn's trickery?

He spoke, anyway. "Is someone there?"

"Evan!" he heard, or sensed, in reply. "Thank God. I thought I was going crazy!"

It was Leo. Mills recognized the other man's voice. Or his vibration. The darkness was still absolute, the silence a blanket that seemed to forbid any real sound. Whatever spell Nunn had laid upon them this time, it was far more difficult to break.

"Do you have any idea where we are?" Leo asked a moment later.

"Somewhere Nunn has put us," Mills answered. He remembered then what the wizard had done to Leo, how the man had been transformed into a pulsating ball of energy clasped in Nunn's hands until the energy, too, disappeared. Mills remembered how angry that had made him.

He was sure Leo was dead.

He couldn't think of much after that, beyond the anger. He remembered charging the wizard. It had something to do with protecting the others. After that, nothing.

Where were they? What had happened to Leo, and to him? Were there others here, too?

It seemed that only after he'd thought of something could he realize it was there. There were hundreds of others here, but none of them came from the neighborhood. All of them were strangers. Many of them weren't even human.

How could he tell this without sight, without hearing? It was all in his head, Mills thought. Like his mind was brushing against other minds.

"Evan!" Leo's voice was full of panic. "It's happening again."

"What?" Evan demanded. "What's happening?"

"I'm being taken away," Leo moaned. "Sometimes, Evan, I change. Sometimes I lose myself."

Leo's voice began to fade, as if he was indeed being taken away.

"Evan! Help me!"

What could Mills do but follow?

○ Thirty-eight

With talking birds and men who looked like trees, this was all too strange for Mary Lou to feel safe. But, for the first time since coming to this bizarre place, Mary Lou felt—well—protected.

She was light-headed, almost giddy, as she marched with her little group toward a reunion with her neighbors. After her experience with the People, it was wonderful just to be able to communicate with others. And she never realized how happy she could be to see her brother. Her dumb old brother Jason; everyone seemed to accept him here in a way he was never accepted at home. And since they all approved of Jason, they approved of his sister as well.

Charlie yapped happily, tail wagging, as he walked by her side, just another dog ready to play. Mary Lou tried not to look into his glowing eyes. Not only was his head changing shape, growing a hard, bonelike ridge above the eyes, but she could swear he was about twenty percent bigger than he had been before. From the way he acted, Charlie didn't seem to realize that anything was happening to him. One advantage of being a dog, she guessed.

The large man, the one Jason called Oomgosh, led the way. Not that the Oomgosh was entirely human. He had a stump where one of his arms should be, and out of that stump was growing a bright green shoot.

The Oomgosh was constantly telling stories, tall tales about how he made sure the rain and sun kept their proper places in the sky. Jason laughed at every other sentence out of the tree man's mouth. Mary Lou couldn't remember when she had seen her brother this happy.

Somewhere up above them, Raven flew, swooping down occasionally to tell them all was clear ahead, both on the ground and in the trees. Mary Lou hoped that meant the People had given up on her.

Of course, the prince was with them, too. Not that she could see him, but, the way he had talked, it sounded as if he felt his destiny and Mary Lou's were intertwined.

She heard a cawing sound above. "The goal is near!" Raven called. "Your destination is only a few minutes' march away." With a flutter of wings, the large black bird descended to land on the Oomgosh's shoulder. "I thought I should return so that we might prepare."

"Prepare?" Jason asked. "Is something wrong?"

"Not if we are ready for it," the bird replied curtly. "Most important, I need to be properly introduced. These people are new to our world. Without the proper arrangement, they may think me no more than a bird."

"That will never do," the Oomgosh said. "I will announce us." He cupped his one hand to his mouth. "Hello, the camp!" he called in a voice loud enough to carry across half the island.

The air before them blurred with silver. Two hands appeared in the opening and pulled it wide. Mrs. Smith stepped through. Her wary look turned to a smile.

"Oh, it *is* you. Obar said you were almost here." Her smile grew broader still as she spotted her neighbors. "Mary Lou, Jason! It's so good to see you again. And this must be?"

The tree man bowed slightly. "The Oomgosh. Only another humble denizen of these woods."

"And Raven!" the black bird called with a note of warning. "Only the most singular Raven!"

Mrs. Smith nodded pleasantly, charmed by the bird's behavior. "Yes, Obar told me how important you are."

"He did?" Raven ruffled his feathers. "Well, of course he did! Obar knows what is important around here."

Mrs. Smith frowned when she looked at Charlie. "And who is this?"

"Nick's dog," Jason answered. "Charlie."

"Oh, dear. He isn't in pain or anything?"

"No, ma'am." Jason looked down at the tail-wagging dog. "Charlie's as happy as I've ever seen him."

Mrs. Smith made soft tsking noises with her tongue. "Well, maybe there's some way we can fix poor Charlie up. First, though, you should join us in the clearing ahead. It is just past those trees."

But she couldn't go yet! "Mrs. Smith?" Mary Lou called.

The old woman's smile returned as she looked at Mary Lou. "Yes, dear?"

"There's someone else that I'd like you to meet." With that, Mary Lou wished the prince was by her side.

There was a moment of silence, but no prince. Where could he be?

"Oh, so I see," Mrs. Smith said, as if nothing had gone wrong at all. "Well, introduce us next time he appears, won't you?" She waved to the others in the party. "I'll meet you all in the clearing. These days, I'm afraid, flying seems much easier than walking." She waved one more time, then popped from existence.

Mary Lou looked at the others and saw Jason staring at her.

"Everything here has gotten weird," her brother said. "Hasn't it?"

"Just different," the Oomgosh replied for her. "Everything here is just very different."

"And Raven," the black bird announced from the tree man's shoulder, "is the most different of all."

The tree man glanced down at Mary Lou's brother. "And what do you think, Jason?"

"I think that's all that needs to be said," Jason replied with a shrug and a grin.

The Oomgosh's laughter echoed across the forest. "Jason, you learn very quickly indeed. Come, let us meet the rest of your people."

It was only a moment more before the trail they walked opened into the clearing. Mrs. Smith stood next to the ice cream man from the other night; Obar, Jason had called him. Mary Lou saw Mrs. Blake and Mrs. Jackson. And there, behind them, was her mother.

"Mom!"

"Mary Lou!" Her mother allowed herself the slightest of relieved smiles. "I'm so glad you're safe! Jason! Come here and let me hug you!"

Jason ran in front of Mary Lou to meet their mother, acting more like a boy of ten than his current aloof fourteen. Mary Lou followed somewhat more hesitantly. Ever since that trouble with her older sister, her mother had seemed to want to keep her distance.

Mary Lou glanced at the others as she crossed the clearing. People looked different than they did back in the neighborhood. Mrs. Smith looked better than she ever had before; positively radiant. The others mostly seemed like they'd been living in the woods for the past couple of days, a smudged cheek here, a torn sleeve there. Even her mother's hair was starting to lose its shape.

"Hey, Mary Lou!" a boy's voice called from farther back in the trees. She looked over and saw Nick. He tried to smile, but the expression didn't seem to want to stay on his face. He looked a little wild, like he hadn't slept in the past couple of days. One of his hands played with something at his belt. It looked like the handle of a sword.

"Hey, Nick," she managed after a moment. She turned back to her mother for the requisite hug and peck upon the cheek.

"Oh, Mary Lou!" her mother gushed suddenly. "I'm so glad both of you are safe."

"We're all together now, Mom," Mary Lou agreed. "Is Dad here?"

Mother frowned and pulled away. "Your father? No, he didn't come with us. You see, we all escaped from this other fellow, Nunn—a terrible man. But your father, he wasn't sure what he should do. You know Harold. He can never make a decision. So"—she paused to take a deep breath—"he stayed behind."

"Dad stayed behind?" Jason cried in disbelief.

"You know your father," his mother repeated, her tone even more disapproving than before.

He can never make a decision. Mary Lou knew what that meant. The only one in her family who could really make a decision—who was allowed to make a decision—was Mom. And if anyone disagreed, or put the family in a bad light, her mother turned away. After her older sister, Susan, got pregnant, it was like she no longer existed. Would the same sort of thing happen to her father, to Jason and Mary Lou, as her mother shut them off one by one? Mary Lou was surprised how clearly she saw this now.

"Charlie!" another voice yelled.

There was terrible pain in that voice: the sort of hurt and anger she felt deep inside but couldn't express. She looked away from her mother. It was Nick. He had seen what had happened to his dog.

"Oh, dear," Obar murmured. "This comes from that light-creature. I'm afraid there's been a—well—a bit of an infection."

That didn't calm Nick at all. "A bit of an infection?" he yelled. "Look at him! He's turning into some sort of monster!"

Charlie barked for joy, happy to see his master.

"Hey, Nick," Jason called. "Charlie's all right! No matter what he looks like! He helped save my life!"

Obar nodded at that. "Inside, I think he's still your dog."

Nick turned away from the others to study the prancing Charlie. The tiniest smile tugged at one corner of his mouth. "C'mere, boy." He waved the dog forward. "You and I can be monsters together."

Charlie bumped his rough head against Nick's knee. Nick scratched his dog behind the ear.

Monsters together? Mary Lou wondered what that meant.

"Things sometimes change in this place," the Oomgosh offered, "in order to survive."

"I won't let it!" Mary Lou's mother burst out suddenly. "Nothing's going to happen to my perfect daughter. Or my fine son!"

"Yes, Mother." Even as she said it, Mary Lou knew that her words—and her mother's words—weren't true. And not just the part about the perfect daughter. Didn't her mother realize that everything had changed already?

"So, did all the rest of the neighbors stay behind?" Jason asked.

This time Mrs. Smith answered. "Some of them did. They're still back with Nunn. Your father, Mrs. Furlong, Mr. Jackson. And I think that a couple of the others are dead. But we're still expecting Todd to join us."

Todd was still all right? That made Mary Lou feel even better. She shouldn't care about Todd at all with the way he treated her. Well, she didn't care about him, really, especially when there was someone as fascinating as the prince around. But she could never quite shake the feeling that, under that rough exterior, Todd had a sensitive side that might really be worth getting to know.

"And we're going to take back some of our own, too," Mrs. Smith continued, "beginning with Bobby."

"Bobby?" Jason asked.

"Nunn's got him," Obar explained. "Not a good situation, oh, no." He looked to Mrs. Smith. "If we're going to try and save him as you suggested, we should go as soon as possible."

"Before Nunn does something really horrible to the boy?" Mrs. Smith asked.

"Both that," Obar confessed, "and I would rather go before I lose my courage. Nunn and I have had fights before, you see."

Mrs. Smith shook her head at that. "But now you have the aid of a second dragon's eye."

"Yes, I do." Obar smiled and shrugged. "Maybe this time will be different. Maybe this time we can do something to Nunn."

Mrs. Smith turned to the Oomgosh and Raven on his shoulder. "Thank you for joining us," she said.

"It was our privilege," the Oomgosh replied. "We don't often meet folk as pleasant as Jason and Mary Lou."

"Or as important!" Raven squawked. "We are all very important now, though perhaps none are so important as Raven."

"Obar has told me a lot about the both of you," Mrs. Smith continued before the bird could grow any more full of himself. "Although I am sure it is but one small fraction of the glorious stories either of you could tell. So we know a small piece of your history." She quickly introduced Raven and the Oomgosh to the others in their small circle of neighbors.

"I am very glad you're here," Mrs. Smith continued to the bird and tree man. Mary Lou was impressed with the way the older woman was handling everyone. You might think she was the one with years of magic knowledge, rather than the somewhat distracted man by her side.

"Obar and I need to leave here as soon as possible," the old woman explained. "I would consider it a great favor if you were to stay here and watch over the others while we are gone."

The Oomgosh nodded his leaf-strewn head. "It would be our pleasure."

"Sounds like a very important task!" Raven agreed.

"Oh," Mrs. Smith added, almost as an afterthought. "Four Volunteers will be coming with Todd. Please let them join us."

"We know the Volunteers," the Oomgosh said.

"Raven knows everyone!"

"I am not always certain that is an advantage," the tree man commented. "We will be wary of all other visitors."

"Good," Mrs. Smith said as she glanced over at Obar. The wizard nodded back to her. "We will be going."

And they were gone.

There was a moment of silence. What did one say, Mary Lou wondered, when someone popped out of existence right in front of you?

"What was that?" Jason asked, looking up at the trees.

So he had heard it, too? Mary Lou was hoping it was just her imagination. Only a few seconds after the wizards had disappeared, Mary Lou thought she had heard faint but all-too-familiar voices, high in the trees.

○ Thirty-nine

"Good boy, Bobby. If you'll—" The voice started to cough.
Nunn frowned. He was having trouble with Leo Furlong.

"Come on, now, Bobby," he said, using Leo's voice to speak
to his son. "Don't you see how much easier it will be if you just
work with—"

The voice stopped abruptly for the second time, almost as if
Leo was fighting him. That was ridiculous! When Nunn consumed his victims, he kept their personalities, but only for his
own use, one small part of the original which he employed for
his own purposes. They were like ghosts that the wizard stored
in the back of his mind, pale shades he could call forward and
use whenever he felt it was appropriate. They were really little
more than memories of the people once alive before they met with
Nunn. Memories! How could a memory fight back?

Perhaps, Nunn thought, this was further evidence of his fatigue.
He smiled at Bobby, his features rearranging themselves to the
countenance he generally employed as a wizard. Furlong would
be stored for use another day.

"Forgive me, Bobby," he said quietly. "My timing seems to be
off. But don't you think it would be better to work with me than
against me?"

The boy said nothing. He stared sullenly into another part of
the room.

"You know, of course, that I could make life quite unpleasant
for you," Nunn mentioned.

"Keep away from me!" Bobby demanded. "I won't talk to you.
I want to see my father, my real father!"

Oh, dear, Nunn thought. It appeared that young Bobby would
need to be taught a lesson. Nunn had to be careful about dispens-
ing pain. He found he enjoyed it far too much. Sometimes it was
very difficult to stop.

"Now, Bobby," he said with the most charming of smiles, "I

will teach you how very bad it is for you not to agree—"

His own voice stopped, as if, for an instant, he had forgotten how to speak. The smile fell from his face. Something was very wrong.

He took a deep breath. Perhaps he'd been holding himself back too much. He'd had other moments of fatigue, even moments when he'd lost the conviction that his plan would succeed. Perhaps he should give in to it, after all. He always felt much better once he'd caused somebody pain.

"Bobby," he said simply, trying not to sound too excited. He reached for the boy's shoulder. "I'm going to punish—"

The lapse came again, as if the sentence he was speaking flew from his head. The hand that had reached toward Bobby tightened into a fist. This was too much, a true warning of his exhaustion. The punishment would have to wait. He'd have to put the boy out of the way and collect himself somehow. Perhaps he'd have to look at those spirits inside him to find out if they weren't quite as dead as he thought. Perhaps he'd have to kill Leo Furlong all over again.

Unless the difficulty didn't come from Leo. Nunn had swallowed Zachs as well, preferring to keep the light-demon inside rather than put up with the creature's ever-more-unpredictable behavior. Nunn could not contain everything. At least not yet.

And another of those damned neighbors had thrown himself at Nunn and was consumed before Nunn was truly ready. In fact, the wizard had been a bit surprised that he had devoured the last human's energy so effortlessly. Perhaps, he realized, the effort was yet to come. He'd need to deposit the boy with his mother and give this matter a bit of an examination.

A door formed in the wall of his study, a door he didn't recall making himself.

"Who?" he demanded. He turned to stare at the boy. Could Bobby have any of the wizard skills? If so, Nunn would have to show him that he wasn't to use them without permission.

Perhaps it was time for a little pain, after all. What would it hurt for the wizard to allow himself one simple pleasure?

Nunn licked his upper lip in anticipation. He sent out a bit of discomfort, a simple spell that would make Bobby's muscles twist inside.

The wizard screamed as the pain hit him instead.

At first, Evan Mills thought he had no idea what he was doing. But his actions all seemed to bring results. Therefore, he decided, his ignorance lay in exactly how these things were really happening.

It began when he had followed Leo Furlong, although he couldn't even say, exactly, how he had done that. Certainly not by anything as mundane as walking. It was more like he *thought* himself from one place to another, like his whole self had been transformed into energy, and could flash anywhere as quick as he could think.

Leo had entered what seemed to be a long corridor, with endless doors to either side. Mills had followed, feeling a bit like he used to as a kid, when he snuck into movie theaters through the back door. Whatever this hallway was, and whoever had made it, Mills felt he was someplace he wasn't supposed to be. He traveled down the hall, with no sensation of his feet touching the floor, or even that there was a floor to be touched. He wondered how long he could go before he was discovered.

A door flew open before him, as if someone else had read his thoughts.

"What are you doing?" a high voice screeched. "No one should be here! No one but Zachs!"

A monkey made of light cartwheeled out into the corridor. Its glowing face grimaced as it came to rest inches in front of Mills.

"Is that so?" Mills replied. He figured he had nothing to lose by drawing this creature out. Nothing, that is, that he could do anything about. "But I am here," he continued. "And I have no plans to leave."

The glowing monkey smiled at that. "Bold human! Zachs is surprised. Humans are afraid of Zachs." It threw its shoulders back and its hands forward, as if it was about to attack.

Mills made no move to leave, or even to defend himself.

"We're not always afraid," he said. "But then maybe I'm a little different."

The bright face stared intently at Mills. "Human's something new. Zachs didn't expect something new."

Apparently, Mills thought, this Zachs creature wasn't going to attack him, after all. Maybe Mills could get rid of this thing before Leo disappeared completely.

"I'm not just something new," he said gently. "I have to go and look for someone."

"You look for Nunn?" Zachs cried in sudden agitation.

Mills guessed that, in a way, he was. He nodded warily. "Nunn, and someone else."

The whole creature pulsed with furious light. "Nunn causes Zachs pain." The glow shifted from a dull red to an angry yellow. "Nunn is so unfair—won't let Zachs eat his full! Wants all the newcomers for himself! Zachs hates Nunn." Yellow slid to a glaring white that made Mills look away. "Nunn should have pain."

"Perhaps he should," Mills replied. He looked past Zachs. He could no longer see Leo in the hallway. "But if I lose my friend, I might lose Nunn, too."

"You look for Nunn?" Zachs nodded its head vigorously. "Zachs looks for Nunn, too! Shows Nunn what pain means!"

He supposed, if this creature would stay truly angry with the wizard, it might work to his advantage.

"I am going," he called as he darted past the light-creature and continued down the hall. "Come if you want."

"Zachs comes!" the light-creature called from close behind. "Zachs will not be closed in! Zachs will not be trapped! Zachs does what Zachs wants. Nunn will know! Nunn will pay!"

Mills tried to ignore the flaring creature behind him to determine where Leo had gone. The doors to either side remained closed, and Mills had the feeling that Leo wasn't behind any of those that they passed. Somehow his neighbor's destination was farther along.

The light-creature was suddenly at Mills' side. "Zachs knows Nunn. Zachs knows your friend. So clear to Zachs now!"

"So you can find my friend?" Mills asked.

"Find friend!" The creature, already far from being calm, seemed to grow wilder with every word. "Zachs once had friends! Nunn took them all away! Find friend! Go now!"

With that, the creature of light sped down the hallway so quickly that its form blurred as it streaked along, then was nothing more than a dim glow in the distance.

"Wait!" Mills called. He panicked, thinking he would lose not only Leo but this strange creature who could lead him to both Leo and Nunn. But the hallway changed again with his thought, and he found himself speeding ahead as well. The light-creature, faint in the distance of this never-ending hall, grew brighter and closer as Mills overtook it.

Zachs glanced over its shoulder, as if it expected to see Mills there all along. The creature pointed down the hall. "Nunn is there."

Mills looked ahead. This corridor did not go on forever. It ended in a door, an open door, with a different sort of light pouring out. While the light that came from Zachs seemed full of heat, the illumination that waited for them ahead was utterly cold.

Mills knew that Leo had opened that door and was waiting inside. He stepped to the doorway and saw his neighbor standing inside, bathed in the frigid light.

"What did you do to her?" someone said. It sounded like Bobby's voice.

A deep chuckle shook the room. Nunn's voice echoed all around them. "She'll be fine, once she meets your father."

Leo moaned softly. His form blended with the cold light, so that it became far more difficult to see.

"Dad?" Bobby asked from somewhere far away as the other room disappeared.

"He's right here, you know," Nunn's voice rumbled.

Mills realized that Leo had disappeared.

"Bobby?" Leo's voice rumbled in the same way that Nunn's had a moment before. "We need to talk."

"Nunn uses Leo," Zachs said close by Mills' ear. "Nunn uses everyone."

"Things have changed around here," Leo's voice said, "but they've changed for the better."

Mills realized then what the creature meant. The magician was able to use Leo's voice, perhaps even Leo's physical form, to say whatever the wizard wished.

"We just have to talk about things," the voice droned on. "We never did talk much about things in the past, did we? That's another thing that'll change. Soon you'll understand."

"Leo isn't saying that!" Mills whispered. "How can we stop Nunn?"

"Nunn? Zachs stops Nunn. Nunn and Zachs very close." The creature of light hugged its arms tight against its shimmering form. "So very close."

Zachs closed his eyes to concentrate.

The next thing Leo said ended in a coughing fit.

The creature giggled. "Zachs and Nunn are so, so close. Whatever comes from Nunn, Zachs can change."

Mills looked at his unlikely ally. He actually could interfere with the magician's speech. Mills wondered if there was some way this creature could rescue Leo, maybe even free both Leo and Bobby from whatever Nunn had done to them. The light-thing did a little dance in the doorway with both its arms and legs. "Nunn has a visitor. Zachs knows this visitor. Zachs will let him in." The creature seemed to be having a grand time.

Leo couldn't complete the next sentence, either.

"Come on, now, Bobby. Don't you see how much easier it will be if you just work with—"

The words ended abruptly this time, as if somebody had flipped an off switch. Zachs laughed and clapped its hands.

A moment later, Mills heard another moan. Leo was again standing in the light. He swayed, as if about to fall. Mills took a step to help him.

A flaming arm barred his way. "No! You go there, Nunn will know you! Let Zachs!" The creature pointed to the swaying Leo. Furlong began to float toward them.

"Nunn taught Zachs!" the creature cried happily. "Zachs learns well!"

Nunn's voice rumbled on as Leo fell through the doorway, into Mills' arms.

Furlong opened his eyes. "Evan," he said hoarsely, as if he had strained his voice. "I dreamed I saw my son."

Mills looked back at his friend. "I think you did, in a way." He looked at Zachs. "Is there any way you can get us out of here?"

"Out of here?" Zachs paused, as if considering something he had never thought of. "Nunn wouldn't like that. Zachs would. Zachs will do it if Zachs can. Zachs will find a way." The creature giggled and danced a shuffle step.

Leo Furlong stared at the glowing monkey-thing. "Whatever's going on here, Evan," he said at last, "I don't think I want to know."

"Nunn is looking for us!" Zachs announced suddenly. "Need a distraction, yes. Zachs will bring the visitor!"

"You know, of course, that I could make life quite unpleasant for you," Nunn's voice reverberated in the room behind them.

"Keep away from me!" the other voice exclaimed. "I won't talk to you. I want to see my father, my real father!"

"Bobby?" Leo asked. "Is that my son?"

"I think it is," Mills said. "But we can't get to him. Not from here."

"He's threatening my son!" Leo said as forcefully as his ravaged voice would allow.

"Nunn likes to threaten," the light-creature mentioned merrily. "But Zachs can help that!"

"Now, Bobby," Nunn's voice began, "I will teach you how very bad it is for you not to agree—"

His voice stopped abruptly. Zachs danced from one foot to the other.

"Bobby, I'm going to punish—" Nunn stopped.

"Who?" Nunn rumbled. At that, Zachs only grinned.

The words shut off again. Zachs smiled at the others.

"Nunn is angry. Nunn wants someone to pay." The creature's giggling grew higher and wilder. "Zachs will make Nunn pay."

The white light surrounded Mills and the others.

The world was filled with screams.

Bobby had never heard anyone scream like that. Nunn writhed on the floor, clutching at his stomach as if he was being torn up inside.

This was the time to get out of here. Bobby turned to the open doorway that had somehow appeared in one wall.

He heard footsteps outside, odd, heavy footsteps, like one of the feet was being dragged. He approached the door more cautiously than he had first intended.

"I know you!" a voice called from the far side of the door. "You thought you'd get away!"

The owner of the voice dragged his foot into view. He had been human once, before birds and animals had pecked at his face and arms, ripping away bits of flesh to expose the bone beneath, and, of course, certain soldiers had stuck a sword in his belly and a bullet in his brain. But even with all the damage and decay, Bobby knew him well.

"No one gets away who screws with my lawn."

Bobby yelled as he was grabbed by Old Man Sayre.

◯ Forty

Mary Lou saw the black bird cock his head to one side. "Some-one is calling you?"

Then he could hear it, too: the strange, high cry of the People as they twisted her name, again and again.

The bird fluttered his wings. "They will get Raven instead." With a single cry, he launched himself from the low branch from where he had watched the neighbors.

"Raven is good at this," the Oomgosh reassured her. "He will assess the situation and let us know what is best."

"Raven is good at everything!" came a cry from high above.

"Certain birds also have excellent hearing," the Oomgosh con-fided in a quieter tone than usual.

Mary Lou's mother pulled her daughter closer. "Why are they calling you?"

Mary Lou quickly explained how the People had found her after she had escaped from Nunn; how she tried to leave but was surrounded by wolves; how the People had come to rescue her but wouldn't let the other humans near her; and how she had escaped a second time for good. She didn't mention the battle with the red furs or the People's feast. Her mother already seemed pretty upset without that.

"What sort of place is this?" her mother demanded.

The great tree man spun about to face them. He wasn't smiling. He looked large and dangerous.

"This is a wild place," he said, his voice as gentle as his face was fierce. "It's the sort of place where you might have to prove yourself every day. It's a place where you'll learn to survive, or you will die."

Mrs. Blake came up behind Mary Lou's mother. "We're together," she said, "and we've all survived so far. I think we can learn, too."

"I hope you're right, Joan." Mary Lou's mother scowled down

at her daughter. "Why isn't your father here?"

What good would her father do against the People? Mary Lou wanted to ask. What good were any of them against the People, if the whole tribe decided they had to get her back? Why, when she had to face up to danger, did her mother think of her father at all? Maybe it was something about having the whole family together. Her mother was always big on that. Or maybe it was just easier for her mother if she had someone else to blame.

She heard the People's voices in the trees again, using her name to urge each other forward on the hunt. Why were they coming now?

Nick stepped forward, the first time he had left the shadows of the trees for the clearing. "They know we've lost our protection."

"What?" Jason asked. "We can still fight."

"With our fists?" Nick asked back. "With the few weapons we have?" He patted the hilt of his sword. "Even if those weapons are special? With Obar and Mrs. Smith gone, we've lost the magic that guarded us. Somehow the People know this."

Nick was right. Mary Lou nodded her head. "The People know all sorts of things."

Calls answered the sound of her voice. Calls from the trees, always closer than the ones before.

But, speaking of magic, where was the prince? He had always shown up before when she needed him. He had said, just before they had reached the clearing, that they were going to be together. Why was he gone for so long?

The Oomgosh stood tall, holding his single arm toward the sky. "We will fight if we must."

"With what?" Mrs. Jackson spoke up. "I'm afraid some of us don't know how to fight."

"Nick's got a sword," Jason pointed out. "Charlie's got his teeth. And the Oomgosh, even with one arm, is twice as strong as anybody I've ever seen. And the rest of us? We've got rocks and sticks to throw at them. The People are small. Maybe we can drive them away."

But the People were also armed, Mary Lou thought, and could sit up in their trees and rain arrows down on them. And, as much as the People wanted her, she didn't doubt they might resort to using a leftover poison stick or two to eliminate anyone who was good at fighting—Nick or the tree man or even her little brother.

She didn't want anybody to die because of her. That would be even worse than being a prisoner.

"Maybe," Joan Blake said, "we could call Mrs. Smith back here."

"She does seem in tune with the rest of the neighbors," Mrs. Jackson agreed. "Maybe she'll realize we're in trouble."

"No one can fathom the thinking of wizards," the Oomgosh added. Mary Lou wasn't sure if he was agreeing or raising an objection.

"Merrilu!" The call was loud enough now to carry over the wind. "Merrilu!"

The great black bird cawed as it swept into their midst.

"The entire tribe is in the trees!" he announced as he landed on Nick's shoulder. Somehow the bird looked like he belonged there. "Raven has seen them! Four hundred and thirty-eight. They are spread out, but only across half the forest." The bird waved his beak to the right.

"So we can get out of here?" Mary Lou's mother asked.

"Unfortunately," the Oomgosh replied, "these creatures can move faster than all but Raven. The best we can do is find some more advantageous place to make our stand."

"But," Mrs. Blake pointed out, "perhaps by delaying our encounter with these things, we might give Mrs. Smith the chance to come back here and help us."

"It certainly sounds better than staying here," Mary Lou's mother said. "Anything sounds better than staying here."

Mary Lou turned. She had heard her name again. But this time the voice had been deep and male. She looked into the shadows of the forest and saw the faintest flash of blue. It had to be her prince.

She pulled away from her mother and walked quietly out of the clearing.

Her prince stepped from the darkness, his faint form even more insubstantial in the shade.

"I came as soon as I knew," he said.

"About the People?"

He nodded. "We can't let them overtake the others. The People are desperate to get you back. The others would be slaughtered."

It was every bit as bad, then, as she had feared. "But what else can we do?"

"Come away with me." The prince's smile peeked through the darkness. "The two of us know these woods. We can move faster than the others. Together, we can leave everything behind."

This was the prince she had been waiting for. "All right. Can I tell the others what I have to do?"

"There's no time. The People are approaching much too quickly. A few seconds could mean the difference between our escape and someone dying."

Mary Lou looked back toward Jason and her mother. She hoped they'd understand. She turned to the prince. "All right. Let's go."

"This way," the prince instructed, floating before her. They were not leaving an instant too soon. The calls redoubled through the trees. They sounded like the People were almost directly above them.

"Are you sure?" Mary Lou asked. If the People were that close, she didn't know how they could get away.

"Of course I am," the prince replied calmly. "Remember how well I know the People."

That was true. For a time there, Mary Lou remembered, she imagined the prince and the People could read each other's thoughts.

Her feet crunched over the dead leaves as she ran, sounding to her as loud as an air-raid siren.

"Hurry!" the prince called.

"Won't they hear us?" she shouted back as she ran even faster.

"The People do not hear in the same way as people do," he answered. "Besides, listen to all the noise they're making themselves."

Mary Lou realized that there seemed to be calls of "Merrilu!" everywhere above them, the whole tribe drowning in the ecstasy of calling her name.

"We're almost there," he called back encouragingly.

Almost where? she wondered. The prince must have found a hideaway safe from the trees, a house of some sort, even a cave. No wonder they had to rush before the People got too close.

The prince's blue robe suddenly grew brighter. He was leading her into a clearing lit by the morning sun.

"We are here," he announced.

It was only when she stopped running and tried to catch her breath that she realized the whole open space was ringed by a circle of the People, silently watching her.

"Mary Lou," the prince said with a smile. "Welcome home."

○ Forty-one

Bobby swatted at the dead man's hands. A knucklebone broke free, clattering against the wall.

"You won't get away from me that easily," Sayre warned. His voice was rougher and deeper than Bobby remembered, like his voice box was rotting away along with the rest of him. "You're one of those damn kids who was always running over my lawn!" The dead man coughed. A large beetle ran from the corner of his mouth. "I bet you thought you'd never have to pay."

Nunn groaned on the floor.

"Talking back, heh?" Sayre said to both Bobby and the whole room beyond. "I don't let people talk back to me anymore. No one controls this fellow anymore!" He brushed at the flies that circled his face. Bits of skin fell away, and maybe a piece of his ear. "You might say I have a whole new view of life!"

Bobby backed away, looking for someplace he could hide.

Sayre leaned down toward Bobby and waved. "Now stand still while I break your neck."

Sayre jerked upright when someone coughed behind him.

"The least you could do," said a voice almost as hoarse as the dead man's, "is to thank me for all I've done."

Sayre managed to turn around, his arms flapping loosely against his torso. His head teetered precariously at the top of his neck as he swayed, but his voice was still strong with anger. "I've had about as much of this as I can stand!"

"I think, unfortunately, that most of us could say that." The newcomer stepped to the doorway, leaning heavily against it, as if the act of taking that single step could use all his energy. This newcomer looked almost as bad as Sayre, his skin dead white, his eyes sunken deep in his face. Bobby felt like he was in the middle of a zombie convention.

"So you don't recognize me," the newcomer said to Sayre. "Well, who would? You see, I'm responsible for giving you life."

261

He muffled a cough before he added, "But that's, of course, after I killed you in the first place."

Bobby looked carefully at the newcomer's face. Almost invisible on his pale flesh was a scar on either cheek. It was the Captain who had taken them from their homes.

"Soldier!" Sayre screamed, sounding even angrier than he had before. "I'll show you how I hurt!"

"I'm afraid I already know that all too well," the Captain replied. "It's time to stop your threats. I also know you, Mr. Sayre, better than you might imagine."

"Then you know I mean what I say!" Sayre shrieked as he lunged toward the other man. He took two steps, then stopped abruptly, his hands inches from the Captain's throat.

"Most of all, Mr. Sayre," the Captain said softly, "I know your mind."

The Captain lifted up his own hands, so that his fingers almost touched those of Old Man Sayre. The soldier gazed straight into the walking corpse's eyes and lifted his hands slightly.

Sayre's hands lifted as well, as if he and the Captain were mirror images.

"Good," the Captain said, and both his lips and the rotting lips of Sayre mouthed the words. The Captain and Sayre both lowered their hands to their sides.

"Your mind and mine are quite close now," the Captain spoke for both of them. "But I imagine you realize that."

The Captain, and Sayre, looked over at Bobby.

"I don't think I can hold him like this forever." As the Captain spoke, Bobby could already hear the strain in his voice. "It's best that you get out of here." The Captain nodded at the unconscious wizard on the floor. "With Nunn in his present state, I imagine you might be able to get out of this castle entirely."

Bobby wasn't so sure about all this. "Why should I trust you? Aren't you working for Nunn?"

"Nunn and I have had a falling-out." The Captain managed a grin. The scars lined up above the smile the way they used to. "My present condition should be proof enough of that. Nunn doesn't take kindly to others going against his orders. Unfortunately, he sometimes forgets to tell others just what those orders are." He grimaced. "I don't want anyone else to have to go through what I have suffered."

He started to cough again. Old Man Sayre coughed in time.

"If I had any real strength," the Captain managed after he'd caught his breath, "I'd get out of this place."

So this was the escape Bobby had been looking for. But he didn't want to go alone.

"My parents—" he began.

The Captain waved at the door. "Your mother is down the hall, with a couple of the other neighbors. I would get out of here now. I'm not as strong as I once was."

His gaze snapped back to lock with that of Sayre. Both began to shake, as if sharing some collective fit. The Captain moaned, and this time Sayre made a noise as well. Bobby decided to take the Captain's advice and get out of there. He ran past the two quivering forms.

As he hurried down the hall, he heard two voices speak in unison:

"My—lawn."

The stone corridor Bobby ran down was featureless, save for a single open doorway. He could hear voices in the room beyond.

"Maybe we should go out there and see what's happened."

"No. Nunn hasn't told us anything. I think we wait for his orders."

"Maybe something's happened to Nunn. Maybe he's hurt—or even dead."

A laugh. "Come on now, Harry. You've seen what Nunn can do. What could hurt something like that?"

Bobby recognized the neighbors' voices. He peeked around the corner of the doorway to see another large stone room like the one he had just left. Jackson and Dafoe stood in the center of the room, talking.

"I don't know, Mr. Jackson," Bobby interrupted. "But something did hurt him. He's out cold."

"Leo?" his mother's voice said from the corner. She was huddled beneath a table, as if trying to hide from the light. Her head turned from side to side, but her eyes didn't seem to focus on anything.

"No, Mom," Bobby replied. "It's just me."

"Where's Leo?" His mother clutched at her skirt, gathering the navy fabric in her fists. "I need my Leo."

"You heard Bobby," Dafoe said. "Maybe this Nunn isn't as all-powerful as you suppose. Maybe we all made a mistake in staying."

"How do we know this isn't some sort of test?" Jackson shot back. "The minute we turn our backs on Nunn, he could kill us all as traitors!"

Bobby didn't have time to listen to this argument. He knew what he had to do.

"Excuse me," he said as he passed the two adults. "My mother and I have to go."

"Leo?" his mother said weakly as he approached.

"I'm going to take you to Leo, Mom," Bobby whispered. It was a lie, but what else could he say? "Me, you, Dad, we'll all be back together again."

"Together," she repeated. She smiled at that.

"Give me your hand, Mom." Bobby held out his own hand for her to grab. She focused on his fingers with a sharp intake of breath, as if even fixating on a set of fingers was enough to scare the wits out of her. Her own hand quivered as she reached out and took her son's.

"Good, Mom." Bobby gently drew her forward, out from under the table. "Now you've got to stand up."

His mother stared at him like he was speaking some foreign language.

"For Dad, Mom," Bobby urged. "We're doing this for Leo."

His mother smiled a shy smile and shifted around so she could stand.

"I think you should stop there," Mr. Jackson said behind them. Bobby looked around. "What do you mean?"

Jackson sneered down at him. "If you think I'm letting the two of you walk out of here, you're crazy."

"Oh, come on, Carl!" Dafoe objected. "What harm can it do?"

"Nunn wouldn't like it," Jackson replied. "Or did you forget we were working for Nunn now?"

There was a shuffling sound outside the door.

"Someone's coming," Dafoe said softly.

Bobby turned back to his mother. "Mom, you really should get up."

Jackson walked quickly across the room toward him. "Leave her there!"

"I will not!" Bobby was getting angry. What right did this guy have to tell him what to do? "My mom and I are getting out of here."

"Oh, yeah?" Jackson stopped directly behind Bobby. He held up his arm as if he was about to clip Bobby's head with the back of his hand. "You take one step toward that door, I swear I'll kill you."

"Ah, now," Nunn's voice said from the door, "that's where your predecessor got himself into trouble."

Bobby looked around to where the wizard sat outside the door, carried in the arms of the Captain on one side and Old Man Sayre on the other. Neither Sayre's nor the Captain's face held any expression whatsoever.

"Still, I think your initiative is laudable," the wizard continued. "That's why I'm making you the new captain of my guard. There are a few simple rules you'll have to obey. I'll explain them to you"—he nodded to Bobby—"after I've cleaned up the messy situation around here."

Nunn waved for Bobby to come closer. "Now, Bobby, it's time for us to complete our negotiations. I imagine we might find we have a great deal in common. Don't you think it's time we worked together?"

Bobby wasn't going to do anything. Now that he had seen his mother up close, he hated the wizard even more.

"I won't!" he screamed back at Nunn. "I won't ever!"

"No, you won't, Bobby," a woman's voice said.

With a soft pop, Mrs. Smith dropped into the room. A second pop, and she was joined by Obar.

◯ Forty-two

Todd wasn't moving anymore.

That was the first thing he realized when he opened his eyes. The second was that he couldn't see any of the Volunteers.

He heard the high cries of the Anno in the trees overhead.

He rolled from his litter and was on his feet in an instant, waiting for a new raft of arrows to fall. But there were no arrows yet, only the singsong voices of the little creatures calling for Mary Lou. And even those cries were growing fainter.

Todd felt a hand on his shoulder.

"It still wouldn't be a bad idea if you stayed down," Maggie said quietly.

Thomas emerged from behind a tree.

"Thought we were going to have another attack," he announced, still studying the trees. "But they must of got what they wanted."

"Unfortunately for whoever that was, hey?" A pile of leaves shook and rose to become Stanley.

Todd pointed back at the litter. "So you just left me out in the open for them?"

"Weren't looking for you," Thomas replied.

"We figured you were the safest among us," Wilbert added with a laugh as he walked from behind another tree. "Why would the Anno want to shoot something that already looked dead?"

The Anno's voices were gone completely now. But other voices took their place.

"Mary Lou!" a woman called from somewhere nearby.

The Volunteers looked at one another.

"I'll do the honors," Maggie offered. She cupped her hands around her mouth. "Hello, the camp! We are friends! May we approach?"

"Yes, you may!" a deep voice called back. "We welcome you!"

"Forward," Thomas remarked with a wave of his hand. All five of them walked in the direction of the voices. There was a clearing ahead, in the middle of which stood the Oomgosh.

"Many welcomes!" the tree man called in that booming voice of his. He waved one of his arms. There seemed to be something wrong with the other one, like it had been chopped off and replaced with a new green branch.

"The Newton Free Volunteers," the Oomgosh announced to the others in the clearing. "Obar told us you were on your way."

"I think Obar knows us better than we do," Wilbert remarked, "for there were a few times we were not so sure we were coming."

"Perhaps we should introduce ourselves," Maggie began.

"Todd!"

He turned at the sound of his name. It was his mother. Deep down inside, he realized, he never thought he'd see her again.

He felt himself smile as she rushed toward him. Still, he couldn't let himself be too happy. Not yet.

"Where's Dad?" he asked cautiously as his mother hugged him.

"He didn't come with us," she said simply. Todd couldn't really tell if this made his mother happy or sad.

"He decided to stay behind with the wizard, Nunn," another woman said. Todd looked up to see it was Nick's mother, Mrs. Blake.

So Dad had stayed behind with Nunn? That was like his father. If he did one thing better than bullying, it was sucking up to the bigger bullies.

But that meant there was no reason for Todd not to be as happy as possible.

"Mary Lou!" Mrs. Dafoe wandered around the edge of the clearing, calling her daughter's name. She didn't look happy at all.

"What's wrong here?" Maggie asked the Oomgosh.

"The girl has disappeared. One minute she was here, then as suddenly she was gone. Raven has gone to look for her." The tree man paused and frowned. "I believe she's in the trees."

"Then she's gone back to the Anno?" Todd asked. That meant she had been here only a few minutes ago. He wondered if he'd ever see her again.

"Why would she do that?" Mrs. Blake asked. "It sounded like she hated those things!"

The tiny leaves rustled as the Oomgosh shook his head. "Sometimes things happen in this place that you wouldn't expect." He grinned and shrugged his working shoulder. "It's not that there are no explanations for these things. It's just that the explanations are new as well."

Todd wondered if the tree man meant that to be reassuring.

"Hey, Todd," Jason called. Next to him stood Charlie. Or was it? The whole shape of his head had changed, making him look half dog and half dinosaur. The mutt was barely recognizable.

"But you mentioned something about making introductions," Wilbert suggested now that things had quieted down.

Todd turned, along with everyone else. Something was crashing its way toward them through the forest.

Nick ran into their midst, stumbling to a halt.

"I saw Mary Lou!"

Her mother rushed forward. "Where is she?"

"Gone?" Nick managed, gasping for breath. "That is, they've taken her away. Those little bald creatures."

He paused for a minute, holding his stomach.

Nick swallowed, and straightened back up. "When I didn't see her around, I went out looking for her."

"Nick!" his mother reprimanded.

"Hey, Mom!" Nick gave his mother a pained look. "I can protect myself if I have to." One hand gripped the handle of the sword. "Obar gave me this thing. I've had to learn how to use it."

God, Nick was sounding full of himself. So he could use a sword! Todd wanted to shove that sword down his throat.

"But Mary Lou," Mrs. Dafoe insisted. "What happened to her?"

"She was struggling," Nick answered, "but there were so many of them. I was too far away to do any good. And I didn't want to draw my sword because—well, I just couldn't."

He looked at the ground for a moment, his breathing finally regular. When he looked up again, he added, "There was something else strange. There was some guy with her that wasn't really there."

Some guy who wasn't really there? Todd really couldn't believe that one. This was the sort of crap you got from Nick. He was the kind of guy who ended up writing poetry for the yearbook.

"The prince," Jason said.

"The prince?" Mrs. Dafoe asked, even more confused than before.

"He was—sort of a ghost," Jason explained. "Sometimes you could see right through him. And he sort of came and went mysteriously. But Mary Lou really liked him. She said he'd saved her more than once."

"Maybe that's why I saw him," Nick mused. "Maybe he'll help her again."

Todd wouldn't trust anything he found around here. If anyone was going to save her, it would be someone from the neighborhood.

"And Mary Lou?" Mrs. Dafoe asked again.

"I saw them take her up into the trees," Nick admitted.

The Volunteers looked at each other.

"No time now for introductions," Thomas murmured.

"We've got to bring her back," Maggie agreed.

"Been too long without a fight, hey?" Stanley added.

"The Oomgosh can help you find them," the tree man offered. "And Raven will scout ahead."

"Ma'am," Wilbert said to Mrs. Dafoe, "we'll have your daughter back in no time."

"I'm going, too," Nick announced, his hand still on his sword. "To overcome those things, you'll need everyone who can help."

Nick's mother started to protest, but instead only gave her son a disappointed look as he walked over to join the others.

"Hey!" Todd said. He wasn't going to be left behind, especially if some feeble lit type like Nick was going. "I've got a knife. And I know how to fight."

"Well, you're not going to leave me!" Jason objected.

"Jason!" his mother began.

"I think we all must go," the Oomgosh interrupted. "We are at our strongest when we are together. We will all do our part to regain Mary Lou. But we must do so now."

"What are they going to do to my daughter?" Mrs. Dafoe asked, her voice edging on panic.

"We can only hope that we are in time," was the Oomgosh's only reply.

◯ Forty-three

Mary Lou couldn't be quiet any longer.

"Why are you doing this to me?" she screamed.

The People answered with that mockery of her name, over and over and over again.

The People had surrounded her, great lines of the small creatures to either side, hundreds of hands carrying her into the trees. They pressed against her like a second skin, making it almost impossible to move. They tied one vine beneath her arms, a second around her waist. The People suddenly fell away from her sides as they swung her out from one tree toward another. She saw dozens of tiny grinning faces waiting for her, and twice as many grasping hands.

"Let go of me!" Mary Lou was starting to sob. The hands grabbed her and pulled her along a new branch. Her name was chanted again, over and over. The People once again pressed against her, lifting her at a silent signal.

"I want to be left alone!" she screamed, trying to be heard over the rising chorus of *Merrilu! Merrilu!*

"Try to be quiet," the prince said at her side. She could barely see him beyond the row of grinning People who transported her.

"Being this upset only makes it worse for you." Somehow she could hear his voice perfectly well, despite the People's chanting.

Mary Lou jerked her head free from the tiny hands that cradled her. "Why did you do this?" she asked the prince. "You helped me to get away. Why did you bring me back here?"

The prince gave her one of his sad smiles. That smile still made her ache, if only a little.

"I've begun to remember. There are certain things that are very important. Unfortunately, Mary Lou, you're part of one of the most important pieces of all. Even without my memory, I realized that."

"I should hate you," Mary Lou replied. She was glad that made him frown. "Why would you do this to me? You said I was very special, that you would protect me. You gave your word!"

"No," the prince said curtly, "I never made that kind of promise." He shook his head, letting his gaze wander past the People to the treetops and the sky. "Back before I remembered, I didn't realize I had that kind of word to give."

"I wish you could give me your word now."

He looked directly at her, his mouth set in a grim little smile. "I wish I could, too."

She realized then how serious he was about this Ceremony. And how little she knew about it.

"What's going to happen to me?"

"I don't know that much about the particulars of the Ceremony," the Prince said all too lightly. "I only know that it has to be done."

She felt as if he was avoiding something. She wondered what he was really thinking behind that smile.

She sighed, and asked the question. "Are they going to kill me?"

The prince looked away from her. "No," he said too quickly. A moment later, he added: "I don't know. I don't think you'll die. I don't think any of us will die, actually, until the dragon wants us to."

Mary Lou frowned. She felt as if something had suddenly changed. It took her a moment to realize that the People were chanting something now that wasn't her name.

"Dagar! Dagar!" they cried, as agitated as they were in the moment before the attack by the red furs. "Dagar! Raven! Dagar!"

With that, a great black bird swooped from the sky. A black bird with great yellow claws that raked at the People as he flew by. The People screamed. Some tried to fight the claws, others scrambled out of the way, a couple lost their balance and fell, shrieking, to the ground far below.

"Mary Lou!" the bird called in a voice that sounded like tires scraping across gravel. "Raven is here!" He fluttered his wings, rising from sight.

Mary Lou realized that all but a few of the People had stepped away. She sat up on the great branch.

"Don't try to move," the prince cautioned. "This Raven will never get you down from here."

The black shape swooped down from the opposite direction. The few remaining People cried out and fled to adjoining branches.

The bird alighted on the branch just below Mary Lou's feet.

"Raven is only the first," he remarked. "There are many who follow. Together, we'll work to save you."

"Again," the prince said, "I tell you, there's no way." He waved to the nearby trees. The People lined the closest branches, and now they held their weapons, bows already fitted with arrows, their strange, short knives, and the last of the poisoned spears rescued from their battle.

The bird ruffled his feathers indignantly. "Raven only has to take to the air to drive them away!"

The People lifted their weapons in unison, ready to attack.

The prince raised his translucent hands.

"Stop it!" he called. "You will not hurt Mary Lou!"

The People hesitated, as if they understood. Even Raven looked a bit startled. Mary Lou had never heard the prince talk in that tone.

The ghost turned to regard the bird. "It's too late to do anything now. The Ceremony's begun. The Anno will fight to the death to see that she goes through with it."

The black bird cocked his beak defiantly. "And who gave you authority? Raven recognizes no authority but Raven." Raven cawed suddenly. "Authority? That's who you are! Raven remembers! Who would question Raven but a wizard!"

Mary Lou looked up at the prince. "What is he saying?"

"A wizard!" the bird called triumphantly. "You are the third! Raven always remembers!"

"It doesn't matter who I am," the Prince replied matter-of-factly. "What matters is that I can't stop the People from shooting you."

The bird considered this. "Raven may be immortal, but he can be inconvenienced." He cawed again. "The third wizard! You were the third wizard!" He flapped his great black wings as he launched himself from the branch. "Raven will find you, Mary Lou! And this time Raven brings friends!"

Mary Lou looked around as the large bird disappeared beyond the nearer trees. She wished she could fly like him. It was probably the only way she could have gotten out of here.

The People hopped from one branch to the next, rushing toward her again with their ecstatic cries. In a few seconds, they would overwhelm her again, pressing hundreds of bodies around her as she was pushed toward their platform and the conclusion of their Ceremony.

"The third wizard?" she said to the prince while she could still see him.

"I'll tell you about it, if you wish." The prince shrugged. "At least, what I recall."

Mary Lou only had one wish, and that was for Raven to hurry back.

⭕ Forty-four

Evan Mills had always considered himself a practical man. Before he had become a vice-principal, he had taught mathematics. Mostly geometry. You couldn't get much more practical than geometry. So, no matter what happened, he always thought it best to look at all the angles, so to speak, before you went for a solution.

He'd never seen angles like this before. He had started this day on a different world. Now he seemed to be in a different reality.

Somehow, Evan Mills realized, he was a part of Nunn. And he was in here with Leo Furlong—or whatever had become of Leo Furlong—and some creature named Zachs. He imagined there were others here as well, maybe behind all those doors. And why did he see doors, anyway? Doors in a hallway, no less. No, no, that line of thought wasn't practical. Doors in the hallway worked as a concept. For now, that should be good enough for him.

Mills also knew Nunn held Leo Furlong inside him for a purpose. He had seen the magician take on the appearance of Leo. Nunn must keep some part of those he'd consumed, ready to wear like so many masks. He wondered if Zachs was held here for the same reason. Somehow, though, the creature of light seemed different, special. And strange.

There were so many unknowns here, even for a practical man.

But Mills knew one more thing. These individuals he had met since coming to this place were now able to act in a different way; and that difference was attributable to him. He remembered the way Nunn had absorbed Leo, the way Furlong had shrunk and Nunn had squeezed. The magician had had no time to do the same sort of thing with Evan. But Mills was in here, anyway. He was the surprise, the fly in the soup, the uninvited guest. That made him sort of a wild card.

Nunn was able to control those he kept within. At least sometimes. But Zachs had shown that it could control some of Nunn's

274

actions as well. Zachs was special, a creature of peculiar powers, but Mills imagined an uninvited guest would be special, too.

And just like Zachs, perhaps Mills could learn to control the wizard as well.

Mills heard a great moan from the end of the hallway. Nunn's moan.

The light-creature made a noise that seemed a faint echo of the one that drifted through the door. "Nunn knows now!" the creature wailed. Its light pulsed from red to yellow to sickly green. "You hurt Zachs! Zachs hurts you!" It paced randomly, making a great circle in the middle of the hall. "Will Nunn be too angry? Nunn can get very angry."

Leo looked up from where he sat on the floor. "Where are we?"

Mills didn't think Leo was ready to hear.

"We are prisoners of Nunn," Zachs answered for him. "Nunn keeps us inside, to use when he wants."

This light-creature seemed to understand their dilemma. And its comment had given Mills an idea.

"But Nunn won't attack us here, will he?" he asked Zachs. "Not when we're inside."

The creature stopped abruptly. "He can't." It giggled, executing a little monkey hop. "That will only cause Nunn pain."

Another groan came from the open door.

"But Nunn will know!" the creature cried, sinking down until its knuckles brushed the ground. "Will bring Zachs out! Will punish Zachs!"

"Maybe," Mills added quietly, trying to keep this creature as calm as possible, "he might bring one of us out. But what if more than one of us could cause him pain?"

Zachs looked up, its glowing eyes large with fright. "More than one?"

"Yes! That way one of us can give him pain first! That way we can protect each other."

Zachs' head rose again. It giggled, very softly this time, as if it only barely dared to think of such a thing.

It cringed when it heard a third groan.

"Sayre," Nunn's voice said this time. "My dear Captain. I need your help."

The light-creature shrieked, throwing its arms above its head. "Nunn is awake! Zachs hides!"

The light that was Zachs streaked away in an instant, leaving the other two behind.

Mills wondered how anyone could hide inside someone. Or, for that matter, how he could expect someone as volatile as Zachs to share its secrets.

Again, speculation like that wasn't practical. There simply wasn't enough information.

"Evan," Leo called up from where he still sat. "I'm afraid I don't understand a lot of this."

"None of us do, Leo," Mills reassured him.

Furlong sighed. "I just wish I could get back to Margaret and Bobby."

Mills was afraid that was impossible. But then, they were in the middle of the impossible already, weren't they?

"Evan!"

Leo clutched at Mills' pant leg. Mills looked where the other man was pointing.

Another door had opened partway down the corridor.

This, Mills thought, could only be an invitation.

"C'mon, Leo." Mills pulled the other man to his feet. "We might as well see what's waiting for us."

As soon as he thought about approaching the door, he was there. Leo stood next to him.

"Do you think this is such a good idea?" Leo whispered.

Heck, Mills thought, it's better than having no ideas at all. He looked inside.

The room was filled with a sky of robin's-egg blue, broken by three white fluffy clouds, and a larger thunderhead of a very deep grey.

Mills realized that the thunderhead had eyes. Two eyes, as blue as the sky. It blinked at them.

"I understand," the cloud said, its mouth filled with a very pink tongue and a perfect set of teeth, "that you want to know something about causing pain."

Mrs. Smith wished she felt as confident as she sounded.

"You will give Bobby to us now." Those words came out of her somewhere.

She wasn't at all surprised when Nunn laughed.

"So nice of you to come and visit." Nunn nodded at the two men who carried him. One, she realized, was Hyram Sayre. The other was the Captain of Nunn's guard. She had thought that the Captain had killed Sayre. Actually, at the moment, neither one of them looked particularly alive.

The two of them slowly lowered Nunn to the ground.

"I trust Obar has brought his dragon's eye? I've been looking forward to adding it to my collection."

"Ah, brother," Obar said abruptly, as if he had only just now remembered how to use his voice. "You should be even more pleased to know that we've brought more than one dragon's eye."

She supposed this was the best time to hold her own gem aloft. She held it in her fist, only revealing it when her arm was fully raised.

"Yes," she said, far more calmly than she felt. "We have two."

"So that explains your power!" Nunn replied with glee. "You've had the stone all along. I was afraid you were something extra-ordinary, something new. Two dragon's eyes? Perhaps we can negotiate."

Actually, Mrs. Smith thought, she had only found the stone quite recently. However, that didn't seem to be the most important point to bring up at this minute.

"Negotiate?" Obar mused. "Oh, yes, oh, my, the threats are gone, aren't they? How different the world becomes when things are equal."

Nunn snorted at that. "Things are never equal. I have allies as well."

With that, Hyram Sayre and the Captain lurched into the room.

Nunn raised his hands. A glowing jewel was embedded in either palm.

"Now," Nunn said calmly, "do you prefer to be killed by my servants or by my eyes?"

Mills was transfixed. A cloud with eyes was too far beyond the practical.

Leo spoke first. "Who are you?"

"The proper question, I imagine, is 'Who was I?' " the cloud replied gently. "I was a wizard, too. There have always been wizards in this place.

"Before that, I was a human, just as Nunn was a human before he developed his skills. Humans and wizards are not so different. We are all the sum total of all those we meet, and all that we consume. The true wizard is only more so— especially someone like Nunn, who consumes so many of those he meets."

The cloud smiled serenely.

"He ate you?" Leo asked.

"Of course. There's really no other way to get rid of a wizard. We just sort of hang around forever. Unless, of course, you're careless around the dragon."

Mills was sure he should be paying close attention to all of this. But he couldn't get Bobby out of his mind, especially since Nunn seemed about to do something to the boy. Nunn had hurt enough people. He wanted to stop him now.

"This is all very interesting," he told the cloud, "but I need to do something now."

"Yes?" the cloud asked.

Mills decided it was best to be direct. "I need to cause pain this minute. To stop Nunn."

The cloud closed its eyes for a second. "Ah. So you do. And after this, I suppose you'd want lessons?"

So this cloud, or wizard, or whatever it was, really would do what he asked. Suddenly, Mills felt overwhelmed.

"Lessons? In giving pain? If it isn't too much trouble," Mills agreed.

"No trouble at all," the cloud replied genially. "I haven't had anyone to talk with in ages."

When Hyram Sayre screamed, it was an awful sound, ragged and raw, with a tone that shifted from a grumble to the kind of high whine you heard in those damn rock and roll songs.

Sayre decided to scream again. It was awful, but he liked it. The way he felt now, he was ready to get back at anyone who'd done anything to him, his whole life long. If he met someone he didn't know—hell, he'd do it to them, too. It was time to let everything out. It was time to make everyone pay.

No one would laugh at his lawn now.

Look at this fat man in front of him, with the long mustache. How'd he like it if that mustache got pulled off his face!

Sayre felt no pain. He only felt how strong his muscles had become, how much they wanted to choke the life out of anything that got in his way.

The sooner he killed these people, the sooner he could get back to his lawn. He'd forget this twerp's mustache. A single twist of the neck would do instead.

"Hyram! No!"

Sayre stopped short. Who knew his name?

He looked over. It was someone he remembered. A lady who lived across the street. Why couldn't he recall her name? So many things seemed to be slipping by him. She never made fun of his lawn. At least to his face. But behind his back, yeah, they all made fun of him behind his back. How could they imagine he wouldn't know?

Still, she'd been nice to him, out on the street. Sayre decided to give her a few more minutes and break the fat man's neck first.

She held something in her hand. It flashed green, pushing away some guy with scars on his cheeks.

Hyram Sayre forgot all about the fat guy's neck. What a wonderful shade of green that was.

He wanted that green, almost as much as he wanted that lawn.

Nunn would win. Nunn always won.

Two wizards with two dragon's eyes could defeat him if it was a direct contest and there were no other elements to confuse the combatants. But Nunn was a master of confusion. And it was that confusion, really, that would win the day.

Power to power, this would have been a fair fight. But Nunn never fought fair. He had tossed his two minions into the fray as a diversion. The poor Captain wasn't much good. Nunn's other plans had almost used him up. The woman brushed him aside with the power of her own dragon's eye.

Ah, but this Sayre fellow was a revelation. Nothing seemed to stop him. Certainly, whatever pitiful spells his brother could muster seemed to do no more than flake off another bit of skin or hunk of bone. Dear Sayre didn't even seem to notice. He might even be able to kill Obar without a bit of help from Nunn. Wouldn't that be jolly. Nunn could think of so many things he could do with as naive a wizard as Mrs. Smith, once she was all alone.

And then dear Constance had actually managed to distract Sayre for an instant. Perhaps his dim, reanimated brain remembered something from the old neighborhood. Obar shot another bolt of energy at Sayre's back. The reanimated corpse staggered as the energy bored a hole through his shoulder. But it was only a small hole, and Sayre kept on moving.

Now, while both Obar and Smith were distracted, would be the perfect time to rid himself of them.

Nunn called to his eyes. He felt the heat of power first in his palms, then flowing up his wrists and arms and across his shoulders to his neck. So much power. The dragon's eyes were excited by the possibilities. The heat was intense, searing his face as it reached for his brain.

It was too much. Something was wrong.
"Noooo!" he screamed as pain lanced through his skull.

"Yes!" Mills exclaimed. "That's exactly what I want."
The inside of the room, which had suddenly shown a view of the battle in the room beyond, just as suddenly shifted back to sky and clouds.
"Good," the thunderhead remarked jovially, "because you're the whole reason this is happening."
"Me?" Mills said. What was he doing besides trying to survive?
"These dragon magics are delicate things," the cloud explained. "Nunn has learned how to use them well. But no one, save perhaps the dragon itself, can ever have complete control of these things. If Nunn has a weakness, it is his confidence. He leaves himself open to attack from unexpected quarters. You are that attack."
"Well," Mills replied, a bit overwhelmed by the magnitude of what he might have done, "I did want to fight him back there."
"And that's what you're doing!" the cloud agreed eagerly. "But you're going to be able to fight him in a way that neither he nor you have ever experienced before.
"By entering Nunn without his proper preparation, you have stirred up the powers that reside in his brain: all those things that he has consumed that stay, ghostlike, in his memory. Suddenly, Leo Furlong can think for himself. That light-creature, Zachs, finds it has the will to move. And an old wizard awakes, and thinks of retribution."
The cloud chuckled. "I think, if we handle this properly, we shall not only succeed, we shall also be properly entertained." The image of the thunderhead faded again, and Mills could see the first outline of the room beyond. "But maybe we should get back to our battle. I think we might be able to adjust the outcome here very easily. Don't you?"
Mills decided for the moment that he was content to shut up and watch.

Oh, dear, Obar thought, this wasn't going at all well. Mrs. Smith's lack of experience with her eye was already showing. And this damned corpse seemed to shake off minor spells. Obar was afraid that if he occupied himself with a major spell to rid them of this pest, Nunn would counter with a major spell of his own when Obar was unprotected.

Then Mrs. Smith called out the corpse's name. The Sayre-thing lurched around and started for her. Obar's attacks didn't seem to have any more effect on the corpse's rear. And what about Nunn?

That's when his brother wizard screamed, without Obar doing a thing. Somehow Mrs. Smith had gotten through to him. She was such a wonderful raw talent. How could Obar have ever doubted her?

Now was the time for Obar to strike.

"Bobby!" Mrs. Smith called as she lifted her jewel. "Get Bobby!"

Oh. Of course. That was the whole reason they'd come here, wasn't it? Bobby first, Nunn later.

"Come on, Bobby," Obar called. "We have to get out of here."

The boy looked up from where he knelt by Mrs. Furlong. "Can we take my mother, too?"

"I don't see any problem with that." Obar looked at the two other men who had backed into the corner as the conflict began. "We can take you fellows, too, if you want to go."

The more nervous of the two looked at the other, a large man who appeared to be angry at everything that was happening.

"What do you think, Carl?" the nervous one asked.

"I've made my decision, Harold," the angry Carl replied. "Nunn is going to win. Look at how messed-up these two others are, and they had surprise on their side."

"But something's wrong with Nunn!" Harold's shaking finger pointed at the wizard.

"So we need to prove ourselves," Carl said. He stepped toward the center of the room, waving for Harold to follow. "Come on. I think we can take them."

Oh, dear, Obar thought. This was getting a bit out of hand.

"Mrs. Smith!" Obar called. "If you could gather the others around you, I'll hold off Nunn." And maybe, Obar thought, he could disable his brother for a while as well.

"Hyram!" Mrs. Smith answered severely. "Stop there, or I'll have to hurt you!" She held the dragon's eye high above her head. It pulsed with power.

"Green," Sayre muttered in reply. "All green is mine."

"Now!" Carl called as he charged toward Obar. Harold followed, somewhat more hesitantly.

"Please," Obar remarked offhandedly. He caused a ring of green fire to seal him off from this foolish attack.

Nunn stood suddenly. From the agony in his face, he was still struggling with whatever spell had attacked him. "I—will—not—be—overcome!"

Oh, drat. This was getting worse.

Sayre lurched toward the stone in Mrs. Smith's hand.

Carl screamed as he hit the wall of magic fire. He staggered back, beating at his chest as green flames enveloped his clothes. He started to scream and ran backward three steps, right into Sayre.

Sayre fell forward, right into Mrs. Smith.

She cried out in surprise as the dragon's eye was knocked from her hand.

"Green!" Sayre yelled in triumph as his rotting hand reached up to catch the stone.

"Not that!" Mrs. Smith exclaimed as she pushed herself forward toward the stone. But Sayre was taller, his reach greater.

Mrs. Smith's hand knocked hard against the other's rotting wrists as he touched the stone.

Sayre grunted. The stone flew across the room. Straight to Nunn.

He caught it with his right hand, closing his fingers so that the new jewel brushed against the dragon's eye buried in his palm.

Nunn started to laugh.

There was only one thing left to do.

"Bobby!" Obar shouted. "Here, now!" He threw his spell over the boy and his mother, whipping it around to cover Mrs. Smith before Sayre could renew his attack.

"Go!" Obar screamed, pulling them all from the room.

The spell worked. They were back in the clearing where they had started, although the other neighbors seemed to have left.

"Oh, dear," Mrs. Smith said softly. She stared at the hand that used to hold the dragon's eye.

It was only now that she probably really realized what had happened. They had lost a dragon's eye, their only chance to fight Nunn on an equal footing.

But they were safe, for the moment. Safe to think of anything they might do to survive, before Nunn learned to control all three of the eyes at the same time.

Once that happened, Obar was quite sure everyone now in this clearing was dead.

○ Forty-five

Mary Lou hoped Raven would hurry. There was no other way she would escape the Ceremony.

"A little adventure," the prince said by her side. "It must feel good to know that so many people care about you."

Mary Lou had had just about enough of her prince. "Why don't you just shut up!" she snapped at the apparition. "If I'm going to die or something, the least you can do is let me have a few minutes' peace."

"Oh," the prince replied. He actually was silent for a moment as the People kept on with their task of carrying her higher and higher, sometimes toting her, at others passing her from hand to hand, but always holding her with so many of their tiny hands that she could never move her arms or legs. They kept on calling her name, too, she supposed. The chanting had gone on for so long that she was beginning not to hear it.

"You do know that I meant it," the prince added a minute later.

"What?" Mary Lou demanded. Actually, she thought, maybe some talk would take her mind off what was going to happen next.

The prince looked down at her with his transparent eyes. "About a lot of people caring for you. I have the feeling that might be something you're not used to."

Mary Lou felt she was going to blush. She decided it was better to be angry. "Sure, you care about me! The People care about me! Otherwise, you can't go through with your stupid Ceremony! It doesn't matter that the Ceremony is going to kill me!"

"I never said the Ceremony would kill you," the prince replied softly. "I quite actually don't know what it will do. I only know that it's necessary."

"Necessary?" Mary Lou demanded. "Necessary for what?"

"For the next stage to begin. For us to gain some power over the dragon. For me to regain some bit of the real me that was lost so long ago." The prince shrugged. "At least that's what I think it's all about. I didn't feign my forgetfulness, you know. And there are still huge parts of my past that I still know nothing about."

"What *do* you know?" Mary Lou found herself interested despite her anger.

The prince gave her the intense look that would have melted her heart only a few hours ago. "That I was one of three wizards that came here, except we didn't start out as wizards." He paused, looking down at his insubstantial robes. "Actually, there were five of us at first. A barber, two shopkeepers, a banker, and me. I was a customer, just passing through San Francisco on my way to Alaska and gold. I found gold of another kind." He smiled. "Once we got here and found what little the dragon left, we also found that three of us had certain powers. It was a shame that the remaining two had to die along the way.

"And an old wizard died, too, one that held three dragon's eyes. Once we'd put him out of the way, of course, that meant there was one eye apiece for the three of us. Or there was, until the other two killed me. Or at least thought they did."

"So they murdered you for the eye?"

The prince smiled down at her. "Oh, I would have killed them, too. The stones meant that much to all of us at first. And we could only find the three. The dragon was keeping the others hidden, keeping the power of the final four for itself." He hesitated for a second, his ghost face graced with the slightest of frowns. "For some reason, that isn't true anymore. A fourth eye has been found, and I'm beginning to feel the others."

Mary Lou had never seen the prince look troubled like this before. "Feel?" she prompted.

He stared off into the trees, his face still solemn. "Once you have had a dragon's eye, you are very close to them, forever. You miss them, you want them, you'd do anything—" His voice drifted off into thought. He suddenly looked back at Mary Lou. For the very first time, he seemed a bit self-conscious. "Sensing these eyes—perhaps it has something to do with the dragon's reappearance. But I think the remaining eyes will be ready for the taking, if you're fast and clever enough."

Mary Lou didn't care much for the eyes. Instead, she asked, "If they murdered you, why aren't you dead?"

The prince laughed at that. "Well, I don't know if I'm precisely alive. And I have the most trouble remembering those days just before I was attacked. But I imagine I guessed that Nunn and Obar—they are brothers, you know, and in those days their family feeling ran rather deeper than it does now—I guessed the brothers would kill me for my gem. And I somehow concocted a spell that would help me survive."

Mary Lou still didn't understand. "But what does all this have to do with the Ceremony?"

"Forgive me, but it's all part of the spell. To complete it, we must have this Ceremony."

"Your spell? But the Anno seem to think the Ceremony will give them something they always wanted."

"That's what the Anno do believe," the prince agreed. "The People are a single-minded species. Once they get something in their head, there's no getting rid of it."

"And you used that," Mary Lou said. "You put that something in their heads, that Ceremony!"

The prince spread his translucent hands. "Guilty. I had to find something that would bring me back. What better than someone brought by the dragon?"

"So you're the one I should hate," Mary Lou said softly, as if she might keep herself from that emotion.

"Hate me or not," the prince said, "I think all of this was destined to be." He laughed softly at a private joke. "All the time, I think it was the People who used to work for me."

Mary Lou looked up and saw the never-ending leaves give way to a vast expanse of blue sky. They had almost reached the People's village at the top of the trees.

This was it, then. The Ceremony would begin, the prince would get whatever he needed. And Mary Lou?

She was surprised to find she wasn't that afraid. In fact, she felt very little at all. She simply knew that, a few moments from now, she might not fear, or hate, or hope ever again.

⊙ Forty-six

The Oomgosh had no doubt as to what would happen eventually, for he could talk to every tree.

The land, the trees, the sky—these always prevailed. And the Oomgosh was a part of this order. Wizards came and went. Even the dragon spent most of his time in hiding. But nature was forever.

Unfortunately, the Oomgosh was not as certain about what would happen now. The world was a much faster place in the presence of these newcomers.

He had not spent much time lately around humans. He had forgotten how much he enjoyed their company. Not that Raven wasn't a joy. He and the Oomgosh were fated to be companions, after all. But even one as ancient and patient as the Oomgosh found Raven's boasting irritating on occasion, despite the fact that boasting was a fine part of the great black bird's nature. Humans, however, were unpredictable, and this newest batch, courtesy of the dragon, seemed to be a particularly contentious and talented lot. Especially the children. The Oomgosh always cared about growing things.

And the Oomgosh hated the taking of life without good cause. When he thought of what might happen to Mary Lou, he grew angry. And when the Oomgosh grew truly angry, he could move the trees, the earth, and the sky.

He listened to the cries in the trees overhead. At first, the Oomgosh thought, the way the Anno chanted on and on, they would lead them straight to Mary Lou.

But the Anno, although they sometimes appeared to have a single mind, were not single-minded. Some of their number split off from their main force above, calling Mary Lou's name to the right and left of them, spreading out so that they might be taking Mary Lou to any part of the forest.

But the trees told the Oomgosh the Anno's secrets. Their

trunks groaned under the weight of the hundreds of little ones as the Anno carried Mary Lou higher. The branches whispered as they shook with the Anno's passing, "This way! This way!" And, as surely as water flowed from root to trunk to limb to leaf, the sighs and groans and whispers of the trees were carried the other way, down to the great mass of roots that covered the whole island. And the Oomgosh could hear these roots, talking far underground.

"This way," the Oomgosh instructed. Jason waved for the others to follow. Of all the humans, the Oomgosh liked Jason best of all. The boy was full of an energy the likes of which the Oomgosh could barely remember, and that in another lifetime. And Jason and he got on well with each other from the first, like old friends from the moment they met. Although they had lived in different worlds, the Oomgosh and Jason were a match.

The Oomgosh looked to the Volunteers, hard humans who knew the way of the wood. "They are taking Mary Lou to their city. I imagine the Ceremony will begin there."

"I'm the best at climbing trees," Maggie announced. The Volunteers still hadn't introduced themselves to the others, but the Oomgosh knew them from long ago.

"And the rest of us are bad, hey?" Stanley chided. "We'll go up there and make short work of them."

"Well, I'm not so good, at least at climbing trees," Wilbert admitted with a pat to the stomach. "Perhaps I can take up the rear."

"Can you tell us where this city is?" Thomas asked as he scanned the trees.

"It covers a large area," the Oomgosh answered, "but I believe it begins quite nearby. I trust that Raven will return shortly and tell us more about appearances."

The remaining neighbors, three women and two boys, caught up with the forward party.

"What's going on?" Mrs. Blake demanded as they approached. "Is there anything we can do?"

"I think the best strategy for now is to stay together," the Oomgosh cautioned.

"Once we know Mary Lou's whereabouts," Maggie began, "those of us who can climb trees"—she smiled at Wilbert—"can form a raiding party."

"Hey, I can climb a tree," Nick offered.

"So can I, jerk," Todd said, more to Nick than the rest of the group.

"Better if you climbed vines," Thomas interjected. He nodded at the thick vegetation hanging from the lower branches. "That's how we really travel."

Stanley squinted at the two boys. "We might be able to use the two of them, hey? There's an awful lot of Anno up there."

"Awful lot of ways for them to get killed, too," Thomas added. "Don't know about this."

"I don't know about this, either," Mrs. Blake said. Her son, Nick, barely glanced at her. He turned back to the Volunteers, his hand on his sword.

"I've learned how to fight with this thing," he said, patting the hilt.

"I'm ten times the fighter he'll ever be!" Todd protested.

"Fighters?" a harsh voice cawed overhead. "We'll need plenty of fighters!"

"My Raven!" the Oomgosh called.

"Tired Raven," the great bird squawked as it swooped down toward them. "Even the most superlative of creatures can find this work trying." He fluttered his wings, landing gently on Nick's shoulder. Nick shuffled a bit under the additional weight, but didn't say anything about the imposition.

"Now, Nick," Mrs. Blake began again.

"You're Nick's mother," Raven said abruptly. She stopped whatever she was going to say and stared at the bird, openmouthed. "Don't be surprised. Raven knows everything. Your son is the most comfortable perch. And young Nick has many other talents nearly as valuable."

"We all have to work together here, Mom," Nick added before his mother could say more. "Otherwise, we won't survive."

Mrs. Blake's frown deepened. She sighed. "I suppose you're right. Remember, Nicholas Blake, if you get yourself killed, I'll be very mad at you."

Nick smiled at that. "I'll try to remember, Mom."

But there was a life to be saved. "Raven," the Oomgosh insisted. "What did you see?"

"Raven has never seen these creatures so excited," the bird replied. "They have thrown all their caution away! The whole tribe has gathered on the platform, except for those carrying Mary Lou. And those who carry her have almost reached their destination."

"What will they do with her?" Mary Lou's mother asked anxiously.

"The Ceremony," Jason answered, then asked, "What's the Ceremony?"

"Raven saw a great pot up there, filled with a steaming liquid."

"Are they going to boil her?" Jason asked.

"The Anno do like to eat," Wilbert offered.

Mrs. Dafoe gave a small, strangled cry. She put her hand to her chest, as if even she was surprised by the noise. She looked to the Oomgosh. "You've got to do something."

"We will all do our part," the tree man agreed. "Raven, do you recall how many lookouts they had? And where they were placed?"

"Raven thinks they're too excited for lookouts!" The black bird flapped his wings as though that excitement was contagious. "A few watched the edges of the platform, but even they could not help but look around at the festivities behind them."

"Maybe we can sneak up on them, after all," Maggie said softly.

"Never expect attack from the trees," Thomas agreed. "Least not from humans."

"So we go now, before the Ceremony starts?" Wilbert asked. He looked doubtfully at the nearby vines. "I could use whatever time's available."

Nick glanced at Todd. "We're coming, too!"

"If you're set on it," Stanley agreed. "But let us take the lead, hey?"

"What about the rest of us?" Joan Blake insisted.

"We will all be needed," the Oomgosh replied gently. "If we do manage to rescue Mary Lou, we may all have to defend ourselves against the Anno."

"Defend ourselves?" Todd's quiet mother spoke up for once. "How can we do that?"

Stanley threw his pack on the ground. "I'll leave this behind for you. There's a few things inside you might find useful. Hey, it's too heavy to climb with, anyways."

"Where are the edges of their city?" Thomas asked as Mrs. Blake knelt by the pack.

"Careful not to cut yourself, hey?" Stanley suggested quietly. Mrs. Blake unfolded the animal skin to reveal half a dozen knives and hatchets and twice as many arrowheads. "Split the weapons up as you see fit. Save the arrowheads for later."

The Oomgosh listened to the trees. "The city is very near."

Raven cocked his head, looking first at the trees above, then at the humans gathered around them. "Raven thinks the platform begins twenty paces from where you stand."

Maggie walked a few feet to grab a vine. "This is as good a place as any to begin."

"Please hurry," Mrs. Dafoe said softly.

"Swift and silent, that's our motto," Wilbert assured her. He grunted as he pulled himself off the ground.

All four of the Volunteers were already making their way up the vines. Todd and Nick hurried to follow.

Raven fluttered aloft as Nick sprang into action. "Raven will fly ahead. Perhaps Raven can cause a distraction!"

The Oomgosh chuckled at that. "You are the most distracting bird I know, my Raven. Go quickly, all of you!"

Before they put poor Mary Lou in a pot, was what he didn't say. If that were to happen, the Oomgosh would become very angry indeed.

○ Forty-seven

It only takes a second, Nunn thought, for everything to change. He cupped both his hands around his newest darling, his third dragon's eye. With this in hand, there was no way he could lose.

"Where'd they go?" Carl Jackson glanced uncertainly back at the wizard, as if unsure he should speak at all.

"It doesn't matter," Nunn replied. "Not anymore." He glanced over at Sayre and the Captain, freezing both in place. They looked like statues, the Captain representing the malnourished, while Sayre stood for death and decay.

He looked back to the living. "I would like to congratulate you, Mr. Jackson, upon your efforts on my behalf." He nodded first at Jackson, then at Dafoe. The second man began to squirm as soon as Nunn looked his way.

"Mr. Dafoe," Nunn added, "I think you could have done better than that." He liked Mr. Dafoe. He liked anyone whom he could make uncomfortable.

"There appears to be a void of leadership in my palace guard," he continued. "Carl, you will be the new Captain. Harold will be your second-in-command. Together, we will run not only my home but this entire world. I will give you further instructions on this—shortly.

"Now you'll have to excuse me." He could feel all three gems pulsing beneath his fingers. "I have other matters to attend to."

With a wave of his hand, he returned to his study, a study once again devoid of doors. Nunn took comfort in the darkness.

A minute ago, he had almost failed. All his enemies seemed to conspire against him, including some he had thought were powerless. A wizard's psyche was so fragile. Encounter someone like this Evan Mills, and you invited disaster. As far as Nunn could determine, Mills had upset certain things within the wizard, his unauthorized entry activating a few of the hundred personalities that made up all those little parts of Nunn. And those personalities were capable of damage that Mills could not even imagine. Who would think a danger like that might come from within?

It was like the arrow he took in the shoulder, Nunn reflected, a surprise attack that got past his defenses, even with the extra strength and speed given by two of the eyes. He was not so invulnerable as he had thought.

But that was so long ago, when he had only two eyes.

Now it was so much better. Now there were three eyes. His speed and strength, doubled before, would double again, and the eyes would allow him to split his consciousness and join with three separate powers, to witness three things at once, or weave three spells into an impenetrable web. There'd be no more arrows, no attacks from within. With the power of these three eyes, he would destroy anything that stood in his way.

He had work to do. It would take a little while to incorporate this third eye, to find the balance with which all three could work together. Once that was accomplished, Nunn would calmly destroy Obar and Mrs. Smith, and gain eye number four. It would be easy after that to gather the other neighbors for his amusement, and his hunger.

The new eye felt warm, nestled between the other gems. And the three parts of the dragon, linked together so, showed Nunn something new.

The other eyes were waiting for him. He had always known they were there somewhere, out among the seven islands, but before this, they had been hidden from him. Sometimes, with two eyes, he had been able to vaguely sense their existence, but now he could feel their pull, as if those last remaining gems wished to join their brothers and sisters. Was this the power of the third gem, already filling him? Or were the gems suddenly free of their hiding spells, another sign from the dragon that he was about to come and reclaim his own?

Nunn couldn't tell. And he didn't care. He only knew that now he could gain all seven of the stones, so that when the dragon came, he could say, "No! You can't have these! I am keeping this power for my own!" For, if that old wizard Rox had survived the last passing of the dragon with only three eyes in his possession, with all seven Nunn should be able to ride on the dragon's back!

Laughter burst out of him. He'd make the dragon dance! But he had to be careful. This new power he held was inebriating.

There were things he had to do before he could claim it all.

Things both without and within.

"He knows," was all the cloud said.

Mills stared at the thing that had once been a wizard. "Are you talking about Nunn?"

"I must make certain precautions," was the thunderhead's only reply. "You would be well advised to do the same."

Mills looked around, as if he might somehow find those precautions the thunderhead referred to. The room seemed to be growing more indistinct, as if everything was becoming part of the cloud.

"Precautions?" he asked. "What do you mean?"

"We haven't even begun the lessons, have we?" the cloud murmured. "Too bad there hasn't been more time. I will see what I can do. In any event, this diversion has been quite pleasant. I never thought I could get back at Nunn. Actually, I hadn't been thinking about anything whatsoever." The thunderhead sighed. "I imagine that will happen again. Remember what we've done. Remember that feeling of success, if you can remember anything at all."

This, Mills thought, did not sound promising.

"What's that?" Leo wailed.

In the corners of the room, the clouds were fading, replaced by blinding light.

"Nunn is doing his housecleaning," the thunderhead remarked. Even the great grey cloud appeared less distinct than it had before.

"Is he going to destroy us now?" Leo asked miserably.

"Nunn doesn't destroy anything completely," the cloud continued, its voice the soul of calm. "He simply seeks to control. Any independent energy you have will be drained away completely. But some part of you will remain."

The light swept across the room toward the thunderhead.

"Goodbye," the cloud said.

The light flooded across the image of sky. The thunderhead was gone. There was nothing but light.

"The light's coming this way!" Leo shouted. "Run!"

"Where?" Mills replied. Perhaps a bit of the cloud's calmness had passed along to him. Or perhaps he simply realized there was no escape. How could they run away when they were trapped inside Nunn?

The light sliced across the room like a knife through paper, a light that would wash away every one of Nunn's woes.

Leo Furlong screamed as the brightness roared toward them. The sound cut off abruptly as Mills was lost in the light.

Nunn smiled.

Things seemed so much quieter now.

The eyes were working together already. As he withdrew from his inner purge, the gems showed him three images at once. There were Obar and Smith, not talking at all in a clearing, as if the two of them were in shock. And that tree man, surrounded by the other neighbors, rushing through the forest on some grand adventure. And there was that annoying black bird, Raven, swooping through the trees above a crowd of the Anno, all dancing about a great cook pot. He blinked, letting his eyes seek new subjects. There was Carl Jackson, yelling at Harold Dafoe to shape up or they'd both be in trouble. There was the King of the Wolves, growling to the remains of his pack about revenge against the humans. And there was a procession of the Anno, marching toward their village, taking great care with something in their midst, carrying what must be a most precious cargo. Nunn could not make out that part of the image, though. It was fuzzy; indistinct. He wondered if the third eye might have some defect. What might be beyond its power?

He realized with a thrill that the Anno must be carrying Mary Lou. It didn't matter that he couldn't see her when he could see everything else. Even she could no longer hide from the wizard's power.

Nunn let the images fade back into the darkness of his room. The three gems seemed to balance each other perfectly, as if they were meant to work together, and he was meant to be their owner. Perhaps, the wizard thought, the dragon was not as neutral on these things as legend claimed. Perhaps that all-powerful creature preferred that a certain type of man would wield the dragon's power, maybe even going so far as to influence the placement of its power so that it fell into the proper hands. Nunn laughed. Perhaps the way this third gem fell into his hands was a sign from the dragon itself, a blessing on Nunn's actions, a harbinger of the greatness that was to come.

Before that greatness could begin, Nunn had to add the third eye to his collection. He had placed the first two in the flesh of his palms so that they would always be a part of him, and he would always share in their power. But, with a dragon eye on his either side, where should he place the third?

Of course, he realized, there was only one place for the newest gem, one spot to display proudly the gift from the dragon, to let all those who came before him know that he was heir to the dragon's power. Once he thought of this, he realized there was no other place for the eye to go.

He felt the heat of the stone as it rubbed against his fingers. His hands tingled with the sensation as he rolled the stone about the other eyes, as the power of all three gems built, waiting for the magic to burst forth. Nunn breathed deeply, letting the energy wash over him for a minute while the stones reached their peak.

The moment was near, so familiar from his use of the two stones, but so much more now with three. The energy seethed from finger to palm to thumb, then spread to wrist and elbow and shoulder. Nunn allowed himself a moment of the fullness the power brought before he concentrated on placing it back into the stone.

Now, he thought.

He brought both hands up to his face and placed the stone against his forehead. Although the stone was dark, it felt white-hot against his skin, for the eye still held all its energy within.

"Now!" Nunn shouted as he pressed the stone into his flesh. He heard his skin sizzle as the great heat burned it away and filled his lungs with the acrid smell of sorcerous fire. He pressed his palms against the newest stone, so that two eyes pressed against the third, heat adding to heat, and heard the bone bubble and boil as the skull melted to make way for the facets of the gem. As the power grew, so did the vibrations that spread from his hands to rack his whole body. And now he could feel those same resonances in that space above his eyes as well, great sweeping tremors of energy that threatened to make him collapse. But he wouldn't stop yet, not before he was truly fulfilled. A final moment of concentration, and he would be done.

Nunn screamed for joy as the dragon's eye pushed into his forehead.

Evan Mills opened his eyes. Or at least he tried to. It was far too bright.

"About time!" a high, whiny voice announced. "Zachs is not to be kept waiting!"

"Zachs?" Mills asked, remembering the creature of light as he repeated its name. He had met the thing somewhere inside Nunn. It felt very long ago. He couldn't remember much that had happened since. He did remember light and then blankness. How had he regained consciousness?

"Zachs hides," the whiny voice said proudly. "Zachs knows Nunn. Waits for the right moment. Nunn gains power. Zachs lives for power!"

"What do you want from me?" Mills asked.

"You woke Zachs!" the thing insisted. "You're Zachs' friend. Now Zachs wakes you! Together, we will use Nunn's power! Together, we will find a way to get free!"

So that's why the creature was here. It knew Mills had somehow been independent of the wizard's power before. Now it wanted Mills to show it some way out.

Except Mills didn't know a way out, didn't even know the exact nature of the place they now were in.

But he did know another thing or two.

"Zachs," he replied, "there is a way out of here. But we will have to wake a couple of the others first."

The creature giggled. "Zachs will wake everyone. Power enough for all!"

"Yes, Zachs," Mills agreed. "Power and freedom, too."

◯ Forty-eight

The King of the Wolves was worried.

He had already lost a part of his pack to these treacherous humans. And he could hear rumblings from those that remained, that he was no longer worthy of leadership, that he should be challenged and killed.

The wolves needed meat. Not that they were truly hungry; they were skilled hunters, and took down small animals and the occasional larger creature, like those three red-furred things that came from another island. But they held a different, deeper appetite. They had been rebuffed by the humans too many times. They needed to tear apart soft human flesh, to taste the salty blood that only came from man and woman.

He scented humans often now. There were many of them in the wood these days. A great group of them had passed through here only moments ago, including a number armed with those sharp flying and stabbing things to cut the life from a wolf. They were not the best place to start.

The King of the Wolves prowled, barking for the others to follow. His pack might grumble against him, but they still obeyed. He caught the smell of other humans on the wind. A smaller group this time, only four, and two of them had the particular stink that came to humans with age. But old meat was better than no meat at all, especially when its real purpose was to lift the spirits of the pack. After they were done with the aged, the two others would give them more tender, juicier fare. Maybe, the King thought, they could keep one or two of them alive in a Man Trap and lengthen their feast. No one would question the King of the Wolves after that.

The King moved forward warily, growling for the others to follow, but at a distance. He would scout this prey himself. He wanted no chance of failure. Yes, he could see all four of them in the brightness of the clearing ahead. They hardly moved at all,

297

instead sitting and leaning against the ground, plainly exhausted. The old man's head kept nodding down, as if he was fighting sleep. The old woman stared up into the trees, perhaps looking for something far away. Another woman of middle years stared at the ground, muttering to herself. The only one who appeared to be any sort of trouble was the fourth, a youngster who spent half his time talking to the woman who looked at the ground, and the other half pacing the clearing.

It already looked like these four had lost a great battle. They appeared exhausted and dispirited, not much of a foe at all. The wolves would have the human meat they needed, after all. And maybe, the King thought, they'd save the boy for later.

The King of the Wolves howled for the pack to follow as he broke into a run. Three of the four in the clearing ahead didn't even seem to notice his cry.

He broke into the clearing with a great growl. It wouldn't do if these humans were too dispirited. Their meat tasted so much better if it had been flavored with a scream or two, just before they were taken down.

"Wolves!" the boy cried.

"Yesss!" the King of the Wolves exulted. "Ssit sstill. It willl be overrr quicklyy."

"What?" The old man started, as if he had indeed been sleeping. "Oh, bother."

He pointed at the King. Green light shot from the man's finger.

The King of the Wolves screamed in pain.

Wizards! Was there no end to this human trickery? He howled a warning to the rest of the pack. The King somehow got his paws beneath him and scrambled from the clearing.

There were no sounds of pursuit. The humans seemed to still be sitting there, as if there had been no attack at all.

He was safe from the wizard, then.

The King was not so sure about his pack. They had been promised human meat. The grumbles would soon become growls, and he would find his throat torn out and be left to bleed to death on a forest trail.

The King of the Wolves roared to all of the woods.

"Frustrating, isn't it?" a voice said behind him. A human voice.

The King spun about, ready to defend himself. But the tall, pale creature before him made no move toward him. He did not look precisely human, either, although he might once have been a man, for he had a great, green jewel embedded in his forehead, a jewel that lit the whole forest around him.

"Whoo arre youu?" the King of the Wolves demanded.

"A friend," the stranger said with a smile. The King didn't like it when humans, or things that looked like humans, smiled. "A friend who has recently acquired a bit of power. I saw your frustration when you attacked those humans. Perhaps there could be a way to lend you a bit of my power, so that you could go back and destroy them."

"Desstroy?" the King growled warily.

"Let us say that this is something I wish to see done as well," the stranger replied. "Because of this, I might be able to give you certain abilities that would make you faster, fiercer, better than you are. Are you interested in making a bargain?"

The King of the Wolves reared up on his hind legs. For once, he was ready to listen to a human voice.

○ Forty-nine

The wolf seemed to have woken them all up. At least, all of them besides Bobby's mother. She smiled as she stared at someplace nobody else could see, murmuring words of comfort to her husband and son.

"Do you have your lunch? I made that sandwich especially. How was your day, dear? Oh, the lines at the supermarket were terrible. And they have to do something about that traffic—" She'd shiver from time to time, but then start her monologue again, reassuring words from the family and neighbors. "Did you see that thing the Smiths put on their lawn? What's happening to this neighborhood? I made your favorite for dinner—"

It felt like this place was too scary for her, and she had to find someplace—the old neighborhood—that was safer. Bobby wondered if she'd ever leave the neighborhood again.

"Obar," Mrs. Smith said quietly. "I'm sorry for losing the stone. I was overconfident. I rushed into this thing without really knowing what I was doing."

"And I'm terribly out of practice," Obar answered with a sad smile. "I was totally exhausted by that confrontation. We'll have to get better if we're going to defeat Nunn."

"Defeat Nunn?" Mrs. Smith shook her head. "How can we possibly defeat Nunn? Thanks to my foolishness, he has three of the dragon's eyes!"

"But we have one," Obar replied reasonably. "And we have your power, which was formidable even before you got the eye. And there are other eyes out there, on other islands, eyes that used to be hidden from us. But this world is changing, maybe because you are here, or maybe because of the dragon. The other eyes should be easier to find, for those quick and willing to find them."

Mrs. Smith closed her own eyes for a second. "There are three more of them, aren't there? In three very different places."

Now it was Obar's turn to shake his head. "And you do that without the benefit of your own dragon's eye." A short bark of laughter emerged from between his lips. "Sometimes I find you frightening."

"My husband used to say things like that to me, too," Mrs. Smith replied with a smile. "It's a shame I'll never see him again."

"You never know," Obar said, suddenly very serious. "That sort of thing is the will of the dragon."

"What is that supposed to mean?" Mrs. Smith asked with her own frown. "This is always so mysterious. How can anybody know the dragon's will?"

"I have a feeling that we will all know far more about the dragon before this is over," Obar added. "Far less mystery, far more blood. But we must plan to find the other eyes."

"As soon as we know that the others are safe," Mrs. Smith agreed. "I have the feeling there is still something we can do for Mary Lou." She looked over at Bobby and his mother. "For that matter, maybe there's something we can do for Mrs. Furlong, too."

Bobby shook his head. His mother said something reassuring to the dirt.

"I think Nunn's done too much to her," Bobby said.

"Anything Nunn can do can be undone," Mrs. Smith answered, some of the old strength returning to her voice. "With or without an extra dragon's eye."

"You are truly terrifying," Obar remarked. "I'm glad we're on the same side."

"And I'm glad that you keep that in mind," Mrs. Smith said with the sweetest of smiles. "Now, what say we try to help Mary Lou?"

Mary Lou never thought she would hate her name.

The cries of "Merrilu! Merrilu!" were deafening as her captors carried her from the last of the trees onto the great log platform of the People's village. Mary Lou didn't want to hear any more. She wanted to cover her ears, to make all of it go away, if only for an instant, a final silent moment for her to think. But her hands were pinned to her sides by a hundred of the People's hands, and hundreds of voices shouted her name.

"It will be over with soon," the prince's soft voice cut through the chanting again.

"Merrilu! Merrilu!" the People called ecstatically as they carried her across the platform.

Soon, she supposed, there would be nothing but quiet.

Charlie barked at the disappearing Volunteers. Wilbert grunted away, reaching the tree line a full minute after any of the others, but still climbing with a steady pace. Nick and Todd were not far behind.

"You want to go, boy, don't you?" Jason said to the dog. He was surprised he hadn't volunteered to join the rescue team himself. But a part of Jason felt it was important to stay with the Oomgosh, as if this was his true purpose in this place. He looked over at the tree man, who also watched the others leave very intently, as if for once he wished he could leave the ground. The Oomgosh's new limb was growing at remarkable speed, its bright green shoot already half as long as the arm that remained. In another day or so, Jason doubted they would even be able to tell which arm the tree man had lost to the poisoned spear. Jason would feel better, too, once the Oomgosh was whole and himself.

"I feel so helpless," Mrs. Dafoe said softly.

"We should arm ourselves," Mrs. Jackson replied suddenly. "I never want to feel that way again. Let's see what Joan has in that sack."

Mrs. Blake looked up from the assortment of knives and hatchets. "We all need to protect ourselves."

Rebecca Jackson hugged her arms close to her body, as if fighting off a chill. "It's not like—" she began. "Some of you have guessed that things were not that good between Carl and myself. Sometimes I was scared of him. A hundred times I swore I'd leave him. But where would I go? What would happen to Todd?" She walked over to get a better view of the knives. "All those worries disappeared when we were pulled out of our homes and brought here. I don't know what's going to happen. But I don't want to be afraid the way I was before." She crouched down next to Joan. "I think I'd like a knife. I sort of know how to handle that. I wouldn't have a clue how to handle a hatchet."

"How about this one?" Mrs. Blake suggested, pulling out a knife big enough to carve a turkey.

"I don't know if I could handle—" Mrs. Jackson paused as she took the knife in her hand. "This is very light, isn't it?" She jabbed the blade up into the air. "Yes, this could do some damage."

"Here," Mrs. Blake added, offering her neighbor the sheath, fashioned from some mottled animal hide. "How about you, Rose?"

"I guess I could take a knife, too," Mrs. Dafoe said softly.

"Just like working around the kitchen," Mrs. Blake said with a smile. She looked back down at the knives spread out before her. She picked up a smaller blade and stabbed it into the air. "Who would think that preparing dinner would lead to a second career?"

Jason stepped over to the Oomgosh. "Is there anything we can do?"

The tree man glanced down at Jason. His smile looked tired. "We will be very busy very soon. For now we wait. Sometimes waiting is the hardest job of all."

Nick heard the shouts get closer as he climbed. These rugged vines had knots and branches that were easily used as foot- and handholds. In a way, pulling himself up this vine was more like climbing a ladder than a rope.

As he climbed, the world changed. The perpetual twilight that surrounded them in most of the forest seemed to brighten with every step he climbed. The great trees seemed far more majestic up here, where Nick could see their limbs spread and cross, surrounded by great sprays of deep green leaves. There were trails through the trees below as well, well-worn paths that ran along the great branches and boles, leading, no doubt, to the same place these creatures were holding Mary Lou. He felt he had entered a world above the world, every bit as strange as the fantasy kingdoms he made up in his head.

He wondered how his father would react to a place like this. He'd hardly thought of his father at all since he'd come to this place. His father, who always yelled at Nick for not facing up to things, but who couldn't face up to his family. His father went away before they'd had a chance to talk. Sometimes Nick was mad at him for leaving like that. And sometimes he just missed him.

"C'mon!" Todd whispered hoarsely. Nick started. He wasn't paying attention to the signals.

Wilbert waved to him from up ahead. He'd gone from his vine to one of the paths that led upward, and wanted them to follow him. Todd joined him on the trail a second later. Nick nodded his head, swinging his weight around to move his vine so that he could join them.

He landed with a thump on the large branch. Todd grimaced at the noise. Wilbert only turned and led the way.

There could be no doubt that they were traveling the right way. The noise was overwhelming before them, a great crowd cheering in their odd, high voices. And the only thing that all the voices called, over and over again, was Mary Lou's name.

Mary Lou's bearers stopped abruptly. They must be near their destination. Mary Lou leaned her head back to see what they had reached.

The crowd separated to reveal a great dark kettle hung over a moderate fire. It looked like something out of a fairy tale, all ready for Hansel and Gretel. Except this time the wicked witch was waiting for Mary Lou.

There were steps at one side of the kettle, and her bearers steered her there. The crowd noises were growing less intense, with most of the shouts coming from those People in the distance. Those in Mary Lou's view seemed only to watch her in hushed silence, as if in awe of what was to come.

They mounted the steps, a dozen People pressed close against either side. They'd give her no chance at all this time to get away. She wondered if the Ceremony started with her being boiled alive. Part of her thought she should be more upset about this, but another part thought this was all inevitable. She was Mary Lou. She was born to be sacrificed.

She wondered if the prince was happy with this. She turned her head as best she could to observe the surrounding crowd. She couldn't see him anywhere around. The thought that he might have deserted her upset her more than anything else about this.

"No!" she called suddenly.

Her voice seemed to wake even the respectful People nearby.

"Merrilu!" they shouted back triumphantly.

She tried to wrench around, maybe jerk an arm free. "Let me go!"

"Merrilu! Merrilu! Merrilu!" The People were really happy to hear from her now.

Oh, God, she thought, this was impossible. She couldn't struggle anymore. She felt like laughing. In a moment, they'd dump her in the kettle, to be boiled like a lobster. Mary Lou, the special of the day.

But her bearers didn't stop at the lip of the kettle. They climbed higher, to a rickety-looking platform some ten feet above the pot.

Mary Lou realized she wasn't going to be boiled, after all. She was going to be steamed.

She laughed at last.

"Merrilu!" the People cheered.

◯ Fifty

Nunn was quite pleased with himself. By making a few simple adjustments on that pitiful wolf, he would develop a new soldier to rid him of petty distractions like his brother, so that he could go after the other jewels.

He had already planted the seed that would transform the wolf in a matter of hours. He should seek out the jewels now, while the others were occupied. The three remaining dragon's eyes were in three far different places, a time-consuming quest even for someone who held three of the eyes already. He would go, too, as soon as he completed some unfinished business.

He would reclaim Mary Lou.

No one ever escaped from Nunn. And no one ever would.

Todd had never seen anything like the Volunteers. The four of them had formed a loose half-circle approaching the Annos' camp. They had tightened that circle, slowly and steadily, calmly and quietly killing any member of the Anno that happened to get in their way. They wouldn't even let any of the dead bodies fall, instead securing them to branches with lengths of vine. Then all four Volunteers would creep forward again.

Nick and he weren't so quiet. Todd didn't know why the Volunteers had to be so stealthy, either. The tribe of creatures ahead was making so much noise, Todd could barely hear his own clumsy footfalls and branch-rustling.

Wilbert put up a hand for the two boys to pause again. The trees broke open a bit ahead, and beyond them, Todd could see a great log platform built high up here, sort of like a tree house gone crazy. And every inch of that platform was covered by the Anno, all facing away from them, pushing toward some spectacle that Todd couldn't see.

Todd was sure it had something to do with Mary Lou. They should be rushing forward to help her. Why were the Volunteers still being so cautious?

Wilbert looked back at Todd and pointed, twice. There, in two different trees, were two Anno, each one sporting a drawn bow. Both glanced back often at the platform and the celebration, but both also turned from time to time, as if reminded that they were supposed to act as lookouts.

"Merrilu! Merrilu! Merrilu!" the People cried.

Thomas and Maggie drew out arrows of their own, each aiming at one of the two lookouts.

They launched their arrows as the People began to shout again.

"Merrilu! Merrilu! Merrilu!"

The lookouts' screams were covered by the ecstatic crowd.

Wilbert waved Todd and Nick forward, until all three had reached a hidden place only a few feet from the platform.

"What now?" Nick asked as he nervously fingered the hilt of his sword. Todd touched the handle of his knife as well, just to be sure.

Wilbert looked to Stanley, crouched in a tree on one side, then to Maggie, who knelt on some sort of rough-hewn bridge of logs and vines on the other. Both nodded as if they understood.

"Now we wait for an opening," Wilbert replied very softly. "There are too many on that platform, even for us. We need a diversion."

What did that mean? "What kind of diversion?" Todd demanded.

"I think I see one now," Thomas replied. He pointed to the sky above the trees, where a great black bird had swept into view.

"Merrilu! Merrilu! Merrilu!"

The People were growing so excited, she could swear she heard a couple of them scream.

Her personal guard had climbed high above the kettle. They had finally had to release their grip as they pulled and pushed her onto the rickety pile of twigs that hung above the great black pot. For the first time, Mary Lou had some freedom to move. She thought about struggling, but realized all that any fight would bring was the platform's collapse, and her quick trip into the boiling liquid below. Out of the frying pan into the fire.

She wasn't at all surprised when the People quickly bound her arms and legs to the branches. So much for her break for freedom. The People who had escorted her scrambled off the platform and back down the stairs.

"Merrilu! Merrilu! Merrilu!"

She could already feel the heat from the kettle. She imagined that the branches below her were widely spaced so that the steam from the kettle could do just that. They had left her head free. If she craned her neck as far as it would go, she could just barely see the edge of the kettle.

"Merrilu! Merrilu! Merrilu!"

The Chieftain raised a great pole adorned with elaborate carvings she couldn't quite make out at this distance. A pair of the People walked forward, carrying a platter covered with a pile of fine leaves, which they proceeded to dump into the pot.

Seasonings? thought Mary Lou.

The liquid below was boiling. And, instead of invisible steam, it was producing a thick, green smoke.

Mary Lou started to cough as the smoke reached her. Maybe, she thought, they would choke her to death instead.

All of the People called her name.

And then they started to call another.

"Ontawa! Ontawa!"

The People punctuated this new cry with a quick stamp of their feet.

"Ontawa!" *Stomp.* "Ontawa!" *Stomp.*

They had set up a rhythm, a rhythm to call something.

For some reason, Mary Lou was sure they were calling the dragon. The prince could read the People's minds. Maybe this Ceremony gave her that talent, too.

"Ontawa!" *Stomp.* "Ontawa!" *Stomp.*

Is this what the prince wanted? Would the dragon make him flesh and bone again? From everything she had heard about this dragon, though, Mary Lou imagined it did not make that sort of bargain.

Or perhaps, she thought, the prince was mistaken, and the People were conducting a Ceremony all their own. Maybe that was why the prince was nowhere around. Maybe the prince was still far too much the People's subject, after all.

The smoke was making her dizzy. She thought she saw shapes in the roiling green around her. People fighting, screaming, dying. What happened, she thought, the last time the dragon came? Why would the People call to something as destructive as that? Did they think Mary Lou could control it?

"Mary Lou!" called a hoarse voice, as different from the cries of the People as Mary Lou was from that high school girl she used to be. She looked up in the sky.

A black shape swooped down toward her. She had trouble focusing on it. Something about the smoke.

"Stay with us, Mary Lou! Help is on the way!"

Raven. It had to be Raven.

But why did she see the great leathery wings of a dragon above her?

"Hello," the thunderhead said.

With that, the blinding light went away. Mills opened his eyes and saw that he was in the room filled with clouds.

"Zachs did good!" the light-creature cheered.

"Zachs opened the way," the cloud agreed. "Now we have to take care that Nunn can never close it again."

Mills was amazed by all of this. "Can we do that?"

"With someone as careless as Nunn?" the cloud asked disdainfully. "It's barely worth asking the question. He gains power without limit, assuming he will easily learn how to control it. More likely, it will end up controlling him!"

The cloud wizard sounded like he could do anything.

"So how do we get out of here?" Mills asked.

"A delicate matter," the cloud replied after a moment's hesitation. "We will need something of Nunn's cooperation. I believe we should first teach him a lesson."

"A lesson?" the creature of light shrieked with glee. "Zachs will teach Nunn a lesson!"

"We all will," the cloud agreed. "We simply have to wait for Nunn to overreach himself."

"And when will that happen?" Mills asked.

"Oh," the cloud replied mildly, "I should say any moment now."

Nunn did like it when his coming caused people to scream. It was reassuring. And when they scrambled like mad things to get out of his way, well, that really showed a wizard his worth.

Of course, these small, weaselly Anno made awfully easy prey. Nunn could crush a dozen of them without even noticing. But even obvious superiority could be the most positive of feelings.

Of course, he wasn't here for the Anno. He was here for Mary Lou. He looked across the platform, finally able to see with his human eyes what his dragon's eyes would not show him. They had propped the girl on some platform made of twigs, above a great cooking pot. Where would someone as primitive as the

Anno get a pot like that? Did they have allies Nunn didn't know about?

"I wouldn't do what you're thinking."

Another human here? Nunn spun about to confront the other. He didn't like being startled this way. He was the one who always brought surprise.

It took him a second to recognize the other man, perhaps because the other looked more ghost than human. But it only took a second.

"Garo!"

"Is that my name?" the other replied with a smile. "Thanks for telling me."

This was most disconcerting. "You should be dead."

"And I very well may be," Garo agreed jovially. "Good of you to notice. All thanks to you and your brother."

This was taking Nunn away from the real reason for his appearance. The People had stopped calling Mary Lou's name and had begun calling the dragon. It was time for Nunn to take her and leave this place.

"It was you," he said suddenly, "who kept me from seeing Mary Lou."

"Was it?" Garo continued in that same maddening tone. "Well, perhaps I still have some powers, after all."

Nunn shot his hand forward, grabbing for the young wizard's neck. His hand passed through Garo's image, as if the young wizard wasn't there. The youngster must be existing on a slightly different plane. Obar and he had been so new to magic when they had tried to kill this difficult fellow; this sort of thing was probably to be expected.

"You can't do any more to me, old man," Garo taunted.

"Can't I?" Nunn replied. "Well, then, I imagine you can't do anything to me."

He turned away from the other wizard. It was time to capture Mary Lou. Or rescue her. It all depended upon your perspective.

This was the sort of thing Wilbert was waiting to hear.

"There's our diversion," Wilbert announced.

The People were screaming as if their world had ended. Wilbert knew the Volunteers would be glad to help that feeling along.

Wilbert glanced to his left. Maggie waved him forward, as Thomas would have done for her. He waved as well, a signal to Stanley and the two boys.

Nick and Todd seemed pretty worldly-wise for boys their age.

Probably city kids. They always grew up faster in a place like that.

Wilbert always thought about the damnedest things when he was getting ready to fight.

He could feel a yell building in his throat as he ran up the trail to the Annos' village.

The pressure was too great. He had to let it out.

Wilbert pulled his knife and let his voice yell for all it was worth.

"Come on, Mary Lou!"

◯ Fifty-one

"Here it comes," the cloud wizard remarked in the same calm voice it used for everything. "Let us see if we can witness the action."

Mills blinked, and the room full of clouds was replaced by a scene of screaming chaos. The short, wizened Anno were everywhere, and they all seemed to have one thought: to get away.

They were looking through Nunn's eyes. The wizard lifted his hands. Tiny green fires erupted from each of his palms.

He turned one of his hands toward a group of the Anno. Twenty of the wizened, pale white creatures screamed as they were consumed by flame.

Mills felt as if he was watching some bad disaster film. "Does he eat those things, too?"

"Usually, he stays away from the truly foreign species," the cloud replied. "They tend to disagree with him. So he destroys them instead."

As soon as the sorcerous fire had reduced the first group of Anno to ash, a second group took their place. They shook spears and knives at the wizard.

"They have gotten over their initial fear," the cloud wizard continued. "They realize they have to protect Mary Lou and their Ceremony."

"They?" Mills asked.

"The Anno always make decisions as a group. Singly, they are none too bright, but in a crowd, they can be formidable."

"I don't have time for this," Nunn's voice rumbled through the cloud chamber.

The Anno shrieked again as they suddenly looked up at the wizard looming over them. Then just as quickly they shrank in size as the platform flew by beneath the wizard's gaze. Mills realized Nunn had left the ground and was flying toward the pot and Mary Lou.

"Nunn always was an exhibitionist," the thunderhead remarked.

There was the girl below. The Anno had tied her to some sort of platform, a structure now surrounded by thick, green smoke. The wind shifted so Mills could see her face. Mary Lou was choking.

"Caw!" a harsh voice interrupted. "Stop right there!"

Nunn's gaze shifted upward. There, hovering in the air before him, was a large black raven.

"Raven will rescue the girl!" the black bird announced. "Leave this instant, or face Raven's anger!"

"Is there no end to this nonsense?" Nunn's voice rumbled in return. He clapped both hands together. Bright green light flashed from his fingers, striking the raven.

The bird screamed as it was tossed away, high into the air.

"Now, Mary Lou," Nunn murmured. The girl on the platform rushed toward them.

"Zachs has never seen Nunn so powerful," the light-creature whined, "or so angry."

"Or so careless," the cloud wizard replied. "There will be some moment soon when he will be taught to respect us." One of the cloud's eyes appeared in the midst of the scene before them. Mills thought the clear blue eye was looking directly at him. "You will have to be ready. I may need your assistance."

At this point, Mills imagined, he was ready for anything.

Once Wilbert started running, Todd followed. He didn't want to think about anything else. Together, somehow, they'd save Mary Lou from these miserable little creeps.

The creatures were screaming already, at something in their midst. What could Raven have done to upset them like this? The way these Anno things were running around now, it would be no problem at all to push right through them.

Wilbert shouted in front of him. He heard Thomas and Maggie and Stanley pick up the cry. Even that wimp Nick was shouting behind him.

Todd grabbed the dagger in his belt and pulled it free. And he yelled, letting his voice give speed to his running feet as they jumped on the platform.

He remembered, then, when he had roared with the dragon. It was something about that anger that had saved him. Something about that anger that the dragon lived for. Something about that anger that would let all of them live, or cause all of them to die.

One of the Anno was in front of him. The thing had a knife. No more thinking now.

Todd held up his own blade, hoping the creature would run away.

The Anno bared its pointed teeth and charged. "Merrilu!" it called. Or maybe all the Anno yelled that together.

Todd knocked the knife arm aside. He thrust his own blade forward, but the creature squirmed past the knife point, its snapping teeth lunging toward Todd's hand.

Todd jerked his hand away, surprised at the small thing's fierceness. But only for a second. One thing he had learned in all those playground fights was never to be surprised a second time.

There was a great scream nearby, and a burst of strange-colored fire. Both Todd and his opponent froze for an instant as a man in dark robes rose above the crowd on the far edge of the platform, levitating above the mass of shrieking Anno.

Todd saw other movement out of the corner of his eye. His own personal Anno had whipped its head about, its teeth set for Todd's wrist. Todd jerked his wrist back, so that the thing's teeth clamped shut on his sleeve. The thing, startled, seemed unable to open its mouth for an instant. It was trapped by its own attack.

Todd drove his blade into the thing's belly.

The creature's mouth opened then to scream. It thrashed about, trying to hack at Todd with its own, smaller knife. But there was no strength behind this last attack. Todd avoided it easily. The creature stiffened for an instant, then went limp. Todd raised one sneakered foot and pushed the thing off his blade.

This, he thought far too calmly, is the first time he'd ever killed anything.

More screams. A pair of Anno launched themselves toward him. Which one? Todd thought. He couldn't cut both. A sword blade flashed forward on his left, slicing easily through one of the attackers. Todd heard Nick laugh.

He turned his attention toward the other, slicing the air with his blade so that the Anno rushed into it. The creature's face erupted with blood.

"This way!" he heard Wilbert shout in his ear. Todd saw Stanley, Thomas, and Maggie all in a line, each surrounded by piles of small corpses. The Volunteers looked like they were going to fight their way along the edge of the platform, skirting the main body of the Anno until they got close to Mary Lou. Todd risked a glance back at Nick. The other boy brandished his sword over his head, the blade so covered with blood that it seemed to glow from within.

"Damn it!" Wilbert suddenly shouted on his other side. "Nunn!"

Todd turned to see a human shape hovering above the place where Mary Lou was tied to the branches. That flying figure had reached her before them. So that was Nunn?

The Anno had stopped fighting for an instant, too, their bloodlust replaced by hysterical calls of "Merrilu! Merrilu!" Maybe they realized that, with Nunn here, things wouldn't work out quite the way they'd planned. But Todd didn't see how the Volunteers could get to her, either.

"Have to move!" Thomas called from the front of their line. "Now!"

Charlie was going wild.

"Is it the Anno?" Jason asked.

"Not yet," the Oomgosh replied. "The dog reacts to something that isn't here yet."

Charlie stood his ground, eyes glowing, as he barked at a bare spot in the middle of the clearing. A second later, Obar and Mrs. Smith popped into existence in the same spot. Bobby and his mother showed up a little bit behind them. Mrs. Furlong didn't look too good. Mrs. Jackson walked quickly over toward her.

"Good dog," Mrs. Smith remarked.

Charlie yipped in surprise. The red embers in his eyes dimmed slightly.

"Are we too late?" Obar asked.

The Oomgosh looked up in the tree. "The battle is overhead. Mary Lou is still there."

"Shouldn't you know all this?" Mrs. Blake asked. "I thought at least one of you was a wizard."

"Well, I'm afraid, Joan, there's been a couple of setbacks," Mrs. Smith replied quietly. "We're running a bit behind."

"We've lost a bit of power," Obar admitted.

"Then you can't save Mary Lou?" Mrs. Dafoe asked.

"No, no," Mrs. Smith answered firmly. "That's the very reason we're here."

"Just needed to reconnoiter a bit," Obar added.

"Speaking of that," Mrs. Smith began.

"Shall we?" Obar agreed.

Charlie barked once as they popped back out of view.

Jason decided that Mrs. Smith was getting every bit as confusing as Obar.

She must be truly becoming a wizard.

Jason went over to Bobby to ask him just what had really happened.

Sometimes the dragon wings were the color of the smoke, a deep, deep green, like the very darkest of leaves. At others, the wings seemed to have no color at all, as if they refused to have light bounce from their scales.

Whatever their color, they were coming closer to Mary Lou. Soon she would be lost completely in their shadow. In only a moment, she could turn her head and see the great green eye of the dragon staring back at her.

"You're not leaving yet," a voice announced. A voice far too human to be the dragon.

Mary Lou blinked. She took a deep breath of smoke-free air. What was happening to her?

The dragon's wing was gone. She looked up and saw a human face. No, not exactly human. The face belonged to Nunn.

"Why, Mary Lou," he said with a smile. "Don't ever leave without saying goodbye."

She shook her head. She had trouble making sense of what he said. "Goodbye?"

Nunn's smile grew even broader. "We'll be leaving now. Together."

She felt something at her wrists and ankles. She looked at her right arm and saw her bonds were untying themselves.

"If you're so polite," another voice interrupted, "why don't you say hello?"

Mary Lou looked up again. There, just past Nunn's shoulder, stood Mrs. Smith and that other wizard, Obar.

Nunn didn't seem the least upset. He laughed instead, a deep and hollow sound. "So you've come to give me your last dragon's eye?"

"If that's what you want to believe, brother," Obar replied. "However, the reality of this situation might be somewhat different."

The Anno didn't even seem to notice them now.

Todd couldn't believe it. One minute, these creatures seemed like they wanted to fight them to the death, and the next, they turned, mesmerized by the drama that took place on the raised dais, where the three wizards hovered around Mary Lou. It was like these creatures listened to silent orders in their heads, telling them to chant, or attack, or simply to watch.

The Volunteers didn't even bother killing any of their enemy. Thomas simply pushed the Anno out of his way, clearing a path for the others as they rushed toward Mary Lou.

"Merrilu!" the Anno chanted. "Merrilu! Merrilu!" As if saying her name would change everything.

A fifth figure appeared to hover about, although the newcomer was not quite so solid as the others. It was Mary Lou's prince.

"Now," the cloud announced.

Mills and the creature of light looked at each other, as if someone must know what the cloud was talking about.

"It's time for a confrontation," the cloud wizard explained. "Nunn will once again call upon his power. And, once he calls his power, we can use it against him. This time, though, I don't think we should settle for something as simple as disabling pain. This time I think Nunn must make a sacrifice."

"You said you would need our help?" Mills asked.

"I'm afraid I will," the cloud agreed. "You see how I am manifested here, with nothing but these clouds and sky. I hardly have any physical presence whatsoever. Until you arrived, I was little more than a figment of Nunn's imagination. Now, though, I have reclaimed my memory, thanks to the difference you have made. You see, the two of you are the most physical presence Nunn has ever allowed within. And I think we can use that physical nature to our advantage."

For a moment, Mills felt like he was listening to something like theoretical physics. "Yes, but what do you want us to do?"

"Simple enough," the cloud replied. "I want you to push."

"Push?" Zachs finally spoke up. "Zachs can push!"

"Right there," the cloud instructed.

The left-hand wall of the room suddenly no longer looked like a view of endless sky, but a real wall. In the middle of that wall was a great green boulder.

"That's what we have to push?" Mills asked.

"Exactly," the cloud continued in that same calm voice. "As soon as Nunn begins to generate his power." The voice paused for a moment. "Ah. Yes, now would be an excellent time to begin."

Somehow Mills and Zachs found themselves directly in front of the great stone.

They pushed.

"In a moment," the cloud's voice encouraged, "Nunn will think twice about eating any of us ever again."

Mary Lou's head was clearing at last. For the moment, the smoke and the dragon were gone. They had been replaced by any number of wizards.

"Mary Lou," a gentle voice said at her side. The prince had returned.

"Good heavens!" Obar whispered. "It's you!"

The prince nodded his head. "Your brother and I have already been introduced."

Mrs. Smith floated forward. "Mary Lou, I think we should get out of this place."

"I've been sent here to tell you to stop this," the prince said to all the wizards floating about. "All your interference."

"Interference?" Obar asked with a frown.

"With the People's Ceremony," the prince explained. "They want you to know that if it is not completed, the results will be regrettable."

"So you *are* working for the People," Mary Lou said. Somehow she'd feel so much better if that was the case.

The prince glanced down at her again. "In some ways, I suppose I am. Frankly, I just don't know anymore."

"I've had enough of this nonsense," Nunn remarked curtly. "I think I'll destroy all of you." He lifted his hands toward the new jewel in his forehead. "Except for dear Mary Lou."

"Mary Lou," Mrs. Smith insisted. "We have to get out of this place now."

"Mary Lou," the prince said. "The People need you here."

"Mary Lou," Nunn smirked. "You'll be coming with me."

Mary Lou quickly looked from face to face. All of them wanted her for different reasons. But not one of them, not even dear Mrs. Smith, asked her what *she* wanted.

Nunn giggled as green sparks flew from his fingers. He was the real danger here. He was the one who had to be stopped.

Suddenly, surprisingly, Mary Lou thought she caught a glimpse of the dragon. Not in any of the wizards, but behind her eyelids when she blinked, as if the great beast hadn't left, after all, but was waiting there to burst forth and destroy everything around it.

She sat up. The image of the dragon gave her strength. She knew she had to stop Nunn. He was keeping her from her destiny.

Nunn floated toward the platform, his eyes daring any of the others to stop him. He had spread his arms wide now, and his fingertips glowed as if they were lit from within. Mary Lou's gaze was drawn to the new gem in his forehead, which seemed to pulse with light. She wanted to touch that light. She felt almost like she had to, like she was ordered by the dragon.

The gem moved slightly, as if it had somehow worked itself loose. Why not, she thought, if it was part of the dragon?

"I'll kill the rest of you now," Nunn said as he hovered above her. "Mary Lou and I will have a much better time in private."

Not with that gem, you won't. She reached up and plucked it from his forehead.

It came out easily.

Nunn screamed, his hands flying to his forehead. "What have you done to me?"

"Only taken something that wasn't yours," Mary Lou replied, surprised her voice could sound this strong.

Nunn groaned. The green fire now lived in his eyes. "You'll give that back to me." Green flame burst from his mouth.

Mary Lou felt like she had been punched in the stomach. The platform of sticks rocked beneath her.

"Mine now," Nunn cried as he grabbed for the gem. "Mine forever!"

A black bird swooped between him and his prize.

"Raven owns all shiny things!" the bird announced as he grabbed the dragon's eye with his claws.

"No!" Nunn screamed, unable to stop his forward momentum. He fell heavily on top of Mary Lou.

The platform of sticks collapsed beneath them.

○Fifty-two

Todd and the others had almost reached them when Mary Lou disappeared.

Raven flew away as Nunn fell toward the smoking pot below. The kettle disappeared a second later. Nunn spun about in the air, whirling around as if his sorcery now controlled him. The wizard made a shrieking noise, so hard and high it sounded like metal scraping metal rather than the sound of some living thing.

Then the wizard, too, was gone.

There was a moment of silence as if no one could believe what had happened before them.

Then the Anno all erupted at once, not with a call of "Merrilu" or any of their other chants, but with a great cry of anguish and loss.

Thomas led the group forward again, so that the Volunteers surrounded Mrs. Smith and Obar. Todd and Nick rushed to join them.

Mrs. Smith leaned against the steps that once led to the platform above the kettle. She looked as if she had just run a mile. Obar was on his knees, breathing heavily. Todd had never seen either of them look so drained.

"Watch it!" Stanley called.

The Anno, so still for a minute, then so full of grief, had begun to run. Most scurried away from them, but a few raced in their direction, as if the humans weren't even there.

As they rushed forward, Todd could see recognition in the Annos' eyes. Their foes were before them, the ones who had taken Mary Lou. The first among them rushed toward Todd with a shriek, not even bothering to draw its knife, all snatching claws and snapping jaws.

Todd managed to catch the thing by the head, flipping it around. He cut its throat with a single slash.

"These things have gone crazy!" he said as he saw most of the other attackers fall under the Volunteers' arrows. One last Anno rushed forward to impale itself on Nick's sword. The metal glowed as somehow the impaled Anno seemed to shrink.

Todd looked around quickly, to see if any more were coming, but all the Anno were gone or dead.

"They're acting like berserkers," Wilbert agreed. "Like they just don't care."

"Without Mary Lou," the ghost-man said, "their lives have lost their meaning. You have taken away their reason for being."

Todd stared down at the bodies littering the log flooring. "We have?"

"So the People think."

Stanley looked at the suddenly silent world around them. "So what are they doing now, hey?"

The ghost-man shrugged his shoulders. "What else can they do? They've gone to look for Mary Lou, no matter what it takes. Unfortunately, I don't think they'll find her anyplace—not on this world, anyway."

This time Mrs. Smith stared at him. "What do you mean?"

"There was a great deal of power used here today. It caught everyone with sorcerous ability, draining them."

"Except you," Mrs. Smith pointed out.

"I'm not quite on this world myself," the ghost-man replied with a slight smile. "It would take something very special to drain away the magic like that. I think we've just witnessed the first visit of the dragon."

Not the first, Todd thought. But he didn't want to say anything to this stranger.

"So the dragon took Mary Lou?" he asked instead.

"It is the only sensible explanation," the ghost-man answered. "We can only hope that someplace, somewhere, the dragon brings her back."

"Then Mary Lou is that important to the dragon?" Mrs. Smith considered.

"We are all important to the dragon," Obar said, looking as if he had caught his breath at last. "That is why we're here."

"At the dragon's whim, hey?" Stanley said caustically.

"Unless we can find a way to turn the dragon's whim around," Obar replied.

"And what's that supposed to mean?" Stanley demanded. "Now do you see why I can't trust wizards? They don't talk with two tongues, they talk with a dozen!"

"Just because we can make magic," Obar answered a bit defensively, "doesn't mean we can explain it." He coughed, a bit nervous to be the center of attention. "When you have a dragon's eye, as I now do, you control a small piece of the dragon's power. Because of this, these eyes are invaluable, but, despite their worth, many of them have remained hidden, beyond our grasp. Until now, that is."

"Now?" Maggie asked. "What do you mean?"

"Now," Obar continued, "these eyes are surfacing, pulsating with power, so that those who have had contact with one of these eyes might be able to find the others. Who knows why this is so? Perhaps the power comes from the proximity of the dragon. Or perhaps they are another sort of signal. Maybe the dragon wants someone to collect all seven eyes. Maybe this time, instead of controlling the world, the dragon wishes for someone to control it."

"Perhaps, perhaps, perhaps, hey?" Stanley scoffed. "I think the magic's seeped into your brain."

Obar smiled at that, as if Stanley's comment was nothing more than a joke. "As far as we know, the dragon has risen and the world has been destroyed countless times, an endless cycle." He paused, lifting a finger to point at the sky. "What if, this time, the dragon wanted to put an end to the cycle?"

"You mean that he'd want to destroy everything once and for all?" Maggie asked.

"Perhaps that," Obar agreed. "Perhaps something else."

"But how are we supposed to figure out something like that?" Stanley called in frustration. "How can we know something about the unknowable?"

"Maybe," Todd said, surprised at the thought, "even the dragon doesn't know."

"But we're forgetting about our friends, the Anno," Wilbert called out with a frown. "What will happen if the Anno can't find Mary Lou?"

The prince also frowned for an instant before replying. "They'll do what they're used to, kill things and eat them. Before, though, they were cautious. Now I half think they'll kill anything that moves."

Todd thought of his mother on the forest floor.

"They'll attack the neighbors!" Maggie said at the same instant. "Down below."

"God, what are we thinking of?" Thomas added.

The Volunteers were already headed down.

For once, Todd hoped he wasn't right.

The trees warned him a minute before the attack began.

"From above!" the Oomgosh warned the others. "Get to the middle of the clearing. As far from the trees as you can!"

Jason called to Charlie as the rest of the neighbors gathered around the Oomgosh at the dead center of the clearing. Mrs. Furlong had to be led by a couple of the others. They placed her so that she was the closest to the Oomgosh's broad back.

He heard the first high shrieks as they formed a tight circle.

"It's the Anno!" Jason called over the rising noise.

"They are not happy," the Oomgosh replied. "The trees tell me they've lost someone they love."

There were maybe a hundred voices, filling the trees all around, voices filled with anger and pain, voices that wanted someone to pay for their grief.

"Watch out!" Jason called. Arrows flew from the nearer trees. But the clearing was too large. All but two of the tiny arrows fell far short, the others far wide of their little group. The Oomgosh saw that someone had shot one of those spears as well; those poison sticks. But the Anno had little experience with them, and the spear had not even made it as far as the arrows.

"They can't touch us," Mrs. Blake said softly.

"Not unless they are very lucky," the Oomgosh agreed. "Or they decide to venture forth from the trees. And the Anno are cowards. The trees give them their advantage, and they seldom venture far away."

The arrows stopped for a moment, and the screaming began anew. The sound doubled, and doubled again, causing the humans to cover their ears.

"I have never heard the Anno mourn this way," the Oomgosh said. When this was over, he would ask the trees what they had lost.

"Oh, God," Mrs. Dafoe whispered.

The Oomgosh saw them, too, then. The Anno were dropping from the trees. More than a dozen of them hit the ground and began to run toward them. They had left their bows behind, but they still held their knives.

"Now," the Oomgosh said, "we will have to fight."

He was ready, if he must. His strength was far more than that of humans, and even greater than the Anno. He could bat them away, break their necks, crush them, even with only one arm.

Their knives would do little more than scratch his barklike skin. With the luck of the dragon, maybe he and his companions could escape this unharmed.

One of the Anno paused in the attack and pulled the poison stick from the ground. The Oomgosh would have to be careful with that one.

All of the Anno screamed again as they rushed the neighbors. Some of the neighbors screamed back.

◯ Fifty-three

"That was a bit more successful than even I had imagined," the cloud wizard admitted.

Mills simply couldn't believe it. "Did we really push the jewel out of Nunn's forehead?"

"Well, indirectly," the cloud replied. "The pressure from you and Zachs set it free. I just slightly redirected the energy. Sort of the magic version of levers and pulleys. All simple machines, really."

Mills imagined that made as much sense as anything.

"But what will Nunn do now?" Zachs insisted. "Nunn gets angry. Very angry."

"Yes," Mills added. "How do you plan to negotiate?"

"Nunn has to deal with us now." The cloud's voice was so reassuring, almost anything it said sounded sensible. Or at least it did until Mills started thinking about it. "We'll talk as soon as he awakes."

From somewhere in the distance, Mills heard a distinct snore.

"But Nunn will be angry!" Zachs insisted. "Nunn will destroy us!"

"How can he destroy us?" the cloud's oh-so-reasonable voice replied. "After all, we're a part of him."

"Watch the spear," the Oomgosh said to the others in the circle. "It is tipped with poison."

The tree man remembered how the last poison stick had felt, how that simple scratch beneath his skin had burned as his arm had withered before him. He wouldn't let that happen to him again, either to himself or to any of the humans he was protecting.

The Anno formed a wider circle around the tight-knit group of neighbors. They advanced slowly and silently, as if all they wanted to do was kill. All of the neighbors except Mrs. Furlong had weapons, too; knives mostly, although Jason had picked a hatchet, which he held with both hands.

"Be ready," the Oomgosh further warned. "They will attack all at once."

A second later, the Anno began their silent attack.

"Oh, God," one of the women said behind him.

"They're small," Mrs. Blake said by his side. "Aim low."

The creature with the poison stick ran straight for the Oomgosh. He guessed the Anno thought the tree man wouldn't make a very good meal.

But the creatures were not closing their circle evenly. The one with the spear was having trouble maneuvering with the long piece of wood before him. The Anno to either side would reach the neighbors' circle first.

The Oomgosh stepped forward and grabbed the nearest Anno with his one hand. He twisted the creature about, flipping it over so it couldn't use its knife, and threw the thing back on its fellow with the spear. Both Anno fell to the ground.

Mrs. Blake screamed at his side. Her knife clanged against the Anno's, metal on metal. The Oomgosh reached for the Anno, who glanced up in fright. Mrs. Blake cut the thing across the chest. It collapsed, dragging itself back through the dirt.

Charlie leapt out of the group to take one of the Anno by the throat, shaking it until it ceased to struggle.

The Oomgosh turned to help the others.

"No!" Mrs. Jackson screamed. "Never again!" She swung the long knife before her like a broadsword. Two more of the Anno went down before her attack. The Oomgosh grabbed another that wanted to sneak back behind her, using his large hand to break the creature's neck.

"Jesus!" Jason called nearby. The Oomgosh turned and saw the boy look up in horror as an Anno staggered away, the hatchet buried in its forehead.

Mrs. Dafoe was holding another of the creatures off, her knife point almost touching that of the creature. The Oomgosh reached forward and dispatched the Anno.

"Hey!" Bobby cried, moving forward with quick jabs of his knife. "Hey!" One Anno already lay dead behind him. Mrs. Jackson yelled again as her knife sliced into another of the creatures.

The Oomgosh saw movement in one corner of his eye. He turned and saw one of the last Anno rushing toward Margaret Furlong, left unprotected when the others had met the attack.

She looked up from the dirt as the thing scrambled forward.

"Leo?" she asked.

The Oomgosh rushed toward the woman, his footfalls shaking

the ground beneath him. He reached forward and grabbed the back of the Anno before it could plunge its knife into Mrs. Furlong's throat.

There was a scream behind him. The Oomgosh knew the voice. It was Jason.

He turned around to see that the Anno with the spear had risen and was pushing Jason toward a large tree at one edge of the clearing. Jason's hatchet was still lodged in the skull of the fallen Anno, and he had completely forgotten about the knife stuck behind his belt.

The Oomgosh felt a pricking sensation at his wrist. He glanced over to see the Anno he'd forgotten trying to stab him with its knife. He tossed the creature to the ground and crushed it with his foot.

The other neighbors were looking to him. It appeared that they had killed the rest of the attackers.

"Stay away from the poison!" the Oomgosh commanded as he quickly ran to Jason's aid.

The Anno looked like it was smiling as it poked at Jason. The boy's back was almost to a tree. There was nowhere he could run.

"Beware, my Oomgosh!" a call came from the sky. It was Raven. But the tree man had no more time to be wary.

He reached forward toward the Anno, watching carefully to see if it would swing the spear.

"The trees, Oomgosh!" Raven called as he swooped closer. "Up in the trees."

The Oomgosh glanced up as two Anno fell from above, their knives drawn. The tree man batted one aside with his hand, but the other grabbed onto the thick branches of the tree man's hair and stabbed at his neck and cheek, reaching for the Oomgosh's eye.

"Noooo!" Jason moaned. The Oomgosh grabbed the creature from his shoulder and threw it against the tree trunk. It hit with a sharp crack.

He turned to Jason. If they had done something to the boy—

But Jason looked unhurt, except for the fear in his eyes. He pointed back at the tree man.

The Oomgosh looked down. The poison stick was jutting from his chest. He felt the fire then, sudden and terrible, as he fell to his knees.

Jason pulled the spear from his chest as a new group of Anno dropped from the surrounding trees.

"Raven!" the tree man called to his oldest friend. "Protect them!"

Then the pain became too great.

◯ Fifty-four

The Oomgosh couldn't die.

Jason jabbed with the spear at the Anno falling around him. "You can't kill him!" he cried. "I won't let you!"

Bobby was rushing toward him, screaming at the top of his lungs. Mrs. Blake and Mrs. Jackson weren't far behind.

Charlie leapt out from the side of the tree, snapping at the Anno. He grabbed one by the leg and pulled it to the ground. Bobby was there now, too, his knife slashing at the three-foot-high creatures. But there were more of them dropping from the trees, dozens of them, as if the whole village had decided to join in the fight.

A black shape rocketed down from the sky. "No, you will not!" it squawked at the Anno. "Raven forbids it!"

Half a dozen of the Anno ran into the forest, as if the great bird's claws were too much for them. The bird flapped his dark wings to pursue them. But it seemed that twice as many of the creatures dropped to take their place.

"Jason!" another voice called. "Step back from the trees."

Jason looked around to see the magician Obar standing next to Mrs. Smith.

"Now," Obar said solemnly, "we will show you what happens when you attack humans." He tossed a ball of fire at a cluster of the creatures. They shrieked as the magic flame consumed them.

The other Anno on the ground retreated, their shrieks echoing up in the trees. But even that high, eerie noise grew fainter, as if the Anno in the trees were retreating as well.

Another Anno fell to earth, ten feet away from them. Was Jason wrong? Would these crazed creatures turn around and attack again?

He noticed this latest invader wasn't moving. Jason walked forward warily and prodded the small thing with his spear. The

Anno flipped over. There was an arrow, a full-length, human arrow, in its back.

"Hello, the camp!" came the call.

"Hello, yourself!" Obar called back up. "Please join us. We've got to take care of the wounded."

Jason realized he meant the Oomgosh. The tree man hadn't moved since he had fallen after taking that spear—that poison stick. Jason was afraid he was dead. He hoped the wizard knew better.

Others dropped from the trees as Obar rushed toward the Oomgosh. This time the newcomers were human—the four Volunteers and Mark and Todd. None of them looked hurt in the least. Why couldn't something have happened to one of them, rather than the tree man?

No, Jason, thought, he didn't want to wish injury or death on anybody. The Oomgosh was just so big, so strong, so cheerful. How could this happen to someone like him?

The wizard knelt over the fallen tree man. He placed his two hands a few inches away from the wound. Was it the poison that made it look that green, or was that the color of the Oomgosh's blood? When Jason had had to hack off the tree man's withered arm, there had been hardly any blood at all.

The wizard's hands glowed green, a brighter color than the damp chest below. Vapors seemed to rise from the tree man's chest cavity, flowing into Obar's fingers.

The wizard groaned and shuddered.

"Is he going to be all right?" Jason asked as Obar stood.

"I got to the poison quickly," Obar replied, swaying slightly on his feet. At this moment, he looked none too healthy himself. "It's good, too, that you removed the spear. He will need a great deal of rest to recover completely. But, with luck, he should do just that."

"Oh, really, wizard?" Nick called. He looked different now, the way he leaned with the sword at his belt. "That's what you said about Charlie!" The dog frisked around Nick's feet, tail wagging and eyes glowing.

"Oh, he has recovered," Obar said simply. "It is just that he's a different dog than he was before. This world does that sort of thing to people sometimes. One of the dragon's little jokes."

"They blame it on the dragon," Stanley said. "Wizards, hey?"

A harsh cawing erupted overhead, as if Raven was laughing.

The great black bird descended from the sky, this time landing on Nick's shoulder. Nick didn't even move. It was like he was expecting it.

"So the Oomgosh will recover?" the bird said as he cocked his head. "The Oomgosh is like Raven. We are here forever."

Jason liked that kind of talk. He wanted the Oomgosh to be better than some stupid poison stick. He still felt like crying.

"He'll do fine," Jason said instead.

The bird nodded his agreement. "Raven has chased the Anno. Now Raven needs to bring something else."

He took off again from Nick's shoulder and flew up to one of the lower branches of a nearby tree. Leaves rustled for an instant as Raven's claws grabbed at something out of sight.

An instant later, the black bird swooped back down, straight toward Mrs. Smith. He flew close above her head, dropping something from his claws.

Mrs. Smith caught the dragon's eye as Raven settled back on Nick's shoulder.

"People should be careful with precious stones," the black bird announced. "One never knows who's going to end up with them."

Mrs. Smith stared at the stone in her hand.

"Thank you," she began. "I don't—" She stopped abruptly, just looking from the dragon's eye to Raven and back to the eye. Before this, Jason had never seen Mrs. Smith when she didn't know exactly what to say.

"The dragon wanted you to have it," Raven answered curtly. "Sometimes even Raven defers to others."

"Wait a moment." Jason's mother stepped forward. "What's happened to Mary Lou?"

Mary Lou hadn't come back with the others. Jason had been so worried about the Oomgosh, he had forgotten all about his sister!

"She's gone," Obar replied.

"Gone?" Jason's mother demanded. "What do you mean, gone?"

"Oh, I'm quite sure she's still alive," Obar added hastily. "I'm just not precisely sure—where."

"Isn't there some way we could find her?" Mrs. Smith interrupted before Jason's mom could object again.

"With two eyes?" Obar asked back. "We could certainly try."

The air just beyond Obar shifted and took an almost solid form.

"You have more than two eyes to work with." It was Mary Lou's prince.

"Wait a minute!" Jason protested. "Weren't you supposed to protect my sister?"

The prince shook his head. "I have to admit that things didn't go exactly as I expected." He looked to Obar. "You need me to come along. I have great knowledge of those other places Mary Lou might be."

"You didn't want us taking her before," Mrs. Smith pointed out. "You didn't want her to leave the Anno."

The prince looked away from her for a second. "My mistake. I didn't want to lose her." He looked back up at Obar and Mrs. Smith. "Mary Lou and I are very close."

"If he knows something," Mary Lou's mother insisted, "you have to take him with you!"

"Do we?" Obar answered drily. "Garo and I have some unfinished business."

"And it should stay unfinished," the prince replied, "until we have found Mary Lou. We can hold off on old feuds until we're ready for the dragon."

"Well," Obar replied, "if you feel that way about it—" He looked to Mrs. Smith. "What do you think?"

"I think we should find Mary Lou before something else happens."

"Let us do it, then," Obar agreed. He seemed very relieved someone else had taken the responsibility.

"If you will allow me to show you the way?" the prince said with a smile.

All three of them popped out of the clearing as Jason stared at that smile. He didn't like that smile at all.

What the heck did his sister see in this prince, anyway?

The King of the Wolves growled.

The wizard had lied. He said he would give the King great power. He never said he would trap the King in a place with great stone walls, a place where the King couldn't move and stalk and kill.

But the wizard had used such words, filled with such promise of power. The pack would follow a king forever who had power like that. A king like that could kill anything at any time, even those foolish humans who turned him away, made him the laughingstock of the pack.

A king had to have power like that.

But what had the wizard done? He had taken the King away from his pack, into this strange dark place. And he had given the King nothing but his glowing green touch, a touch that had taken all the wolf's energy and made it feel both hot and cold, as if winter and summer were happening all at once. And then that wizard had left the King here, without another word.

The King stopped pacing. He felt another one of those pains, deep inside. That was something else the wizard hadn't told him about.

Something was growing, deep inside the King of the Wolves.

○ Fifty-five

"Where are we?" Constance Smith asked. This place was full of colors, shimmering one after another, as if they had stepped into the middle of a rainbow.

"One of the other places," the man called Garo said. In this place, he looked quite solid. "The dragon exists in many different dimensions and times. Some say the creature might exist everywhere. In the place where we just came from—the real world, I suppose—the dragon only reveals itself when it is about to destroy. But the dragon always exists somewhere. In one of these places, the dragon rests and waits."

"Is that what we just left?" Mrs. Smith asked. "The real world?" Until a couple of days ago, she would have thought that island the strangest place she had ever seen. Now she was in a whole other world of colors rolling across a great plain, yet a world still dotted with fields and rivers and trees like the countryside at home.

"The more you know about the dragon," Obar murmured, "the less you will use that word—real."

"And this is where we'll find Mary Lou?"

"Only the dragon could have taken her with that kind of power," Garo said.

This was all very well and good, but Mrs. Smith realized that she was totally out of her depth here. How could she hope to find the dragon if everything around her was beyond her comprehension?

"What are we looking for?" she asked Obar.

The older magician mulled his answer a moment before speaking. "A certain vibration, a faint odor of burning, even a certain quality of fire. Evidence that the dragon is somewhere near."

"Mary Lou was taken by the dragon," Garo continued, stating it even more directly than before. "And we must get her back." He looked to Mrs. Smith, for once without his sardonic smile.

333

"My life depends on it," he added. The smile flickered back. "Not that Obar would care much about that."

"Oh, yes," Obar replied suddenly, looking as if he had been caught in the parlor being too friendly to the maid. "Well, you know, that was a long time ago. We were different people then."

"Some more different than others," Garo agreed.

"What are you two talking about?" Constance demanded.

"Oh, well," Obar sputtered. "That time my brother and I killed him. Or at least tried to."

The older wizard sighed, waving his hands about in the air as if they might do his explaining for him. "You see," his voice finally chimed in, "it was a matter of self-preservation. Or so we told ourselves at the time. Garo was a much faster study than either of us. If left alive, he would have eclipsed us in no time. He would have become the great wizard, and we would have died. So you see, naturally, well—" His voice stumbled to a halt as he looked imploringly to Constance.

"You know, Mrs. Smith, you are better even than Garo."

"Really?" Constance was taken aback by this honesty. "So will you have to kill me, too?"

"For a while, I thought that," Obar admitted. "But I don't think that selfish behavior is going to help us defeat the dragon." He glanced about, as if the colors floating by held the answers. "I suppose, in some way, my attitude has changed ever since my brother has started trying to kill me."

"That sort of thing can be a revelation," the younger wizard agreed.

"Yes," Obar added, "I think in some way, we will all work together, although I doubt any of us realize the exact nature of the job."

"We will work together," Garo agreed solemnly. "This time we will probably live or die together. But we're wasting time. There is nothing here." He waved for the others to follow. "Come with me. I know certain darker places."

Nunn opened his eyes.

Two of them were human. The other two came from the dragon.

He had barely made it back to his fortress before he collapsed. It was probably for the best. Otherwise, his rage would surely have destroyed something—or someone—he might have a use for later. There was so much to do, so quickly. He could not let his anger get the better of him. He had to cherish every resource.

He smashed his fist down on the table before him.

First, Mary Lou had escaped. Then she had stolen the eye, popped it from his forehead, with so much pain—he would show her pain—

He had to be careful, to calm his anger, or he would let his rage toward the girl overwhelm his larger plans. If he only followed his original plan, and collected all the eyes, she would be lost in dragon fire with all the others, wiped from the face of this world like the inconsequential dust mote she was.

It was not enough for Nunn.

He would feel as if he had been taken. Bested by a teenage girl. Almost like he was still human.

Of course, he would have his victory. But he needed to make her suffer before that. He needed to humiliate her, to strip her of her pride and power and make her realize she owed her whole existence to Nunn. He had done that to those much more powerful than Mary Lou. It would be little trouble to add her to his list.

"Nunn."

He looked around. Had someone else invaded his study?

"Nunn. Answer us."

He suddenly felt cold, and barely suppressed a moan. The voice came from inside.

"What is this?" he demanded. He remembered Mills. Somehow that damned newcomer had wreaked havoc with his subconscious. But only for a few moments. Nunn had wiped Mills from his head.

"We need some answers from you first."

Nunn's fists closed over his eyes. He would not be dictated to by voices.

"What are you doing in my head?" he demanded.

"We are your past," the voice added with a maddening calm. "You can never escape from us. We are the first person you took, and the last, the wizard Rox and Leo Furlong, and all those hundreds in between. You have left us silent for too long. We are clamoring to be heard."

Truly, Nunn thought, he must be going mad.

"You don't think you lost that jewel on your own?" the voice chided. "How could that dragon's eye break free of your spell?"

Nunn felt the rage build up within him again. "What? How dare—I will purge you from me forever!"

"If you destroy us," the voice responded with everlasting calm, "you destroy yourself."

This was perhaps the strangest thing that had happened even to him. Yet it made a certain sense, or as much sense as anything made in this magic realm. How could he purge something that was a part of his mind? Nunn was afraid, this time, that the voice was right.

Not that he was defeated.

He simply had to figure out some way to separate himself from these voices, so that he could destroy them.

In the meantime, he would send his new guard to seek out the other eyes, with a little help perhaps from his sorcerous allies. Not that they would ever touch the stones. Oh, no. Only Nunn ever touched the stones.

But first Nunn had to take Mary Lou, from wherever she had gone.

His true eyes, the eyes of the dragon, would show him everything.

"Perhaps," he said to the voices in his head, "we can work out something."

"We will not wait forever," the voice reminded him.

Fair enough, Nunn thought. You'll only have to wait long enough to die.

The first thing Mary Lou was aware of was a deep rumble. Something that she both heard and felt, something that seemed as real as anything she had ever experienced.

At first, the rumble frightened her. There was no light here, and no real sound, only that constant vibration. After a while, though, she found it oddly reassuring, as if that deep noise was something she could always depend on.

Mostly, the rumble made her remember.

She remembered how much she was afraid of upsetting her mother, and how many times she would hide in her room or stay after school, so she could have a life of her own. She remembered how, as Jason grew, her mother and father would do extra things for him—the typewriter, the special summer camp: "Men need to get ahead, dear." And she remembered how, after her sister had left to have her baby, no one in their family could talk about her, as if she had never existed.

Mary Lou remembered: How the prince had wanted to use her, not for herself, but for something for him. In the end, it didn't matter if she lived or died. And how all the great wizards of this place had fought over her, not for herself, but for how she might help each of them.

It was the same here as it had been at home. In the end, it only mattered what she did for others. Or so she had always been taught.

Not anymore, she thought.

The rumbling grew.

This rumbling, she realized, came from the dragon. The creature must have brought her to this place.

Would it kill her? She felt the vibration, waiting for some sign. Mary Lou knew that no one saw the dragon and lived.

But the dragon was only nearby. With luck she wouldn't see it; with fortune she would only have this one brief brush with power, as if one edge of the creature's mind grazed against her thoughts. Her brand-new thoughts.

The rumbling was in her head. The dragon thought with her.

Not anymore, she thought.

She felt the answer rise up in her, full of anger and pride, parts of her she'd never known were there until now.

No one will think for me again! No one!

And her answer was written in fire.

○ Fifty-six

Jason woke with a start. It was the middle of the night. The second night he had been in this place. Two days and two nights. It felt more like months or years.

The Oomgosh slept at the edge of the clearing, beneath his beloved trees. Jason crept over to be nearby. The tree man's regular breathing was reassuring, like the sound of waves breaking on a summer shore, or a gentle breeze whistling through a field.

"Jason?" the Oomgosh whispered in his deep voice. "Is that you?"

Oh, heck. He shouldn't have come. "I didn't mean to wake you," he whispered back. "The wizard says you need your rest."

The Oomgosh chuckled. "What do wizards know? There will always be an Oomgosh." He sat up with a grunt and regarded Jason for a moment in the darkness. "But you sound worried."

"You were hurt!" Jason protested.

"Hurts come and go. I think it's time for a story."

"But—" Jason began. He really didn't mean to disturb the tree man like this. The Oomgosh should be thinking about himself.

"Nonsense," the Oomgosh replied, as if he had already heard any objection anyone could make. "A good story will help us both get back to sleep. Let me tell you about the time the Oomgosh first came face-to-face with cold and winter."

Jason was just as glad the tree man wouldn't listen to him. He always looked forward to the stories. He just liked the way the tree man's voice, even when he whispered like this, would wash over him and make him warm like a blanket.

The tree man smiled and began his story.

"It so happened that the Oomgosh left his valley home and climbed the nearest hill. But beyond that hill he found another, taller than the first, and beyond that hill a third that was taller still. So did the hills grow, each one dwarfing the one before, until they ceased to be hills and became mountains, with their proud heads lost in the clouds.

"Still did the Oomgosh climb, and, as was his custom, he talked to the trees that he passed, for, as much as humans, the trees were his brothers and his sisters.

" 'Joy!' the trees shouted on the hills. 'The sun warms us, the rain nourishes us, the wind allows us to display our fine leaves to every living thing. Truly, it is a wonder to be a tree, that grows from the earth and reaches to the sky.'

"So was the Oomgosh content, until he met another, who walked down from the mountaintop as he was walking up: a strange woman, dressed all in white, with a hood and a veil, so that all the Oomgosh could see was a bit of pale skin about her colorless eyes. And the trees about her shuddered as she passed, their branches whipping about as their leaves turned the colors of flame and fell to the ground.

" 'I am Winter,' the pale woman said when the Oomgosh asked her her business. 'All listen to Winter's call. The wind grows swifter, the sun backs away, the rain freezes. Leaves and grass will die, and lie buried beneath the snow.'

"The Oomgosh objected, for he hated to see the end of such joy, but the woman named Winter was unmoved.

" 'It is the way of things,' she replied. 'Now you must turn around, or you will feel my touch as well.' And with that, she brushed his hand with her cold fingers and blew her icy breath upon his cheek.

"The Oomgosh backed away at that, for he could feel the flesh of his hand grow hard and brittle beneath her caress, and the tears he cried for the joyless trees froze upon his cheek. He turned, and fled to the warm valley far from the mountainside.

"But once the Oomgosh had left Winter behind, he felt as if he had betrayed the trees on the high hillsides. Surely, there was some way to reason with Winter! But he did not know how.

"So it was that, in coming to his valley at last, he met a second woman, dressed all in green, with wildflowers in her hair, and skin and eyes the color of rich earth. She smiled at the Oomgosh, and a bit of the sun seemed to shine there in that smile.

" 'Where do you travel so quickly?' the young woman asked.

"And although it made the Oomgosh ashamed, he admitted, 'I am running from Winter.'

"At that the young woman laughed, a sound like a brook after it has rained. 'I have had some difficulties with Winter, as well,' she admitted. 'She does not approve of my arrival. My name is Spring.'

"And Spring brushed against his hand, and her sweet breath blew across his cheek. And the Oomgosh saw that the dead spot on the back of his hand was green again, and once more could tears flow from his eyes.

" 'Winter wants to keep me away,' Spring confided. 'But you have seen her. Why not turn around and guide me, and we will tell her it is time to go?'

"So the Oomgosh turned about, and guided this young woman through the hills, each one higher than the one before. And, as she passed, the trees gained new buds and the ground sprouted with flowers and new blades of grass. And, while they marched, the Oomgosh could see the veiled Winter just before them, and, while her expression was harsh and her laugh bitter, Winter gave way before them, climbing back to her mountain home.

"The trees grew leaves again, and took joy in the sun, the wind, and the rain.

" 'See?' Spring said, once the Oomgosh had led her as high as there were trees that bloomed. 'All things have their season, and you and I are no different. But, if we are patient, our season will come again.'

"And with that, Spring fled back to her home in the South. But the Oomgosh no longer worried, for he had the trees and the sun and the rain and the wind and a new woman named Summer, and he knew that Spring would always come again."

The Oomgosh nodded to say the story was finished.

"A great story!" another voice squawked nearby. "Raven approves!"

Jason turned, surprised to see the black bird by his side. "I didn't hear you arrive."

"You would have if Raven had fluttered his wings. But Raven knows when to be quiet, too." The bird proudly fluffed his feathers. "Sometimes even Raven walks."

"Sometimes all the best things will," the Oomgosh agreed. "Now I think it is time we all went back to sleep."

Jason returned to the pile of leaves he was using for a bed. He wished that all of this place was as pure and clear as the Oomgosh's stories.

He ran a hand through his hair as he settled back down to sleep. A leaf had gotten caught up there. He grabbed the small piece of green between a couple of his fingers and plucked it free.

"Ow!" he cried.

He looked at the leaf. It was a tiny thing, with an equally tiny branch attached. It must have really been tangled in his hair. The way it hurt when he pulled it free, it felt like this little branch had been growing right out of his head.

◯ Fifty-seven

"It was as simple as that?" Mills asked.

"Nothing is ever simple here," the cloud replied. "We have alerted Nunn to our presence. Now, of course, he plans to betray us." The cloud snorted. "Can you imagine that? We are in his head! What kind of wizard would I be if I couldn't read his thoughts?" The cloud's tone shifted, becoming so soft as to sound conspiratorial. "But I do believe I can get us outside."

"Outside?" Zachs piped up. "Zachs prefers outside." The light-creature flashed crimson. "Except—if we get outside, Zachs may eat you." The crimson light shifted to blue. "Sometimes Zachs gets hungry. Sometimes Zachs can't help itself."

"Very nice of you to tell us," the cloud remarked.

The light-creature flashed yellow. "Zachs tries to be honest with friends."

"As, no doubt, does Mr. Mills," the cloud remarked reassuringly. "And myself, of course. But I don't think we're going to leave here in the same way we arrived. We have reinvented ourselves once. We will do so again."

Mills realized he hadn't seen his other neighbor since Nunn tried to kill him. "Is Leo all right?"

"I don't think he's any worse off than he was before," the cloud answered.

"Can Leo join us?" Mills asked. "I mean, outside?"

The thunderhead considered his reply for a moment before speaking. "Well, at the moment, Leo Furlong is not quite as independent as the rest of us. I think it might be best if we leave him here for safekeeping. Once we are more sure of ourselves, we will come and fetch him."

The creature of light did a little dance in front of the cloud. "Zachs is ready! When do we leave?"

"I believe we will give Nunn a little time to mull us over before springing our final demands," the cloud replied. "After all, I do know what he is thinking."

With that, the thunderhead closed its eyes. They vanished in the shadowed oval mass.

Maybe, Mills thought, this was more than a cloud. This was the first time he realized how much the thunderhead looked like a brain.

Nick didn't want to open his eyes. It was morning, and he had to decide who he was going to be.

It seemed like he was two people now. One was the high school student who got along, who lived a rich fantasy life to keep him away from a reality that included a father who was long gone.

But the other Nick had been taken over by the fantasy. And a certain enchanted sword. At first, the sword had scared him, especially the way it liked the blood of his enemies. Actually, that still frightened him some. But he also found that the sword made him more than he was before.

In the beginning, he had been jerked around from one place to another as the sword guided his moves. Now he was starting to anticipate the swing of his blade, when he should step forward, when he should shuffle to the side, when he needed to raise his hand in defense. This sword was training him to be a swordsman. And Nick was a little frightened to realize that he liked it.

At first, Nick wanted to get rid of this sword. Now he was afraid someone would ask him to get rid of it.

He opened his eyes and looked up at the too-green morning sky. No one was going to take his sword until all this was over. He sat up and looked around.

"Hey, Nick!" Todd called. "Nice of you to join the living!"

Nick gave the other boy a sickly smile, the high school kid all over. Todd was always going to be a wiseass. But the day before, they had fought side by side. Todd had been pretty good with that knife. Of course, Nick could have taken him in a minute with his sword. Nick could take most anybody with that sword.

The Volunteers had gotten a fire going and were roasting some sort of small animal over a spit. Nick could hardly believe it. They were actually going to have breakfast.

He stood up and stretched. His mother waved at him from over by the cooking fire, where she was talking with Maggie. Nick stumbled in her general direction, doing his best to wake up.

"A long way from our backyard barbecue, huh, Nick?" his mother called. "No charcoal briquettes here!"

"And nobody wearing a 'Dad's the Chef!' apron," Nick agreed.

He was sorry as soon as the words came out of his mouth. Why did he have to remind himself about his father?

"You surely come from a different part of the country," Maggie said. "What in heaven's a backyard barbecue?"

Nick's mother laughed at that. "Oh, you have to have done that! Instead of cooking the steaks on the electric stove, where they'd get done in no time at all, you take them out to a grill on the patio. That's where you've got the briquettes burning, which take forever, and you can never get them started without lighter fluid. And of course, if you use too much lighter fluid, the whole thing will blow up—"

His mother stopped abruptly when she realized all four Volunteers were staring at her.

"Maybe they don't come from the same place, after all," Thomas murmured.

"Well, maybe they just come from the big city is all," Wilbert added. "We're just a bunch of country folks from the wilds of New Jersey."

"There aren't any wilds in New Jersey," Todd said. "My grandparents live there. Well, the pine barrens, maybe. And there's some farmland in the west."

"That's Newton," Wilbert agreed.

"One of the bedroom communities," Todd said.

"What the hell is a bedroom community?" Stanley demanded.

The Volunteers didn't seem to understand half of what the neighbors were saying this morning. It really was like they came from two different worlds.

Nick had an idea. "You say the dragon snatched you in western New Jersey?"

Wilbert nodded. "That's right. In the woods ten miles outside of Newton."

"When did the dragon take you?"

"December," Wilbert answered. "Cold day, too."

That still wasn't what Nick wanted to know. "What year?"

"Why, 1906, of course."

Nick exhaled. Even though he had suspected this, he still didn't want to hear it.

"You're kidding!" Mrs. Dafoe burst out. "You've got to be. That's crazy."

Nick looked over at Mary Lou's mother. "What isn't crazy around here?"

The Volunteers were looking at each other as if they might want to get out of this place before somebody else went crazy.

"What?" Maggie asked for all of them. "What's the matter here?"

"We come from 1967," Nick's mother told them. "Mid-August 1967."

The Volunteers all stared for another moment.

"Yep," Thomas said after a moment. "That's crazy, all right."

"None of us are getting home, are we?" Todd asked, his voice a little strained. "Why are we stuck here? I never asked to be here! Who the fuck has the right to put me here?"

Nick moved over to the other boy. Todd was getting hysterical.

"Hey, Todd, cool down," Nick cautioned. "Yelling isn't going to solve anything."

Todd turned on him. "How would you know? Nicky Blake, the Goody Two-shoes of the neighborhood, always following your mother's skirts. You can't yell, Nicky. You gotta get your mother's permission!"

"C'mon, Todd," Nick replied. God, this guy could be an asshole.

"Come on where?" Todd was suddenly in his face. "You want to fight? Goody Nicky always ran away. You need your mother's permission to fight, too?"

Now this guy had gone too far.

"I don't need my mother's permission to do anything."

"Nick!" his mother called. Nick turned away from her. He had to handle this himself.

"Hurry up, Nicky," Todd called in a high, affected voice. "Run to your mother, Nicky."

"Get off my case!" Nick yelled.

Todd shoved him. "You got no case to get on."

Nick almost fell. He'd show this asshole.

"Oh-ho," Todd said softly. "We're getting serious now."

It was only then Nick realized he had drawn his sword.

○ Fifty-eight

Nunn considered the King of the Wolves. The wolf was coming along nicely, a tiny bit of the dragon's power festering inside that would make the wolf ten times stronger than before. The King would make a fine servant in the battle to come.

But the King was still untested. Nunn would rather use someone whom he had seen in battle, someone with a will of iron.

The King paced in the room where Nunn had placed him, impatient to be free. When the creature looked up at the wizard, Nunn could see the first traces of green fire in its eyes.

"You will have your chance at battle soon enough," Nunn said quietly. "I have a group of humans that you will enjoy tearing into little pieces."

The King reared on its hind legs. Already, it was almost twice the size of its former self.

"Ennnjoy!" the King agreed.

The wizard removed himself from the room, passing through the wall into the adjoining chamber.

"Mr. Sayre?" he asked gently.

Sayre rapidly turned his head, which bobbed as if his neck muscles weren't all they used to be.

Sayre shook a finger at Nunn, a finger that had lost a good part of its skin. "What do you want now? This dark is no good. My lawn needs light!"

Nunn smiled like a father. "Oh, Mr. Sayre, you'll get all the light you want. And you can do whatever you want with your lawn. I only need you to do one job for me."

Sayre looked at Nunn warily. "Job? Who are you to tell me I have to do a job?"

"Only someone who can give you a better lawn, a bigger lawn, than you ever dreamed of. Look here."

He let both of his dragon's eyes glow. Sayre's frown vanished as the light filled the room.

"Green," Sayre murmured as if mesmerized.

"And this green can be yours. Here, let it touch you."

"Green," Sayre agreed as the light poured into him. He grunted as the light shook him, forcing his decimated body to stand straight and tall.

Sayre coughed, expelling a couple of small, flying things. "Haven't felt this good in days."

He looked far better, too. Almost human. It was unfortunate how wisps of green seemed to leak out of the hole in his stomach.

"Now can I work on my lawn?" Sayre asked in a tone that said he did not like to request permission.

"Would you like more?" Nunn held his hands up, palms forward, so Sayre could see the glowing gems.

"Green!" Sayre agreed. "Green for my lawn!"

"I'll be glad to give you more," Nunn said cheerfully, "as soon as you do a little job." He closed his hands into fists.

Sayre blinked. "Well, why didn't you say so? I always like a man who appreciates a good lawn." He made a small, hiccuping sound as a salamander slithered from his nostril. "But those who defile my lawn will still have to pay!"

"Oh, they will, my dear Sayre," Nunn replied. "They'll pay deeply."

Mrs. Smith had been many of these places before. She had to have passed through here to do those things she had accomplished back on the island. It was only now, though, that she really opened her eyes to see them.

One of the places was filled with light, as if fire and lightning and the stars above all vied with each other to see which could be the brightest. Another seemed to hold all the sounds in the world, perhaps all the worlds: bells rang, engines grumbled, birds sang, creatures cried and screamed; a cacophony one instant, the sweetest blend of melody the next.

The place Garo led them through now seemed defined by darkness. Not that Mrs. Smith couldn't see. The dragon's eyes took care of that. Perhaps the dragon provided its own kind of light, everywhere it went. But her real eyes saw nothing, so that she had to let the dragon gem lead the way.

"This is more like it," Garo whispered.

She wondered what he meant by that. There was another sound, a deep rumbling, very far away. Was that what Garo had been searching for?

She had begun to wonder why she was here. Oh, she had a certain power, and she had wanted to free Mary Lou. When this youngster had suggested flying to fight the dragon, she agreed, caught up in the spirit of the moment.

But this rescue was not taking mere moments. In fact, Mrs. Smith seemed to be losing all track of time. They had left the neighbors behind, defenseless against an attack by Nunn.

In fact, this course of action seemed even less well conceived than their fight against Nunn. It was as if, as soon as these magicians were confronted by some magic, they immediately took leave of their senses, gallivanting off on one adventure after another. And she was no better than the rest of them, blindly following, never raising her voice. This would have to stop now.

"She's very close," Garo announced before Mrs. Smith could speak.

"And the dragon is, too," Obar added.

The stone felt warm in Mrs. Smith's hand. Perhaps something would happen, after all. Now that they had gotten this close, even she didn't want to turn back.

But how could they hope to find Mary Lou in a place as dark as this?

"Mary Lou!" Garo called out loud.

There was no answer but the rumbling, although that seemed closer now.

"I thought it was worth a chance," Garo whispered. "Perhaps there is some way your eyes could lead us to her."

Her dragon gem was pulsing, in time to that low rumbling that seemed to fill this world.

"What?" a voice called back, full of echo, as if the sound came from the end of a great tunnel. "Did someone call my name?"

"Yes!" Garo shouted. "Mary Lou!"

There was another pause before her voice shouted back. "Prince. Is that you?"

The prince smiled. He was a very handsome young man when he smiled. "So you call me. We've come to rescue you!"

Another moment of silence, as if her voice came from a great distance. "Why should I trust you after what you did?"

What he did? Garo had neglected to mention anything about that. Mrs. Smith was beginning to like this less and less.

But the young phantom's smile was gone. For the first time, he seemed genuinely worried. "It's not just me!" Garo answered. "Obar is here! And Mrs. Smith!"

The pause seemed even greater this time.

"Well," Mary Lou replied at last, "maybe—"

Her voice was lost under another noise as the deep rumble rose to shake everything around them, and then rose some more, into a roar so deafening Mrs. Smith was afraid her ears would burst.

The roar ended as abruptly as it had begun, leaving behind a silence that seemed even more terrible.

"Mary Lou." Garo, her prince, mouthed her name silently, as if afraid to say anything else aloud. Perhaps, Mrs. Smith thought, he was afraid he'd never see Mary Lou again.

Not that Mary Lou was all they had to worry about. For, in getting her attention, Garo had also gained the notice of the dragon.

○Fifty-nine

"Mr. Mills, I presume."

Evan Mills looked up with a start. He must have been dozing. He was astonished that he needed sleep. Funny, after all that had happened, that sleep would be the thing to surprise him.

It was Nunn's voice that he heard.

The cloud had opened his eyes as well.

"You can call me that, if you wish," the cloud said solemnly.

"Then you don't claim responsibility?" Nunn's voice sounded amazed. "I know it was you who started all this, going where you didn't belong."

"So you say," the cloud replied.

"This is absurd!" Nunn protested. "How can I have a conversation with a creature who's invaded my head? I won't feel right until I'm talking to you face-to-face!"

"We want no less," the cloud agreed.

"We?" Nunn's voice was growing more tense from one word to the next. "What is this 'we'? I know you are Evan Mills, and I'll have you out of there!"

"If you can do it," the cloud replied in the same mild tone.

"If I—" Nunn sputtered. "No. This anger does neither of us any good. My creature Zachs comes and goes from me at my will. I am quite sure I can do the same for a common human being."

"So you will set us free?" the cloud asked. "What happens then?"

"What happens? Ah, I see." Nunn chuckled. "On my honor as a wizard, I will not lay a hand on you. Now, if you will excuse me, I must make preparations."

Mills waited a moment before asking a question. "Does Nunn mean it? About not laying a hand on us?"

"Of course," the cloud answered in that same maddeningly serene tone. "Not that we could leave his fortress alive. But he'll let somebody else do the killing."

"Zachs knew it!" the light-creature erupted. "When Nunn is angry, people die!"

"So he's going to have us killed?" Mills asked, trying to stay calm himself.

The cloud made a soft tsking sound. "Just because Nunn wants something does not make it so, no matter what the wizard believes. I believe, Mr. Mills, that we will have some say in this as well."

The lawn was everywhere.

Sayre opened his eyes. Everywhere but here, that was. The endless fields of green he saw when his eyes were closed were replaced by these bare stone walls, walls where nothing would grow.

Sayre hated things that wouldn't grow. He hated them almost as much as those who ruined his lawn. But Sayre did more than hate. Since the world had changed, Sayre made them pay.

He had a special punishment for people who'd defile his lawn. He'd pluck off parts of them the way they'd pluck his grass, smash them beneath his heel the way they'd smash down his grass with their tires, strangle their laughter and unkind words out of their throats. And, when he was done with them, he'd have the greatest lawn of all.

"Are you ready?"

Sayre jerked around to see the tall man in the dark robes. He didn't like where the tall man had put him. But the tall man had filled him with the green. Yes. It felt so good. Sayre didn't need to kill the tall man. Yet.

"I need you to get rid of somebody," the tall man said. "An old neighbor."

Neighbor? He hated the neighbors. They almost all made fun of his lawn!

"Once you're done with that," the tall man added, "you can have as much green as you want."

"Green," Sayre said. He frowned. If he concentrated, he could still make sentences. "I'd like to get to work on my lawn."

"And you shall," the tall man reassured him. "Now your neighbor is going to appear here suddenly. He may even look like he's somehow coming out of me." The tall man laughed as if this was the most foolish of ideas. "I don't want you to be alarmed."

Things like that would never alarm Sayre. Nothing in here could compare to his lawn.

"And then I want you to kill him."

Sayre nodded. It seemed simple enough.

"It will only be a minute," the tall man murmured, "and everything will be yours."

Everything was ready. Nunn looked inside.

"Mr. Mills, are you there?"

He saw the image of a man, almost lost among the thousand other images that waited in this corner of the brain. He saw a flash of light, a reflection of Zachs, perhaps? And there was something else, behind the tiny Mills, something that looked like a cloud.

"I'm here," Mills answered.

"Good. I think I see you. Stay still, please, and I'll bring you out. This may hurt a bit."

Nunn concentrated, repeating the same pattern he used to withdraw Zachs from his inner self.

He thought he heard a single word, in a different voice. The word was "Now."

Nunn couldn't let his concentration waver. Who knew what fragmented personalities remained in that corner of his cortex? He had to bring Evan Mills out of Nunn's separate reality, and into the reality of this greater world.

There. He had him.

Mills screamed in pain as he was reborn.

He looked up from where he crouched on the cold stone floor.

"Can't be helped, I'm afraid," Nunn murmured. He couldn't help but grin.

Mills groaned as he pushed himself to his feet.

"See?" Nunn remarked, to show he had kept his part of the bargain. "Safe and sound."

Mills nodded doubtfully. He looked down at his body, perhaps to check that all the pieces were there.

"Oh," Nunn added casually, as if it was an afterthought. "One of your neighbors is here. I'm afraid he has a little unfinished business."

The thing that was once Hyram Sayre shuffled from the shadows.

"Lawn," Sayre said.

Nunn had no time for small talk. "Make short work of him. You know your reward."

With that the wizard stepped through the wall, headed to his next task. Even if Mills was somehow important to the dragon, he was too much of an irritant to let him live.

Enough of Mills. It was time for Nunn to do something important, not just for him but for the dragon. One more short stop, to make sure there would be no more interference, and to regain those other humans who were the dragon's pawns.

Then, even if it meant snatching her from under the nose of the dragon, it would be time to retake Mary Lou.

Sayre stared at Evan Mills. Mills never had any time for his lawn.

"Hyram?" Mills asked. "What have they done to you?"

Sayre looked down at his hands. They glowed green in the dim light.

"Only made me better," he said. "Haven't felt this good in years. In fact, I've never felt this good." Somehow this feeling seemed even bigger than his lawn. New thoughts were flooding into him, one jumbling in after another. He looked up at his neighbor. "Evan, I don't even know if I'm human."

Mills yelled as his hands started to glow as well with a bright, yellow light. He shuddered. "Zachs," he whispered.

"Are you listening to me?" Sayre demanded. He hated when people didn't listen.

"So," Mills muttered. "This was what the cloud meant by 'we.'"

Mills obviously wasn't listening. Sayre found he was getting angry.

"Evan!" he shouted. "Let's talk about my lawn!"

But Evan Mills had started to laugh.

"No!" Sayre screamed. "No one laughs at my lawn!"

He threw out his arms, letting his anger burst through his fingers. A bolt of green flew from his hands, soaring above Mills' head to crash into the wall beyond.

Mills had stopped laughing. "I'm sorry, Hyram. What did you say?"

"Never mind," Sayre replied. His bolt of energy had smashed a hole through the wall, showing the outside world. The green outside world. He didn't need to fight in a musty old castle when the outside world waited for him.

"Excuse me, Evan," he said as he let his power lift him from the ground. He floated toward the opening. It was a huge gaping hole; he'd fit through it easily. If he was going to fight anybody else, though, he'd have to work on his aim.

He floated through to the other side. Floated right off the

ground! He was right. He was no longer human. He felt more like a god, surrounded by green.

It was time to leave foolish things like Evan Mills and the wizard Nunn behind. Hyram Sayre set himself down beyond the walls of the fortress. He sighed. There were far too many trees.

The lawn god had work to do.

○ Sixty

The human who was not quite human had come back to the King's prison.

"Come," Nunn said to the King of the Wolves. "You're ready. It's time to leave this place and make you king of all the woods."

He would be free. This wizard would keep his word at last. The King threw back his head and roared. The sound shook the walls. Sparks flew as the King scraped his fine new claws against the stone floor. The King knew he only had to reach out with his powerful new arm, and he could slice the wizard in half.

"I willl be grreeaterr thann alll humanns," the King declared. "I willl roamm the woods forreverr!"

"Yes, you will," Nunn agreed, "after you complete your promised task. I will come with you. After this is done, the island is yours."

"Miinne!" the King agreed.

"I will need you to kill a few humans, and someone who is not quite human. There will be others that have to be delivered to me. But after that, your debt is paid."

The King of the Wolves barely listened to this wizard prattle on. He would be free. He would taste fresh blood. He would find his pack and rule to the end of time.

What more could there be to life?

The walls faded around them as the wizard called upon the stones in his hands. The King would do what he had been called upon to do.

After this, the King would take orders from no one, not even a wizard.

This, Garo realized, was where he belonged.

The three of them—Garo, Obar, and Constance Smith—stood in a place that seemed different from all the places he'd ever seen, and exactly like every place he had ever been.

355

If you looked at this spot in a certain way, it seemed like a featureless plain, some corner of a never-ending desert. There was light in the distance, light so bright Garo had to squint even at this range. But the spot where they stood was lost within a great shadow, a shadow of something unimaginably large.

But his view of this world was different when he closed his eyes.

Every time he blinked, he saw a different place, a different world, skies of blue and green and red and yellow, trees with violet leaves and seas of molten gold. He saw a crowd of the People, and then great hordes of humans rushing who knew where, and next a field full of strange, two-legged beasts covered with yellow fur, all standing perfectly still, except for the movement of their eyes and tails. Every time he blinked, he saw a different scene, a different reality, maybe every world the dragon had ever seen. Because he had no doubt that these visions came from the dragon, visions far more real than the place where they stood, as if he could only see the truth when he closed his eyes.

He looked at the others. They seemed frozen, uncertain of what to do before the dragon. Could they see these visions as well? Or did the dragon mean these things only for him?

He blinked his eyes and saw Mary Lou. She looked even more frightened than she had when she had been taken by the People. Garo frowned. He had never meant for her to suffer like this. But then, he had never thought of her suffering. He had only thought of becoming human again, leaving this twilight world no matter what the cost.

He thought of Mary Lou's smile when she used to look into his eyes. A way she would never look at him again. His fever to become human had cost him something, too.

He blinked. She was still there, in the space behind his eyelids, but now a vast shape towered behind her, hoarding her, keeping her for its own.

He opened his eyes and saw shadow all around him. How could the creature be standing with Mary Lou, and still be hovering overhead? Somehow he couldn't look at what hovered above, as if looking directly at the dragon might be as blinding as looking into the sun.

He closed his eyes, and Mary Lou stared straight at him. She smiled at him suddenly, in that open way she had. After all he had put her through, she still smiled.

He felt an emptiness then, an emptiness that he longed to have filled. He realized how much he felt for her. That maybe

Mary Lou, and not the dragon, had been his key to becoming human.

"Constance!" Obar said suddenly.

Garo was pulled back to that place that he shared with the others.

"We have to leave here quickly," Obar said. "We have gotten too close to the dragon."

Mrs. Smith grimaced at that. She lifted her head, but stopped before she truly looked above her, as if she shared the same fear with Garo.

"What will it do to us?" she whispered instead.

Garo thought of all the stories he had heard of the dragon.

"Devour us, no doubt. Even a dragon needs a snack." He grinned despite himself. This moment was as funny as it was terrible. "It goes ages between meals."

Mrs. Smith didn't see the humor. "So we came all this way to be devoured by a dragon?"

Garo shrugged. "Who knew the dragon would treat Mary Lou as property?" Who had known anything about the dragon? he now realized. Certainly not Garo the ghost-wizard. Then why had he felt it so important to lead the others here?

The other two cringed as another roar shattered the world around them. Obar looked like he wanted to run.

Mrs. Smith shook her head. "We're not going anywhere."

She waved for the others to look behind them. Somehow they had reached a wall, a wall that seemed to go up forever.

Garo suddenly felt cold, as if this wall had sucked all the warmth from this place. "I think this is from the dragon," he said softly.

"Perhaps it is simply one of the dragon's claws," Obar agreed.

"We only see bits of the dragon," Garo explained, surprised at how much he knew. "It is not truly ready to come back to the world. But we have disturbed it." He sighed and smiled. "Someone will have to pay."

"Pay?" Mrs. Smith repeated. "So that's what the dragon wants? A sacrifice?"

It was so obvious. Garo abruptly stopped smiling.

"No," he replied, "the dragon wants a particular sacrifice."

He closed his eyes and thought of Mary Lou and her smile. They all had their purpose under the dragon. His purpose was about to be fulfilled.

"I'm the one who should do this thing." He spoke slowly, but his voice gained power with every word. "I led us here. And I led Mary Lou to this place as well. All in an attempt to regain my physical body. The dragon should take *me*."

Mrs. Smith wasn't so certain. "Are you sure this is what the dragon wants?"

Garo tried to smile again. It almost worked. "With the dragon, who knows? But I am the only one who cannot hide. The dragon has already half claimed me. I am the only one who can't escape into the physical world."

With that, the roar came again, so loud that Mrs. Smith fell to her knees. Even Garo covered his ears, but the roar seemed just as loud, as if the sound started inside his head instead of without.

"No matter where I go," Garo said softly, "the dragon will find me." He wondered if, with that roar, the dragon had agreed to his offer.

"Maybe," he added quickly, "if it takes me, it will spare Mary Lou. I've spent too long as a wizard. Let me do something honest for a change."

"Very well," Obar said for both of them. "Constance, it's time to leave this place." He grabbed the old woman's hand before she could object. There was a flash of green, and they were gone, jumping to another reality.

Garo was alone with the dragon.

The dragon had already half claimed him. Maybe, by letting the dragon take all of him, he could be human again. This was Garo's destination. And Mary Lou had shown him the way.

It was time he came full circle.

He hoped Mary Lou would smile for him again.

He took a deep breath, filling his lungs. He felt as if he did not breathe air, but fire. The dragon roared again.

Garo opened his mouth to shout. What came out was half a cry of joy, and half a scream.

Jason felt his arm the moment Nick drew his sword. The scratch was still there from the day before, when the sword lashed out because it wanted blood.

Now Nick had drawn the blade again. And the sword would have to taste blood before it would return to its scabbard.

Nick looked down at the sword in his hand, as if just now realizing what he had done, almost as if the sword had drawn itself. He looked at Todd. Todd tried to smile, but Todd knew about the sword, too.

The Oomgosh pushed himself to his feet with a groan. "Nick and Todd. Do not—"

Raven crowed from above. "Forget your battle! We have visitors!"

Jason turned around to see Nunn, standing at the clearing's edge. But next to Nunn was something that looked even worse, something that stood like a man but was taller than a man, and whose body was covered by hair and teeth and claws.

"Lordy!" Stanley called. "What is that?"

Nunn smiled at that. "You've met him before." He waved his hand grandly at his grotesque companion. "Say hello to the King of the Wolves. I've just helped him to be more regal."

"Not for long," Thomas said as he shot an arrow into the King's chest.

The giant wolf-man looked down at the shaft sticking from its chest. It gave a short, barking laugh as it pulled the arrow free.

"You may kill all four of those with bows," Nunn remarked to the King, "and that odd fellow who looks half like a tree. The others belong to me."

The King of the Wolves smiled, revealing teeth as long as Jason's hand. He took his first step toward the Volunteers.

Nunn looked to the others. "If you don't want to be killed by the King, you'll have to come with me. We will meet the dragon together. If you are left behind, you belong to the wolf."

"Meeaat!" the King agreed.

"We're not going anyplace!" Nick shouted, running toward the King with his still-drawn sword. The great wolf reached out ready to take Nick's head off with its claws.

"Nick!" Jason shouted. He found he was running, too. "You don't have a chance. Get away from there!"

A great, hairy foot stepped in front of Jason.

"Tenderrr meeat!" the wolf announced.

"Not Jason!" the Oomgosh shouted. In three great strides, the tree man was before the wolf.

"Noo matterrr whoo I killl firrst," the King announced. He leapt forward onto the Oomgosh, all biting teeth and gouging claws.

The tree man wrapped his one good arm around the great wolf and squeezed. The wolf had opened a great wound in the Oomgosh's side. Its jaw snapped onto the tree man's neck.

But the Oomgosh would not let go of his hold. The wolf began to squirm and then to whimper. The tree man's grip grew tighter, and the great wolf wailed in pain. The Oomgosh groaned as his muscles grew tighter still.

There was a sharp crack. The wolf hung limp in the tree man's arms, its spine broken in two.

The Oomgosh let his opponent fall.

"Is it dead?" Jason asked.

The tree man managed a smile. "I'll tell you that story, someday, the story of how the Oomgosh found death." The great green man grimaced. "When I'm better—"

The Oomgosh fell down.

"Nunn!" Obar's voice cut through the silence. He and Mrs. Smith had returned.

And Nunn was gone.

But none of that mattered to Jason anymore.

○ Epilogue

The world shook. A great wind blew from high above, a hot wind that brought with it the smell of fire. The wind roared, causing the people to fall to hands and knees. Even Raven took shelter behind one of the great trees, huddling there as the wind broke huge branches from the trees above, tossing them away like twigs.

Jason remembered this. It was a sign from the dragon. A much larger sign than the one before.

Jason was the first to see her as she drifted down to earth. She was surrounded by flames, but none of them seemed to touch her.

"Mary Lou!" her mother called.

"Not now, Mother," Jason's sister replied firmly. "I have something to say. Something I have been sent to say."

She took a deep breath as her feet touched the ground, and the flames vanished.

"The dragon is near," Mary Lou said. She tried to take a step forward and almost stumbled. Jason was back on his feet. He rushed forward to help his sister. She waved him away.

"Unless it finds what it wants," she said slowly and deliberately, as if repeating someone else's words, "it will destroy us all."

"Anger!" Todd said as he stood himself. "It has something to do with anger."

Mary Lou nodded. "The dragon is angry. It was so close. It doesn't want to have to destroy everything—so soon." She frowned as if the words had deserted her. "If it can find—the one—the missing—it needs to take someone—"

"Nick!" Mrs. Blake called.

Jason turned around. Nick Blake was gone.

"Someone else." Mary Lou managed to smile. "The missing piece."

Her eyes closed as she fell, limp, into Jason's arms.

361

• • •

This had to be a dream.

When Nick opened his eyes, he knew he was home. Back on Chestnut Circle. In his living room, or almost his living room. Some of the furniture had been moved around, and there was a brand-new chair in the corner. But most of it was just the same.

A man walked out of the kitchen. A man Nick knew.

"Dad?" Nick called. He looked older, as if he'd lost a bit more hair, filled out a bit more around the waist.

His father looked up and dropped the plate he was carrying.

"Nick!" his father said. "God, I thought you were dead!"

His father rushed forward, ignoring the food he had spilled on the floor.

"Nick!" he said again as he grabbed his son's arm. "When everybody disappeared, the whole goddamned street—"

Nick could feel the pressure of his father's fingers. It certainly felt real.

"I don't know, Dad," Nick replied. "We were all—taken away—" If that had been real, Nick thought.

He looked in his right hand. He still held the sword. The hilt felt warm in his palm, as if it was impatient for blood.

"Nick, you're sure about this?" There was the tone in his father's voice criticizing his son's flights of fancy. "Where did everyone go?"

There was a deep rumble outside the house.

"What the hell was that?" his father asked.

Nick pulled the sword away from his father. He knew that sort of noise. He had not gone home, after all. Instead, home, and his father, had come to him.

Nick looked out the window. The neighborhood wasn't there. Instead, he saw a great, dark globe before him; a globe so large it took him a moment to realize that it was an eye.

A dragon's eye.